THE BARREL MURDER

a Detective Joe Petrosino case

based on true events

Michael Zarocostas

The darkest places in hell are reserved for those who maintain their neutrality in times of moral crisis.

Dante Alighieri

Note to the reader:

This novel is based on an actual murder that occurred in New York City in 1903 and the criminal investigation that followed. Several of the main characters are real persons or inspired by real persons. Joe Petrosino, the central character, was the first Italian-American detective in the NYPD's Central Bureau appointed in 1895 by Teddy Roosevelt (then President of the Board of New York City Police Commissoners). Petrosino and a few other brave men protected the immigrant masses and fought against the most feared criminals in the city's history. Their story begins here.

Prologue

The East River lapped at the foot of 11th Street where a dock rose and fell on black water. The rain had swelled the river until it seeped into the street and onto the steps of a tenement on Avenue D. Frances Conners came out of the tenement, shielding herself with a shawl from the rain. She was dreading the thought of cleaning the saloon on Fourth Street. Her empty stomach burned as she walked through the muck, watching a soiled diaper float next to her in the gutter. She passed a pile of lumber left out for seasoning in front of the New York Mallet and Handle Works. Then a large barrel on the curb. One of its hoops was missing, as if it had just fallen off a delivery wagon.

Some Long Island farmer dropped it, she thought, in a hurry from the ferry.

The barrel bulged with the promise of something large inside. She moved closer and saw an overcoat covering the lid.

"What are you looking at, darlin'?" a man's voice said. She could smell the whiskey on his breath before she saw his big smiling teeth.

He nudged her away from the barrel and blocked her path.

"No time for it, McCafferty, you hear? I've got real work to do."

"No time for extra silver?" He jingled coins in his pocket and licked his lips.

"Not even sun-up and you're soused." She looked around the empty street. "Right here?"

"Right here." He opened his trousers and exposed himself. Already excited.

"You bastard," she said, glancing up and down the street

through the rain. "Make it fast."

She moved behind the pile of lumber and tried to pull up her worn petticoat, but he was already yanking it down. He pressed her up against the barrel and grunted in her ear. He went fast, and she snickered mockingly at him and counted panes in the Mallet Works windows until he finally convulsed and slumped against her.

"A flash in the pan as usual, McCafferty." She pushed him off and pulled up her petticoat, glancing around again. "Let's have the money quick. You made me late now."

"You got all you're getting from me, whore." He brushed off his trousers.

"Why, you no-good bastard." She grabbed his lapels. "Maybe your Chief would like to hear what you're doing in the wee hours?"

He grinned and shoved her hard, backwards. She fell against the barrel and toppled over. A hand jutted out to her. She reached for it, planning to pull McCafferty down in the muck with her, but the hand was rigid. She let go and saw that the hand came from a body crumpled inside the barrel, folded in half, the head dangling from the torso.

She heard herself shrieking as she pushed her heels into the mud, trying to move away. She tried to stand and yelled at McCafferty to help her, but he was nowhere in sight.

A distant police whistle pierced the air.

Then a watchman ran up to her. His eyes fixated on the barrel as he covered his mouth, whispering, "It's the devil's work."

The police whistles grew louder and carried in the wind. She covered her ears and made the mistake of looking at the face. The eyes were open, and the mouth was stuffed with something bloody. Entrails or worse.

She recognized the familiar shape and retched a string of liquid from her empty stomach.

The World.
EVENING EDITION

"Circulation Books Open to All."   "Circulation Books Open to All."

NEW YORK, TUESDAY, APRIL 14, 1903.

KING
LOSE.

ult Gets a
from Her
s Wealthy
uting Her

. SPITE.

MAN WHO WAS FOUND MURDERED IN A BARREL, HIS CLOTHING
AND SOME OTHER ARTICLES THAT MAY HELP TO IDENTIFY HIM.

MAN
WA
TH

Investigati
Was Sta
Before
Cutting

DECOYEI

Detectives
Secret
sion by
Conceal

BIG STRIKE ON "L" ROAD
IS NARROWLY AVERTED.

Dissatisfied Committee and Men Were
Actually Voting Last Night on the
Proposition to Tie Up the Entire
Manhattan System To-Day When a

ROOSEVELT HAS

THIS ASSAULT

I

THE LUNATIC DOCTOR

Chapter 1

Petrosino had been staring out his window all morning. The night sky had turned a rusted blue, and the rain tapped on the glass as he sighed and looked down at the corner of Lafayette and Spring. Rain fell in silver arrows on Adelina's black dress as she dragged an ash barrel to the curb in front of Vincenzo Saulino's Ristorante. Wet tendrils of hair curled at her lips as she glanced up at his window, then slipped inside. He sighed again and sipped from the bottle of wine they had opened the night before.

As the sun shouldered through the clouds, Petrosino checked his pocket watch and finished the rest of the wine in one long tilt. He had bathed and shaved and doused his hair with tonic, but he could still smell her. He fought off the urge to yawn and doused the lamps as sunlight sifted through the rainfall and the windows, leaving a grey pall on the furniture.

He put on a derby and an overcoat and took out a .38 caliber Smith & Wesson. He looked for a shadow beneath his front door, pressed his ear against the wood, and gently turned the lock. He cracked open the door. The stairwell was empty. He pocketed the gun and descended the three flights back to earth.

❧

Petrosino tried not to look at Saulino's as he walked into a wind that howled like a she-wolf. The wine was roving through his veins, staving off the cool air. He took a deep breath of New York as the peddlers rolled pushcarts down the street, jockeying for position along the rainy sidewalks, and the headscarves and shawls of the women fluttered black, violet, red, and indigo in the misty breeze. A lazy rooster crowed late, and newspaper boys sang out morning headlines in Italian and English. Bootblacks lugged shine boxes with brass footplates, their skinny fingers permanently stained shades of black and ox-blood. He watched some of the boys head south towards City Hall Park and thought about how little he used to charge when he was a kid. Now it was a small fortune, a nickel for a spit shine and a dime for an oil polish. He felt footsteps closing and looked around for anyone suspicious. More boys ran by him, in the same northern direction he was going.

He scanned familiar faces on the streets, making quick eye contact. His network included young and old, and, in exchange for their ears on the streets, he would give them anything from gumdrops to a handful of coin to his solemn promise to personally handle a family affair. The lines of communication were like the strings of a violin, and he had become a maestro at strumming the right ones to make them sing.

He approached a banana seller. The stool pigeon's unshaven face was so full of grime that only the gleam of his eyes and a country pipe were visible. As poor and honest as an Augustinian friar, Petrosino thought. If the banana seller had the goods, he would tap the clay pipe. No signal. Petrosino kept walking, winking subtly at a White Wing in his ivory duck suit. The young street cleaner leaned over his shovel and three-wheeled cart full of brooms and water cans. A quick shake of the head. No news.

Then he saw the familiar face of an elfin fourteen-year-old boy, Izzy, one of his stool pigeons who could never keep his hands still, fidgeting and flying around. Izzy was busking for a couple of older toughs, who smiled at each other and encouraged him. The older ones looked about sixteen years old, Italian boys he'd seen before in the neighborhood. Petrosino could see their game coming a mile away.

"A nickel if youse sing that song for us," one of the toughs said to Izzy and grinned at his friend. "Listen to dis little bum croak like a toad."

Izzy sighed in resignation, then sucked in a deep breath. He exhaled a Yiddish song that Petrosino didn't understand, but had heard a hundred times before on the East Side. The toughs clapped and nudged Izzy, making him dance while he sang. A few passers-by stopped and listened to Izzy's lilting lament. When Izzy finished, he bowed, and the pair of older boys laughed.

"You got your tune, fellas." Izzy patted them amiably. "Now where's my nickel?"

"Nickel? I'll give youse a nickel, you dirty Yid!"

The smaller tough held Izzy, and the bigger one spat in Izzy's face.

"Let him alone!" Petrosino shoved the older boys onto a patch of horseshit and gave the bigger one a hard kick in the pants. "You make me ashamed to be Italian, you shitbirds. Get outta here or I'll break your ass."

The pair ran off, flipping Petrosino the finger.

"What the hell'd ya do that for, Joe?" Izzy wiped spit from his forehead. "You scared em off for good!"

"Don't you want them to let you alone?"

Izzy's sweet face turned impish. "I want them bums to rough me up a little. Lets me get closer to 'em, see?" Izzy reached into his pockets and showed Petrosino a handful of loose change. "The schmucks didn't even know I was sneakin' 'em. Now who's laughin'?"

Petrosino bit his tongue at the trick. "Clever, kid. But what makes you think I'm gonna let you get away with it? I'm the law, aren't I? So now you gotta pay tax. Tell me what you've heard today." Petrosino halfheartedly grabbed Izzy's collar and gently shook the boy.

"Say, take the paws off, Joe. I got my ears to the ground, I can hear trains coming."

"What?"

Izzy pushed away from Petrosino and straightened his collar. "You don't read nuttin', do you, ya big dope? It's in them Western novels. The Injuns put their ears on the ground, and they can hear a cowboy fart from ten miles out!"

Petrosino snorted. "So then, who broke wind today on the East Side?"

Izzy looked up and down the street, then whispered dramatically, "While you were snorin' your head off, some louse got snuffed out. They found the body on Avenue D. I heard they stole the innerds to make a curse. They say. . ." Izzy swallowed hard. "They say it was the devil's work."

"Devil's work, he says." Petrosino chuckled. "What else you hear, kid?"

"That's all. The rest is on interest." Izzy rubbed his fingers together.

"Nuts. If I see you snatching purses, I'll show you the devil's work myself. Now scram."

Izzy gave him the Bronx cheer and sauntered off.

At Elm and Prince, Petrosino turned right, past two ragpicker's carts piled high with moldy sacks of clothes. On the corner of Mott and Prince, Father LaValle was sweeping the entrance of Old St. Pat's. Petrosino walked up the front steps and embraced LaValle, then dipped his finger in a marble bowl of holy water, making the sign of the cross. The cold water evaporated on his forehead, and he felt suddenly alone as he prayed to St. Michael.

When he left Old St. Pat's, Petrosino realized that a man across the street was shadowing him. The shadow was reading a newspaper, and Petrosino could only see the upper half of his face: gold spectacles, fret lines in his forehead, and a thinning tuft of brown hair. The shadow wore an expensive blue suit and white spats over new shoes. Not like the usual crook from the Rogues' Gallery, Petrosino thought, but then crooks were dressing more like dandies these days, so it was hard to tell. The shadow made Petrosino think of T.R. When he was Commissioner, T.R. would always brag about what he would do if an assassin ambushed him in the streets of New York. "Stab him right in the heart, that's what *I'd* do!" T.R. had said, pretending to strike with an invisible dirk.

Petrosino smiled now and glanced once more behind him, convincing himself that no crook worth worrying about would wear white spats in a storm. He quickened his pace through the stinging pricks of rain until 300 Mulberry Street stood before him. Police Headquarters was called the Marble Palace. Four stories of ragged window awnings and American flags with forty-five stars fluttering wet with rain. Petrosino walked up the Palace's high stoop and through the anteroom, where the desk sergeant slurped coffee and an old doorman waved excitedly.

Petrosino nodded and walked past the railing.

He unlocked his cubbyhole of an office and hung his derby and overcoat on a rack next to a picture of President Roosevelt. He sat down at his blotter, a basket of reports, and a stack of letters. He yanked open a musty drawer with cold fingers fidgeting in anticipation of a warm Cuban cigar. He slipped one in his mouth to forget the taste of Adelina's lips.

The old doorman hobbled through the open door, saluting anxiously.

"Morning, Strauss," Petrosino said, not looking up.

"Don't bother sittin', Detective. The Chief's on his way from Union Market and wants to see ye. Wants to see all the Central Bureau dicks. Some kind of madman went on a rampage on the East Side. Gutted a man like a fish."

"I'll be damned, the kid was right." Petrosino bit off the end of his cigar and spat it into the brass spittoon on the floor. "Let's go see what's doing."

Chapter 2

"All right, listen good, this is what we know so far," Chief Inspector "Gentleman George" McClusky said, playing with his braided vest and a gold watch chain with hanging jeweled trinkets. "At 5:30 this morning, a scrubwoman found a dead man stuffed into a barrel on East 11th and Avenue D. The witness's name is Frances Conners. She came out of her tenement on 160 Avenue D near the Mallet and Handle Works building at number 743 East 11th. When she passed the sawmill, she noticed a pile of lumber left out in the yard. Then she saw a large barrel that caught her eye. She mentioned a ferry. . ."

McClusky paused and glanced down at a report, lips moving silently.

Petrosino licked his pencil, scribbling down notes. Word had been traveling as quickly as the telephone switchboard operators could gossip, and he and a dozen other dicks were stuffed in McClusky's office, huddled around his neat desk, listening intently to what the new Chief had to say. The office had Roman busts, Oriental rugs, and oil paintings of the Chief and his family. Adjacent to the Chief's desk was the museum or "cold chamber" displaying artifacts taken from captured crooks during their confessions. McClusky looked up as the heavy footsteps of dozens of reserves from three stationhouses shuffled outside his door in the outer office and hall, waiting for their marching orders.

"That's right," McClusky continued, "she said it looked to her like some Long Island farmer must've dropped the barrel from his truck in a hurry from the 10th Street *ferry*. She thought it might have something valuable inside. Probably a thief herself. When she got closer, she saw an old overcoat covering it. She was going to take the coat with the notion of making a scrub rag. But, when she pulled the coat aside, she slipped in the rain and knocked the barrel over. Out came a mutilated corpse." McClusky grimaced and shifted in his lumpy leather chair beneath an Irish flag and an oil portrait of himself in full parade uniform. He had aged poorly since the portrait was painted. His once rugged chin and cheekbones sagged with loose skin the color of a potato, and his jagged teeth were yellow from tobacco.

Petrosino hadn't trusted McClusky since his first day as Chief Inspector. McClusky was mean-spirited and morose. The opposite of T.R. Whether T.R. was down-dressing a police captain or needling a reporter or simply reading a book in his office, there was always a broad smile on T.R.'s face. The gift of the gods to Theodore Roosevelt was joy.

McClusky was saying, "The dead man's body had been jammed inside the barrel, folded in half. The head was twisted severely at the neck, gashed and bleeding all to hell. And this is the worst part, boys: the mouth was stuffed with the son of a bitch's own cock and balls."

The detectives in the room eyed each other, and someone whistled in disgust.

"She also said the coat and the barrel were hardly wet, even though it had been raining all night and morning. Patrolman O'Dell was the first on the scene. Detective McCafferty was next, and he summoned an ambulance surgeon from Bellevue. They packed the body on ice and took it to Union Market. They say the victim is respectable looking, could be a merchant or a banker, a citizen in good stead. So I want all our ears pricked up.

"Since the victim was found on the East Side in the First Inspection District, the case falls in The Broom's bailiwick." McClusky glanced up at Inspector Max Schmittberger, the tallest man in the room at six foot five. Petrosino caught Max's eye, and they winked at each other. "But, because of the nature of the case,

General Greene himself put me on the job. And I'll be damned if I leave one stone unturned. I summoned the Brooklyn men here because I think the body may have been brought to 11th Street from across the East River. The goddamn rain's washed away any footprints or wagon tracks or any other clues on the ground, so it's no use going back to the scene. I figure that, since no patrolmen saw a wagon carting the barrel through Manhattan, it may have been dumped there by boat from Williamsburg or Greenpoint. McCafferty was on a case near Avenue D at 4:30 a.m. and said he never saw any such barrel."

Petrosino didn't buy it, but kept his mouth shut. If McClusky were right, the barrel would have been unloaded at the foot of East 10th and transported by wagon two blocks to the spot in front of the Mallet Works. Why would the murderer have gone to the trouble of a boat *and* a wagon? And McCafferty may have missed the wagon easily. Petrosino had pounded the pavement for years as a roundsman, and there were times when it took a good hour to circulate back to the same corner on his patrol. An hour was plenty of time to dump a body when no bull was lurking, he thought.

McClusky was still barking out his ideas, looking at a few of his favored Irishmen.

"Attorney Garvan and the Coroner went to look at the body at Union Market and thought the man might be Italian, Greek, or Armenian. It's been transported to the Morgue since, and we'll get a chance to examine it and pick the doc's brain. I got a gut theory about the victim being a socialist agent or a pot-stirring union man. If so, he could be from any of the colonies on the East Side. Maybe Syrian because of the dark features, pointed nose, and earrings." McClusky pointed at a group of his Irishmen. "I want you boys under McCafferty to scour every corner of the Syrian immigrant quarters. Becker, I want you to turn the Greek and Armenian colonies upside down. You men from Old Slip precinct take the Poles and Slavs. And don't talk to the press. Leave the newshounds to me."

"Chief, what about me and my Eldridge Street boys?" Schmittberger asked.

"Hell, I don't know, *Broom*, aren't you more suited to 'sweeping up corruption'? A murder case may be too much for a *reformer* like yourself. Might rattle your nerves, boy-o." McClusky aimed a derisive grin at Schmittberger. Some of the Irish dicks chuckled. "Tell you what, I'll leave the Dagos and Yids in the Ghetto to you. Petrosino can help you 'sweep up' the shit there. We'll see if your motley crew of Jews can solve it faster than my lads. Dismissed."

"Yes, sir, Chief, leave it to us," Schmittberger said with a sweet tone, "we like sweeping shit up. I got a shovel and barrow ready."

McClusky grunted.

Schmittberger lingered outside McClusky's outer office and pulled Petrosino aside. Petrosino nodded, and the two men walked two flights down and then stopped on the worn marble steps of the stoop on Mulberry Street. The big flat feet of McClusky's men shuffled past them and plodded into the light rain toward the Syrian and Slavic colonies.

"He skipped over things," Schmittberger mumbled out of the corner of his mouth. "Why do you think McClusky's keeping clues to himself from that report?"

Petrosino looked up and down the street. "He's been demoted and promoted by Tammany plenty. Got sent off to Goatsville twice. And he just made head of the Central Bureau a month ago. So I figure he's playing this one close to the vest because he's not itching to go back to the sticks if it's botched. But I ain't buying what that snake oil man's selling."

"Especially one in a Saks suit, and did you see when he took off his jacket? Wearing red garters on his sleeves like a riverboat dealer. Son of a bitch is as dumb and chesty as a peacock. This killing happened in the Red Light District. That's my district!"

"Well, at least he fancies you, Max." Petrosino smiled.

"Sure. Ever since I blew the whistle on his brothers to the Lexow Committee. That was ages ago, but he's not letting it go, is he? At least I made a clean breast of *my* graft. The Micks hate me because they still collect 'sugar' from the disorderly houses, and this McClusky can't wait to lay a trap for me."

"You'd best forget that. You only made Inspector this year, and he's the brand new Chief Inspector. Chain of command."

"Right, and I still outrank *you*." Schmittberger smirked. "Did you know McClusky was *last* on the eligible list when we were both Captains and I made Inspector ahead of him."

"How'd he leapfrog you then and make Chief Inspector?"

"How else? Tammany. Don't get me cross thinking about him. What's your gut say about this case, you little Italian wiseacre?"

"Act of passion. Or maybe a blackmail killing. My stoolies say a lot of rich Italians are getting threatening letters telling them to pay off or end up like Luigi Troja and Joe Catania. But it could be anything. Another saloon squabble gone wrong or even a madman escaped from Blackwell's. I'd like to see the body to start." Petrosino realized something and crossed himself. "Whoever did this had no qualms doing it a day after Easter Sunday."

"Probably even went to see the flowers at the Fifth Avenue parade. Why do you think the killer put the victim in a barrel?"

"Not sure yet. Maybe as an easy way to transport him. He had the sawdust already inside the barrel to sop up the blood, then he puts it on a wagon, dumps it. But, if it's a saloon brawl, or if it's a gang squabble like the Catania job, then why dump the barrel in the street for everyone to see? And right in the middle of Little Italy, to boot? He went to a lot of trouble and could've been spotted."

Schmittberger thumbed at a horse carriage. "While these fools are playing in the rain, we should find out exactly what's inside the barrel and speak to Weston about what's inside the dead man's body. Give us something to chew on."

"Agreed."

Chapter 3

"Gentlemen, please have a seat," Dr. Weston's portly young assistant said. "The doctor is finishing up shortly." The assistant disappeared back into the examination chamber.

Petrosino and Schmittberger waited in the sitting room outside the death chamber. They hadn't been able to find Izzy, and none of Petrosino's other stoolies knew anything yet. The owners of a saloon, a dry dock storehouse, and a manufacturing tenement near the Mallet Works had seen nothing. Petrosino was hoping by night, after the evening papers spread the news and the pictures, that someone would have some wine and start singing.

"*In vino veritas*," Schmittberger said.

The pair passed a cigarette back and forth, preparing for the cold examination chamber with its smells of spoiled meat, sweat, and formalin. Schmittberger stopped stroking the thick bristles of his grey moustache when Chief Inspector McClusky and two of his lackeys came next through the door, suits damp from the rain. Max tipped his hat, and McClusky grunted in return. Captain Becker and a Brooklyn detective were the last to arrive, shaking hands with everyone and saying they had no luck finding a solid clue. They said that the police captains in Williamsburg checked with ferrymen and barge skippers, and none of them had brought any barrel across the East River that morning.

Schmittberger flicked a smart-aleck wink at Petrosino, which meant, "McClusky's angle isn't panning out." And Petrosino nodded back at him with a half-frown, meaning, "We knew that."

Weston's assistant reappeared from the examination chamber.

"The doctor is ready to discuss his findings. Please rub out your tobacco."

They filed into the room and huddled around a table beneath a buzzing white bulb. The scent of strong briny pickles hung in the air. Petrosino scanned the body. The barrel victim was supine on the slab, completely naked, bare arms lying at the sides of a brittle ribcage. The skin appeared eerily green in the glow of the spot lighting. A large Y incision from each shoulder converged down to the breastbone and ended at the pubic bone. The stitched markings where he had been cracked open and sewn back together made him look more like a leather bag than a man. And the neck wounds left no doubt. This was worse than any other murder Petrosino had seen in the Italian colonies. There were multiple holes, too many to count it seemed. A rampage of bloodlust.

"Excuse me, gentlemen," Captain Becker said, "but I need to . . . I need. . . air."

Becker's lips were the same color as the body, and he turned and lurched for the door.

"Becker's always had a weak gut," McClusky said. "I heard the police surgeon shit himself when they found the body, too."

"Can't say as I blame them." Petrosino held his notebook tightly and gazed at the neck, knowing he wouldn't need to write down a description. The image would be burned in his memory.

Puncture wounds, ranging in size from pins to dimes, pierced the front and sides of the throat. Some were deep, others were mere pricks. All of them oozed a pink fluid. A slashing wound split the Adam's apple, traveling from ear to ear. It was so deep that Petrosino could see inside the gullet, through a knot of red tissue and membranes, all the way through to the bony outline of the man's spinal cord. The edges of the slashing wound had yellowish flaps fringed with black blood. The head was tilted back on the table, barely hanging onto the body by a few shreds of skin and tendons in the neck. At the end of the Y incision, the pubic bone had no penis or testicles. Only a strange empty gash and a nest of veins that looked like raspberry jam in greying pubic hair. But the face was worst of all. It was pristine, well-groomed, and clean with curly dark hair receding just above the temples. The nose and the cheekbones were prominent and angular. The eyelids were thick, the eyes halfway open, almost at peace, belying the torture inflicted on the rest of the body. The face reminded Petrosino of his own father, and he knew it would haunt him forever.

The sound of running water came from the corner. Dr. Weston was furiously washing up and examining his fingers. He toweled off his hands and wrapped iodine cloth around a finger.

"Gentlemen, one moment," Dr. Weston said. "Gave myself a little cut on the hand. Did the same thing a couple of years ago and got blood poisoning. Nearly had to amputate the limb."

With the influx of immigrants over the past decade, Weston's job had become an unrelenting queue of the desperately poor and criminal traveling across his table, and his face showed the fatigue as plainly as his white coat showed streaks of red and brown.

"Let's get started on this barrel tenant." Weston moved to the head of the slab and stood over the victim's face. He tossed the iodine cloth on a long table to the side, next to his scalpels, bone saws, and a weighing scale.

Petrosino noticed the implements for the first time, and a chill rushed through him. Beside the tools was a bowl containing the severed genitalia, shriveled and ugly. The genitals had random patches of grey, but the hair on the man's head was dyed black.

"Earlier today," Weston said, "an inventory of the victim's possessions revealed clean and good quality clothing. Upon arrival from the ambulance wagon, we took the body off ice, removed the clothing, and measured it as best we could in its current condition. The man was five and a half feet tall and weighed one hundred sixty-seven pounds. He appeared well-nourished and in good health prior to receiving the fatal wounds. Both ears, which are small and well-shaped, were pierced for rings. The victim's hands are soft, white, and tapering, and the nails manicured in a gentlemanly fashion. Evidently, he hadn't done hard labor in quite some time and, given his grooming, may have been in the barber trade."

Petrosino looked at the hands. Not one callous and the cuticles were perfect half moons.

"Got the hands of a little Florodora chorus girl," McClusky said.

Dr. Weston nodded. "Yes, George, he's almost as much of a 'dude' as you."

McClusky grumbled, and Petrosino tried not to smile at Weston's jab.

"As you can see," Dr. Weston continued, "the victim's facial features appear foreign in origin. Coroner Scholer is the eugenics expert and thought perhaps Middle Eastern. It may be difficult to tell at this point, but the victim's skin tone is olive. His eyes are wide set, and his hair is brown and wavy. His moustache is neatly trimmed, and I note the forehead is high, sloping and beginning to bald, indicating middle age between thirty-five and forty years old. There are two scars on his left cheek, each an inch long." Dr. Weston pointed with his small finger at the victim's face. "The two marks come together like a small V. These are old scars however."

"Did you find anything that can help identify him?" Schmittberger asked.

"Patience, Max. I would have told you that first. Now, look carefully at the man's injuries. You'll see the obvious multiple slashing and puncture wounds on his throat. The blows are barbaric and indicate a great deal of violence. But take a look at his hands and forearms. Notice anything peculiar?"

McClusky said, "He ain't married?"

"He has no defensive wounds," Petrosino said, "which means he didn't fight."

"Correct," Dr. Weston said. "There's no sign of a struggle, and that is very peculiar given the numerous stabbings to the throat. I counted eighteen knife wounds to the neck, but nary a scratch or bruise on the hands and arms. Even if he had been sleeping, the muscles would involuntarily contract upon being attacked and the arms would naturally come up in a defensive posture." Weston mimed a defensive pose. "I would venture he wasn't asleep, but held down on a chair or over a table, unable to defend himself, and then tortured to death."

"When did he die?" Petrosino asked.

"It was slow. No man living could tell which wound happened first. It appears that whoever did this took pleasure in the killing and wanted to make the victim suffer consciously. But I would say he died between eleven last night and one in the morning. I looked inside his stomach and found he'd eaten a meal just before he was killed. Beans, beets, and potatoes."

"That's a bum's supper," McClusky said.

"Any alcohol or drugs in him?" Petrosino asked.

Dr. Weston shook his head. "None that I can tell."

"Can you tell how many weapons were used?"

"From the nature of the wounds, there appear to be two, maybe three. And I would say possibly two men if not more. Though one man could use different knives if he made this a torture session. The chief wound was just above the laryngeal prominence, the Adam's apple. The knife thrust penetrated all the way to the spinal column." Dr. Weston pointed at the different shapes and depths of the wounds. "The victim was likely held down and made defenseless with a narrow deep stab, four inches deep, under the left ear and another through the front of the throat. After being subdued, he was tortured with a dozen punctures and the coup de grace, a slash from an exquisitely sharp blade like butcher's steel from the left ear around the throat to the right ear. A little deeper and I'd have his head on another tray next to his genitals. Of course, you know the genitals were in his mouth, but I removed them to conduct my exam."

"Is it possible one man did this?" Schmittberger asked. "Could he have drugged the victim?"

"Possible? Yes. But unlikely."

"So then two weapons?"

"One stiletto, at least, for the punctures and a very long and sharp knife for the near decapitation. There may be another smaller, double-edged knife for these linear stabbings here close to the collar bone."

"He never had a chance," Petrosino said, feeling cold all over. "Doc, can you take his Bertillon measurements? Maybe we can circulate them to other cities for identification?"

Schmittberger nodded. "We should send them to the Secret Service boys here, too. They've got a file on everything. Can you put him back together, Doc, and cover his neck for the police photographer? We could use a good picture for the papers."

"Stop barking out orders, goddamnit!" McClusky said. "Mind your place, *Broom*."

"Yes, sir, Chief. I'm sure you were about to say the same things."

Petrosino spoke quickly to divert McClusky's ire, "Do you have his clothes, Doc?"

"Of course. When we look at the clothing, notice the victim's shirt collar. It's a thick three-ply linen, but the blade swept clean through it, leaving an incision a quarter inch deep. That would have taken a strong hand, someone possessed of great muscle. Or perhaps great madness. There's also a square of gunnysack cloth that was wrapped around his neck. I believe that was done to stem the bleeding and to conceal the wounds on the victim to transport him."

Dr. Weston called for his assistant.

The assistant wheeled in another table with underclothing, a black worsted overcoat, a black tweed waistcoat, black and white striped trousers, a pleated shirt with blue checks, a white turn-down linen collar, a green necktie with black squares, laced shoes and overshoes, handkerchiefs, a gunny sack, a pair of gloves, cheroot cigars, a rubber stamp, small coins, a silver watch chain, and a necklace and crucifix.

The detectives looked over the items as Dr. Weston told them that the soles of the shoes bore the maker's name, "Burt & Co.," and the man's linen collar appeared to bear the name, "Marl." Petrosino looked closely at one glove and pulled it inside-out to see the trade name, "Laird." He then examined the necklace and Latin crucifix with the titulus "INRI" and an engraved image of a skull and crossbones.

"What's that lettering on the cross?" McClusky said. "*I-N-R-I*? And the skull and crossbones?" McClusky raised an eyebrow at Petrosino. "Some kind of Dago witchcraft?"

Petrosino was about to explain the meaning, but the words "Dago witchcraft" hit him in the forehead like a prizefighter's jab. He felt a flush of anger and said quietly, "I don't know, Chief."

"Could be the son of a bitch's name? Or the name of a secret society?"

"I'm a Methodist, sorry, George," Dr. Weston said. "Besides the necklace, we found that silver watch chain with no casing in the victim's waistcoat. There wasn't much else of value. He had a bandana and two handkerchiefs. The smaller of the handkerchiefs, the white one, has a noticeably strong odor of women's perfume. That may help put you on the scent, so to speak."

Petrosino jotted down in his notebook a description of the clothing and his belief that the watch and any money were stolen by the killer. He also wrote down that the square-cut cigar looked like a cheap Toscano to him. The detectives took turns sniffing the ladies' handkerchief.

McClusky said to his men, "Check the red lantern clubs in the Ghetto and see if any whores know anything about this hanky. Slap 'em around if they play coy."

Dr. Weston pointed out a charred fragment of a letter found in the victim's topcoat. Someone had obviously tried, and failed, to burn the letter. The detectives took turns reading the paper, but all of them except Petrosino shook their heads. The note on the scrap of paper was written with a fanciful but shaky script: *Giorno che venite subit l'urgenza.*

"It's Italian," Petrosino said, "it means something like, '*Come at once.*' Could be a woman's hand, maybe she lured him to his death?"

"Sounds like a Dago love triangle," McClusky said.

"Of course," Dr. Weston said, "there's also the barrel." He pulled a sack cloth off a barrel in the corner of the room. "We waited for you gentlemen to sift through it."

The barrel had a marking in black stencil, "W&T," on the bottom, and "G228" on one of the staves on the side with an address, "366 Third Ave." McClusky's lackeys sorted through the sawdust inside, emptying everything into a sack. Petrosino wrote down that the barrel contained a few cigars and cigarette butts, a tobacco box with a Turkish label, and traces of blood. Typical sawdust for an East Side saloon. While the other men talked over the barrel, the perfumed handkerchief and the note triggered a memory from Petrosino's childhood.

Petrosino tapped Schmittberger's shoulder, and they slipped out while McClusky and his Irish lads played in the dead man's sandbox.

Chapter 4

No one knew anything. Petrosino and Schmittberger had walked the East Side a second time, checking in with every stool pigeon they could roust. Still no Izzy. They canvassed the streets, questioned shop owners and saloonkeepers, and sent their best informers to the Morgue to view the victim. Even if no one could identify the body, they wanted their stoolies to memorize the grotesque image for any later rumors.

At noon, they came upon a stickball game on Second Street. Petrosino recognized the young man pitching as Bimbo Martino. Bimbo had thick eyebrows and the beard shadow of a man ten years older. He was only eighteen, but his physique was that of a beautifully wild creature. Even the cords in his neck muscles stood out. Bimbo's Swamp Angels were playing the visiting Ten Eycks gang, and the Eycks had the bases loaded. First base was a fruit peddler's stand; second was a trampled Boston Beaneaters cap in the street; and third was a rickety milk crate. A pale boy practiced swings with a short broomstick at home plate, a sewer grate, while a swarm of Swamp Angels danced in the "outfield" among pushcarts on the sidewalks.

Bimbo kicked at a small pile of sawdust under his feet and called out formally, "Seven to three. Bases full, tying run at the plate, one out. Look out below!"

Bimbo blazed a fastball past the Eyck boy.

"You see the big kid hurling?" Petrosino said to Schmittberger.

"How could I miss him?" Schmittberger tilted his fedora up to get a better look. The rainfall had subsided to a mist. "He's as solid as a column at the Tombs."

"That's what the police surgeons said when I took him in for the physical. He passed the exam like Caruso passing a voice lesson."

"He's one of your bastards then, is he?"

"He's not from my loins, Max. I wish I could make a son like that. He's almost as tall as you and maybe two hundred twenty pounds. Not an ounce of blubber either."

"What's his name?"

"Bimbo. From *bambino*, 'the kid.' I knew his mother from The Mabille."

"I bet you did." Max whistled as Bimbo whizzed another pitch past the batter, and the poor catcher dropped the ball and rubbed his hands together in pain. "Hot potato!"

The batter struck out and threw his stick on the cobblestones in frustration.

"I never knew his mama in a 'professional' capacity, Max. She got scarlet fever in the bordello and died years ago. They say the boy is the bastard son of that Italian boxer who won the Golden Gloves and almost beat John L. Sullivan. When his mama died, he ended up on the streets. I caught him stealing figs from Old Man Balducci and hiding in water tunnels on Cherry Street. I've been looking out for him ever since. He wants to be a bull now, imagine that."

"Imagine that. I wonder where he got that idea?" Schmittberger studied Petrosino's face and frowned. "Joe, he ain't a puppy you can just take in. Don't get attached to the notion. You know how the Ghetto works."

"Easy for you, Max, you got six sons and a daughter. There's no harm in me teaching him what I know about the job. Watch." Petrosino took off his jacket, handing it to Schittberger, and rolled up his sleeves. He walked over to the sewer grate, picked up the broomstick, and shouted, "Let's see what kinda twirler you are with a *man* at the plate, shitbird!"

"You're on, old man!" Bimbo laughed, and the Swamp Angels in the outfield trotted back further down the street.

Petrosino took a couple of practice swings and hunched down over the plate.

The chant of "batter, batter" started, and Bimbo stood up tall, reared his right hand back, and lunged forward with a grunt. The ball appeared for a second and flew past Petrosino's stick as he swung furiously and spun in a full circle.

"Strike one!" Schmittberger shouted from the curb, laughing. "This batter's no matter!"

The chubby catcher cackled as he flicked the ball back to Bimbo, and Petrosino spit in both hands and gripped the wood tightly. He pointed the stick at the baserunners. "All you Eycks are coming home soon."

Bimbo played with his grip on the ball. "Two outs, no balls, one strike. Here's another strike!" He leaned back far, and all six-feet three inches of the kid seemed to spring forward with his right arm snapping like a whip. Petrosino started his swing early, his back foot planted hard, and he could see the rubber ball clear like a red tomato. Big and ripe, and ready to be smashed. Petrosino chopped through it and the ball towered up into the air, flying down the street, with all the outfielders scrambling backwards to catch it. By the time it landed in a fish monger's basket, the base runners had come in, and Petrosino was sprinting, hearing his own wheezing, slipping on wet cobblestones and laughing as he made the turn. He kicked the milk crate at "third" base and barreled for home, hearing Max shout, "SLIDE, DUMMY, SLIDE!" At the sewer grate, Bimbo caught the ball and blocked home plate like an Ivy League footballer. Petrosino thought it was time to test Bimbo and see just what kind of cop he'd make.

Petrosino flicked off his derby hat, lowered his head, and jackknifed straight into Bimbo's chest. There was a whoosh of air as the wind came out of Bimbo, and Petrosino's vision went black for a moment. A trio of stars rolled across the blackness. He tumbled over the sewer grate, slapping it with his hand, slowly coming to his senses.

"YOU'RE OUT!" Schmittberger shouted.

Bimbo was sitting on the sewer grate, still holding the ball. Grinning.

"The son of a bitch tagged you, fair and square, Joe!" Schmittberger dusted Petrosino off and handed him his hat and jacket. "Joe, you all right? Seeing little birdies?"

"Nuts. I'm fresh as a daisy." Petrosino pulled Bimbo up by a hand. "You okay, kid?"

"You bet your ass, Sarge." Bimbo held the ball up and shouted, "The old man's out at home! Seven-six, Swamp Angels win! Now all youse Ten Eycks can fuck off!"

Schmittberger held out his hand and shook Bimbo's. "So you wanna be a bull?"

"Bimbo, this is Inspector Schmittberger," Petrosino said. "He's over Eldridge Street Precinct, which could be your station if you make the list of candidates for patrolman."

"Took the skull test last month, sir," Bimbo said to Schmittberger.

"Did you now?" Schmittberger tested him. "What's the Deadline?"

"That's easy. That's the line at Fulton Street. Any crook crosses it south, they get pinched. To keep the banks and jewelers safe."

"Oh yeah? What's the Bertillon Method?"

"Rats. Ain't that when you measure a crook's arms and legs, how big his noggin is. . . I think it's twelve things you measure to identify them if they got disguises?"

"Close. Eleven measurements." Schmittberger smiled. "We could use a swell specimen like you on the street. We better get you before Ebbets signs you up for the Brooklyn Nationals. Or maybe you wanna be a slab artist for that new American League team at Hilltop Park?"

"Nah, that American League won't last. Besides, I wanna mash crooks not baseballs."

Schmittberger patted Bimbo's shoulders. "How'd you get so big?"

"All that macaroni in the Ghetto made me strong."

Schmittberger laughed. "Come here a minute." He led Petrosino and Bimbo away from the other kids. "We're on a case. A man was butchered and stuffed in a barrel on Avenue D this morning. If you get a tip for us, it might grease the skids for you."

"Even if I failed the skull test?" Bimbo's thick eyebrows arched up.

"Sergeant Petrosino and I will be your 'rabbis.'"

"But I ain't Jewish."

"No, we'll be your 'sponsors.' Won't cost you a cent either." Schmittberger leaned closer. "When I was your age, a couple of Tammany bosses saw me in a delivery uniform and liked my looks. So they paid my way into a bluecoat on a lark. Those were the old days." Schmittberger winked. "Now, what's the word on the street about this murder?"

"Nothing yet. But I'll do whatever you want. Just say the word."

"Go down to the Morgue," Petrosino said, "and get a look at the victim's face. Put it to memory, every hair on his head. Then find out who he is." Petrosino patted Bimbo's face.

"Will it help me make patrolman?"

"Maybe." Petrosino put his arm around Bimbo. "And when you start walking your beat, stay at the curb. Don't walk under the eaves, because your old pals will toss down bottles and bricks once they see your uniform."

"We call 'em 'East Side Missiles,'" Max added.

"Go on now," Petrosino said, "get to work, son."

Bimbo stood silent for a moment, committing the advice to memory, and then he shook both men's hands before heading back into the street.

"All that baseball made me hungry," Schmittberger said. "Saulino's then?"

Petrosino's neck muscles began to ache, and he wondered if it were from crashing into Bimbo or the thought of seeing Adelina again, in front of Max this time. He shook his head.

"I'm not hungry yet. Why don't we shake the trees a little more?"

"Joe Petrosino not hungry for Vincenzo Saulino's I-talian food? Nuts. That kid must've knocked you senseless. Come on, you work better on a full stomach. I'm buying."

Petrosino sighed and began dusting himself off and straightening his clothes, secretly preening himself along the way to Saulino's.

☙

Vincenzo Saulino's Ristorante always smelled sweetly of garlic and onions frying in olive oil. It was the kind of East Side restaurant that allowed shirtsleeves on warm days and had no formalities except for a clean red and white gingham cloth on every table. Petrosino and Schmittberger went in and sat at their corner table next to the kitchen, where they could smell the cooking and see the front door at the same time.

"I-N-R-I on the victim's crucifix," Petrosino said, "is from the Latin phrase, *Iesvs Nazarenvs Rex Ivdaeorvm*: 'Jesus the Nazarene, the King of the Jews.'"

"Why didn't you tell your dear old Chief Inspector McClusky?"

"Because he asked if it was 'Dago' witchcraft. Sooner or later one of his Irish Catholic boys will tumble it out from their catechism days."

"I've got two theories on that perfumed handkerchief," Schmittberger said. "One, the victim was lured to his death by the woman with the perfume. Maybe a badger game, and, when they robbed him, it got ugly. Or, two, the victim had a gal who was married, and the cuckolded husband got his revenge. Her hanky was the tip-off. Like *Othello*?"

"How do you mean?"

"Othello thought his wife gave her strawberry hanky to another man and killed her."

"Haven't read that one yet, professor."

"Maybe you should read something besides *Tanner's Memorandum of Poisons*?"

Petrosino smiled. "What if the victim's not from New York? That handkerchief made me think of when I was a little kid. My father was going somewhere, I was too young to remember, but I remember seeing my mother give him a handkerchief so he wouldn't breathe the smoke in the tunnels. When the train started, my father hung out the window and waved the hanky like an old lady. I never heard my mother laugh and cry so hard."

"So how's that figure in with our barrel victim?"

"It means he could have had a gal back home, gave it to him as a memento. Could have been waiting the day he returned, like the note said. *The day that you come. Quick.*"

"I like my *Othello* angle better."

"Me too."

They both finished off a roast chicken, pasta slathered in tomato sauce with fresh basil, and "veal" cutlets of cheap beef pounded tender and coated with egg and breadcrumbs. As they ate, the kitchen door swung open and shut, and Petrosino could see Adelina pounding away at tough meat with her mallet, sweating in her widow's dress. She must've noticed him by now, but she said nothing. He ate and pretended to listen to Schmittberger and secretly watched her swirling in and out of the kitchen, turning from table to table with dishes on her black-sleeved arms like a whirling dervish. Her face was ruddy as if she'd been stooped over a hot oven baking a fresh loaf of bread.

"Joe?" Schmittberger snapped his fingers. "What are you daydreaming about?"

"I can't get the victim's face out of my head. Reminded me of my pop." Petrosino looked away from Adelina and thought of the dead man's face. The slashed neck. The genitals on Dr. Weston's table.

"You have a chance to visit the family lately?"

"I saw them for Easter. They don't understand why I got in with a bunch of Jews and Irish cops. They say I've brought a curse on the family because they all get death threats now."

"You were probably a curse to them already." Schmittberger grinned.

"What do you think the others are doing? On this case?"

"Becker's gathering up witnesses to take them all to the Morgue, and I'd wager McClusky's favorite son, McCafferty, is scooping up shopkeepers from the Syrian quarters, slapping them silly to see what they know. At the Morgue, the Brooklyn dick whispered to me that McClusky told his Irish crew not to lay heads to pillow until they had solid clues."

"The Chief doesn't know what to do with us. But he's gotta keep us since no one else will touch the Dago colonies."

"I want to solve this case before that bastard even gets his boots on."

"Why was our victim put on display like that?" Petrosino said. "With the son of a bitch's cock and balls in his mouth?"

"That's what we've got to tumble out." Schmittberger shoved his plate aside and stood.

He paid for the meal, and Petrosino shook hands with Saulino and watched Adelina out of the corner of his eye. Saulino held up the five dollar note that Schmittberger had given him, studying the portrait of Chief Running Antelope in his war bonnet.

"You pulling my leg, Vincenzo?" Schmittberger asked.

"Can't trust anyone these days," Saulino said, making change.

Adelina apologized with her eyes and gave Schmittberger sugar candies for both of them. But not a word to Petrosino. He thought of her mourning dress on his bed, and how long it had taken him to undo her corset, her giggling the whole time. Petrosino looked away from her now, irritated, and he noticed a patrolman rushing through the door and signaling to them.

"Sirs, the boss wants to see you both. About the barrel murder."

"The Chief Inspector?" Schmittberger said.

"No, sir. The Deputy Commissioner."

Petrosino and Schmittberger glanced at each other in surprise and followed the patrolman out the door. Petrosino turned back to Vincenzo and Adelina. "*Don* Vincenzo, thank you for the meal, and, Miss Adelina, it's been too long. *Ciao*."

She bit her lip and smiled.

MURDERED MAN'S BODY FOUND IN A BARREL

Woman's Perfumed Handkerchief and Scrap of Letter with It.

Victim Stabbed Eighteen Times and His Throat Cut—Efforts to Establish Identity Vain—Secret Society Crime, the Police Theory.

An atrocious murder was revealed early yesterday morning when the body of a man was found in a barrel in front of the building at 743 East Eleventh Street, near Avenue D. The man's throat had been cut from ear to ear—the head almost severed from the body—after eighteen knife wounds had been inflicted in the neck.

Who the man was, why he was killed, or when, or where, or by whom, and how or when or by whom the body was conveyed to the spot where it was discovered are questions the police cannot answer. All day and all last night one of the largest details of detectives ever assigned to a single case in this city, scoured New York and its environs, following a multitude of clues.

But those clues disappeared as they were pursued, and the authorities early this morning admitted that they were entirely in the dark, and that they were waiting for the identification of the body until

NEW YORK TIMES

Chapter 5

The rain came back again colder, stinging their faces. The trio of Petrosino, Schmittberger, and the young patrolman squinted and held onto their hats while the clouds hung over their heads like dark swollen sponges spilling filaments of water.

Petrosino saw the shadow again. The man was standing outside the Marble Palace, rain beading on gold glasses, a newspaper still covering half his face. Petrosino nudged Schmittberger and whispered, "Have you seen that character before?"

Schmittberger kept walking, but glanced over his shoulder like a veteran jockey, and mumbled, "Looks familiar, but that paper's in the way. Not too clever, is he?"

"Is he a crook, you think?"

"Could be. But everybody's a crook these days, Joe. Most of us is so crooked we get cramps in our beds at night."

Petrosino laughed. He glanced back in the rain, but the man stopped following them. When the patrolman walked south past the Marble Palace, Petrosino and Schmittberger looked at each other with slight confusion.

"Say," Petrosino said, "why aren't we going to Headquarters?"

"Just a bit further down Lafayette, sir. The Commissioner said he wants me to bring you there." The patrolman pointed vaguely south toward storefronts two blocks away.

Petrosino and Schmittberger eyed each other again, but kept walking. The patrolman stopped in front of a three-story brownstone with hot steam pumping in bursts from three chimney pipes. There was a half-flight of outdoor stairs leading to a blood red door and a sign that read, *Lafayette De Luxe Turkish Baths 10¢.*

"Well," Schmittberger said, "I guess these old bones could use a rub-down."

Petrosino asked the patrolman, "You sure this is the right place?"

The patrolman nodded, pointed at a large man in a Tombs Keeper uniform waiting at the door. He was all red hair and red eyelids and three hundred pounds of pasty blubber.

"I know him," Petrosino whispered to Schmittberger. "Everyone calls him 'The Scotch Whale.' He's a superintendent at the Tombs."

"I know him, too. A little thick, but on the level."

The patrolman saluted the Scotch Whale, and the Whale nodded and motioned for Petrosino and Schmittberger to come inside the bath house. They climbed the stairs, and the Whale shook their hands and held the door for them. The first thing Petrosino noticed was the tremendous heat inside the place. He could feel the steam blanketing him, coiling around his neck, and making the air in his lungs heavy.

They passed by a pair of attendants in a long marble hallway that led to a door. The Whale knocked twice, and a voice asked him to enter. Inside, the room had marble floors, white brick walls, buckets, and large furry sponges strewn on the floor around a central table. Along the left side were two rowing machines and an electric camel for exercise. The floors were wet with steam rising from a box pit of hot rocks, and the air was buttery with heat. Petrosino could hear himself breathing more heavily as he unbuttoned his jacket and loosened his collar.

The prone man on the table came into view through wisps of steam: Deputy Commissioner Duff Piper. He was naked on his stomach, and a burly "rubber" stood over him, kneading hairy forearms into Piper's back. A small towel covered Piper's rear, and Piper had his eyes closed, grunting and groaning, his pale white skin pinkened in splotches from the heat and the rub-down. He looked like a big glazed ham. He opened his eyes, crow's feet deepening, and smiled through a sweaty red beard thick as an antebellum general's.

"Gentlemen, come in!" Piper propped himself up on his elbows. He turned back to the rubber, mumbled something, and the rubber came around the table, naked except for a white loincloth and sandals. The rubber helped Piper into a fluffy white robe, and Piper walked with an undisguised limp, leading the men into the cooling room. They sat on wicker chairs beneath a large fan, and a Negro butler brought a tray of teas and seltzers. Piper took some bromo seltzer before waving away the butler and the Whale. Piper stirred his concoction with a spoon, then appraised the spoon, nodded approval, and slipped it in his robe pocket.

Petrosino and Schmittberger glanced at each other in amusement.

"They say the great evil of the police force is intemperance," Piper said with a wry smile and sipped his bubbly concoction. "So I'm taking a little bromo for last night's sins. Like the H2O crowd says, 'I will not become a drunkard even for twenty-five dollars.'"

"'Get from behind me, Satan,'" Schmittberger chimed in, and he and Piper chuckled.

"How have you been, Max? How's Sarah and the children?"

"Couldn't be better. And Gerty, she's well?"

Piper looked distressed. "As well as I've come to expect. She can't sleep without that infernal *medicine*." Piper turned to Petrosino. "Excuse us, Detective. Max and I go back to the days of old Inspector Byrnes. Byrnes and I were in the Zouaves regiment back in the War of the Rebellion, and, after it ended, we built up the PD. Max here was but a pup when we made the PD what it is, isn't that right?"

Schmittberger nodded. "The Deputy gave me my first big collar. He had a tip on a white slave trader, some Arab pimp in Cockran's Roost."

"That's right, boy-o," Piper said. "I made a bull out of him. Sure, he had his dark time with Lexow, but look how he's come out of it? T.R. called Max his 'Big Stick.'"

"I know, sir," Petrosino said. "T.R. made me Sergeant."

"That's right, forgive an old man's memory."

"Well, Duff," Schmittberger said, "we're plumb in the middle of a murder case-"

"The barrel murder, I know. That's why I wanted a word."

"Why not talk at the Bureau?"

"Because I want this kept between us. Spies lurk within." Piper took a gulp of his seltzer, burped. "I want to be able to trust the two of you. The other lad, the big fat bull who brought you in here, that's my nephew. Sandy. You remember him?"

Schmittberger nodded.

"Truth be told, Sandy's got the brains of a chicken, but he's as loyal as a hunting dog. Like the two of you. That's why I bid you hither. I can't trust a soul at the Marble Palace. Everyone's a spy in there, and every time I say something, I hear it in the hallways an hour later. There's leaks all over my office."

"Why don't you put a detective on the job?" Schmittberger smiled.

"Detective? Detective! Hell, what I need is a *plumber*."

The three men laughed.

"So what's the tip, Duff?" Schmittberger took off his fedora, shook the rain from it.

"First things first. What do you think of your new boss, *Gentleman* George McClusky?"

Schmittberger grinned. "I'm sure he's a real peach once you've known him... for thirty or forty years."

"I'm sure." Piper crossed his legs beneath his thick white robe and chewed on his lip. The wicker creaked in the silence as he studied Petrosino. "How about you, Sergeant? George McClusky's been the Central Bureau sachem for a month now. You like your Chief?"

Petrosino shrugged. "Sir, I do what I'm told and follow chain of command."

"Aye, I don't like him either. So I'll cut to the chase, lads. You know how this city operated before Mayor Low got elected, before Reform set in. The political excrement from Tammany Hall flowed sideways to the Mayor, then down to the Commissioner, and then through the Commissioner's three deputies. Am I wrong, Max?"

"Right as rain, Duff."

"Tammany's made me a museum piece, shoved me to the side trying to retire me. I've been outcast since I stood with T.R. and the Republicans. And this new Chief Inspector McClusky is Tammany to the core. That peacock's more concerned with luncheons at Delmonico's and whether his suits are the latest from Lord & Taylor. He's not like *us*. He doesn't care a lick about the job. He's a climber. First he makes Chief Inspector, then maybe Commissioner, and then, who knows with the Green Machine behind him, maybe Mayor? I won't stand for it! Tammany men are harpies feeding on the City's vital organs, they're a vile, lecherous, rum-soaked, and corrupt lot!"

"I'm with you, Duff," Schmittberger said, "except for the rum-soaked part."

Piper smiled and offered them tea. They drank and stirred, spoons tinkling.

Piper whispered, "I know you're on the level, Petrosino, because I've seen your work. You've knocked out more teeth than a dentist, and T.R. wouldn't have made you detective unless you were honest." Piper patted Max's knee. "And I know how hard it's been since you came clean to Lexow and T.R. reinstated you. There's a wicked lot of Tammany scoundrels who'd like to see you take a splash."

"I was a kingpin in the police system of graft," Schmittberger said, sipping tea, "but I gave up that jig a long time ago. I'm on the square now, boss."

"I remember you testifying back then. The tall handsome Captain on the stand in full uniform saying he was the bag man of the Tenderloin who paid up to Clubber Williams. Confessing in exchange for immunity was a smart move, lad. I don't judge that, not a wee bit."

"Gave the whole system away." Schmittberger sounded rueful. "Names, dates, prices, rules. So I know what you mean when you say you feel cast out. I am *the* outcast in the PD."

"What was it, $300 for a gambling house to operate in your precinct?"

"That was the 'initiation fee.' There was also an annual payment to the 'Gambling Commission,' and all kinds of monthly payments, too, for protection."

Piper eyed him cautiously, watching Schmittberger's every facial expression and movement. Then Piper cast his eyes away, pretending to look at his tea cup nonchalantly.

"Max, do you miss the old days? Do you ever wish you had your old 'Steamboat Squad' back and that the rules could be bent again?"

"Hell no, Duff," Schmittberger said vehemently, stiffening in his chair. "I wouldn't put my family through it again, not for a million times what was in it for me. Not on your life."

"Good." Piper nodded, seeming relieved by the answer. "You two are on the outside of Tammany, that's why I trust you. McClusky's got pull with Big Tim Sullivan, and Tim's not just a crook, he is a *grand* crook."

"A lot of men are on Sullivan's string," Petrosino said.

"But Duff's got an axe to grind against McClusky," Schmittberger said.

"You still know me well, Max." Piper grinned. "McClusky was captain in a Goatsville precinct on the Hudson. That precinct was where my nephew came up. Sandy had all the talents to be one of our best, but he caught another cop trying to make love to his wife, and Sandy did what any man would do in the circumstance. Now, the other cop lived, so there was no injustice there. But McClusky made an example of Sandy by booting him out. I've tried to help Sandy, got him a fine job at the Tombs, but that doesn't square it, lads. I want McClusky to lose his post, I want him shamed and sent off to doorman duty in some Tammany saloon in the sticks!"

"And how do we figure in?"

"This barrel murder is a gruesome scandal. It's front page fodder. And a good lead in a case like this makes a man's career. And guess who has the kingmaker of all leads, lads?"

"What is it, Duff? Spill." Schmittberger wrung his fedora and leaned forward.

Piper's voice came out in excited spurts, "I got a call from the alienist at the River Crest Sanitarium in Astoria. Over Easter, a wealthy physician named Duncan Primrose went crackers in Union Square. He believed his wife was having relations with their Dago carriage driver. So when she prepared a nice roast lamb for supper, he showed her the dish he had prepared: a bloody pair of testicles served up on a silver tray. He said they were her lover's, but it tumbles out they were just a fresh pair from the butcher shop. Now the wife didn't know that, and she starts weeping in fear, but Primrose thinks she's mourning her lover. So he goes beserk and throttles her and all the female servants. Meantime, the driver's gone missing…"

Schmittberger said, "So you think Primrose's driver is our victim?"

"It's a sure bet he's your victim, but Primrose's family has been quick to hush it all up. Apparently, Primrose has never been right in the head and has cracked up before. This time, the family's lawyer made sure Primrose was committed to an asylum pending a court hearing, and if they delay long enough, the charges will be reduced. But the asylum's alienist is a friend of mine, and he tipped me off that Primrose has confessed to something big." Piper paused and smiled at them. "Primrose says he killed his carriage driver and stuffed him in a barrel."

"Duff, if this madman's in an asylum under proper legal process," Schmittberger said, "what would you have us do?"

"I want you to go to River Crest and bring that lunatic doctor back in irons. And I want you to tip off the gossip vendors so everyone knows that this heinous crime was solved by the hard work and big brains of a Jew and an Italian and not that bastard George McClusky!"

"Well, I don't ordinarily like seeing my name in print," Schmittberger said sarcastically and rose to his feet, "but I will make an exception for you, Duff."

"Just remember," Piper said, "when you set the city afire with this arrest, I was the matchstick. And another thing. If anyone asks, you got the tip about Primrose from a stoolie. I am Dicken's ghost of Christmas past. Nowhere to be found."

Schmittberger shook Piper's hand. "We'll have our man on the front page of the evening news."

"Aye, I'm well pleased, lads." Piper shook Petrosino's hand, too. "But just so you know, I'm going to treat the two of you rough in public. We can't have anyone know we're in league against the Chief Inspector."

"Agreed," Schmittberger said. "McClusky won't be the wiser."

"Go on then, lads, and shove it high up that lace curtain Irishman's arse."

Chapter 6

Schmittberger had gone off in a frenzy to retrieve a set of shackles and his day billy in case Dr. Primrose put up a fight at the sanitarium. The rain had waned, and Petrosino was waiting at the curb of the Marble Palace when he saw the shadow again. That same pair of eyes behind gold spectacles and a newspaper. Petrosino tried to get an angle on his whole face this time. The man was looking in a café window, smoking a cigarette, and, in the reflection of the glass, Petrosino could see the man's fingers tremble in the Spring chill.

Petrosino pulled his derby low over his brow and crossed the street toward the man. He got within reach of the newspaper, ripped it from the man's hands, and grabbed his Eton collar.

"Curse the fishes," Petrosino muttered and let go of Lincoln Steffens' neck. "I thought you were someone else. What the hell are you shadowing me for, Steffens?"

"A story. . ." Steffens coughed and placed a fresh cigarette on his lips, between his brown moustache and goatee. He had keen eyes behind his thick, smudged glasses and a haughty smile, as if he knew things that other men didn't know.

"Here." Petrosino flicked a matchstick across his fingernail. The flame licked at the curve of his hand, lighting Steffens' cigarette until it glowed amber. "Why didn't you just call?"

"I missed seeing the ugly mustard walls of the Marble Palace in person." Steffens straightened his collar and bow tie and handed Petrosino a linen business card. It had his name under *McClure's* and an address. "You walk so damned fast, and by the time I catch up, you're with other dicks I'd rather avoid. I've been waiting for the chance to catch you alone. Had I known the Third Degree was waiting. . ."

"You ain't seen the Third Degree yet. What's doing?"

Steffens pointed at the street, as if to ask whether they could take a stroll. Petrosino nodded, and they walked slowly. Steffens puffed his cigarette and swaggered as he spoke, "I'm doing a series on political corruption. The kind of tales that would knock your socks clean off. I'm not a regular newsman anymore. I'm an investigator now for a high-flying magazine."

"An *investigator*, you don't say?" Petrosino smiled at this, wondering if Steffens could solve a petty larceny if his life depended on it.

Steffens' cocksure smile cracked. "Well, I'm a reporter leastways."

"Why would a fancy writer like you want to talk to *me* about corruption and politics? I've got nothing to do with either."

"Oh, I think in an unwitting way you just might."

Petrosino became annoyed and stopped walking. "What's that supposed to mean?"

"No offense. I don't think you're corrupt or politically hinged at all, but the system is, Detective. And we're all in the system. Look, I'll be frank. I like to tell people I'm an investigator, a sleuth, but I know I'm not. That's a fact. My greatest fear is that someone will expose me, expose the fact that I don't know much about corruption or crime or anything I endeavor to write about. So I've been tramping around each city I visit, looking for men who actually are sleuths, men who do know what they're talking about."

"Why me exactly?"

"My old friend Jake Riis said he's known you since you were a bootblack shining shoes in front of Headquarters. He said you're a square man with guts, a fighter. He said that if you had an army, if you had a minority, no, if you had ten men, I mean *men*, then you would whip the whole crooked bunch of us. Besides that, you're an expert on Italian crime, and you could help me with my next article." Steffens held up his hands like a showman pointing at a billboard. "*The Shame of New York.*"

"Riis knew me when I was a greenhorn. I don't have an army or even ten good men. And Italian crime ain't the only *shame* in this town."

"Why, of course, I agree. The real 'shame' I mean to reveal is not Italian crime, but corruption endangering New York's good government. To that point, my boss and I would like to talk to you about a great octopus stretching its tentacles from the Old Country to our dear old New York."

"Is that right?" Petrosino's curiosity was snared now. He looked back at the shadow of the Marble Palace behind them. "If you want a whistleblower, you've got the wrong man. I'm not throwing my badge away for a yarn."

"I would never ask that. Besides, you'd remain anonymous, and it would only involve our investigation of this malevolent octopus."

"What 'octopus' is that?"

Steffens adjusted his spectacles and looked squarely at Petrosino. "Have you ever heard of an Italian secret society known as 'the mafia'?"

Petrosino snorted. "Of course, but it's no 'octopus.' Some gangs here try to use the ways of Sicilian *mafiosi*, sure, but they're small potatoes."

"We disagree, and that's what we'd like to talk to you about."

"Well, I can't talk. I've got a new case. You might've heard of a man being butchered with dirks and stuffed in a barrel on the East Side?"

"I've heard quite a lot about the barrel tragedy. But then again, I have all sorts of colleagues with their fingers on the pulse of the latest crimes." Steffens put his hand on Petrosino's forearm. "I could be a great asset to you, and you to me."

"The mafia, huh?" Petrosino took a drag of his cigar. "You know, there are hill people in every country who hold vengeance as their only way of justice."

"Like the mountain folk of Kentucky and West Virginia with their 'blood feuds.'"

"That's my point, Steffens. Sicilians have a long history of being oppressed, so they distrust the law and take justice in their own hands. But the real mafia died a long time ago. I'd say nowadays it's like a mountain feud or a sort of local Tammany Hall in its worst form."

"What you just said," Steffens whispered, eyes brightening like oil lamps, "that's exactly why we want to meet with you, Detective. I can't say much more here."

Petrosino contemplated it. The certainty in Steffen's eyes and the mystery of the proposed meeting swayed him. Before Petrosino could answer, Schmittberger walked up, carrying a rucksack that undoubtedly held a variety of restraints and weapons for Dr. Primrose's capture.

"Well, if it isn't Mr. Lincoln Steffens," Schmittberger said, "the grand muckraker late of *The Post* and *The Commercial Advertiser*? I thought they canned you a long time ago?"

"Hello Max, good to see you again, old friend." Steffens held out his hand to Schmittberger, who grudgingly shook it. "Still handsome and taller than I'll ever be."

"And you've lost more hair since I last saw you, Steff. Shouldn't you be in another town writing about the 'shame' of this or that politicker?"

"Ahh, so you've read my articles in *McClure's*?"

"Not a damn one." Schmittberger grinned. "What the hell are you doing here?"

"I've come back to my dear old New York. It's a great big swimming hole to me. Every day I can dive in and swim around to see what or who I can get, to make a story of them."

"Like you did with me?" Schmittberger's grin still there, but wolfish now.

"I treated you square, Max, you know that." Steffens patted Schmittberger's shoulder. "You should read my new articles. I'm achieving some fame writing about government and police corruption. You must have heard of *The Shame Of Minneapolis*? Or the latest one, *The Shamelessness of St. Louis*? I can get you copies."

"No thanks, Steff. I don't have the education to read your ten-dollar words, and we're all stocked up on toilet papers at home."

Petrosino tried not to laugh. "Steffens, maybe you could speak to Max about your story."

"I'd love to bend Max's ear some time," Steffens said uncomfortably, "but my boss sent me out to catch hold of you, Petrosino. You and you alone. No offense, Max."

"None taken. In fact, I'm glad I'm not the subject of any more tales written by you."

"Our office address is on the card I gave you, Detective." Steffens tipped his hat to them and quickly walked away down the street.

"Son of a bitch." Schmittberger spat in the street. "What are you talking to him for, Joe? Are you giving that wormy muckraker a news beat on the barrel murder?"

"No." Petrosino looked down at the linen business card. He memorized the Washington Square address and pocketed the card. "He wants to talk about the mafia society for a story. Did you read his articles?"

Schmittberger nodded. "Of course I did. But I didn't want to give him the satisfaction."

"What's with you and him?"

"It goes way back. From before you and I knew each other."

"Lexow?"

"I'll tell you another time, but you'd be wise to be careful with Lincoln Steffens, Joe. He thinks he knows everything and, worse, he aims to prove it."

"Don't worry, I will. I think it's high time we visited River Crest Sanitarium."

"Swell idea." Schmittberger pulled out the sleeve of a strait jacket from his rucksack. "Our mad doctor will be traveling in the finest of criminal gent's fashion."

⅋

They took a ferry from Manhattan to Astoria sitting by themselves in the last row of a starboard bench beneath advertisements for Pabst Malt Extract. Ships were lining up at every pier circling the island with masts and smoke stacks piercing the sky. The river lapped at the ferryboat's hull, and Max kept giving him that Cheshire cat smile.

He pointed his long finger. "You've got yourself a woman, don't you?"

Petrosino shook his head adamantly, but smiled at Max's intuition.

"Yes, you do. That's why you've been distracted. No matter. You'll confess in due course. Then I'll want details. Perfume, bosom size, whether she does the French whore's suck."

"You're demented, you know that?" Petrosino said, trying not to laugh.

"Well, I hope she is, too." Schmittberger nudged him. "When I came up, I worked a Negro district. One time, a prostitute comes out and presses a ten-dollar bill in my hand. I was so green I didn't know what to do with it. I asked an old bull who said, 'The Cap put you in a fat district so you can make a little on the side. He likes you, wants to fatten you up.' I was so damn foolish I took the money to the Captain and said, 'I've had plenty to eat today and don't need fattening up, sir. This money's for you.'"

"What did he do?"

"He was madder than a wet hen. He shouted, 'I don't take chicken feed!' Then he cooled down and told me it was just a tip, part of the job. Next time I see that Negro girl, she giggles, waves me upstairs. Here I am expecting another tip, but she gives me a different kind. Or I guess you could say I gave her the tip." Max grinned.

"You're off your damn rocker." Petrosino turned away, looking at the mist hanging over the East River. It smelled of garbage. "I don't have a girl. I wish I did, but I don't."

"Sure. You know, Piper used to be a real Casanova with the gals."

"Was that in olden times when you were children together?"

"Oh sure, we went to Sunday school together with George Washington. I'm younger than he is, you bastard."

Petrosino laughed. "I never came across him much, but I'm glad he's with us."

"Duff's a red-headed St. Nick. You know the story behind his limp?"

Petrosino shook his head. "He said he was in the War."

"He was, but no," Schmittberger said as the ferry bounced over a ripple, nearing Ward's Island and the rough tidal strait. "After the War, he started out as a cop in Satan's Circus. One night, a man was pistol-whipping a prostitute when Piper came on the scene with his nightstick. The man takes his .22 and shoots Piper in the leg, but Piper still manages to crush the man's skull with one billy blow. Drops him dead. Then, leg bleeding to hell, Piper carries the girl to a hospital. Almost had to amputate it he lost so much blood. Here Duff was, survived the War without a scratch, then almost dies on the job from a goddamn pimp."

"That's a hell of a story."

"And get this: the whore in the story is… Missus Gertrude Piper. Nice Christian society lady nowadays, even introduced me to Sarah at a maypole dance. Now you know why Piper understands us rank-and-file men. Keep that between us, Joe."

"What was Piper saying about his wife's *medicine* in the bath house? She sick?"

"Ah that." Schmittberger sighed. "Poor old Duff and Gerty tried like hell to have kids. Nine times she got pregnant, and nine times she had a miscarriage. If you ask me, it had something to do with her working days in Satan's Circus."

"So they've got no kids at all?"

"Nope. That's why he dotes on that big fat nephew of his. And Duff's poor wife is still so broken up about never giving him kids that she weeps all day and takes morphine to go to sleep at night. That's the *medicine* Duff was talking about."

"That's a shame," Petrosino said.

"Yeah, he's had it rough, and now he's toothless as a house cat in his old age. Hates Tammany. He fears what I fear: that we'll be beaten soon and Tammany will come back."

"What makes you say that?"

"My gut. But if Piper gets us a gold star and a raise for this collar, I don't give a damn about the why or what for. As long as we ram a hot poker up McClusky's ass."

"I don't think Tammany will come back, Max, at least not like before." Petrosino sighed, doubting himself, wondering what would happen to the cops who played the Reform game.

They navigated the curve around Pot Cove and landed on a pier near Hell Gate, about the same distance north as East 100th Street in the City, only they were on the eastern shore of the East River now. It smelled different here, the salt smell of the sea. The City's horse manure and garbage scows were a faint memory. Ward's Island was directly west of them in the middle of the river. Petrosino got off, stared back across at the island and further off at Italian Harlem in the distance. The sun was beginning to crawl down to the shanties and the gunmetal grey horizon. Schmittberger looked at the darkening sky, too, and checked his pocket watch.

"You afraid to go to the madhouse at night, Joe?"

"I am." Petrosino waved at a cab driver, and they climbed inside the hansom.

The carriage ride was only a few minutes to River Crest Sanitarium. Dust kicked up from the roads, and long planes of soft green grass and rows of sycamore led up a gentle hill to the estate on Merchant and Wolcott Avenue. New saplings had been carefully arranged in a semicircle on a crest overlooking the East River.

Schmittberger said, "Hell, this place looks more like the Ivy League than the loony bin. Look at all the fancy buildings and flower gardens. It must cost a fortune to be crazy here."

Petrosino scanned the grounds. There were seven buildings that looked like guesthouses or hotels and a main office building in the center that looked more like a private estate with red gables and a white painted porch running all the way around. Their carriage slowed and arced around the horseshoe driveway, stopping at a whitewashed sign: *Welcome to RIVER CREST, A Sanitarium for Mental and Nervous Diseases.* They got out, and Petrosino read the smaller print on the sign: *Separate Buildings for Alcoholic and Drug Habituation. Physician Wm. E. Dold.*

Schmittberger had one hand on his rucksack and another on his hip, admiring the bucolic scenery like a hunter before the fox is released. "By God, Joe, would you look at that?" Max pointed at curved swaths of woodland and manicured greens with flagsticks. "They've got a damn golf course."

"And we haven't seen one guard yet. Something's fishy in Denmark."

A squat man in a uniform flew out of the main building and down the front porch.

"Spoke too soon," Petrosino said. "Maybe they've got guards after all."

The hospital guard waved his arms at them. Petrosino noticed that he had a freshly broken nose and ringlets of blood caking in his nostrils. They hurried across the front circle, and the guard stumbled as if he were fresh from a boxing match that didn't go his way.

"Are you the law?" the guard asked, panting.

"We are." Petrosino nodded.

"Thank the Lord!" The guard tripped on the first porch step and righted himself, saying woozily, "Dr. Dold just sent word. He got loose."

"What the hell are you talking about?" Schmittberger said.

"Primrose is loose, and he's got the devil in him."

New York City Office
616 Madison Ave.
Corner of 58th St.
Telephone 1470 Plaza.
Jno. Jos. Kindred, M: D.,
Consultant.

RIVER CREST SANITARIUM,
ASTORIA, L. I., N. Y. CITY.

Established 1896
by Jno. Jos. Kindred, M. D.

Office hours
at New York City Office.
3-4 daily.
Sanitarium Telephone 820-821 Astoria.
Wm. Elliott Dold, M. D.,
Physician in Charge.

River Crest Sanitarium

Chapter 7

"Where the devil are the rest of you all?" That was Dr. William Dold's first question. He dashed onto the front porch of River Crest Sanitarium in a whirlwind of silver hair, eyebrows, and sideburns. With a honeyed drawl, he said, "In his current condition, he'll be more of a load than any two men can handle."

"If that's so," Petrosino said, "then why don't you have more than two guards here?"

Dold hemmed and hawed.

"Is the only way off this place by ferry, doc?"

"Yes," Dold said, "and the next one isn't due for hours."

"We heard Primrose confessed to you. What did he say exactly?"

Dr. Dold hesitated. "Gentlemen, there's no time for this. Duncan is in a psychopathic state, and we must find him for his own sake."

"Just tell us what else you know about this loon, and make it quick so we can snatch him up and leave this country club. Go on, spit it out, goddamn it."

Dr. Dold stopped pacing and pointed at Petrosino. "*I* am the physician in charge here, and I don't take kindly to blasphemy. The patient was duly committed here by court order, and we certainly are not a 'country club' as you say. I was a Valentine Mott medalist, and I am a renowned alienist in this-"

"Valentine Mott," Schmittberger interrupted, "well hell, why didn't you say so?" Schmittberger put his long hand on Dold's shoulder and leaned over him like a preying mantis on a fly. "I don't give a sewer rat's tits about your medals or your golf course or how much money you make from this racket. All I want to know is what this killer was doing here, and what happened? Now sing before it gets dark, for shit's sake."

Dold shrunk back into the cocoon of his white coat and spoke quickly, "I was asked by the judge and the family's defense attorney to conduct an inmate psychopathic evaluation of Dr. Primrose. Duncan was transferred here on Easter Monday. I was told he had killed a servant, a carriage driver, I believe. Evidently, Duncan said the body had been mutilated because his wife had cuckolded him. However, I hadn't-"

"Wait," Petrosino said, "did you get his confession in writing?"

Dold shook his head. "No, I hadn't completed my psychopathic report yet."

"So no signed confession. Did Primrose describe how he killed his driver?"

"He said he 'castrated the little Dago.'" Dold gave Petrosino an apologetic smile. "His words."

Schmittberger said, "What else? Did he say he used a stiletto or a kitchen knife or a spoon? Did he go to the poor fellow's home? Did he drug him first? Did he have help?"

"He may have mentioned something about subduing his victim, about knocking him out."

"Aha." Schmittberger poked Dold's shoulder. "But the coroner didn't find any trace of drugs in the victim's system nor a lump on the head."

"What difference would it make? He was just some poor Dago… I mean, an unfortunate fellow from the Ghetto."

"Just another Dago, doc?" Petrosino said.

Dold's face flushed as he hissed, "Shouldn't y'all be searching the grounds now?"

"What the hell is your hurry?" Schmittberger said. "There's only one way off, and he ain't swimming the East River."

The sanitarium's front door opened, and Dold seemed relieved by the interruption. He waved over a pale and bloodied duo that shambled onto the front porch. A nurse and a sturdy guard. The nurse had the furry face of a rabbit and pink handprints on her shriveled white neck. The guard was holding a sopping wet, red towel against his right ear and whimpering.

"This is my staff who tried to subdue him," Dold said and turned to the nurse. "Miss Anna, tell these lawmen what happened."

"He was locked in his room during the after-luncheon nap," Miss Anna said calmly. "The windows are locked tight, but he must have jimmied one open. I was in the staff office when I heard a man shouting, 'I'm the Czar of Russia, you can't keep me bottled up in here!' I went outside to the porch and saw him standing right here in his nightshirt and patent leather shoes. I held his arm, trying to calm him down, and said it was a nice time for a walk. He said, 'All right, you little Jap.' We walked up and down the porch for a quarter of an hour. Then I told him it was time to return to his cot. That's when he loosed his arm from me and threw me to the ground like so much chaff. I started screaming, but he choked me."

Petrosino imagined this old nurse trying to control a grown man. She was small enough to walk beneath Schmittberger's outstretched arm.

Petrosino looked at the guard and asked, "Where were you?"

"I heard a rumpus and run out to help. He tossed Miss Anna aside and came at me. Look what he did." The guard removed the towel and showed them a bloody hole where his right ear was supposed to be.

Petrosino grimaced and waved at the guard to put the towel back.

"Duncan is strong, he was a crack Harvard jumper," Dold said, almost admiringly, "and, in his current state, he has the might of five men."

"And he has a knife now, too?" Petrosino said.

"I don't know what it was," the guard said, sobbing. "We still ain't found my ear."

"For shit's sake, stop the waterworks," Schmittberger said. "This nice lady here got strangled, and she ain't crying. Now which direction did he go? And what's he look like?"

"Clean and fair, average height, build," the guard said, trying not to whine. "He doesn't look like much, but he's wild. I think he was headed to the river bank again. It's near the Gas Works, just below us. Kept saying he was going 'home.'"

Petrosino turned to Dr. Dold, "Why wasn't Primrose in a strait waistcoat?"

"I didn't see the need for a strait jacket. When he was admitted, I gave him heavy opiates. They must have had no effect, which is unusual because they worked well before."

"Wait a second," Petrosino said. "Your guard says Primrose went for the river 'again,' and you call him 'Duncan' like you're old chums and now you say he's been here *before?*"

Dr. Dold paused, looking down as if he'd stepped in manure. "Duncan has suffered from 'nervous prostration' in the past and usually took the 'rest cure.' So it was no surprise he was sent to us for treatment and for a psychopathic evaluation after this latest episode."

"*Episode* indeed," Schmittberger said. "Was it a *surprise* to you that he'd castrated a man and could have canned his parts for sausage?"

Dold stared malevolently at Max. "That is not what I meant."

"He should have been put in the Tombs," Petrosino seethed. "Not this resort."

Schmittberger glared at Dold. "I heard he got here on a 'long green certificate'? How much did your affidavit cost to get him sent here instead of jail?"

"Gentlemen, I suggest you do your jobs and look for him now." Dr. Dold turned for the door, but Schmittberger grabbed his wrist.

"If we don't find Primrose," Schmittberger said, "we'll be back for you, *Dolt.*"

Schmittberger and Petrosino took the earless guard with them and headed for the river.

Ↄↄ

The River Crest watchman was snoring off an afternoon cocktail in his watchouse, a shack on the river's edge. Petrosino, Schmittberger, and the earless guard took him by surprise.

Petrosino kicked the chair he was slumped in, and the watchman growled, "Fuck off."

"Get up, shitbird," Petrosino said and punched his ear.

The watchman quickly realized he was talking to the law and stood up, but the liquor was coming off him in fumes. "Ask the Gas Works man, he was the last to see him."

"I know you," Schmittberger said, "no wonder you left the Department for this job, *sarge*. Drunker than ten Injuns at midday. Have you looked for him yourself?"

"Not on your life. He's raving-"

"Shut up. Did you see him? Does he have a knife?"

The watchman held up his hands pleadingly. "I don't know. Ask the Gas Works man. He went that-a-way. He must be hiding, there's no way off here without a boat."

"You just stay here safe and warm then with your one-eared pal." Petrosino slapped the watchman again for good measure, and he and Schmittberger left the earless guard behind. They made their way to the neighboring property to the south and saw a man's dusky silhouette in the distance. He was wearing denim and a moleskin coat, standing in the grass and looking toward a stand of trees and an endless patch of brush sprouting all along the river.

"You looking for that loon?" the moleskin man called out. Petrosino and Schmittberger nodded and hurried to him. He shook their hands. "I'm Moylan, superintendent of the Consolidated Gas Works. I seen him a little while ago. I think the damn fool jumped in."

"In the East River?"

Moylan nodded. "I had a few men look for him in the bushes. But we found naught. Then I heard someone shoutin', 'Save me, save me! I'm drowning!' But we ain't found no one. Must've drowned hisself by now. I hope."

"There goes our picture in the paper, Joe. Maybe we should get grappling hooks in case we have to drag the river?"

Petrosino felt his fists tightening. Nightfall was a half hour away, at most. He looked around at the terrain and the river again, noticing a small tug coming down the water from the north. "What does the Gas Works do with its rubbish?"

"Some of it gets dumped in the river. But if we can sell anything, we put it on a scow."

"What about a dock? They have a dock for hauling?"

Moylan pointed past the scrub at a leaning pier of old tree trunks and warped planks. Petrosino thought he saw a tug at the Gas Works pier and grabbed Schmittberger's shoulder. He started running for the river bank and circled around the trees and the scrub brush. Fresh tracks ran along the bank, and he followed. A quarter mile later, there was a pair of patent leather shoes, muddied but new and good quality. He pointed them out to Max, who had a fierce glow in his eyes. They ran further south down the bank to the Gas Works pier, where they saw the tug starting up, three scows hooked to it, ready to make the trip across the East River to Manhattan.

Petrosino grabbed Max's forearm and pointed. A figure was coming out of the water, climbing onto the last scow. It was a blond man in a cream nightshirt stained with blood, doing a crab walk, inching his way across piles of garbage toward the second scow.

"Curse the fishes!" Petrosino shouted.

They made for the pier, shouting at the tugboat captain to stop. But the captain had revved his engine, and the sounds of the tug and the bell and the river kept him from hearing. Duncan Primrose had scampered across two scows now, and he was jumping onto the scow closest to the tug. In a matter of seconds, Petrosino thought, he'd be surprising the tug captain, and who knew what havoc he'd do?

Schmittberger ran ahead of him like a galloping ostrich and screamed over his shoulder, "Move those little Dago legs!"

They ran to the end of the pier just as the last scow was sliding by, and they both leapt onto it. Petrosino's stomach hit hard, knocking the wind out of him, and he slid back, his feet dangling in the water. He shouted at Schmittberger, who grabbed him by the back of his jacket and yanked him on. Petrosino's derby went rolling across the garbage and he snatched it before it could drop into the cold ink of the East River. They had no time to catch their breaths, up and crawling again, sliding through filth and coal dust and broken metal parts.

By the time they reached the tugboat and threw their legs onto the deck, Primrose was holding a deckhand from behind, forearm under his throat, and his other hand holding a sharp piece of metal against the deckhand's chin. The captain was at the wheel, glancing back frantically, saying something to Primrose.

Petrosino and Schmittberger took out their billies and approached the wheelhouse.

"The Czar's orders must be obeyed!" Primrose shouted. "Take me to see my wife or I'll cut this one's nose off! DO IT, you Jap cockeater!"

"Easy there, Primrose," Schmittberger said.

Primrose turned to the back of the boat, still manhandling the deckhand. Petrosino could see the "knife" wasn't a knife at all. It was a shoehorn, but the smaller end of it had been sharpened to a deadly point. As Primose tensed, the shoehorn punctured the deckhand, and blood beaded and trickled down the deckhand's cheek.

"Stay away from me!" Primrose shouted. "I'll take his Jap head clean off if you move an inch! I'm the Czar of Russia!"

"Sure, you're the Czar," Schmittberger said. "Why, you're the President and Mayor all in a bunch. Now, let him go, Primrose, or you'll be the Man in the Iron Mask, too."

"Hang it, Max," Petrosino whispered, "not now damn it. Don't set him off."

"I'm a rich man," Primrose said, eyes unblinking and bright sea-green. "I can pay you $50,000 if you just let me be. When we land in Manhattan, just let me go and don't follow."

"That sounds like a fair bargain, Duncan," Petrosino said. "But you can't hurt anyone, all right? We'll just finish our boat ride, then we'll all be on our way. Deal?"

Primrose didn't answer. The men tensely held their positions as the boat neared 12th Street. Petrosino and Schmittberger held their billies down by their thighs now, watching Primrose's hand on the sharpened shoehorn. Primrose quieted down for a moment, on the verge of tears. His eyes fought to stay open, both wild with rage then suddenly pathetic with fear.

Schmittberger whispered, "He's getting tired, Joe."

Primrose convulsed with tears, cheek to cheek with the deckhand. "I just want to see my wife! What's taking so damn long? You're trying to kidnap me! Land now!"

"I'm supposed to go all the way round past the American Line piers to West 45th," the tug captain said, looking back at the detectives, and they shook their heads at him and mouthed the word, LAND, as they passed under the Brooklyn Bridge. "Fine fucking mess, this is. All right, it'll get me canned, but I'll try that little pier there."

"You agreed not to hurt him," Petrosino said to Primrose, pointing at the deckhand.

"Yes," Primrose said calmly, "just land. I need to see my wife."

As soon as the tug was within twenty feet of the pier, Primrose threw the deckhand at Petrosino and Schmittberger and snatched up a bale stick. He struck the captain across the mouth, and the captain fell on his knees, clutching his face. Primrose took four strides and leapt onto the dock, making the jump easily before sprinting full speed into the city.

By the time the tug was close enough for Petrosino and Schmittberger to jump onto the pier, they lost sight of him. But they followed a string of screams until they found Primrose barefoot in the street in his bloody nightshirt, squawking, "The Czar's orders must be obeyed! Death to the disobedient Japs and Dagos!" He had the bale stick in one hand and the shoehorn in the other, threatening passers-by.

Petrosino put away his billy and took out his .38. Max nodded and kept a billy in hand as they marched through a crowd swirling around Primrose, who swung the bale stick at a storefront and shattered a plate glass window. An old woman passed too close, and he struck her on the head and knocked her out cold. The crowd shouted at him and followed his whirlwind path, and Petrosino and Schmittberger shoved people out of the way as men picked up stones and hurled them at Primrose. But Primrose was unfazed. He lunged again and again, and the crowd danced backward.

"Where's a cop when you need one?" Schmittberer muttered, pushing through. "Cover me, Joe, so I can get one good lick with my billy, and he'll fold straight up."

Petrosino fired a warning shot in the air, and the crowd opened up.

Primrose shouted, "Let the War of 1812 begin!" and threw a livery driver to the ground and stood over him with the shoehorn. Petrosino covered Schmittberger as Max dove in and smashed Primrose's arm. The shoehorn clinked to the street. Schmittberger clubbed Primrose on the head, but Primrose stood straight up and swung back with his bale stick. Schmittberger ducked and tackled him to the ground, and Petrosino holstered his gun and piled onto both men. They rolled around in the gutter for what seemed like hours to Petrosino, and finally Primrose wilted and began giggling like a child.

"My wife is the Czarina. She's fixed up with the King of Italy to assassinate me. But I still love her!" He looked at Petrosino, who was sitting on his chest with Schmittberger. "Go on, you dirty Dago spy, do me in!"

Petrosino said to Schmittberger, "Even the loons?"

"I keep telling you, Joe, it's the garlic."

"You said one good tap with your billy? He's still moving." Petrosino struggled to stay on top of Primrose. "You used to be an artist. You used to hit 'em once, and they'd flop down like a fish. You're losing your touch."

"You're hurting my feelings, Joe. Loons are different, they're always strong as a bull moose. Hold him. No time for the strait jacket." Schmittberger snatched up irons from his rucksack, and they cuffed him. Then Schmittberger patted him down and stopped when he reached inside the nightshirt pocket. He wiped his fingers on the nightshirt and slapped Primrose. "Joe, look inside his pocket."

Petrosino didn't want to, but he couldn't resist. He pulled open the pocket, saw a fresh ear caked in bright blood, and muttered, "You crazy bastard."

"Add petit larceny," Schmittberger said as they dragged him through the crowd.

"I'm a millionaire," Primrose pleaded. "I'll pay you both $100,000 to let me go!"

"Shut your fucking hole, you loon." Schmittberger slapped Primrose.

A boy shouted, "The old woman's dead!"

Angry cries erupted, and men came forward with a noose. Petrosino pointed his pistol at the first one's nose, and the lynch mob retreated. A delivery wagon drove by, and Schmittberger snatched the horse's bridle and shouted at the driver to halt. They tossed Primrose onto a pile of flour sacks, hopped on, and told the driver to whip up the horse quick. Petrosino and Schmittberger held down the lunatic doctor as he curled up on a flour sack and sang:

> *"Hello Central, give me heaven!*
> *For I know my mother's there.*
> *You will find her with the angels*
> *Over on the golden stair."*

Chapter 8

McClusky's Irish boys were still at Headquarters when Petrosino and Schmittberger processed Dr. Duncan Primrose in the basement. They made cracks at the smell coming off Petrosino's clothes and at Primrose's hospital gown. Primrose was a limp bundle of chains on a wooden bench, momentarily lucid, staring wide-eyed at them all as if he'd just rubbed a nightmare from his bleary eyes.

"Say, pal, am I dreaming?" Primrose asked Petrosino.

"Nope, you're pinched for murder in the first and six counts of assault."

Detective "Handsome" Jimmy McCafferty watched Petrosino write the arrest report, smiling with his big mocking teeth. Despite his mouthful of piano keys, he had a reputation as a "masher" or Casanova. Even the puritanical police matrons doted on McCafferty, always running their hands through his wavy black hair and pinching his dimples.

Petrosino glanced at McCafferty's lush head of hair and self-consciously raked his own receding hairline.

McCafferty's teeth sparkled as he whispered over Primrose's shoulder, "I can't believe that you, a genteel fair-haired doctor, a white man of all people, stooped down to massacre a Guinea on the East Side. The Italian niggers in Sing Sing will eat you alive, boy-o."

McCafferty called out to the other dicks with a voice like a pistol shot, "Can you believe it, boys?! Can you believe this nice Caucasian doc is a stone cold butcher? Maybe we ought to cut *his* balls off and see how he likes it? Just one of them for fun, eh?"

McCafferty poked at Primrose's crotch, and Primrose cowered meekly and began weeping in spasms.

"Jesus, he's a fucking nancy," McCafferty said to Petrosino. "How'd you find him, Joe?"

"Sleuthing," Schmittberger answered from behind a newspaper, sitting at a desk adjacent to Petrosino. "You ought to try it some time, Jimmy."

McCafferty snorted. "That's swell advice, Inspector."

"I'm innocent, I tell you!" Primrosed cried out.

McCafferty spun and kicked Primrose's crotch. "That's what they always say. 'It's not me, judge, I swear on me mudder's grave!'"

The Irish dicks cackled in the background.

"The old woman you attacked is alive," Petrosino said to Primrose. "So that charge is a molehill compared to the killing. Why'd you butcher that man?"

Primrose said nothing, and the Irish dicks goaded him, "Come now, Nancy!"

"Why'd you put him in the barrel like that?" Petrosino asked. "Did someone help you?"

Primrose slumped on the bench in his irons and pissed himself.

"It's no use, Joe, let's have a word upstairs," Schmittberger said, putting down his newspaper and rising. He said loudly to McCafferty, "Sergeant, clean up that piss and then let *The World's* man take the prisoner's picture."

McCafferty half-saluted.

Schmittberger pointed at McCafferty. "Do it again, the right way."

McCafferty scowled and gave Max a full military salute.

Schmittberger nodded at Petrosino, and they left Primrose shackled to the bench with the other Central Bureau dicks taunting him while the pair slipped upstairs to Petrosino's office.

"I couldn't stand listening to those Irish punks anymore." Schmittberger shut the door. "Let's telephone our *rabbi* and give him the dope. Ask him if he thinks we should hold him here or send him to the Tombs where they can have a police alienist examine him."

Petrosino picked up the telephone receiver in his office.

Schmittberger shook his head. "Across the street, use a public line. The telephone switchboard operators are the worst gossips in all of Greater New York."

"You think the T/S girls would leak the connection between us and our tip?"

"Does JD Rockefeller have a million dollars?"

"I'll say." Petrosino stood and hesitated. Something had been gnawing at him. "You ever solve a big one like this so quick, Max?"

"Sure. Remember that Sicilian prostitute last Christmas? Only took us an hour to find her father with his hands still wet with her blood. Why, what's wrong?"

Petrosino shrugged. "I don't know."

"He confessed. And Weston said the killer must have been strong as hell to slice through the victim's neck the way he did, remember? The two of us could barely hold Primrose down."

"True. But Weston said more than one weapon and maybe two killers or more."

"'*Convinced myself, I seek not to convince.*' That's Poe." Schmittberger wiggled his eyebrows and bristly moustache. "We got the collar, Joe, don't look a gift horse in the mouth."

Petrosino sighed and slipped out of Headquarters to a public telephone booth in a boarding house down the block. He rang Piper at home and advised him that they had captured their man after a chase and that they would tip the "Poker Club" of reporters at Headquarters so the morning would have front-page screamer headlines. Piper told him not to mention his name and to send Primrose to a padded cell in the Tombs.

"I'll make sure Sandy has an alienist take charge of the prisoner at the Tombs and assess his sanity," Piper said on the telephone. "The less control George the Peacock has, the better. And I want you two to know how pleased I am. Don't be surprised if you get letters of commendation and an extra day off a month, perhaps even a pay bump, lad."

Petrosino hung up the telephone. They'd solved the biggest murder in the city in less than a day, and not a single Irishman would get credit for it. For a moment, he was distracted with dreams of promotion and glory. From bootblack to White Wing, he said to himself, and now Sergeant and maybe Captain someday? A decade ago, he never would have dreamed of the possibility of an Italian running an entire precinct. But now in the twentieth century, it didn't seem so absurd. Look at Max, he told himself, a Jew Inspector.

"*Captain* Petrosino," he whispered as he walked back to the Marble Palace, oblivious to the gusts of cold air that buffeted his derby. There was always this euphoria after a solved case, then the reality of his position and melancholy would settle on him like so much coal dust. It must have been what the opium fiends felt like when they visited their dragon dens in Chinatown for a moment of bliss and then a long sad sleep.

☙

Primrose was still crying when McCafferty and two patrolmen took him in a Black Maria to the Tombs. Schmittberger and Petrosino saw him off in the street, making sure their prey was carted off in one piece and in more chains than the Handcuff King himself, Harry Houdini. Like henpecking mothers, they reminded McCafferty a dozen times to have Primrose put in a strait waistcoat once he was in a cell at the Tombs. Then they winked at each other and headed down Mulberry Street. As they passed The Mabille, Schmittberger pointed at the young men and women in bright make-up and sheer gowns who beckoned them.

"The fairies have come out early tonight. It's a *Midsummer Night's Dream* in April."

They laughed and kept walking to the Florence Saloon.

"You think Primrose is some kind of escapologist?"

Petrosino shook his head. "Only a lunatic."

"This is a big collar, Joe." Schmittberger clapped Petrosino's back. "You know, if I keep up this brilliant pace, I'll be Commissioner soon. And I just might let you ride my coattails."

"Maybe the Italians are next? What do you say?"

"Oh, sure, they'll have an Italian mayor, too, and a Negro governor."

"They'd never let him in," Petrosino said. "The only thing they think is worse than a Dago in New York is a Negro. He'll become mud in the bricks of progress."

"Yeah, and so will we. Who are we fooling? Let's get some suds."

They walked into a saloon through a wave of smoke and chatter and bellied up to a tin counter. They had two rounds of beer with rye chasers before they took a deep breath and looked at each other, basking in the day's accomplishment.

Petrosino was still doubtful about Primrose. He stared at the foam on Schmittberger's moustache and the frown hiding beneath. "You don't look pleased, Max."

"We always do this. Even though we know we ain't going nowhere but eighty hours a week on the East Side and then straight to hell. Same difference, I guess." Schmittberger ordered another round and skipped the beer to down the shot first. "We're fooling ourselves. I get giddy at first like you, but then I think that T.R. is long gone to Washington, and Reform will be over and out soon. Tammany will be back. Then what do we get, Joe? We get the axe, that's what. They'll send me to Devil's Island like that French Jew, Dreyfus."

"Why do you keep worrying? Mayor Low's not going anywhere. He'll win again this year, and Tammany will be done for."

"You think so?" Schmittberger took a sip of beer. "God, I hope so for our sake."

"Cheer up damn it. You're starting to talk like Steffens." Petrosino drank half his brown bucket of beer in one gulp and plunked it down on the counter.

"What did that tenderfoot say to you?"

"That Low's Reform government was in danger. Corruption and Tammany. Same old thing. Why are you so sore about Steffens anyhow?"

Schmittberger tilted his bucket, swallowed an entire beer, and burped. "All right, I'll tell you about ole Lincoln Steffens. Then maybe you won't be so impressed with that know-it-all muckrake. Sarah and I are *friends* with him and his wife."

"If that don't beat all." Petrosino laughed and lit a cigar. "You sure don't act like it."

Schmittberger took a puff from Petrosino's cigar and handed it back. "Back in '94, when the Lexow Committee was investigating police corruption, Steffens was at *The Post* and he'd become good friends with Reverend Dr. Parkhurst and the Society for the Prevention of Crime. *The Post* never printed crime news or police gossip. Too good for it. They always printed stuff about Wall Street and high society. But then when we were under fire during Lexow, they had Steffens turn up everywhere to expose us and clean us out as rascals. This was before you made Sergeant. Steffens was the one who sang one damn song all day long, '*Get Schmittberger!*' He went around telling the Reformers, the police, the public, that if I squealed, I would deliver everybody and everything."

"I would've throttled the son of a bitch."

"Oh believe me, I wanted to." Schmittberger smiled cruelly. "After Lexow, I got sent out to the sticks, Riverside-on-Hudson. One day, I'm on mounted patrol, and I see Steffens and his wife on bicycles. He waved, and I ignored him. But then his wife invited us to dinner, and Steffens eventually saw what a swell fellow I was."

"So he got you back on the job?"

"He did after a while. At the time, the good were against me for grafting, and the underworld was against me for squealing. Everyone wanted my head. But Steffens saw his chance to make a moral experiment of me. Could a dishonest man be reformed? He convinced them all, Parkhurst, Roosevelt, the papers."

"You don't feel like you owe Steffens anything?"

"Sure I owe him for getting me back on the job, but it was all to stroke his own ego. And I resent the hell out of him for it."

"He was playing puppetmaster."

"Exactly. Men like Steffens and Parkhurst, they like to sit back and pull wires just to see the puppets jump. You be careful with him, Joe, or he'll make an example of you, too."

Petrosino sat back on a stool, seeing the anger dull the blue glint in his friend's eyes.

Schmittberger ordered another round. "He doesn't know what I've been through. He's never had his kids sit silent at dinner, nudging one another on, and then pass the buck to the oldest boy, the one I always wanted the respect of. And then my oldest swallows a big lump in his throat and blurts out, 'I say, Pop, is it true this stuff they're saying? That you're a . . . crook and . . . a squealer, too? It's all lies, ain't it?'" Schmittberger stopped talking, his lip quivering.

"Max, let's talk about something else. Tonight we're the two biggest dicks in New York, and we'll be the talk of the town tomorrow: *Handsome Dago And Dim-Witted Inspector Solve Barrel Murder*. Let's drink to that. Let's have a snootful and talk about cunny or when cattle got loose from that ship and nearly trampled you. We can talk all night, damn it. We just pinched the devil who did the barrel murder!"

Schmittberger handed Petrosino a beer and lifted another to clink buckets together. The twinkle was back in his eyes. "You're a good friend, Joe. You're right to make me talk of better things. We can say in all humility that we are the finest dicks this City of whores has ever known. Speaking of which, did I ever tell you about the prettiest young twins who ran a badger game in the Tenderloin? The only way I could tell those gals apart was a nice mole right here." Schmittberger turned and pointed at the crack of his ass.

They laughed and drank to Schmittberger's toast, "To the milky white arses of Eileen and Eleanor Fischbein, may we dream of them tonight."

Chapter 9

When Petrosino woke, his head throbbed, and his stomach was lurching up to his throat. He slowly rolled out of bed and opened the window curtain. He held his hand up to the frayed sunlight and cursed as the thirst hit him. He drank straight from the tap, almost choking on one long breathless gulp. Then he washed and shaved quickly over the wash stand. The face in the looking glass still seemed gloomy. He'd grown more anxious about the barrel murder case, and his queasy stomach growled over it as he dressed.

Outside, Bimbo was waiting in ambush for him a block north at Prince Street with a group of smaller newsies swarming like gnats. Petrosino pretended not to see the kid coming.

Bimbo rushed up and saluted, rigid as a flagpole.

Petrosino saluted back. "At ease, kid. What are you all atwitter about?"

"The best day of my life," Bimbo exhaled, waving a stack of newspapers that looked small in his muscular arms. "You solved that barrel murder, *Detective Sergeant*, sir."

The other boys buzzed around them, hanging on their every word.

Petrosino said, "Let me see the paper."

Bimbo held out a copy of *The World* with the headline: *DERANGED DOCTOR ARRESTED IN BARREL MURDER TRAGEDY – Believed Victim In Tryst With His Wife*. Petrosino quickly skimmed the article. He and Schmittberger were mentioned as having made the arrest, and there were halftone photos of the victim's face and of Primrose weeping in irons in the Marble Palace's basement.

Petrosino smiled and gave Bimbo a dollar.

"That's too much, Joe." Bimbo held the money in his palm.

"I'm gonna buy more copies, kid. What else you got?"

Bimbo fanned out the papers, and Petrosino picked out *The World*, *The Times*, *The Sun*, and *Il Progresso*. He folded them into a bundle and hid it in his overcoat.

"You still gave me too much," Bimbo said.

Petrosino started walking toward Headquarters. "You'll pay me back soon enough."

Bimbo tagged along. "They said the killer put up a fight. Did you lick him?"

"Inspector Schmittberger and I whipped him real good, kid."

"How'd you find him?"

"Good sleuthing." Petrosino waved him closer. "I'll learn you something, come here."

Bimbo leaned his ear in, and the other boys tried to squeeze closer.

Petrosino pointed to a shabby man across the street, loitering at a fruit peddler's cart.

"You see that fellow over there? A crook moves different than an innocent citizen. He'll walk at a jerky pace, turn his head slyly, take quick sidelong glances, and he won't look you in the eye. There's nothing calm about a crook unless he's very good. That's for free, kid."

Bimbo and the other boys were staring at the shabby man, and the man saw what they were doing, put down an apple, and quickly walked off.

"Why," Bimbo mumbled, "you're the Italian Sherlock Holmes, Joe. What else are youse gonna teach me now that I'm a bona fide bull."

"A bull?"

Bimbo unfolded a wrinkled letter and held it up.

Petrosino stopped in his tracks and read the first sentence: "*Dear Sir: We have certified the results from the civil service examination, and we are pleased to inform you that you have made the list of candidates for patrolman in the Police Department for the City of New York.*"

"Well, kid, I guess you ain't a shitbird after all." Petrosino took out his billfold and gave him several bills. "You gotta pay for your uniform and equipment from the quartermaster. And get good socks. The old brogans will kill your feet if you don't have good socks. I'll speak to Schmittberger about getting you into the Red Light District."

Bimbo looked at the money, dumbfounded.

"What the hell are you looking at, kid? When you get your sixty-five bucks a month, you can pay me back. Now scram before I kick your ass… *patrolman*."

Bimbo ran down the street with a cowboy yelp, "Hi yi yi!"

 భ

The smile on Petrosino's face disappeared when he walked up to the Marble Palace and checked his pocket watch. He needed to get down to the basement for roll call at the "Mulberry Street Morning Parade." The prisoners who had been arrested the night before were paraded in front of the Central Bureau dicks. The detectives would wear black masks as the prisoners were displayed and identified, and the lawmen were supposed to commit each crook's face and crime to memory, in case they crossed paths again in the future. Petrosino normally enjoyed the ritual, but all he could think about was the barrel murder. A voice shouting from above startled him.

"Yeah you, Sergeant!" Chief Inspector McClusky's rough voice rained down. Petrosino took two steps back and looked up at McClusky leaning out of his office window. "Get your ass up here, on the double!"

The window slammed shut, and pigeon feathers fluttered down.

Petrosino sighed and made his way up the three flights of stairs to the anteroom of McClusky's office. Early morning was when the Chief Inspector received complaining citizens, department heads, reporting captains, and the press. Petrosino glanced at the suits, dresses, and uniforms in the anteroom waiting for instructions from the desk sergeant who regulated foot traffic. The door to McClusky's inner office was shut.

"Well, look who's here." Schmittberger peeked from a fedora so low on his head that Petrosino could barely see his eyes. "Bought yourself papers, too, to see your name in print."

"You look like something a tomcat dragged in," Petrosino said.

"Yeah? Well, I got here before you did, didn't I. You can't outdrink me on your best day, greenstick."

Petrosino sat down with his papers and hat next to Schmittberger.

"He's been in there a half hour with the press," Schmittberger said.

"How much credit will we get?"

Schmittberger made a big O with his hand, closed his eyes, and leaned back in his chair.

"You know that boy, Bimbo, playing stickball yesterday? He made the list."

"Bully for him. I suppose you want him to start on the East Side."

Petrosino nodded, then whispered, "I've been thinking on the case."

"Me, too, Joe. Don't say it. Let me enjoy it for a little while, would you? My noggin' hurts. I wish I could find an ice truck and just dunk my head in the back of the wagon for a couple of days. You got any headache powders?"

"No. You thinking what I am about the case?"

"I was, but I'm not gonna make waves. We close it, it's good for all. Especially us."

Petrosino looked around the room at the innocent faces of the civilians, the greasy smiles on the politicos, and the worried cops scratching pencils on reports and erasing mistakes. The air was stale, and he thought of taking off his overcoat if it weren't for the bundle of newspapers.

"We ought to get Dr. Primrose's wife to identify the barrel victim," Petrosino whispered. "Make sure it's their driver."

"She's taking the 'rest cure.'" Schmittberger smirked, eyes still closed. "At a sanitarium upstate. Exact location undisclosed."

"How do you know that?"

"One step ahead of you. I sent Weiss to the Primrose household. No one would talk, and the wife is gone. She was distraught over her husband's crack-up and went away. She's committed no crime, so we can't force her to talk or even stay in the city. So her lawyer says."

Petrosino shook his head. "Weston said there were two knives at least, maybe three."

"I know, Joe. I was at the post-mortem. But then I reasoned that Primrose is a doctor and probably drugged our victim like Dold said. Then Primrose tortured him with different dirks and stilettos. Just for kicks. He's crazy enough, you saw him."

"You believe that?"

"Joe, he confessed to Dold." Schmittberger opened his eyes and hunched over, elbows on his knees. "And you saw how he sliced off that guard's ear, with a shoehorn for shit's sake."

"What about our victim's fancy clothes? He kept himself in better stead than me."

Schmittberger grinned. "That's not saying much. Besides, you've seen rich folks' servants. They dress better than most of us. Maybe Primrose's carriage driver dressed like a dandy and wore derby hats, to make himself look taller?"

"Wise-ass," Petrosino whispered, thumbing his own derby on his lap. "Where did Primrose kill him and why put him in a barrel on Avenue D? And do you think our lunatic doctor dragged him to the East Side that night?" Petrosino snorted. "Come on, Max, my gut's in knots over this."

"You've got buyer's remorse. Remember *Othello*."

"What?"

"My *Othello* theory makes it fit. Primrose is already off his rocker, then add jealousy to the fire. The driver is new to the work, an Italian just off the boat, cheap and handsome, soft hands, too. He takes any job he can get, which is carriage driver for a rich doctor. Thereafter, Primrose's wife fancies the new Italian and starts giving him the French on the side, but Primrose finds out somehow. So he goes to where this Italian lives, some shithole flophouse on

Avenue D, and confronts the man, and that's what the note and handkerchief were about."

"The note was in Italian."

"Yeah, well maybe our victim wrote it as a love letter to Primrose's wife. Or maybe Primrose's wife knows Italian. One of those educated society gals, been to Europe on a steamship, studied Italian art history or somesuch."

"Yeah, but…" Petrosino saw the desk sergeant trying to get their attention, waving them to the Chief's inner office door. "Why the barrel? Why out in the open?"

"Why does he call himself the Czar of Russia?" Schmittberger stood, buttoned his suit, and smiled graciously at the desk sergeant. "Let's go, the Chief awaits."

A slew of reporters exited McClusky's inner office and pressed them for comments, but the pair shook their heads and went inside.

♐

Chief Inspector McClusky pretended to be writing at his desk, too busy to notice them. Petrosino and Schmittberger stood there silently. Schmittberger crossed his eyes, and Petrosino bit the inside of his cheek to keep from laughing.

"Well, if it isn't Shylock Holmes and the Dago in the Derby!" McClusky boomed, setting aside his paperwork. "What a fine pair. One's six and half feet tall and built like a railroad tie, and the other's five and half feet and squat as a fireplug. Don't just stand there. Sit."

Petrosino and Schmittberger sat stiffly on the edge of two chairs in front of McClusky's desk. McClusky leaned back in his chair, drummed his fingers on the desk.

"What is it you like about being a cop, Broom?"

"Taking care of the folks in my District and the East Side."

"Horseshit." McClusky turned to Petrosino. "What about you, you little Dago mongrel?"

"Respect, sir." Petrosino squinted at McClusky's face, scaly like a lizard's, the cracked lips parting to smile. "They don't have to like me, sir, but they damn well better respect me."

"Now there's an honest answer, and from a Dago, would you believe it? Sure, you want respect. Because those Sicilian gangs wouldn't let you in when you were a kid in the Ghetto. You couldn't join 'em, so now you wanna beat 'em, is that it?"

"No, sir." Petrosino shook his head, hating McClusky in that moment. The Chief had done some checking up on him.

"Double horseshit. I know just as much about you, you little pie-faced mutt, as I do about this Jew squealer here." McClusky stood and paced behind his desk. "I've got reporters coming in all morning ambushing me, making me feel like a goddamn buffoon. I've got the most foul murder in the city, a mutilated cockeater crammed in a barrel in plain view, and what do I know about it? Not a goddamn thing. The Chief of the Central Bureau is completely in the dark. Now, I'm as honest as they come, and I reward good work, but I will not coddle a couple of no-good mutts holding out on me."

"Chief," Schmittberger said, "we brought the prisoner in late after you'd gone home."

"You should have called when you went for the arrest. And don't play me the fool. Even a greenhorn patrolman knows if you can't find me, the watch commander knows where I am."

"Sir, we gave you all the facts, chapter and verse," Petrosino said calmly. "We put our report in the pigeonhole in your anteroom last night."

"If the report's not on my desk, it didn't happen."

"You didn't get the report?" Petrosino asked, baffled.

"Where'd you two get the tip to pinch this Dr. Primrose?"

Schmittberger and Petrosino looked at each other, and Schmittberger spoke up, "My lead, Chief. A confidential informant heard the lunatic was hauled in for castrating his wife's lover."

"What's the informant's name? Bring him to me."

"Can't do that, Chief. Only know him as 'Chicken Charles.' He's a fly-by-night hawk, drives a rickety hack late at night all over the city. Jumpy little fellow. Sometimes disappears for months on end. Only contacts me when he's got dirt."

"Chicken Charles." McClusky laughed hard. "This collar in the barrel case, that's a fine feather in your cap, boys. Got your names in the yellow journals, too. But I'm the Chief around here, and you will be brought to heel. Understand? I was brought up in the old days under Byrnes. He established the 'deadline' at Fulton so no thief dared go downtown, and Wall Street held him in high regard for it. Everyone followed chain of command till he got pushed out during Lexow. Goddamn Lexow." McClusky kept pacing, but pointed at Schmittberger. "He brought me up, and now I'm over you, Broom."

"I'm sorry you lost Byrnes' stock tips, Chief." Schmittberger smiled politely.

"You've got some goddamn gall. Let me tell you smart alecks something. Reform is a wave, and you rode it. But Tammany is not a wave. *It is the sea itself.* And I'm not going to fall out altogether with what stays to follow a bunch of climbers who pass on to Albany and Washington. Ole 'Silk Socks' Roosevelt is gone. He's used you up to make his career, and you've got no pull anymore. I have a career to make, too, only mine's right here in New York."

"If that career involves solving murder cases," Schmittberger said coldly, "then maybe you ought to congratulate us on a job well-done instead of upbraiding us?"

"Is that what you want, Broom? Well, maybe when you start working *for* me instead of *against* me, then you'll get a pat on the head. Now I think I've made my point clear as day, so let's talk about what's all over the papers. Do we have enough to turn this goddamn barrel murder over to District Attorney Jerome?"

"Maybe," Petrosino said.

Schmittberger grimaced at Petrosino. "We have *plenty* of evidence, Chief."

"Which is it then?" McClusky said. "I thought the killer confessed and there's a witness? What was his name, Dr. Gold at the sanitarium?"

"Yes, Dr. Dold," Petrosino said. "So then you got my report, sir?"

The question stopped McClusky's pacing. He stared angrily at Petrosino, then nodded slightly. "I want this evil case to go away. I want us all smelling like roses. You hear?"

"We've got enough evidence, Chief," Schmittberger said, turning sideways and gritting his teeth at Petrosino. The signal to shut up. "We have a madman with a history of violence, his wife was having an affair with their Italian driver, the madman throttled his wife and servants, then he cut off a guard's ear at the sanitarium and finally confessed the barrel murder to the alienist."

Petrosino couldn't help himself and said, "Sir, that's all true. But we don't have one person yet who's positively identified the victim. We don't even have his name, and Primrose's wife has skipped town."

"Goddamn it!" McClusky pounded his desk. "First you break the thing without telling me, and now you tell me it's not broken? Are you shitting on my case?"

"No, sir, Joe's just leaving no stone unturned." Schmittberger patted Petrosino's back roughly. "We'll get an affidavit from Dold, and I'll have my men find out the victim's name. The Bureau will have its biggest murder case closed, and everyone will be pleased."

Petrosino shook his head. There was a long silence while he and Schmittberger looked straight ahead at the Chief Inspector, waiting for his answer and seething at each other.

"I don't give a damn if the victim goes down as John Doe, close the file." McClusky grunted, then pressed a button on his desk, and the anteroom sergeant came in to hold the door for Petrosino and Schmittberger.

"Stay behind, Petrosino," McClusky said.

Petrosino turned and went back in alone. McClusky waited until Schmittberger left.

"About your friend," McClusky said, looking over his papers again, "you know what I always hear the other men saying?"

"No, sir."

"They say, 'Tammany will be back. Then we'll get the cops that soaked us and first that big Jew.' You'd be wise to steer clear of him."

McClusky never looked up.

Petrosino was too angry to speak. He left the Chief's office, kicked over a spittoon in the anteroom, and went looking for Schmittberger.

Chapter 10

"You're as stubborn as an army mule, *Sergeant*," Schmittberger said, standing toe-to-toe with Petrosino on the rear entrance stoop of the Marble Palace. There were two empty Black Marias parked on the curb and hardly another cop in sight.

"You wanna pull rank now, *Inspector*?" Petrosino said, standing his ground.

Schmittberger poked Petrosino's sternum. "Watch yourself."

"Go on, *Inspector*, take a swing. Just remember, I'm a filthy Dago. I'll bite your ears and tear your mustache off. I'll make Primrose look like a chorus girl."

"I bet you would, too, you little runt." Schmittberger smiled and shoved Petrosino back gently, making room to sit in on the steps. He took off his fedora and punched it in frustration.

"You know the case isn't solved yet," Petrosino said. "So why feed bull to McClusky?"

"Because it's good for us, Joe. Can't you see that?"

"And if we're wrong, then what? Then we'll have egg on our faces." Petrosino sighed, trying to calm down. "They'd love to see us stumble. They've got it in for us."

"Not *us*. Me. Just once I'd like some ink for solving a crime instead of being a squealer. That's why I want this collar… so I can say, 'You ain't so clever yourselves, boys.'"

"Goddamn it all, Max, we've still got holes! He hasn't even identified the victim."

"It doesn't matter. We've got the right man." Schmittberger took a hip flask from the inside pocket of his jacket and uncapped it. He took a swig, then held it out. "Hair of the dog?" Petrosino shook his head. "We've got the right one behind bars, Joe, and we've got the Deputy behind us. Men are taking sides, and you're supposed to be on mine. Do I have to order you to stand down?" Schmittberger took another swig, held up the flask again.

"*Order* me? No, sir, if you say the barrel murder is closed, it's closed. Now I've got other work to do while you crawl inside a bottle and feel sorry for your pitiful self."

Petrosino started up the stairs, but Schmittberger put a hand on his chest, stopping him.

"Joe, we're pals, but you're forgetting your place. Maybe it's time I reminded you?" Schmittberger pocketed the flask, took off his jacket, and towered over Petrosino. "After I lick you, it's done. No more arguing, no more of you playing holy crusader. Deal?"

"Deal." Petrosino put up his fists. "I'm dying to sock you, you bullheaded bastard."

A carriage trotted up just before they started fighting. The horse clip-clopped to a halt and snorted loudly at them. Petrosino quickly put down his hands, and Schmittberger slung an arm back in his jacket as two men got out of the carriage in navy blue suits and straw boaters.

"Secret Service," Petrosino mumbled. He recognized the older and bigger of the two by the trademark American flag ribbon on the brim of his straw hat. Agent Willaim J. Flynn. He looked like an overstuffed, bow-legged tent revival preacher.

"Joseph, what's doing?" Flynn shook hands with Petrosino and introduced himself to Schmittberger. "William Flynn, Secret Service."

"Inspector Max Schmittberger."

"Looks like you two were about to scrap? Agent Ritchie here was putting odds on the Inspector when we drove up."

Ritchie looked as clean and green as an altar boy from Old St. Patrick's.

"Naw," Petrosino said, "we were just playing out how we arrested a man recently. He put up a wild fight, and we were bragging on it."

Flynn nodded. "Is that the barrel murder case?"

"It was, why?" Petrosino said.

"Ritchie knows your victim. We've come calling on your Chief Inspector about it."

❧

Chief Inspector McClusky had been warned that the Secret Service men were calling unannounced. He kept everyone out in the anteroom, and, by the time they entered his inner office, McClusky was in full parade uniform, black duds with gold embroidery. He almost had an aristocratic air about him now. A reporter was on his way out, and McClusky smiled at the Secret Service men and waved them in along with Schmittberger and Petrosino. When the departing reporter lingered in the doorway, McClusky stood tight-lipped, blood vessels streaking red in his eyes, muttering under his breath.

"So no progress at all on identity?" the reporter said. "Next of kin?"

"I told you, he's a John Doe," McClusky said. "What matters is we've solved it, and we're going to put the mad doctor away. Give my best to your editor." When the reporter was out the door, McClusky's jaw muscles tightened, and he mumbled, "Parasites."

The four visitors sat down, and Agent Ritchie forced a phony chuckle.

Agent Flynn said, "So Joe told me the barrel murder is closed?"

"Like a lead pipe cinch," McClusky said, turning to Petrosino. "You know Bill?"

"Yes, sir. I lent a hand in a Treasury investigation of a counterfeiting gang. We suspected them of killing a Brooklyn grocer. I knew Mr. Flynn before that, too, when he was Second Deputy Commissioner under T.R."

"Pardon my manners, George." Flynn pointed at the younger agent. "This is my field agent, Lawrence Ritchie."

McClusky shook hands, then retreated behind his desk and sat. "So what can I do for His Majesty, Teddy Roosevelt's Secret Service?"

"What do you know about this barrel murder?"

"Well, I know it's solved." McClusky took a long cigarette from a gold case.

"Yes, you said that. What else?" Flynn listened, stroking his moustache and severely-parted brown hair. He had a fat pensive face and a perfect triangle of a mustache, which made him look like an austere walrus.

"There's not much to tell. The killer is a doctor named Duncan Primrose, thirty-two years old, well-off, but mad as a fucking hatter. He confessed to his alienist. Apparently the victim was an Italian driver in his employ who was plowing the wife. Simple enough."

"Can't say I miss the colorful language of the PD." The small nose of Flynn's beefy face flared. "Looks like you stepped right into our Treasury case."

"How's that? This ain't a federal case, it's a murder."

"We know who the associates of your victim are."

"Come again," McClusky said, cigarette hanging from his saturnine mouth.

"My men have been surveilling a counterfeiting gang of Italians long before this murder of yours. We think the victim recently appeared at the gang's haunts. One of my boys, Ritchie here, read about the barrel murder in the papers and went to the Morgue to view the body."

"Yes, sir," Ritchie said, "I recognized his mug. It was photographed on my brains. Without the family jewels in his mouth, of course." The Secret Service men smiled morbidly.

"So then what's the victim's name?" McClusky asked anxiously. "That's the only piece of the puzzle we haven't tumbled out."

"We know the gangsters' names," Flynn said. "We call them the Morello Gang after their boss, Giuseppe Morello. The whole lot was squared away to be arrested for counterfeiting."

"I know of Morello," Petrosino said. "Has a restaurant near Elizabeth Street?"

"Yes, one of those spaghetti joints. Stinks like the ninth circle of hell. You can smell the garlic off these heathens for miles."

Petrosino said, "What may be hell for you, Mr. Flynn, is heaven for us Italians. But, then again, I never fancied boiled cabbage and potatoes."

"No offense." Flynn nodded uncomfortably. "In any event, this gang has counterfeiting headquarters at a café called the Star of Italy on Prince and Elizabeth Street. Next door to the café, Morello runs his restaurant and a saloon. Ritchie can brief you on the crooks and how we spotted your barrel murder victim."

Ritchie looked at McClusky, whom Petrosino could tell wanted none of their briefing. Ritchie cleared his throat and began, "Morello believes he's a born leader like the Caesars of old. He and his cohorts are all from Corleone, Sicily, about twenty miles from the capital of Palermo. Corleone means 'lionheart' in Italian."

Petrosino listened to Agent Ritchie's pronunciation of Corleone. Quite good.

"This Morello is called '*Don* Piddu' or 'The Clutch Hand' by his men because he has a deformity from birth. His right hand is disfigured, it's got only one good finger. He's rough and cunning as a fox. We think any violence done by the gang is okayed first by him. We arrested him three years ago for carrying false silver certificates and again six months ago. Then three months ago, we arrested four of his underlings for passing fake five-dollar notes from the National Iron Bank of Morristown. But Morello always slips our grasp."

"Slippery as an eel," Flynn said. "We've never been able to pin a conviction on him."

Petrosino was watching McClusky's reaction to the information. The Chief sat rigidly behind his desk, his brows sunken, making him look more dim than angry.

"Why should I care about this Morello?" McClusky exhaled smoke in frustration. "My two sleuths and I have already solved this murder, and I don't need anyone mucking it up."

"This isn't mucking," Flynn said with a twinge of malice. "These gangsters may know how your victim came to meet his end. What if they witnessed his death? And no God-fearing man wants to die a John Doe, George. Tell him about the 13th, Ritchie."

Agent Ritchie continued, "We'd been tailing the gang for months and knew all their faces till April 13th. That night, they went to a butcher shop at 16 Stanton Street. Morello was at the shop with two other thugs, Antonio Genova and Nico Pecoraro, the main counterfeiting experts. The Italians were having animated conversations in the rear of the shop, and we noticed that a new face was at the front, separate from the others. We call him 'the Newcomer.' The Newcomer was sitting on a box, fidgety as a footpad at a billfold convention. We sent a man inside to buy beef chops and get a description of the Newcomer for our file."

"So what of it?" McClusky said impatiently.

"So the Newcomer is the same man as your barrel victim," Ritchie said proudly.

Petrosino felt a tingle of vindication that there were more leads. He wanted to say, *I knew it*, but he kept a poker face, not wanting to rile the Chief Inspector or Schmittberger, who had been sitting unusually still the whole time.

"Tell him the rest, Ritchie," Flynn said.

"We became concerned when one of the gangsters came to the front of the shop and hung a piece of butcher paper over the glass in the front door. A short time after, a rickety covered wagon pulls up. Two other gang members entered. After two hours, they came out and split up into three groups. The Newcomer went with Morello and Pecoraro, arm-in-arm, to the Bowery."

"So this Newcomer, the man you claim is the barrel victim, he made it out of the butcher shop alive," McClusky said. "Where'd they take him after that?"

"When they split three ways, we didn't have enough men to safely follow, so we stopped shadowing their movements."

"That was your mistake," McClusky said, "and now he's dead." He snubbed out his cigarette, and his voice sounded confident now, almost flippant as he looked at Flynn. "Seems plain to me that if this Newcomer of yours is our barrel victim, you botched it.

You were all probably snug in bed when Dr. Primrose chopped him up." McClusky grinned yellow teeth.

Flynn's walrus face bunched into a frown. "George, your opinion doesn't make a lick of difference to me. This is my investigation, and I want to know who the victim is."

"Of all the goddamned gall, Bill."

"Please don't take the Lord's name in vain, George."

McClusky wavered, and it looked to Petrosino like he was trying to figure out if Flynn were serious. "Look, Bill, you can't waltz into my office on a murder case of all things, a solved one at that, and tell me what to do. Why don't you just go home and let us amateurs in the Police Department close our case. You big-wigs in the Secret Service don't need the bother."

"George, I'd be glad to get out of this crooked chamber of horrors and let you grope around in the dark. But not until Ritchie sees Primrose and questions him."

"He's not here," McClusky said, eyeballing Schmittberger and Petrosino. "I sent him to the Tombs last night. I wanted to have an alienist examine him since he's not in his right mind."

Schmittberger spoke up, "Mr. Flynn, this Primrose is loony as a seagull. We questioned him for hours, from the time we pinched him till we sent him to the Tombs. Besides, he's already confessed so it's no use pestering him."

Flynn ignored Schmittberger and said to McClusky, "If I went upstairs to Commissioner Greene, it would look like you're not cooperating with your federal brothers. And I know that's not your intention, George. You're not a stingy Jew. You're a Christian, and a Christian shares the fruits of his success. Luke 6:38 says to give and God will see that others give unto you."

McClusky's eyelid twitched before he finally huffed, "Fine. These two will take Ritchie to the Tombs." He hit the button on his desk, and a sergeant opened the door to let them out.

Petrosino stood and led Ritchie out of the office, but Schmittberger was slow to follow. He put on his fedora and, from the doorway, turned and spoke absent-mindedly to Flynn, "Was it

Shakespeare who said, 'The devil can cite Scripture for his purpose'?
By Jove, I think it was-"

Petrosino pulled Schmittberger away before he got them both
canned.

"The Tombs" detention center

Chapter 11

Schmittberger and Petrosino sat side-by-side, across from Ritchie in the carriage on the way to the Tombs. It would have been a good walk, but Ritchie insisted on riding. There was a rush of traffic on Centre Street, and the clatter of metal and carriage wheels on the roads was deafening, making conversation almost impossible. Petrosino was examining the young Secret Service agent's face along the way to the detention center. The kid was in his mid-twenties, light brown hair straight as thread, yellow-green eyes, and freckles stippling his cheekbones.

Petrosino shouted inside the carriage, "Ritchie, the way you said Corleone in the Chief's office, you must be Italian."

"I'm American, born in Jersey." Ritchie looked irritated. "My father's name was R-I-C-C-I, but I changed it to R-I-T-C-H-I-E. What's it to you?"

"Nothing, but being Italian ain't a disease, kid."

"It is to me," Ritchie said stone-faced.

"To each, his own," Petrosino said. "So you really think Primrose was mixed up with a counterfeiting gang?"

"Maybe, maybe not," Ritchie said, like a kid mocking a teacher. "We do things different in the Service. We spend a lot of time on surveillance so we can nail a case down."

Over the street din, Schmittberger said, "Some wealthy Italian merchants have been getting extortion letters from gangs in Little Italy. You think that angle plays here instead of our love triangle?"

"Could be. But… nevermind."

"But?" Petrosino raised his eyebrows. "But all the other extortion cases involved wealthy Italians. And Primrose is an American, a doctor at that. He wouldn't be as susceptible to idle threats from immigrant thugs. And he'd be more likely to go the police, right?"

Ritchie shrugged, still playing coy.

The carriage stopped at the rear entrance of the Tombs, and the guards recognized Schmittberger and Petrosino and waved them in. They vouched for Agent Ritchie, but Ritchie still insisted on showing his federal tin. The trio weaved through the maze of stench and gates. Doors were unlocked before them and clanged shut and locked behind them, and they slipped deeper into the darkness and cramped tiers. When they entered the wing where the lunatics were held, Sandy the Whale popped up from a stool, like a giant white ghost with a shock of red hair. He had a five-pound can of chocolate creams and six of the little brown globules in his mouth and smeared on his chin. He smiled and shook hands with sticky fingers.

"Long time no see, Whale." Schmittberger tried to wipe off his hands.

"We got him in a padded cell," Sandy said with a broad smile and hooked his thumbs in his pockets. "In a straight waistcoast the whole stretch, just like ye ordered. See fer yerself."

Petrosino smiled kindly at the Whale, wondering how the big dullard did his job, much less tied his shoes. They went to the end of the hall, through another locked door to four small cells, two on each side. The prisoners were on the floor sleeping, perfectly silent. The last cell on the right was where Petrosino noticed a white cloth tied to one of the slimy black bars. It was knotted tight, but he couldn't see the rest of the murky cell until they came right up to unlock it.

Sandy gasped, "Jesus, Mary, and Joseph!"

"What the hell happened?" Ritchie said, covering his nose.

Petrosino and Schmittberger nudged them both out of the way. One sleeve of the strait jacket was tied to an iron bar, and the other sleeve was a noose. Knotted around Dr. Primrose's neck. He was sitting in a puddle of excrement and urine on the floor, slumped over, his face frozen in a dark blue grimace. His head hung taut from the sleeve, a few feet from the iron bars, suspended in mid-air. The eyes were open, looking up to heaven, blood vessels broken. There was a scrap of paper on the ground near the clenched fist of his right hand.

"Harry Fucking Houdini," Schmittberger said.

"He must've wriggled out of it," Sandy muttered in shock, crossing himself. "Poor bastard's stuck in Purgatory now."

"Open it," Petrosino and Schmittberger said at the same time.

Sandy fumbled with a ring of keys and unlocked the cell. Ritchie started in, but Petrosino grabbed him by the collar. "Stay put."

Schmittberger nodded at Petrosino, and Petrosino stepped inside the cell, walking a careful swath around Primrose's body.

"Check his pulse," Ritchie hissed.

"He's fucking dead, kid," Petrosino snapped. He crouched low and touched Primrose's hand. Ice cold. He carefully went through Primrose's clothes and searched the folds of the strait jacket. Nothing. Then he picked up the scrap of paper with handwritten capital letters in pencil.

"Block print," Petrosino said to Schmittberger. He read it to himself and then held it up for the other men to see:

I KILLED THE MAN IN THE BARREL.
MAY GOD HAVE MERCY ON MY SOUL.

"Son of a bitch couldn't take the guilt," Schmittberger muttered.

Petrosino put the note back down where he found it and went outside the cell, closing the door. He pointed at the Whale. "Lock it tight, and call Central to send an evidence crew. Don't let anyone near here until we collect the clues and get pictures."

Sandy waddled off and back through the main door.

Petrosino turned back around and squinted at the note on the floor again. "Wait…"

"Do you recognize him?" Schmittberger asked Ritchie.

Ritchie shook his head. "I've never seen him before. But it

looks like you had the right man all along. He confessed by his own hand now."

"He's right, Joe," Schmittberger said grimly.

Petrosino tugged on Schmittberger's arm, leading him to the other end of the corridor. He waved him close and whispered, "Max, it's a stage job."

"Joe, you think someone framed up a suicide in here with all these locked doors and all these guards? You can't admit that you were wrong, can you? For shit's sake."

"You ever see a doctor write in block print? They don't write legible script, much less block print. Anybody can write block print. And we just so happen to find him dead after we find out that our victim was last seen with a mafia gang?"

Schmittberger held the bridge of his nose, frowning as he thought it over. "You're losing your mind, Joe. Primrose did the murder."

"Where's the pencil he wrote the note with?"

"You're tired and hungover. Let me take care of the scene here."

Petrosino felt like he wanted to punch Schmittberger again. He stared at him, trying to understand what his friend saw that he didn't. "Max, collar or not, this is horseshit!"

"I said I'll take care of it. Let it be, Joe. Go get some air."

Petrosino gritted his teeth and glanced at Agent Ritchie dumbly staring at Primrose's corpse. "Get some air? What's wrong with you, Max? Maybe Steffens was right about you."

"Go to hell, Joe." Schmittberger shook his head and walked back to Primrose's cell.

"You first," Petrosino said as he stormed out of the Tombs.

Chapter 12

The office was east of Washington Square, a four-story red brick neo-classical with bright flower boxes overlooking the park. Petrosino flashed his badge, and the doorman let him in. He walked up to the top floor and hooked a left. At the end of the hall, his knees ached as he read an engraved placard, *Minerva & Company*. The door was ajar, and Petrosino peeked in at two desks against a wall of windows on the left. Steffens leaned back at one desk, daydreaming at the window, and a secretary dressed primly in a high shirtwaist and long skirt was at the partner desk, glancing at a book, scribbling notes. There was a rolltop in the back with a bald man typing away, the boss maybe. The air clicked with the typographic machine and smelled of ardor and pipe smoke, and the room was Spartan and clean with an efficiency that impressed Petrosino. He was about to knock when he noticed a mezuzah nailed to the office door.

"Say, look who's here!" Steffens popped up from his chair and pointed at the mezuzah. "I'm almost a Jew. I worked the Ghetto so much in my *Post* days that I became as infatuated with them as eastern boys are with the wild west."

"That so?" Petrosino entered the office, taking off his derby.

"The music moves me the most. Sometimes I think I was born to follow the sad feelings of the Jew and the beautiful old ceremony of their orthodox services. Come in. Let me give you the tour." Steffens pointed out the windows at the view of the park. "Look there. You can see Stanford White's marble arch to Washington and over there's the bronze of Garibaldi drawing a sword, your unifier.

Oh, I almost forgot. Congratulations for the barrel murder. We were talking about you over the morning papers. Bully for you, sir."

Petrosino nodded and paid more attention to the other two people in the room. He wanted to avoid any conversation of a murder case he felt was unraveling. In his pocket, he was carrying *The World* picture of the barrel victim's face, like a key to an unknown lock.

"Where are my manners?" Steffens pointed to the woman. "This is my boss. Ida Minerva Tarbell. Minerva, this is Detective Joe Petrosino."

Petrosino hesitated before saying, "Pleased to meet you, Miss Tarbell."

"You didn't expect to meet a woman in charge, did you?" Tarbell stood from her desk. She was a tall lady in her forties, prominent nose, frizzy hair tied back and bundled, but luminous eyes. Starry and focused at the same time. "That's Frank McAlpin, my assistant. He doesn't talk much, but men of few words are the best kind."

McAlpin bobbed up from the rolltop and waved, plumped with an air of excitement and nervous energy. He was young, but bald as a bocce ball.

"Frank's always steamed up," Steffens said, pulling up a chair for Petrosino.

Petrosino sat facing Steffens and Tarbell. "You said you worked for *McClure's*. Don't they have offices on Park Row?"

"Sam McClure is a menace." Steffens pointed at a framed picture of a stern man on the wall. "So we rented out this private office where he can't invade our work."

"I see." Petrosino nodded at their adjoining desks. "You two are partners?"

"She's like another fellow, a good-humored fellow to me." Steffens smiled warmly at her. Petrosino noticed that Tarbell had a humbling effect on Steffens' ego. "There's no feeling of man or woman in our office, but she's the smart one and the better writer."

"I am not, Steff."

"Yes, she is. Don't let her petticoats fool you. She was the only girl in her freshman class at Allegheny College. Studied Greek, Latin, French, German, botany, geology, and geometry."

Petrosino forced a smile at this sharp woman who wore no wedding band and was taller than he was. "You did all that schooling to become a muckraker, Miss Tarbell?"

"I don't like that new label. I prefer 'investigative journalist.'" Tarbell sat back down on a bentwood chair with baskets of paper in messy heaps in front of her. "We are not yellow journalists either. We don't depend on exaggeration or grisly sensations. We depend on facts."

"Ah, another investigator like Steffens here?" Petrosino raised an eyebrow. "And just what kinds of sources do you use when you go sleuthing, Miss Tarbell?"

"You'd be surprised by the breadth of my, what do you call it, dope?" Tarbell smiled. "I track down hot tips, review court documents, I spy on folks, I interview people with information. Stoolies, you call them? I have contacts, reporters all over the country and Europe, I know dignitaries and foreign officials. Why, I even use public and government libraries in New York, Washington, and Paris. You'd be surprised what a woman can find in the public record, sir."

"You might be a sleuth, Miss Tarbell." Petrosino turned to Steffens. "Unlike Steff."

"But we don't practice the Third Degree," Tarbell said with a smile that was beginning to win Petrosino over. "There are many different kinds of monsters to slay, Detective. I intend to bring down Standard Oil, for one. Have you read my stories against Standard and J.D. Rockefeller, or, as I call him, The Wolf in a Prayer Shawl?"

Petrosino chuckled. "No, but I imagine you're making plenty of enemies in that line of work. Aren't you afraid they'll come after you and ruin your magazine?"

"Horsefeathers. For them to do that would be an indictment of themselves."

"She's got so many enemies now that we started writing in cipher," Steffens said. "We send Frank out to get the dirt, and he sends his research back in code because of sabotage."

"Sounds like more trouble than it's worth. May I?" Petrosino took out a cigar.

"Please do," Tarbell said. "We love the smell of a good cigar, don't we fellas?"

Petrosino looked at her as he lit the cigar. "How about the smell of a cheap one?" She giggled. "So what's this *Shame of New York*, Steffens? And why talk to me about it?"

Steffens perked up, turning his chair around backwards and resting his forearms on the chair back. "Frank, could you run across the street and get us all some sandwiches? Some of those big pickles, too? And some hot beef tea for the Detective."

Frank was out the door before Petrosino could say, "I can't stay long, Steffens."

"That's all right. I just wanted privacy so I can say it flat out. The story we've been working on involves the police. So I must know that you'll keep it in strict confidence."

"I'll keep mum, but don't expect my help."

"Joe, I grew up believing in government of the people, by the people, for the people. Instead, I've found we are a government of the people, by the rascals, for the rich. You see, I fear that New York's Reform government is doomed to defeat in the fall elections. Seth Low is a fine mayor despite the fact that he's an educated and honest businessman. But the voters are unhappy, and Tammany is in the whisperings in the wind."

"Why should the voters be unhappy? The police are good, the laws are pretty-well enforced, and graft is at a minimum."

"That's just it, Joe. The laws are being enforced, and there's less graft. But that hurts business, and bad business affects everyone."

"Maybe so, but I don't believe Reform is on its way out."

"Well then, answer me this: how is it that 'Chesty' George McClusky was just installed as Chief Inspector at Police Headquarters?"

Petrosino couldn't think of an answer and shrugged.

"Backroom dealing has returned for everything: streetcar lines, garbage collection, public water supply, gambling, saloons, brothels. And do you know which is most profitable?"

"I wouldn't know."

"Gambling. *Everyone* gambles. Faro, poker, the lottery. And the gambling houses rig the odds and fix the wheels, and then they share the profits with corrupt officials. The racket is worth some five millions a year. Maybe more. And do you know who runs it?"

"Who?"

"Why, it's the police!" Steffens boomed with such astonishment and indignation that it gave the impression it was the first time he'd heard it himself.

Petrosino shook his head. "Those days are over, Steffens."

"Oh no they aren't. Certain politicians and police brass are running a Syndicate, making four to five hundred thousands a month from the gambling houses and pool rooms alone."

Tarbell nodded. "If Tammany were incorporated and its money earnings gathered together, its dividends would pay out better than Standard Oil."

"Worse yet," Steffens said, "they learned from Lexow. The graft is so concentrated now that the divvy is between only three or four men at the top. The rest get chicken feed."

"Which men?" Petrosino's foot started tapping. He began to wonder about his friends on the job. His empty stomach growled as he waited for an answer.

"We can't go that far with you yet, Joe. Let's just say that we think it's a triumvirate, maybe a quartet, of very powerful men. They need a ward boss to control the underworld, an alderman to control the honest folks and pull political strings, and a high-ranking cop to turn a blind eye to their crimes. Maybe even a federal lawman."

"Yesterday you said something about the mafia? Now you're saying corruption?"

"We think the Syndicate is using the mafia society as muscle for its gambling racket."

"But why?" Petrosino said. "The mafia is a relic from the Old Country."

"What do you know about the mafia, Mr. Petrosino?" Tarbell asked, a notebook open on her lap. Petrosino thought that she looked like a handsome teacher about to grade him.

"The mafia supposedly came from the old days when the French invaded Sicily. They say a young married couple was having a picnic to celebrate Vespers, and some French soldiers came upon them and took advantage of the girl and killed the boy. That started a revolt by the Sicilians, who eventually kicked the French off the island. Since that time, the mafia became a secret society to protect Sicilians against foreign invaders and corrupt overlords."

"An old romance story. You're quixotic, Mr. Petrosino."

Petrosino blushed. "No, Miss Tarbell. The mafia today is mostly bands of brigands in the mountains of Sicily. They live off fear of a greater myth of its power."

"We think it's more than a myth. Our Italian sources say that branches of the mafia society exist in every town in Italy and that all Italians are in dreaded terror of it. And our own federal government says the society's tentacles are reaching across the ocean to form a network of gangs here, where immigrants are easy marks. What do you say to that?"

"The mafia in Italy is dangerous. Like I told Steffens, Sicilians are hill folk that use vengeance as a way of justice. They don't trust the law, so they take it upon themselves. But in America, it's small gangs feeding on immigrants. The mafia isn't organized to run a big racket."

"But isn't it?" Tarbell asked. "Sicily has always had a feudal system in place from Roman times. A few governing families organized like Caesar's rule of the Roman Empire that enforce payment of tribute, discipline, and the bandits' code of silence. What's it called, Steff?"

Petrosino was reminded of Agent Ritchie's description of the Morello gang. *They thought of themselves as Caesars.* He absentmindedly answered Tarbell, "*Omertá.*"

"That's it," Tarbell said. "The mafia has the same vertical structure of power anywhere. Landowners lease territory to *gabelloti*, and they in turn hire collectors who collect 'tribute' from the people. And if someone doesn't pay, the collectors have armed gangs, the *campieri*, that use violence to command respect and enforce payment of tribute."

"True," Petrosino said, "but mafia muscle are called *picciotti* or 'kids.' Collectors are *capos*, and estate managers are *Dons* who get their territory from a legitimate source. What you're saying may be true in Sicily, but it's weaker in America. I know all the crooks in New York, and I've seen *mafiosi* here. But they're brutes, Miss Tarbell, not masterminds."

Steffens patted Petrosino's hand. "And the Syndicate is using these brutes."

"But why would this Syndicate use Italian muscle?" Petrosino said. "Before Lexow, the crooks used Irish gangs for muscle. Sometimes Jewish gangs or even rotten cops, if they had to. Why Italians? They can't even talk their language."

"That's what we were hoping *you* could tell *us*. That and whether you could find out anything about rotten cops mixed up in the Syndicate."

Petrosino mulled it over, snubbing out his cigar on his shoe sole. The ash fell as he thought about Schmittberger. "Yesterday, when I mentioned Schmittberger, how come you didn't want to talk to him? He was in the game a long time ago. Maybe he could help."

"We don't want him involved." Steffens looked sideways at Tarbell.

"Why not?" Petrosino leaned forward, squinting hard. "Don't you trust him? Aren't *you* the one who said he could be reformed and got him back on the job?"

"That was a long time ago, Joe. When I was naïve."

"That's horse… feathers. He's not what you may think. Not a chance."

Steffens adjusted his spectacles and swallowed hard. "I'm not saying that. I'm saying that he and his 'Steamboat Squad' used to collect monthly payments from gamblers and prostitutes and pass the money up to the brass. Sometimes he forced payment with his expert use of the billy. Back then, the payments tallied $20,000 a month. And he bought a nice house back then, which he and his wife still live in, which they can never pay off now. Not on an honest salary."

Petrosino felt like all the air had been sucked out of him. "Look, Steffens, I came here because you mentioned the mafia to me. And it just so happens that I have another case that involves a Sicilian gang. So I thought if you scratched my back, then I'd scratch yours. But I don't know anything about any Syndicate, and I don't wanna know about them either."

"When I was a boy," Steffens said, "the smartest men I knew were blacksmiths and niggers who handled mules and kicking horses. They always said the safest place to be was close up to the beast's heels."

"So you want me to be your nigger and stay close to the beast? If I didn't know you better, Steff, I might be offended."

"Would you at least keep an ear open for us, Detective?" Tarbell touched his hand.

"I won't promise you a thing and I won't hear another word about my friend. But I might keep both ears open on one condition: you scratch my back, too."

"What do you need, Detective?" Tarbell said.

"I want you to reach out to your friends in high places and tell me what you can about a Sicilian crook named Guiseppe Morello from a town called Corleone."

Tarbell asked for the spelling and jotted down the name in her book.

"I knew you'd come through," Steffens said, standing and pumping Petrosino's hand.

"Don't thank me, Steffens. I think you're all wet on your Syndicate. I'm just playing along because I want some dirt on that Sicilian. Good day, Miss Tarbell."

Chapter 13

Sandwiches and hot beef tea had sounded good to Petrosino, but he wanted to escape Steffens' office as quickly as he could. He felt like a snitch just for talking to Steffens and Tarbell about their theories of a Syndicate and rotten cops. He wondered if he would have been so friendly if Tarbell hadn't been there. There was something pleasant and disarming about her. He wouldn't have minded lunch with her, but instead he left alone and found a café where he ordered hot beef tea, a corned beef sandwich, and two pieces of apple pie with fresh cream. The lunch exorcised the demons of beer and rye that had possessed his stomach the night before. He took coffee with him and went back to his office at the Marble Palace refreshed and more worried than ever about the barrel murder and Schmittberger.

He sat at his blotter for a while, ruminating. He had plenty of other cases on the East Side. At the top of the list was an assault on ten Jewish workers in their garment sweatshop. Petrosino had already fished out the facts. The workers had gone on strike to protest long hours, and so they were beaten by Pinkertons and off-duty bulls hired by the sweatshop owner. But Chief Inspector McClusky had issued orders not to interfere with businesses "managing" labor, and, besides, the strikebreaker case had none of the mystery of the barrel murder.

What is Max thinking? Petrosino thought.

He heaved a loud sigh and unlocked the bottom drawer in his desk. He took out a dusty bottle of cheap whiskey and nursed it while he did paperwork until sundown. He grew woozy and more agitated about the barrel murder and decided to slip down to the basement. Police stationed all over the city reported fires and crimes in their precincts to Headquarters, and the reports were briefly posted in the basement telegraph office. The Poker Club of loafer reporters were down there, playing cards as always. They smelled of cheap beer and carried cynical smiles and blunt pencils.

Petrosino skimmed the usual fare of bulletins. A roof chase for a burglar, a baby fallen off a fire escape, and a sweatshop fire. For some reason, he had hoped there would be something he could connect to the barrel murder. But there was nothing. He started for the stairwell as he heard Schmittberger's voice dodging questions from the Poker Club.

A reporter asked, "Has the Coroner confirmed that Dr. Primrose committed suicide?"

"What else it would be," Schmittberger said, "he hung himself."

"There's rumors that the man found in the barrel was working undercover for the Secret Service and was exposed and killed. Is that why federal lawmen are here now?"

"Why, you ought to get your eyes checked for specs. Secret Service? Why would they work a murder? They only count money over at the Treasury, didn't you know?" The reporters laughed, and Schmittberger looked over their heads and noticed Petrosino. "Gents, have to go."

Petrosino pretended not to see him and started up the stairs.

"Joe! Where you going? Hey, sourpuss!"

"What?" Petrosino stopped halfway up the stairs, clutching the rail.

Schmittberger walked faster. "Why didn't you stop?"

"I didn't see you."

"Nuts." Schmittberger caught up to him on the stairs. "I was looking all over for you. Jesus, you smell like … say, you got soused without me? I'm hurt."

"Good." Petrosino started upstairs again.

Schmittberger followed. "Now you're pouting like a toddler, Joe."

Petrosino made the next floor's landing and started for the hallway to his office.

"Stop, damn it!" Schmittberger shouted, still in the stairwell. "We've got another meeting."

"What the hell for?" Petrosino turned around.

"The straw boaters are back about the murder," Schmittberger whispered, adding a wink that made Petrosino hopeful. "Let's go watch McClusky shit his drawers."

☙

McClusky was waiting for them, syphoning a cigarette down to a half-inch nub. A semi-circle of chairs faced the desk in his office. The Chief Inspector had apparently directed his underlings to spruce up the place with extra chairs and trays of cigars, teas, and bottles of mineral water. Petrosino noticed that there was now a photograph of President Roosevelt on the wall next to McClusky's painted portrait. And McClusky's favorite detective, Handsome Jimmy McCafferty, was sitting in a chair to McClusky's right, notebook in hand, awkwardly holding a pen with three fingers. A teacup steamed on a sideboard next to him.

"The goddamn Secret Service is back," McClusky muttered.

Schmittberger and Petrosino nodded, but both must have stared too long at McCafferty.

"Jimmy's gonna be my fly on the wall from now on. That spread eagle jingoist Flynn thinks he knows all. Son of a bitch said I was 'groping around in the dark' last time. He's just sore because we solved the barrel murder and left him out in the cold. I told him we'd hear him out, but that's it. I'll be damned if we're going to re-open that case, especially now that Primrose confessed in his own hand and killed his damn self over it."

"What does Flynn want us to hear out, Chief?" Petrosino asked eagerly.

An electric bell on McClusky's desk jingled, and he tossed his cigarette in a spittoon and scowled at them. "Don't agree with him. Just listen and yawn." He hit the button on his desk, and the anteroom sergeant opened the door and let in Agents Flynn and Ritchie. The Secret Service men nodded hello, but said nothing. Ritchie carried a small leather portfolio.

"I'm missing supper for this," McClusky said, "so it better be good, Bill."

Flynn and Ritchie sat down, and Flynn gave McClusky a shake of the head. "No, it's not good. You won't like it one bit, but I feel obligated to let you know: Your killer is still aloose."

"That's a fine how-do-you-do." McClusky took out a fresh cigarette. "So it's true then, what the rumor mongers are saying? That the victim was one of your men undercover?"

Flynn scoffed. "Nonsense. We'd never botch an undercover job like that." Flynn looked over at Schmittberger first, then hesitated and turned to Ritchie. "Go ahead, Ritchie, tell him what we've uncovered."

Ritchie opened the portfolio and drew out a report. He placed it on McClusky's desk, spun it around, and patted it. "It's all in my report, Chief Inspector."

"Well, spit it out, boy. You think I wanna read the god… the damn thing?"

Ritchie sat back down and said, "The barrel victim, who we call the Newcomer, was last seen alive at eight o'clock at night on Easter Monday, April 13, with the Morello gang. The first we heard of this Dr. Primrose was when your men pinched him. But it seemed queer to us that a man we'd never seen could've killed the Newcomer. So we did a little digging."

"Into what?" McClusky asked, the cigarette flattened between his teeth. "Primrose confessed and committed suicide. What the hell is there to dig for? His grave?"

"Well, sir, a lot," Ritchie said smugly. "We checked with the sanitarium. The intake records. And they show that Primrose was admitted at 10:15 p.m. on the evening of Monday, April 13. A ferry to River Crest takes-"

"A good half hour or more," McClusky said. "So what? The

victim was last seen at eight o'clock, you said so yourself. That's an hour and a half window. Plenty of time to kill."

"Chief, they may have a point," Schmittberger said with a gloomy frown. Petrosino could see that he was laying it on thick, but no one else noticed.

"What point is that?" McClusky said.

"The Coroner's report, sir. Dr. Weston said that he examined the victim's stomach contents and that he'd just eaten a meal, potatoes or somesuch."

"So what?" McClusky pointed his cigarette at Schmittberger.

"I'm guessing Mr. Ritchie is about to tell us about the time of death."

Ritchie nodded. "That's right. Time of death was fixed at somewhere between 11 o'clock on Monday evening and 1 o'clock Tuesday morning, the day he was found. So there's no chance that Primrose could have killed him because he already would have been at River Crest Sanitarium for almost an hour."

"Miles away in Astoria," Flynn added, with a bit of relish. "You fell for a false confession, George. Even your own Coroner opined that there was more than one weapon and perhaps more than one killer."

Petrosino wanted to say, *I knew it.* He shifted in his chair, gripping the arms tightly.

Schmittberger raised an eyebrow at him, annoyed by the fidgeting.

McClusky quietly snubbed out his cigarette and licked at his scaly lips, smiling slightly. "What are you trying to do here, Flynn? You got something against me?"

"Justice is God's work. I'm only trying to find out what happened, George."

"You can have that back, boy." McClusky shoved the report across his desk until it fell on the floor at Ritchie's feet. "I'm still running this Bureau, and I'll make sure we get our man."

"See, George, that's where you're wrong. The only suspects now are the men last seen with the victim. The Morello gang. And that's *my* bailiwick."

"Horseshit. Let's see what General Greene has to say about your trying to railroad me." McClusky picked up the receiver from his Upright telephone. "Get me the Gen-"

"Go ahead and ring the Police Commissioner. I spoke to him about this case, and he's already given Treasury his blessing. It seems he doesn't want the bad press for any bumbling with the Primrose angle. He doesn't mind us Secret Service taking the heat for a little while. So you'd do well to defer to me on this, George."

McClusky squeezed the receiver, then rammed it back into its hook.

Flynn ignored him and said calmly to Petrosino, "Joseph, you're acquainted with the Italian gangs in the City. Does it tally with any other killings? Like Luigi Troja or Joe Catania?"

"Hang on," McClusky said, "what do they have to do with this?"

"Luigi Troja was stabbed in his Harlem saloon last year," Flynn said. "Catania was an Italian grocer killed in Brooklyn a few months ago. Word on the street was that Catania was possessed by the liquor devil and wont to open his mouth freely about the affairs of a mafia gang he was in and their criminal exploits. We think that particular gang is the Morello outfit."

"Those cases were before you made Chief Inspector, sir," Petrosino said, glancing at McClusky's suspicious eyes. "Catania's body was stuffed in a potato sack and thrown over the cliff in Bay Ridge. Four little boys found him with his throat cut from ear to ear."

"Do you think it's related, Joseph?" Flynn asked.

"Wait a damn minute." McClusky snapped his fingers. "How do we know that Primrose didn't hire someone to kill the victim? Maybe he paid off this lot of Dagos?"

"Possible," Flynn said, turning back to Petrosino. "What do you think?"

"I don't know," Petrosino said. "The barrel killing is more personal. The killer here butchered the genitals clean off and shoved them in the victim's mouth. Then there's the torture signs on the neck. Catania's wound was one fatal slash, which seems like a mercy killing by comparison. And if this was a gang snuff or even a murder contract, why would they put the barrel victim on display in the middle of the street and chance being caught?"

"Well, I think there's only one way to get more answers at this point."

"And what way is that, Bill?" McClusky asked facetiously.

"My men can swear an affidavit that the victim was last seen with the Morello gang on Easter Monday. So I'm inclined to round the gang up now unless anyone objects? George?"

McClusky stared bitterly at Flynn, brooding. "Fine."

"Sir, we could pinch the entire gang and squeeze them until one of them sings," Petrosino said. "But, if we do, we better take them all at the same time or else they'll send a signal through the East Side so the others can fly the coop."

"Then it's settled." Flynn turned to McClusky. "Get every available plainclothes man to poke up early tomorrow morning. Muster here at 7 o'clock. My agents will spot the suspects' locations and keep a tail on them through the night. We'll take them all at the same time if we're not too late." Flynn stood, donned his straw boater. "We have a lot of fox dens to raid tomorrow. Sleep well, gentlemen. The Lord loves the just."

Flynn tipped his hat, Ritchie picked up his report from the floor, and they both left. Schmittberger and Petrosino tried to follow them, but McClusky said, "Hold it, goddamn it!" They spun slowly and lingered in the doorway, as far as possible from McClusky's big desk and leaden eyes. "What the hell was that?" McClusky asked Schmittberger.

"That? Why, that's the federals doing what they do best: shitting all over us, Chief."

McClusky seemed to like that response and cracked a smile. He went back to frowning quick. "Just the same, I told you not to agree with them. Both of you sold me a false bill with that Primrose angle, and I don't want either of you sharing any information or even giving those cocksmokers the time of day. We're still gonna break this fucking case. Us. Not them. That's why I've got my best man on the job now. Isn't that right, Jimmy?"

McCafferty said, "Ain't a thing that a Yid or Dago can break that an Irishman can't fix."

"Oh, that's good to know, Jimmy," Schmittberger said. "Maybe you can come by the house later and tinker with my phonograph? It skips…"

"Clear out," McClusky said. Petrosino pulled Schmittberger out and down the stairs until they were outside on Mulberry Street, shuddering beneath a black starless sky.

"Okay," Petrosino said. "Spill."

"What?" Schmittberger said resentfully. "You think I wanted to keep looking at your sourpuss and listen to your crying?" He poked Petrosino in the chest. "Don't make me take the high road again. You got at my conscience and made us lose a big collar, you stupid little Dago."

Petrosino clenched his fists and stuck out his chin. "What're you blaming me for?"

"Because I listened to you, that's why. You happy now? Now we're in the shithouse worse than before." Schmittberger took off his fedora and wiped sweat from his brow. Petrosino hadn't noticed it before, but Schmittberger's collar and the rim of his hat were soaked.

"You caught the time of death, didn't you? That was your find, not that federal kid's?"

Schmittberger sighed. "After we had our squabble, I went to Piper about it. Said we had some doubts and wanted to dig a little more. He said he expected no less of us. So I thought about what you said, that something didn't feel right. And I remember we didn't have time to look at the intake records at River Crest. So I went back by myself."

"Why didn't you report it to McClusky yourself?"

Schmittberger tapped his head, grinning, and walked down the street. "You might be a dick, but I'm a *sleuth*. If I tell the Chief that our collar is a bust, who does he shit on?"

"Us." Petrosino followed him. "But if the Secret Service tells the Chief, then…"

"Then he's the one who gets shit on. Sure, sooner or later it'll flow down to us, but at least we've kept our heads down and our holes shut. Or so he thinks."

"I might kiss you, Max, you know that? You had me worried." Petrosino clapped Schmittberger's back. "I was beginning to have doubts about you, that you might be hiding-"

Schmittberger punched him in the jaw. Petrosino stepped back, held up his fists, and said, "What the hell was that for? I know you're not a crook, you stupid schmuck."

"That's not why I hit you. That was because you were right about the barrel case, and I was wrong. You can't one-up me. I outrank you. Now did you badmouth me to Steffens, too?"

"No, damn it. I talked to him about the mafia. How'd you know I saw him?"

"Like I said, I'm a *sleuth*." Schmittberger put his arm around him. "Now put your paws down. Let's find a grog shop. I'm not sore anymore."

"That's swell, because now *I'm sore*." Petrosino elbowed him hard in the gut, and Max doubled over and began laughing.

"I'll buy the suds, Joe, but just the one. We gotta poke up early to pinch our Sicilians."

II

THE MORELLO GANG

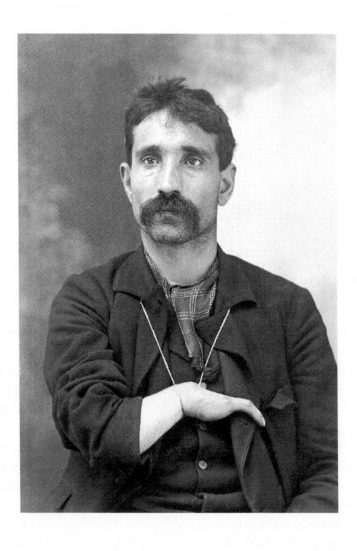

Chapter 14

"The next two suspects are the most dangerous in the entire gang," William J. Flynn said to the group of twenty detectives and four Secret Service agents in the muster hall at 300 Mulberry Street. Everyone had bleary eyes and wore ugly suits to fit in with their targets. Some had rubbed dirt into their hands and fingernails, and some smelled like armpits and beer. Petrosino and Schmittberger had cut their night short at one in the morning, so they looked fresh as daisies by comparison. They sat next to each other in plainclothes, and Petrosino could smell yeast from Schmittberger's moldy suit.

McClusky began mumbling behind Flynn, telling someone to fetch him a cigarette.

"Pipe down," Flynn said in McClusky's direction, making Petrosino smile. "At the top of the list is 'The Clutch Hand' Morello himself, who has a hideout at 178 Chrystie Street and also lurks about his restaurant and tenement on Elizabeth Street. Ritchie, pass out Morello's particulars." Agent Ritchie handed around a Bertillon card with Morello's picture and physical measurements. Flynn paced in front of the men, waving his finger emphatically as he spoke.

"Morello is the ringleader, thirty-four years old and of unusual intelligence. You can't miss him. He has a deformed right arm with hardly a finger on that hand. He's hairy and has beady little eyes, average height at five feet seven."

"Average maybe for a Dago," McCafferty said, and snickering followed.

Petrosino said, "We make up for it in cock size."

"Pipe down," Flynn said. "You might not think much of him, but be careful with the Clutch Hand. He's just as likely to slit the throats of backsliding members of his gang as his enemies. And he's got a bodyguard with him at all times. The guard's name is Tomasso Petto. He's one of those physical culture types who's done carnivals and strongman sideshows. We've shadowed Petto for a while now, and we've seen him use kettle bells and do calisthenics like Eugen Sandow in Edison's moving pictures. Petto's fellow gangsters call him *Il Bove*, Sicilian for 'The Ox.' We don't have a Bertillon card for Petto, but Ritchie obtained this bill for our files. Pass it around so you get a good idea what this Ox looks like."

Agent Ritchie handed around what looked like a carnival poster, and men laughed as the picture circulated the room. Petrosino and Schmittberger grabbed the bill at the same time. They grinned at the image of Petto in a leopard skin loincloth, holding a club and posing for a strength show and male beauty pageant. They nodded at each other as if to say, *Let's take him.*

"Laugh now," Flynn said, "but at one of those carnivals they tied a horse to each of Petto's arms, slapped their backsides, and he kept the beasts from running off and pulling him apart. He's also been known to break iron chains from around his neck. George, let's have your roughest pinch Morello and his Ox."

McClusky puffed his chest out, pointed at two men sitting in front. "McCafferty and O'Farrell there. They'll bring down The Ox like he was Mary's little lamb."

The duo bobbed their heads, and McCafferty said, "You can count on us, Chief."

Petrosino watched as Flynn examined the best of McClusky's Irish lads, tubby and red-faced, sticking out their jaws like prizefighters in a stare-down. Flynn seemed unimpressed.

"Let's have another pair of men to make it an even two-to-one advantage."

Petrosino and Schmittberger looked at each other. "We'll do it."

"The Broom's fine," McClusky said, "but I need a bigger dog in that fight than Petrosino."

"Joe's the Bulldog of the East Side," Schmittberger said. "He's tougher than my wife's flank steak."

A couple of men laughed, and someone in the back gave a Bronx cheer.

"But, Chief, if they come along," McCafferty said, "we'll end up on a wild goose hunt for a loon!"

A dozen men snickered, and Petrosino and Schmittberger smirked.

"Can it back there!" Flynn said. "You want to take on your countryman, Joseph?"

"Sure," Petrosino said, "I'll give him a little *cerviletto*."

"What's that?"

"That's Italian for *billy club to the spinal column*."

Schmittberger laughed.

"All right then," Flynn said, "Joseph's the fourth man on that team. Moving on to the rest of the suspects last seen with the murder victim in the butcher shop at 16 Stanton Street. Vito Laduca owns the butcher shop. He was arrested in Wilkes-Barre two months before for counterfeiting, but was eventually released and returned to New York. Pietro Inzerillo owns the Star of Italy café at 226 Elizabeth Street, where the counterfeiters regularly meet. Those two men, along with Antonio Genova, were seen with the 'Newcomer,' and they were the ones driving a wagon up to the butcher shop in the last hours before the killing. The other low-level gang members are the Lobaido brothers, Vito and Lorenzo, and Giuseppe Fanaro. I want two of you for every one of them. Many of these gangsters have been in prison before, and it's natural to assume they aren't going to turn to gospel singing for a living."

The men laughed.

"I can tell you to a man that they will *not* want to go back to prison. Be on your toes and call in every quarter hour to get the signal. May the Lord be your shield and your stronghold."

The teams of men split up and funneled out separately onto the back streets to begin tailing their assigned targets. Petrosino,

Schmittberger, McCafferty, and O'Farrell walked casually toward Chrystie Street, making wisecracks about Petto's caveman picture while they checked their service revolvers and saps and short "day" billies they had hidden in their pockets. Petrosino felt inside his suit coat pocket, comforted by the weight of his .38 pistol and Max's long shadow beside him. They passed the graveyard next to Old St. Patrick's and crossed themselves. Even Schmittberger.

Petrosino tilted his head at him. "What the hell was that, Max?"

"Can't hurt."

Petrosino smiled and said a prayer, "Saint Michael the Archangel, defend us in battle. Be our protection against the wickedness and snares of the devil. May God rebuke him, we humbly pray." Then he thought of the barrel victim's face and added a silent prayer for the dead man's soul. "In the name of the Father, the Son, and the Holy Spirit. Amen."

Schmittberger groaned. "Jesus, can we get on with it now, *padre?*"

℀

The rain was light, soaking quickly into cobblestones and dissolving in sunlight cutting through pewter clouds. Petrosino and Schmittberger watched it vanish. They had made camp in an empty café across the street from Morello's place at 178 Chrystie Street. McCafferty and O'Farrell had split up from them, O'Farrell strolling among pushcart peddlers, and McCafferty in a milliner's shop trying on every single hat in the place.

"Slugabed must be sleeping the day away in his rathole." Schmittberger stirred cold coffee and glanced out the window at the façade of Morello's tenement as people trickled past it. "Look at that cunny fiend."

Handsome Jimmy McCafferty left the millner's and stood outside a bordello. A young woman came out and handed him something, and he tipped his hat and slid whatever she gave him in his hatband.

"Looks like he's got a friend in that house." Petrosino watched McCafferty through the window. "You used to be a pussyhound yourself, don't forget."

"Yeah, but at least I was a gentleman about it. And he's smart as paint. When he took the civil service exam, he said County Cork was one of the original thirteen colonies."

They laughed, then slowly sunk back into waiting and watching the East Side Ghetto hustle past the window. There were wagons, barrel organs, and tinkerers, but most of all pushcarts. Always peddling something. Gumdrops, candied peanuts, fruit, pretzels, combs, shoestrings, paper hats, macaroni, portraits of royalty from the Old Country, and carp. The three-cent-per-pound mongrel of a fish was the staple of life on the East Side. Petrosino could smell it now as people washed across the damp sidewalks, buying and selling carp.

Petrosino kept one eye on Morello's building, trying not to be distracted by the cart traffic on Chrystie Street. He took out a picture of a man from his billfold.

"Who does this look like, Max?" Petrosino took out *The World* clipping of the barrel victim's face, a profile shot from chin to crown. The photographer had cropped it to avoid the gruesome holes in the victim's neck.

"I'll be damned," Schmittberger said. "Looks like your old man, don't it?"

Petrosino put the clipping away. "Our victim was someone else's papa or son, too."

"Yeah." Schmittberger shifted in his chair, uneasy. "I try not to think of that hole in the crotch."

"We have to get close to the victim and figure out why he was tortured like that. The killer put him on display to thumb his nose at us. That's not a gang's doing, Max."

"Primrose was a nice white American, but now that Flynn's put the finger on a gang of Dagos, it bothers you, eh?"

Petrosino shrugged. "Maybe."

"Was it true what McClusky said? In his office, when he asked why you became a cop."

"Partly." Petrosino squinted at Max, who had that all-knowing smile in his eyes. "When I first came here, I took to following some older toughs in the neighborhood. I thought they were grand. They spoke Italian with funny accents, and their leader, this kid named Ant, wore a fancy derby. They took me in like a pet for a while, and then one day, Ant turned on me. He licked me real good, and then he held a knife to my throat and said I better never show my face again."

"Why the hell for?"

"Because I wasn't Sicilian. He said I wasn't rough enough to be one of them." Petrosino tapped the derby on the table. "A couple years later, I knocked out all his teeth and took his hat."

"That's Ant's hat?" Schmittberger grinned. "Jesus, McClusky had you pegged. And then Steffens asks you about the mafia society, too? No wonder you're cross." Schmittberger looked out the window, but his eyes darted back. "What did you talk to Steffens about, exactly?"

Petrosino could read his mind. "Not you, Max."

"What then? About the barrel murder?"

"Nope." Petrosino noticed that Max was acting indifferently, staring harder at Morello's building across the street. He was keen to know, Petrosino thought. Too keen. "Steffens asked about the mafia. Has a theory that there's a big crime Syndicate."

"Does he now? That's a gas. What'd he say?"

A man shouting at a crowd of boys caught Petrosino's eye. "Steffens thinks three or four men control the gambling in the city and that the mafia is their muscle, but he was being cagey."

"Who do you think would be in such a Syndicate?" Schmittberger turned and studied Petrosino now, lifting his cold coffee, wetting his moustache with it.

"They'd need a ward boss. Or *the* ward boss. I'd say Big Tim Sullivan could control a whole mess of gambling in this city."

"Me, too. Did Steffens say he had proof on Big Tim? And what about the other two? Where's he coming up with his dope? Did he say?"

Schmittberger's questions came fast and made Petrosino suspicious. Schmittberger sensed it, too, and the tension hung taut between them like a clothesline in the Ghetto.

Petrosino said, "Steffens thinks there's a city aldermen and a lawman, maybe even a federal. Since Big Bill Devery's gone, I couldn't think of another cop who could fit the bill."

"Hmm." Schmittberger stroked his dun whiskers. "If I were still in the game, I'd put my money on the top dick in the Central Bureau. He could start or stop any investigation he wanted in all of Greater New York. That's the best insurance against any arrests or raids."

Petrosino knew that Schmittberger was speaking from past experience and chose his words carefully, "Is that how it was when you were in the Tenderloin?"

Schmittberger nodded. "Madame West ran a bordello on West 51st, and the neighbors started complaining about the traffic and the, ahem, noise. So being a fool, I go there and wave my billy around and threaten to shut her down. The next day, Chief Inspector Byrnes calls me to the rug. He says the woman was not a madame, nothing of the sort. She was just a mistress of a political friend of his, and the house was just a private residence owned by the politicker. He told me he'd have my head on a pike if I ever bothered her again. Afterwards, I found out she was paying $30,000 a year for protection, and that her politician *friend* was raking in the profits from the whorehouse. See, the Chief Inspector can always call off the dogs…"

"Chief Inspector, huh?" Petrosino chewed on it. "You might be onto something there, but I was thinking of something else. Flynn and his federal boys have been investigating Morello for a year, but they never pin a thing on him. Makes you wonder, doesn't it?"

"It does. But I wonder a lot. Like why you saw Steffens after I told you about him?"

"Max, it wasn't to spite you. When Flynn talked about the Morello gang, I wanted to see if I could use Steffens to help us. Met his 'boss,' too. Get this: his boss man is a boss *woman*."

"You don't say. Is she a crabby old spinster?"

Petrosino shook his head, and something in the street froze him. He glanced over at the back counter and made sure the café owner was still in the back.

"Don't look. Forty feet south, down the street, playing marbles with four boys. The son of a bitch's shirt collar sticks out like wings because of the size of his neck."

Schmittberger let go of his spoon. His face fell into a chalky frown. Petrosino could see that it took all of Schmittberger's strength to keep from craning his neck. His lips formed the name, "Petto," and Petrosino nodded and said, "Should we pinch him?"

"We've only got one mark in sight. The last thing we need is a fracas with the bodyguard in the street while the *capo* slips away."

They both casually looked at him. Everything about Tomasso Petto was broad. His face, his hands, his back, even his smile. He expertly flicked marbles with big thumbs, laughing heartily and tousling the hair of his playmates.

"He's dark as a Moor," Max said. "I bet he and his boss will go to one of their haunts. Laduca's butcher shop is on Stanton. Inzerillo's Star of Italy saloon and Morello's restaurant are two blocks away on Elizabeth and Prince. Everything in walking distance. Clever bastards."

Petrosino nodded as his eyes stalked Petto. The Ox was oblivious, crouched over a ring of small boys, more enraptured than the kids with the marble game.

Schmittberger checked his pocket watch. "Fifteen minutes past the hour. Your turn."

Petrosino reached for a coin from a pile that sat between their coffee cups and pulled his derby low over his brow. He quickly walked outside and down a half-stairwell to a New York Telephone Company public station inside a druggist's basement shop. He asked for Spring 3-1-0-0, the Central Bureau, and the switchboard girl plugged him into the Chief's line.

McClusky and Flynn were breathing through the other end of the receiver. "Speak."

Petrosino said, "No bid yet on the Hand. But we spotted an Ox. What are our orders?"

Chapter 15

"Stay put, hold your vantage," Flynn's voice crackled through the telephone.

Petrosino hung up and reported back at the café. He and Schmittberger were flustered. They drank more coffee, banging spoons on the table, counting and stacking a dwindling pile of dimes, and watching Petto play more children's games. When their prey slipped further down the street, they moved to a saloon two buildings down. The Ox was animated and rowdy as he played jacks, ignorant that he was being watched. Two hours passed until another target showed.

At the top of the entrance steps to 178 Chrystie Street, a gristled and moustached man in his thirties appeared. He was about five and half feet tall, slender, wearing a weathered Homberg hat and a grey wool shawl draped over his shoulders and concealing his right hand. He had lifeless eyes, tiny and black as peppercorns, that surveyed the crowded street. Morello.

Petto was sitting on the bottom step, his broad back hunched over an Italian newspaper. As soon as Morello appeared from the tenement, Petto turned and dropped the paper. Morello used his left hand to wave Petto up. Petto took two steps at a time, kissed Morello's unshaven cheeks, and the pair disappeared inside the hovel.

Petrosino never saw the right hand, but he was sure it was Morello. He looked at his pocket watch, waited for his heart to stop hammering. "Let's make the next call now."

"What's doing?" Schmittberger turned quickly toward the window, but there was only an old woman in a yellow shawl gingerly descending the steps at 178 Chrystie. "I'll make the call," Schmittberger said, "then you give the others a nod."

Schmittberger's chair screeched backward, and he hustled to a druggist's telephone. Petrosino reached inside his jacket, feeling the pistol. A minute later, Schmittberger came back, breathing heavily, "They nixed it. Damn fools. They're still waiting for the butcher to show."

"Curse the fishes." Laduca was already on the lam, Petrosino thought, and sooner or later they'd all slip through the law's hands. Petrosino looked at the windows across the street. Garlands of brightly colored laundry crisscrossed window sills and air shafts, fluttering above fire escapes loaded with broken sewing machines, washtubs, cast-off mattresses, and soap boxes planted with basil and tomato plants. There was no back entrance to 178 Chrystie, and so they sat and waited for the signal from Headquarters.

At eight o'clock at night, they moved to the covered entrance of a cellar. Petrosino was incessantly opening and closing his pocket watch as if he could will the arms to spin faster. His head was barely above street level. Schmittberger had a piece of coal and was playing tic-tac-toe with himself on the brick wall. The sky had turned the color of a fresh bruise, and Petrosino was afraid the crooks would all be gone if they didn't arrest them soon. The streets were no longer overflowing with peddlers and urchins and wagons. Older men were playing cards in the cafés, younger ones prowled the sidewalks, and ragpickers sorted through castoff wares and rotten fruit left behind by the pushcarts. Alleys exhaled the stenches of the night, and drunks were bedding down, fighting over street corners and gutters. There were few women in sight, except for slatterns hanging out windows and screaming down at waifs in the street. Or rough women leaning out disorderly houses, smiling between unnaturally red lips.

"Look!" Petrosino whispered.

Tomasso "The Ox" Petto came out the front door of 178 Chrystie Street, wearing a tan suit and a yellow fedora that barely clung to his thick head. Petto shifted on the balls of his feet and gave a quick look down Chrystie before he glided down the steps and onto the sidewalk. He loitered, licking his big dumb lips and ogling rough women passing by. The front door opened again, and Giuseppe Morello came outside. The Clutch Hand wore the same Homberg hat, but had a loose-sleeved corduroy jacket over a plaid wool vest and trousers. His right hand was pulled deep inside the brown sleeve, invisible. When Morello descended the steps, Petto escorted him south to Delancey Street.

Schmittberger chucked the coal into a rubbish bin. "Let's move."

They began tailing the suspects, and Petrosino noticed two other men down the street playing the "fingers" drinking game, guessing odd or even, and holding liquor bottles. He gave them a tip of his hat, and Jimmy McCafferty and O'Farrell took sips of their bottles, noticing the approach of Morello and Petto on the other side of the street. They waited for Petrosino and Schmittberger to reach them, and then the two Irish detectives lagged behind. Near Delancey and Forsythe Street, Petrosino flicked open his pocket watch. Almost a quarter past eight o'clock. Morello had stopped on the corner to talk to an elderly man.

Petrosino subtly motioned to the other three detectives to stay put. He fished a dime out of his vest and ducked into a Raines Law hotel with a public telephone station. Rag music drifted in from the hotel piano, and he covered his ear, struggling to hear through the receiver.

The T/S operator at 300 Mulberry put him through to Flynn and McClusky.

"Forget the butcher," Petrosino said. "The Hand is moving. It's now or we lose him."

Flynn's voice crackled, "We just got word the others are moving, too. Take them."

Petrosino hung up and hustled out to Delancey Street, where Morello was still talking and Petto was standing ten feet away, eyes on his boss. Petrosino walked up to Schmittberger and nodded at McCafferty and O'Farrell who were circling the suspects.

Morello and Petto began moving again, backtracking west toward the Bowery as a string of wagons and hacks clattered past them in the street.

Petrosino shouted, "Now!"

McCafferty and O'Farrell were within hand's reach of Morello's corduroy jacket, but they went for The Ox instead.

"What the hell are they doing?" Schmittberger muttered. "The Ox is *ours*."

"We'll have to nab Morello now," Petrosino hissed.

They hustled up from behind and grabbed Morello by the collar.

Morello yelled out in Italian, "Take your hands off me!"

Petrosino put his gun to Morello's temple, and Morello fell silent as Schmittberger started to take out a pair of handcuffs. Up ahead, Petto pirouetted and flicked the fedora off of his head as he stampeded toward them. McCafferty and O'Farrell had bumped into a bum begging for coin, and they moved too slowly as they latched onto Petto's arms. Petto easily shrugged off the two big Irishmen, and in that split second, Petrosino thought of the Coney Island carnival horses trying to tug Petto apart.

Schmittberger yelled, "Hold the ugly one, Joe! I got this Ox!" He put up his hands for fisticuffs, but Petto charged full steam, shoulders big as battering rams, and bowled him over.

Petrosino had never seen his giant friend knocked down so easily, and he gasped in awe. Morello was wriggling out of Petrosino's hold as he watched Schmittberger fall back onto the street. McCafferty ran up and tried to grab Petto from behind, but The Ox flipped him over his shoulder. Then Schmittberger rose on wobbly legs, trying to catch his breath. Petto tackled him again, grabbing his hair and furiously banging his head against the cobblestones.

"Here, hold Morello!" Petrosino punched Morello in the kidney and shoved him at McCafferty and O'Farrell, who greeted him with merciless swings of leather saps.

A small mob began circling the scene, but Petrosino only saw them as a blur. He had tunnel vision as he aimed his .38 at Petto.

No clear shot. Petto began choking Max until the big Inspector's tongue hung out and panicked eyes rolled back in his head.

"Police, stop!" Petrosino shouted. "*Basta!*" He pointed his .38 at the struggling pair. His finger came off the trigger, and he charged in and smashed the pistol against Petto's ear.

Blood spurted from ruptured cartilage, and Petto released Schmittberger. He held a hand against his bleeding ear, glared at Petrosino, and rose up. Petrosino rained the butt of the pistol down on the strongman's temple, but the blow only seemed to anger him. Petto tackled Petrosino and took them both to the gutter. The Ox's massive arms encircled Petrosino's torso, trying to crush him in a bear hug. Petrosino brought the metal gun down like a hammer, again and again, but Petto wouldn't let go. Petrosino found himself on his back, gasping for air, his ribs feeling as if they would splinter. The sickening crackle of broken bone split the air. Petrosino's vision blurred as he heard McCafferty shouting, backing off the mob. A woman shrieking. A dog barking. Everything turning black. He dizzily struck a fifth blow, too weak.

Then Schmittberger's grey moustache smiled above, and his big hand brought a billy down on Petto's skull. Petto's head split open like an old walnut, blood spurting in bright red filaments onto Petrosino's clothes, and the Ox's powerful arms slackened and dropped to the ground. Petrosino staggered to his feet and held his side, wheezing. He felt faint and bent over, hands on his knees. He touched his ribs and a thunderbolt of pain shot through his whole body. He fought the urge to vomit and stood over Petto, trying to kick him.

"I wish you'd pulled a weapon!" Petrosino shouted. "Give me an excuse to put you to bed with a shovel." Schmittberger pulled him off and tried to calm him. Petrosino cradled his ribcage and yelled at McCafferty, "You two were supposed to pinch Morello! Petto was ours. That was the plan, you stupid fucking Micks."

"Aw, quit yer crying," McCafferty said. "We got 'em, didn't we, you runt?"

"Shut your fucking mouth, Jimmy," Schmittberger said, waving his billy club anxiously, like a lion waving its tail as a warning. "Not another word unless you want a lesson from me."

"No, sir." McCafferty backed off.

"You all right, Joe?" Schmittberger coughed out.

"Swell, how's your neck?" Petrosino dusted off Schmittberger.

"It's still here." Schmittberger pointed at Petrosino's ribs. "You need a doc?"

"Aw, ain't they pretty?" McCafferty said to O'Farrell. "I wonder when the nuptials are."

Schmittberger pointed his billy at McCafferty, and he shut up. They pulled Morello and Petto off the ground and handcuffed them. McCafferty searched them, finding a .45 revolver in Morello's jacket and a stiletto hidden in the waistband of his trousers. Morello had put a cork on the stiletto's point to avoid pricking himself. Petto also had a .45 in a holster and a sheathed knife in his pants. McCafferty knelt and took some other objects from their jackets. He whistled at the arsenal as he pocketed their things. Then he slapped a woozy Petto back to his senses.

They began towing the prisoners back toward Headquarters, and a throng of people curled around and followed them down the street. Schmittberger moved to the front and cut a path through the mob, tossing people aside and brandishing his billy. McCafferty and O'Farrell had one hand on Petto and another hand on their guns. The Ox was cowed now, head hung low.

An old man stepped out of the crowd and hissed at McCafferty in Italian, "You son of an Irish whore!"

McCafferty asked Petrosino, "What are they saying?"

"They're thanking you for cleaning out the scum from their neighborhood."

The old man was still following, cursing in Italian, "May you roast in hell!"

McCafferty smiled at him. "You're welcome, sir. Just doing our job."

Petrosino shouted to the crowd in Italian, "These men are murder suspects! They're not worth the horseshit on your shoes, so clear out of our way!"

"My God, that cop is Italian," someone said. "He betrays his own people. Curse the devil of a priest who baptized him!"

"*Hey signore*," Petrosino shouted, "*VAFFANCULO!*"

The mob burst into laughter, and then it slowly made way for the detectives. Arms cleared a path, and hands reached out of the darkness to pat their backs. The other three detectives gave Petrosino a bewildered look as they turned onto Mulberry Street.

Schmittberger asked, "What the hell did you say, Joe, to calm them down?"

"I told them to go fuck themselves in Italian."

The detectives laughed and kept moving.

McCafferty shouted at Morello, "Know why we pinched you?"

Morello lifted his head up, and his little eyes looked as sharp and black as obsidian. Morello's lips twisted into a smile, and McCafferty's face blanched.

"Keep walking, shitbird," Petrosino said, pushing Morello forward. "Jimmy, he wouldn't confess to you if you were St. Peter himself."

On the steps of the Marble Palace, patrol reserves were waiting to let them inside and fend off the crowd. The other teams of detectives were also coming in with gang members in tow. The dicks congratulated each other and reenacted the arrests, showing off their battle wounds. Then they took the prisoners into the Rogues' Gallery with its vast wooden panels of photographs. Newsmen carried accordion cameras on tripods and rushed into the hall for "the mugging of the suspects." They tinkered with glass plates and flash powders while the cops roughed up the prisoners and forced them to pose in front of the battery of flash bursts. When the rumpus subsided, McClusky and Flynn appeared in the Gallery and clapped.

"All right, let's stop holding each other's cocks," McClusky said. "Time to put 'em in the sweat box and give 'em some of the ole Third Degree."

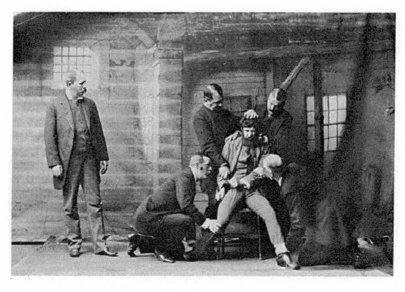

"The Mugging of a Suspect"

Chapter 16

McClusky and Flynn slurped coffee as they stared at Vito Lobaido. Petrosino watched from the outer office through the cracked door. The thrill of the arrest had subsided, and his ribcage burned hot now, making him sweat. They picked on Lobaido first, the youngest of the gang. McClusky asked the twenty-four year old a dozen simple questions, but Lobaido shrugged and repeated "no understand" while his eyebrows arched innocently beneath a swirl of hair on his forehead. McClusky opened his gold case and offered him a cigarette.

Lobaido licked his lips, but shook his head.

"You know Giuseppe Morello, don't you?" McClusky made a crude pantomime gesture, mimicking a deformed right hand. "The Clutch Hand, goddamn it?"

Vito's eyes narrowed, and his head shook vehemently. "No understand."

"Enough of this horseshit." McClusky waved at the patrolmen standing at his door. "Bring me *my* Dago. He'll straighten out these crooked Dagos for us."

The patrolmen opened the door to let Petrosino inside McClusky's inner office. Petrosino paused for a long moment, removed his derby, and looked Lobaido up and down. The moustache on the boy's cherubic face looked out of place, trying to conceal his fragile youth. Petrosino pulled up a chair and sat directly in front of Lobaido. He grabbed the arms of Lobaido's chair, and Lobaido recoiled, trembling fingers shielding his face. Petrosino exhaled deeply like a father disappointed in a wayward son.

"Listen to me, Vito," Petrosino said in Italian, "you can't play dumb anymore." The young gangster was thrown off kilter by a detective speaking his tongue. "You were the only one we arrested who didn't have a weapon. You're lucky. If you cooperate with us, you can save yourself a lot of trouble. Here, let me loosen those for you."

Petrosino took out a key and unlocked Lobaido's cuffs.

Lobaido fidgeted with his free hands on his lap.

Petrosino said, "We found a dead man in a barrel near the Mallet Works on 11th Street."

"I don't know anything about such things, *signore*. I don't know any dead man or why he's dead. You have to believe me."

"Did you ever meet an American man named Primrose? A blond fellow?"

Lobaido shook his head.

"How about a doctor? Did your friends say they ever spoke to such a man?"

Another shake of the head. Petrosino clucked his tongue. He reached into his jacket pocket and unfolded the newspaper clipping of the dead man's face from the front page of *The World*. "You've seen this man before, haven't you?"

"Never." Lobaido's eyes shifted to McClusky and back. "I don't know anything."

"Don't play me the fool, Vito, because I want to help you. This is the most important day of your young life. You're going to make decisions today that will affect the rest of your days." Petrosino pocketed the clipping and patted Vito's face, lifting it up so their eyes met. "What if your brother, Lorenzo, was killed? Would you want justice?"

Lobaido's eyes searched the room for an answer. Petrosino shouted, "Look at me! That poor man was found in a barrel like garbage, and his family wants justice."

"I don't know anything, *signore*." Lobaido turned away, eyelids clamped tight. "I swear to the Virgin Mother and all the Saints in heaven."

"Now you'll go to hell for sure." Petrosino loosened his own collar and drew out a crucifix, dangling it in front of Lobaido. "You helped kill that man one day after Easter Sunday. Easter, of all days. There's blood on your hands, Vito."

"No." Lobaido pulled his hands together under his chin as if to pray.

"Do you know what the Bible says happens to murderers? You'll be in hell, Vito, boiled in oil for an eternity." Petrosino held Lobaido's chin and stared through the kid's watery eyes. "No matter how many masses your mama pays for, your soul will be damned forever."

Lobaido screeched, "I know nothing! I've never hurt a soul, I don't even like knives."

Petrosino looked over at McClusky and Flynn, translating, "He just said he doesn't even like knives. But I never told him the victim was stabbed to death."

McClusky said, "Keep going," with a dark glimmer of satisfaction in his eyes.

Petrosino patted Lobaido's naïve face and whispered, "Who said anything about knives? I said a dead man had been found in a barrel. I never said he was stabbed."

Lobaido's eyes froze and stared vacantly for a few moments. His head slowly wilted between his narrow shoulders, and he mumbled, "The Fox will kill me now." A teardrop formed thick and heavy and trickled down Lobaido's cheek. A rivulet followed.

"Who's the Fox?" Petrosino slapped him hard. Lobaido's head bobbed back up, and his glassy eyes danced around in their deep sockets. He still said nothing. "Who's the Fox? Why'd they kill that man, Vito? Tell me!" Petrosino punched Lobaido in the stomach, but his heart wasn't in it. He knew this wasn't the way through to the kid. Lobaido only wilted more, coughing and holding his stomach, whimpering louder.

"He's as limp as a carp on Hester Street," Petrosino said to McClusky and Flynn. He held back the kid's mumbling about *Il Volpe*, The Fox. "He knows more than he's letting on, but this little one's too weak to have done any killing."

፠

Pietro Inzerillo stalked into McClusky's office with flecks of grey in a grotesquely bushy moustache and a beard that stippled up to the temples of his head. He smelled of sweat as he hunched over his chair like an old stray dog cornered and outnumbered, pulling at his handcuffs. He gave McClusky a vulgar sneer and spat out in Sicilian, "Your mother fucked a monk."

"What'd that cocksmoker say?" McClusky asked.

"You don't wanna know, Chief." Petrosino sat directly in front of Inzerillo and spoke in Italian, "You own the Star of Italy, right?" Inzerillo snorted and shook his head. "The barrel murder victim was last seen in your place on Monday night. How do you explain that?"

Inzerillo looked over at McClusky and Flynn. "No understand. Me speaka *Siciliano*."

"'No understand,'" McClusky said angrily. "That's all these animals know how to say." He reached in a drawer, tossed a set of brass knuckles on the desk. "See if he understands that."

Petrosino eyeballed the knuckles, then Flynn. Flynn looked down, brushed dust from his shoe. McClusky said, "Would you rather use a set of keys? Ain't that your specialty, Sergeant?"

Petrosino wondered how the Chief knew. The last time he lost his temper in an interrogation, Petrosino had taken a set of keys in his fist and knocked out nearly every tooth in the man's head. The thought of all those teeth on the floor agitated Petrosino now as he watched Inzerillo's eyes shifting back and forth between McClusky and the brass knuckles on the desk.

Petrosino said to Inzerillo, "The dead man in the barrel deserves justice, Pietro. What if your father was killed? Or your son? Wouldn't you want the police to find the killer?"

"You wouldn't understand, you dog. A Sicilian would never ask another man to defend his honor. We have a saying, 'If I live, I will kill thee. If I die, I forgive thee.' But you'd go cry to the police instead of acting like a man. You're nothing but a monkey dancing for *them*."

"*They* think all of us are like you," Petrosino said. "No good, dirty rotten fucking Dagos. And I despise you for that. Now talk. Tell me who the man in the barrel is."

Inzerillo spat on the floor. "Go shit in your hand and slap yourself!"

Petrosino snatched up the brass knuckles. "Once more: who's the man in the barrel?"

"You're their monkey, asshole. Go on, dance for your Irish organ grinders."

Petrosino reared back and pummeled Inzerillo in the mouth.

Inzerillo spat a jagged brown tooth onto McClusky's neat oak desk and cursed at Petrosino, "You should've never come out of the whore's cunt you call mamá."

"What's he saying?" McClusky asked.

"Nothing, Chief, just cursing." Petrosino tossed the tooth in McClusky's cuspidor, and it landed with a ding. Petrosino then buttoned Inzerillo's shirt collar up and lifted the lapels on his filthy duster so they covered his neck.

"What are you doing?" Inzerilllo asked.

"So there won't be any marks." Petrosino took off his own tie and wrapped each end around his fists. Then he moved behind Inzerillo and looped the tie around his neck and pulled gently. Inzerillo began choking. "Who's the dead man in the barrel?" Petrosino asked.

"Joseph, take it easy," Flynn said.

Petrosino tightened the silk garotte and whispered in Inzerillo's ear. "Go on. I don't care if you say anything about the barrel murder now. Say something else about my mother. Go on. Show me how rough you are. I wanna see your eyes shit right out of your head."

Inzerillo was kicking and squirming in the chair now, his face so flushed that even his beard looked red.

"For the love of God, Joseph, give him air," Flynn said. "Turn him loose."

"Hell, Bill, he ain't gonna die," McClusky said. "They usually pass out first."

Petrosino could feel himself wanting to put the man to sleep, but he willed his hands to let go of the tie. Inzerillo wheezed and sputtered, then cackled madly.

Petrosino sat down and calmly put his tie back on. His hands were numb and grooved from where the silk cut off the blood flow. "He'll take some time, Chief, *if* he talks."

"My patience is running thin, goddamn it. Bring in The Clutch Hand."

The two patrolmen at McClusky's door carted off Inzerillo, who hissed curses on the way out, and the patrolmen quickly returned, shoving Giuseppe Morello in the chair facing Petrosino.

❧

"Well, well, look at the almighty Clutch Hand now," McClusky said. "How's it feel to be pinched for murder instead of counterfeiting? See, I'm not the counterfeiting police, I'm the *murder* police, you greasy little Guinea."

Petrosino translated, and Morello stared straight ahead, calmly, as if there were no other people in the room. McClusky must have been riled by Morello's stoic demeanor. He came around his desk and slapped Morello. Morello's left eye twitched. There were two egg-sized knots on his forehead above that eye, and Petrosino could see that Morello was trying not to show any pain. The bumps must have come from McCafferty and O'Farrell's saps.

"You ever heard of a man named Primrose?" McClusky asked. "*Americano?*"

Morello spoke in a quiet monotone, with lips barely visible under a dense black moustache, "No understand."

McClusky sat on the corner of his desk, nodding at Petrosino who translated McClusky's question and added in Italian, "*Figghiu di una brutta strega.*" You son of an ugly witch.

Morello looked up at McClusky and shook his head.

"Were you at a butcher shop on Stanton Street on the thirteenth of April?"

No answer.

"What's the name of the dead man in the barrel?" McClusky made a fist as Petrosino translated, and he pressed it against the knots on Morello's head. The muscles in Morello's jaw tightened, but he still said nothing. McClusky punched Morello's forehead, toppling him and his chair backwards to the floor. Petrosino bent down to set Morello and his chair back up, and a shooting pain clawed its way across his ribs and clamped the air in his lungs. He growled at Morello to hide the urge to wince.

"This one's as dumb as an oyster," McClusky said and sat back down behind his desk. "Try some Italian on him, Sergeant."

Petrosino said to Morello in Italian, "My name is Petrosino." Morello yawned. "I know you're a clever man, Giuseppe. You're a leader of men, and I respect you for that." Petrosino could sense the vanity. Even the most brutal ones had it, and he tried to tap into it. "I can see it in you now and in the way your friends show respect for you."

Morello was still silent, but he looked content with himself.

"But there's something in your behavior I don't understand," Petrosino said.

Morello's dark eyes gleamed curiously.

"When I arrested you, you knew I spoke Italian and could understand you, no?"

Morello involuntarily, just barely nodded, *Yes.*

"And, yet, the whole time we were together, when I took you under arrest, you never asked me 'why'? You see, men always ask me why when I put them in jail. But not you, Giuseppe. No. You didn't ask me one question about *why* I pinched you. Isn't that queer?"

Morello's sharp obsidian eyes dulled and blinked. Petrosino leaned in face-to-face, whispering, "Tell me." Morello began to speak but quickly stopped. In that moment of weakness, when there was nothing Morello could say, Petrosino believed that Morello knew all about the murder. He thought of what Ritchie had said, about Steffens and Tarbell comparing the mafia to Roman rulers, and he appealed to Morello's vanity again: "You are a Caesar among your men, and Caesar can do no wrong. So if you speak to me, it's your privilege to say what you want, and no one would ever dare dispute that privilege. Who's 'The Fox'? You?"

Morello's eyes hardened again, stabbing angrily at Petrosino as if he'd been tricked.

McClusky thudded a letter opener against his desk. "What is it, Joe? What'd you ask the bastard? He looked pale as a ghost for a second there."

"He did." Petrosino was looking at Morello's face, but the flicker of weakness had vanished. "I asked him how come he never asked why we arrested him. He couldn't answer."

McClusky grinned at Morello. "Maybe you're not such a clever Dago after all, huh?"

Petrosino continued in Italian, "Who was that man in the barrel, Giuseppe? Did someone hire you to kill him? What did he do to deserve that?" Morello shook his head, almost smiling now. "You put him out of the way, didn't you? But with that weak little claw of yours, you probably had someone else do your dirty work for you. You're a wicked little monster."

Morello shifted his deformity in the cuffs, trying to hide it, then said, "Petrosino, what a name. 'Pitrusinu.' 'Parsley' may be good for the police, but it gives us Sicilians indigestion."

"I'll give you indigestion if you don't start talking."

"You go against your own kind on the East Side," Morello whispered. "Tsk, tsk. Trouble is coming to you, Parsley, don't you worry."

Petrosino grabbed Morello by the throat. "From you, you piece of shit?"

"What the hell is that Dago saying?" McClusky asked.

Petrosino still had Morello by the throat. "Nothing, Chief. He wants a lawyer."

"Does he now? There ain't no Constitution in here! Tell the bastard that."

"George," Flynn said, "if he asks for counsel, we ought to give him one."

Petrosino immediately regretted saying that Morello asked for counsel.

McClusky growled, "Bill, what do you care about his goddamn counsel? Go find him a shyster on Centre Street if you like." McClusky pointed at Petrosino. "Keep going, Sergeant."

Petrosino whispered to Morello, "*Omertá* won't save you. You gave yourself away."

Morello smiled sleepily. Petrosino squeezed his throat harder until he stopped smiling.

"George, that's enough," Flynn said angrily. "This evildoer won't talk. They view police as minions of Old Country oppression and keep mum. Especially him, he's shut tight as a clam."

"Then let's put him back in the box and see if that changes his goddamn mind."

"Let the prisoner go, Joseph," Flynn said.

Petrosino took his hand off Morello's throat. "You'll break, Morello. Maybe not now, maybe not tomorrow, but when you do, I'll be there waiting."

❧

"George, you can give them the Third Degree for a year," Flynn said. "They'll never talk. I know these crooks better than you ever will. Besides, we can't hold them forever without charge. Why, it's un-American, un-Christian even."

"Horseshit, Bill, they *ain't* American," McClusky said, his wingtips on his desk. He was burning matchsticks down to his fingers and tossing them at his cuspidor.

Petrosino, Schmittberger, and McCafferty were standing on the Oriental rug, waiting for them to make a decision. It was almost one in the morning. They had interrogated all the suspects twice using every trick in the Central Bureau book, and Petrosino was losing focus.

"We'll do just fine with a few more days of the Third Degree." McClusky waved at Schmittberger. "Broom, go back through the suspect's homes and sweep 'em out."

"Sir, my men already tossed 'em. It's one in the morning. Everyone's asleep."

"Good. Wake up their families and tear the places apart again. Don't stop till you find something on these gangsters. You're not to lay ear to pillow tonight."

Schmittberger nodded. "How about an ear to bosom, Chief?"

"Get the hell out."

Schmittberger snapped a salute, frowned at Petrosino, and marched out of the office.

"I've got an idea, Chief," Petrosino said. "Let's turn one of them loose."

"You wanna loose these terrorists back on the street?" McClusky said through a cloud of burning sulphur. He licked his fingers and put out another match. "Go home and sleep till your head's on straight."

"Not all of them, Chief. Just the youngest one. Vito Lobaido. The first time we turned the screws on him, he almost cracked. And now he's whining like a baby in The Box."

Flynn and McCafferty were glancing at a clock on the wall.

"Chief," Petrosino persisted, "the only reason he hasn't reached The Break here is because he's scared of his fellow gang members. They're the ones keeping him shut tight. I've got a feeling about him."

"Not a chance," McClusky said. "He'll be on a steamship to Italy before you can say, '*Won't you come home, Bill Bailey.*'"

"Not if we tail him, George," Flynn said.

"That's right," Petrosino said. "We'll turn him loose on a witness bond. Tell the rest of the gang he was the only one who didn't have a weapon on him. They'll buy that."

"I don't like it," Jimmy McCafferty said. "We should move Lobaido to a dorm room in the House of Detention for Witnesses. That way he won't skip."

"Yeah, why wouldn't he skip, Petrosino?" McClusky asked.

"Because he'll go home and lick his wounds," Petrosino said. "Then he'll seek guidance. He's too green to know what to do. At the least, he'll spread the word that the gang needs a lawyer and try to get them sprung. It could lead us to bigshots we don't know about."

"And we'll know if he goes on the lam," Flynn added, "because we'll have a tail on him."

"No, I'd rather keep him in here and make him sweat." McClusky snuffed another match on his wet finger. "Petrosino had his chance trying Italian on them. Now I'm gonna let McCafferty have a go, speak some *Irish* to them."

"Chief, it's only one day. We turn him out, put a tail on him, and let him get a taste of freedom. He'll think he's gotten away scot free, and he'll be comfortable. Then tomorrow night, we'll give him a surprise visit with a tap on the head. He'll squeal quick then, because his friends won't be around to clam him up."

"George," Flynn said, standing and putting on his overcoat, "you're going to turn Lobaido loose. That's the long and short of it."

McClusky gave McCafferty an irritated look, some furtive conversation in the way they nodded at each other and wouldn't look at Flynn.

"All right, Bill, I'll have McCafferty tail Lobaido," McClusky said. "Go get your beauty rest. We'll keep the fires lit and do your job for you."

Flynn said, "Good night," unfazed, and left.

McClusky said to Petrosino, "We'll see if Lobaido breaks when he's alone like you say."

Petrosino didn't like the idea of McCafferty keeping watch on Lobaido. He stood up and thought of saluting and leaving the office, but stopped. "Chief, I should tail Lobaido. I know his language, and I know the East Side like the-"

"You got your way in front of your Secret Service pal. But you won't tell me who to send on detail. Not you or that big Jew.

McCafferty's on the job, end of telegram. So why don't you just go home now, Sergeant, and let me run the Central Bureau for a while?"

As Petrosino left the office he heard McCafferty whisper, "Fuckin' Dago."

Chapter 17

Petrosino barely slept. His right side was swollen, but it was anxiety over the murder that kept him awake. At sunrise, he took a cold bath, aspirin, and a shot of whiskey to numb the pain and crackling noise in his ribs. Then he headed to the Marble Palace eager to see Schmittberger. He shuddered in the morning chill, seeing his breath form a mist as newsies cried out, "Mafia gang arrested for barrel murder! Read it here!"

He picked up *The World* and skimmed it on the way. The front page was crowded with mugshots of the Morello gangsters, and an article said that the police had botched the arrest of Dr. Primrose and that his death had been ruled a suicide by the Coroner. Chief Inspector McClusky commented that they had the killer among the batch arrested, but he wouldn't say which one. Nor would he comment on whether Primrose was still a suspect or a false confessor. The article concluded that the Central Bureau was still in the dark about the victim's identity, and this agitated Petrosino because it was true.

Petrosino walked up to the back entrance of the Marble Palace where he found a detail of police reserves leaning against the stair railings and lampposts, twirling their billy clubs around their wrists. The brass buttons on their long blue overcoats shone in the morning sun, and their eyes squinted sharply from beneath their tall thimble-shaped helmets. A crowd milled about in the street below.

Schmittberger stood at the top of the steps, watching it all.

Petrosino walked up to him. "Max, what's doing?"

"McClusky was mad that the press said we botched the Primrose collar and that we still don't know who the victim is. So he's decided to parade the Morello gang and show the public we got 'em."

"Last night," Petrosino said, "he didn't want to let *one* of them out on bond. Now he wants to parade them *all* and risk an escape?"

"I wonder... like I said before, Joe. Maybe he wants them to escape?"

Petrosino considered it as the rising sun warmed his shoulders and stretched out over the horizon. The crowd grew with the sunlight, and the police reserves began practicing swings of their billies and pointing their sticks at the louder voices in the restless throng.

Petrosino whispered, "I wonder about Flynn, the way he was acting last night. He insisted that we cut the Third Degree short and give them lawyers."

"Is that so?" Schmittberger stroked his moustache. "You know, Ritchie was following me all last night like a lost dog. I get the feeling the Secret Service is waiting for us to botch it so they can have their case back."

"If they've got the goods, then how come they've never convicted Morello once?"

More reserves poured out the Marble Palace's back doors and formed two long columns of thirty men. Petrosino and Schmittberger stood aside on the rear portico as O'Farrell led Irish plainclothes men with the Morello gang in tow, handcuffed in front and holding onto each other like a great metal centipede. The gang trudged in lockstep with bruised faces.

Schmittberger laughed at Tomasso "The Ox" Petto, who had a bandage around his massive head and a left ear swollen like a purple cauliflower.

"Wait till we get lawyers!" Petto roared in Italian. "Then we'll see who laughs!"

Petrosino said, "You'll be laughing from Sing Sing, jackass."

Giuseppe "The Clutch Hand" Morello looked over and drew his deformed, handcuffed claw across his own neck. The Death Sign. Petrosino smiled broadly at him.

There must have been five hundred people in the crowd now, and they gasped as the phalanx of police reserves surrounded the prisoners with synchronized precision and marched forward with billy clubs held high.

"Fancy," Schmittberger said.

O'Farrell shouted to his blue phalanx, "Use your billies on the rabble to make a hole!"

The reserves drove back the agitators in the crowd, and one red-faced bluecoat swung wildly, knocking a boy to the ground. The crowd yelled, "Shame, shame!" And a half dozen men taunted the police and blocked the procession. The Morello gang egged on the crowd.

"Should we lend a hand?" Petrosino said.

While Schmittberger considered it, the cops and spectators began shoving each other.

"T.R. just said in the papers, 'Talk softly and carry a big stick,'" Schmittberger said. "You know he was talking about me, don't you?"

Schmittberger marched down the steps, banging his daytime billy club on the railing. He waded into the fracas, a head taller than everyone, and shouted, "Make way! These men are going to Jefferson Market to have their day in court! I said, 'MAKE WAY'!"

The crowd paused for a moment until a boy swiped the billy out of Schmittberger's hand and ran off. Then the crowd turned on the giant Inspector and came at him with fists. He tried to fend them off and shouted to Petrosino, "Don't just stand there, ya schmuck! Throw me a billy!"

Petrosino tossed a locustwood nightstick, and it looked as it might hurtle over Schmittberger's head. But he reached up, snatched it out of the air, and snapped it down on the nearest man's head. He tapped five more on the crown, and they each closed up like a jackknife. Petrosino moved in with his pistol and fired a shot in the air. The crowd made way en masse, undulating backward like an ocean tide. Schmittberger and Petrosino escorted the parade to three Black Marias waiting at Mulberry and Bleecker Street. The wagon doors flew open, and the bluecoats quickly tossed the prisoners inside. The police wagons sounded their gongs and sped off to the courthouse.

"Now that the Micks are busy," Max said, "let me show you what I found last night."

❧

Petrosino and Schmittberger walked east on Spring Street toward black plumes rising from the factory smokestacks and steamships on the East River. The smoke melded into a bleak canopy of clouds as they turned left on Elizabeth Street and walked north. The Star of Italy café was on the corner of Prince and Elizabeth Streets, a block from Old St. Patrick's. The gusting wind carried the aromas of fresh bread, horse manure, and burning coal.

Outside the Star of Italy, they found a patrolman sitting on a crate, devouring a large pretzel and gleefully watching an urchin turning handsprings and cartwheels. The patrolman was clapping at the little boy until he recognized the Inspector and Detective Sergeant on the sidewalk before him. He snapped to his feet and saluted.

Schmittberger said, "At ease."

The Star of Italy café's awning had "LAGER BEER" signs, and the windows bore the establishment's proprietor, *P. Inzerillo*. Inside, the *pasticceria* looked like a familiar East Side lunchroom with sawdust on the floor and tables and stools scattered across uneven floorboards. Petrosino turned up any light he could find and walked along the bar counter and through the tables and chairs. He looked for a trace of blood or a knife gouge in the tabletops. The only other place to hold down a grown man was the floor.

Petrosino sifted his hands through the sawdust on the floor, shaking his head. "I don't see any blood here."

"We found new linen collars on Morello's bedroom bureau with the four-letter tradename, *Marl.* Just like the barrel victim's collar."

"A lawyer will say it came from a sweatshop that sold thousands of collars just like it. What else? I know you've got something better than that, Max."

"Come look at this." Schmittberger walked over to the cellar door. It sat crooked in the jamb, and he had to wrench it open.

They went down the steps and flicked on a single bulb to see a storeroom of barrels, burlap, and tin cans. Petrosino bent down and stared closely at the ground. Not a single red drop.

"You won't find any blood." Schmittberger pointed at the barrels. "But look at those. They're all marked 'W & T.' Just like the one our victim was in. Wallace & Thompson are bakers at 365 Washington. Problem is, they supply pastries to a whole lot of saloons on the East Side. These barrels are as common as lampposts."

"This is the place, Max. The killers stab him, put him in one of these barrels, then. . ." Petrosino pointed to burlap scraps in the corner. "Use some burlap over there to wrap it around his neck. They have a wagon waiting out front, it's a cakewalk. He drew his last breath here." Petrosino shivered at the thought.

"I think that's right. And the way they cleaned up makes me think it was a professional job. But it gets better. Come on."

Schmittberger led him back upstairs to the bar counter. They filled two mugs from a keg that still had some suds left. Schmittberger gulped his beer and said, "We found a batch of letters hidden behind a loose brick in Morello's wall. They were like union circulars addressed to cities all over. Talked about the plight of Italians in America and how the 'Palermo Society' should be stronger in politics. I memorized part of it: '*The Irish and Jew have paid for their voices in the courts, city hall, and American police precincts. So should the Italian lest he remain as downtrodden as the Negro.*' Then it proposed a convention in New York to discuss '*Nostra Causa.*' What's that mean?"

"'*Nostra Causa*' means 'Our Cause.' Sounds like a socialist handbill."

"Ritchie thinks it's a crime syndicate. Next thing I know, the Secret Service glory hounds take all the letters as evidence in their federal case."

"Curse the fishes. I wonder if it's the Syndicate that Steffens was talking about?"

"I don't know, but I found something even better right here. Swiped it without Ritchie seeing." Schmittberger went around the bar counter and pointed at the wall beneath a framed picture of a half-naked chorus girl. He tapped on several bricks until he found one that jiggled. He had a hard time pulling it out, but, when he did, it revealed a deep opening in the wall. "Nothing in here now, because I have it on me." He drew out a folded sheet of paper from his jacket. "What's it say, Joe?"

Petrosino took the note and read the handwritten ink in block print:

FRQVHUYDCLRQH DO ODYRUR. PD FRPXQLFDUH H GLIHWWRVD SHU ODYRUR. LO EXH GHYH IDUH XQ HVHPSLR GHO EXIDOR.

"The last word, *exidor*, is that Latin? Max, I haven't a clue." Petrosino looked up from the note. "Let me copy it down and see if I can tumble it out."

Schmittberger nodded, and Petrosino jotted the message in his butcher book. Schmittberger folded up the note and slipped it in his jacket pocket.

"What if it's an extortion letter?" Schmittberger filled their mugs with more beer. "I like the angle that the dead man was a rich merchant with a hard head who refused to pay."

"Say, I know someone who might be able to translate it."

"No, don't say it, Joe. Don't even mention his name."

"Not him. His boss lady. She studied a dozen languages…"

"Finish your beer. I've got one last surprise."

"You were a busy man last night, huh, Max?" They emptied their mugs.

"While you were having fun beating the snot out of crooks, I was working." Max stood. "Let's visit Morello's concubine next door."

☙

They walked to the neighboring tenement. The columns framing the entrance had rotted away at the base and appeared to hang in the air, and there was a sign on the door that read: *Hebrews, consumptives, and dogs not allowed.* Inside, the hallway light bulb was smashed, but they could still see the outline of a rusty water pump in the common area. They groped their way up a banister covered with grime. The place smelled of must and ripe sweat.

On the third floor, Schmittberger pointed at a door, and Petrosino pressed his ear against it. He could hear a baby wailing and a woman trying to sing over it.

Petrosino knocked and said, "Open up, it's the law."

The woman shooshed the baby. Petrosino knocked again, louder, and locks clicked open. A stream of light fell into the dusty corridor, and a woman peeked her striking face in the gap. Beneath wisps of oily hair, one of her eyes wandered, making her appear to look at both of them at the same time. Another woman hovered behind, plump with big shoulders, a faint moustache, and tight clothes meant for a thinner girl.

Schmittberger whispered, "You can have the one with the moustache."

The woman at the door said, "*No parlo* Eng-lish."

Petrosino said in Italian, "Where's your man?"

She answered in the Sicilian dialect, "I don't know." She took a brief glimpse of Schmittberger and gave him the *malocchio.* The evil eye.

"We turned this place upside down last night," Schmittberger said, "so she doesn't fancy me very much. I was hoping you could get something out of her. The only thing I got is that she's Marie and her hairy sister there is Federica."

Petrosino saw a small dumbbell on the floor next to Federica. He pointed at it curiously, and Federica lifted it up and showed him how she exercised.

"Say, she's just like you, Joe," Schmittberger said, "strong and ugly."

Petrosino bit his lip and asked the pretty one in Sicilian, "What's your man's name?"

"I don't know," Marie said.

"Your man is Giuseppe Morello, no?"

"I don't know."

"Where was he the night of Easter Monday?"

"I don't know."

"Well, *signora*, tell me, is that your baby I hear crying inside?"

"I don't know."

"My God, dear woman, is there *anything* that you do know?"

"My dear policeman, I know that with or without a rooster God will still make the dawn. I know that and nothing else!" And she slammed the door in their faces.

"Charming gal."

They walked back down to Elizabeth Street and pondered their next move. Petrosino stared at storefronts across the street and wondered what they might have missed. He saw a mortar and pestle over a druggist's store, a picture of a coffin over an undertaker's parlor, and a cluster of three mystical golden balls over a pawnbroker's shop.

"There must be a thousand pawnshops in Little Italy." Petrosino stood entranced by the copper balls, as if they were soothsayer's orbs, and he thought of the barrel victim's possessions. Silk handkerchiefs, a pair of gloves, a rubber stamp, cheroot cigars, the silver watch chain, the necklace and crucifix. "Max, what if they pawned something?"

"Brilliant, Joe," Schmittberger said. "Why don't you go see your scholarly chums and translate that note while I go through the evidence again to see what the gang had on them."

"You sure you don't want me to look with you?"

Schmittberger shook his head. "Trust me. We can cover more ground this way."

Chapter 18

Petrosino would have liked to sort through the evidence with Schmittberger, but it made sense for them to split up and do separate tasks. Still, he had a twinge of doubt. He tried not to think about it as he passed through Washington Square and tipped his derby at young women strolling by with frilly parasols.

The doorman rang up to Minerva & Company and let him into the stairwell. Petrosino walked the four flights and cursed the building for not having an elevator. Before he went in, he dabbed sweat from his face with a handkerchief and took off his hat. He realized it was because of Tarbell. Had they all been men, he wouldn't have bothered. Steffens, Tarbell, and her assistant, McAlpin, were at their desks same as before, only with more papers piled up. McAlpin waved, but went back to typing loud as a warhammer with only two fingers.

"Joe, good to see you." Steffens jumped up from his chair. "You received my message at Headquarters? I've got a remarkable tale for you."

"No, I've been out," Petrosino said, "I came to see you about something else actually. Nice to see you, Miss Tarbell." Petrosino took her hand and bowed.

"Congratulations again on the barrel murder," she said. "That's some feather in your cap, though we're all confused now about who the culprit is."

"You're not alone." Petrosino sat in a chair closer to Steffens.

"Your ears must've been burning," Steffens said.

Steffens thumbed at Tarbell. "We just ate at Lyons on the Bowery with an old Italian friend who was a crime reporter in the Old Country. Sure enough, he had the dope on Morello or… *Terranova*. See, Morello's pop died young, and his mother remarried a man named Terranova. So there's some doubt about his surname."

"He probably used that to his advantage when he crossed over here."

"I'm surprised you can't get that information from the Italian authorities, but then again, Italy's economy and crime rate are so bad, our friend says they don't want their own crooks back. Did you try the Immigration Commisson on Ellis Island or the Secret Service?"

"Secret Service? That's a swell idea." Petrosino smiled to himself, wondering what else Flynn was holding back. "So spill. What's this remarkable tale of yours?"

"It's about Morello. He used to run with cattle thieves in the Ficuzza Woods in Sicily. Some captain of the Sylvan Guard, name of Vella, put Morello under house arrest while he waited for a farmer to muster the courage to testify against Morello. Morello was stuck in his mama's home in Corleone, wasn't allowed to drink and cavort, and had to account to this Captain Vella for his whereabouts."

"Like most men," Tarbell said, "he couldn't live without drinking and cavorting."

"Mind you it's us men, Minerva, that make the world go round."

Tarbell wagged a finger. "If three quarters of you men were killed, we women could replace you with the other quarter. Mind yourself that, Steff."

The three of them laughed, and Steffens said, "Anyhow, Captain Vella went out one night drinking with friends. He almost made it home, a few paces from his front door when BANG. Someone shot him in the back right through the left lung, fatally wounding him."

"Morello would've shot lefthanded," Petrosino said.

"That's right. A woman named Anna Di Puma said she saw Morello in the same spot where Captain Vella fell. She was going to testify, but she gets two bullets in her back, too."

"Was Morello tried for the killings?"

"He fled to America. Say, do you think he's really mixed up in the barrel murder, instead of that mad doctor?"

"Could be." Petrosino thought of Morello's soulless eyes and withered hand. "I'm ashamed to ask, but I need another favor from you. Actually from Miss Tarbell."

"Your turn first," Tarbell said. "What have you gotten for us about the Syndicate?"

Petrosino sighed, fidgeted for a cigar, and chewed it. "The Secret Service thinks the Morello gang is part of a crime syndicate, but I doubt it's your Syndicate. It's more of a Sicilian band of crooks they call the Palermo Society. And, well I... I don't want this to leave the room." Petrosino looked over his shoulder at McAlpin still pounding away on the typographic machine.

"Frank's sound as the dollar," Tarbell said. "Besides he can't hear a pip when he types."

Petrosino nodded. "The Secret Service and the Chief, well, things are being done queerly in this barrel case. Something's fishy. And one of the gangsters let slip that he's afraid of a man who goes by 'The Fox.' I thought it was a crook's alias at first, but... what if it's a rotten cop?"

"That's not much," Tarbell said.

"Well you've kept me at arm's length, too," Petrosino said. "I might be able to help more if you told me more about this Syndicate. Like who you think is behind it."

Steffens and Tarbell looked at each other, and she nodded.

Steffens said, "All right, Joe, *quid pro quo*. We told you there was a triumvirate or maybe a quartet running the Syndicate, right? Well, we're certain that Big Tim Sullivan is one."

"Makes sense, a ward boss like him would run the gambling rings on the East Side."

"We think there's a politicker, too, who owns the gambling dives themselves. We found some real estate records and know spies who worked in Alderman Murphy's offices."

"That makes sense, too. Murphy owns plenty of Raines Law hotels and saloons."

"We're still digging for the third and possibly a fourth boss. Tammany needs a lawman to replace the old crooked Chief, Bill Devery. You knew that. We've got a man in the Mayor's office who tips us, but the problem is that some of the arrows point to the federal building."

Petrosino conjured up Flynn's tense face in the interrogations. "How so?"

"Because a federal man could easily slip the muscle in and out of the country if they were using immigrants to do their dirty work for them."

Petrosino's cigar had become a soggy mess. He wrapped it in his handkerchief and hid it in a pocket. "Why are you so interested in this Syndicate? You're not the law."

"We do it for the same reasons you do," Tarbell said. "You don't do this for promotion or pay, do you? You do it because it's right, because you can't do it any other way, yes?"

Petrosino looked into Tarbell's smiling eyes, and he blushed.

"Corruption is not a mere felony," Steffens bellowed, "but a revolutionary process. If we can trace it to its source, then we might just find the cause. And then the cure."

"Why don't the two of you publish what you've got then? Expose the crooks now?"

"For a detective," Tarbell said, "you don't know overmuch of humanity, do you? Why would we confront the criminal about the skeleton in his closet, instead of finding the bones first, studying them at close range, and collecting evidence to prove their deathly existence?"

"Point taken," Petrosino said. "Listen, I need one more favor of someone smarter than me." He drew out a piece of paper with the words he copied from Schmittberger's note. "Miss Tarbell, you studied a dozen languages in college. What's this say?"

"Is it Cyrillic... no." She harrumphed and copied down the words in her notebook. "Perhaps a phonetic spelling of another language or a cipher. I just can't say." She looked up, her brow knitted in almost angry frustration.

Petrosino found it strangely attractive. "Not used to being stumped, Miss Tarbell?"

"No, I'm not, Mr. Petrosino. As a girl, I loved looking at things under a microscope, rock salt, insects, hangnails. I was very curious to know about everything."

"Made you feel heady, didn't it? I think you like outdoing others, especially us men."

She seemed to blush now. "I like being equal to the task of knowledge." She sat up tall in her chair, chin held high, and patted her notebook. "It's nearly tea time, Mr. Petrosino. Would you like to come to the soda jerk down the street? I could invite a linguistics professor I know, and we could have egg creams while we translate your note?"

"I would, but I have much to do. And I can't let you show the note to anyone else. Maybe a word or two, but we can't trust anyone with all of it since we don't know what it says yet. I hope you don't mind?"

"No, no, not at all," she said, but the smile in her eyes dimmed. "Steff and I will look at some books to see if it compares, and I'll maintain your confidence, as you wish."

Petrosino tipped his hat, but Tarbell was already digging through her shelves for a text.

❧

Petrosino felt strange about wanting to take afternoon tea with Tarbell. He pondered it as he walked up Lafayette Street toward the Marble Palace until he saw the sign for Saulino's. It was the lull between lunch and dinner, and Saulino's chairs were upside down on the tables, the door locked. He swallowed his pride and knocked gently. Adelina answered wearing that somber widow's dress, but she seemed pleasantly surprised.

"Did I disturb your afternoon catnap?" he whispered.

"No, I was preparing the menu for dinner. Where've you been?"

"I could ask you the same thing. Come out, I'll treat you to a nice egg cream."

She held her hand out the door to test the weather. "Let me get my hat and umbrella."

The clouds blotted out the sun, and a silvery mist fell as they walked toward the pink-and-white striped awning of the soda fountain on Houston Street. Adelina hummed to herself and spun her umbrella on her shoulder, unfazed by the gloomy skies. She wore a hat festooned with silk lilacs. When he held her hand, she looked at him suspiciously.

"Why are you trying to butter me up, Joe? You guilty about something?"

"Always." He held open the door to the soda fountain and winked at her.

She closed her umbrella and spun it, spraying him with rainwater.

She giggled as he wiped the mist from his face and followed her swishing black dress inside. The sweetness of egg shakes and cocoa hung in the air. They breathed it in and smiled at the marble counter full of cakes and jars of hard candies. Bow-tied soda jerkers passed over each other on a sliding ladder along a wall of bottles. A glossy mosaic of phosphates, seltzers, Apollinaris minerals, ginger ales, grape juices, syrups, limeades, bromides, bouillons, and bitters.

Adelina sidled closer to him, her hips rubbing against his. "This kind of place can make you forget there are such things as murders and crooks."

"Sure," he said, glancing over her shoulder.

Two men were staring at them, murmuring between stiff lips. They looked like they belonged in a saloon, not a soda shop. The younger of the two was handsome despite a brown velveteen suit from the Old Country and a pint of tonic in his curly black hair. The older one had dark circles under his eyes and a hounddog look about him. He wore a black suit and a tie knotted severely at his throat, as if he enjoyed the feeling of strangulation.

"You go first, Joe," Adelina said, "I can't decide."

"Egg shake with cream," Petrosino said absently, still eyeing the two men.

"Plain ole egg cream? That's something my father would have." Adelina studied the chalkboard of specialties and asked the jerker, "What's that one, the Sasparilla Sunset?"

"Yes, ma'am, that's sasparilla, swirls of cream, orange juice, and a yeller marshmallow that'll sink down in your drink like the sun."

Adelina beamed approval. Petrosino nodded, but looked over his shoulder for the men.

The hounddog one was outside the front window now, resting lethargically against a lamppost, indifferent to the rain sheeting down. Steam came off him like a dying soul. The handsome one was gone. Petrosino turned back to the counter. The jerker spun out bottles and a mortar and pestle and mixed their exquisite sodas with nimble hands that reminded Petrosino of a pickpocket like Izzy. They sat at a table in the corner and sipped their drinks.

"I saw Max by himself the other day," Adelina said. "He's such a handsome man."

"Where did you see him?"

"Outside your apartment building. If I didn't know better, I'd say he was snooping."

"You sure it was him?" Petrosino said, wondering what Max could have been doing.

"Yes." She ate a spoonful of cream. "Why do all the cops hate him?"

"Says who?" Petrosino wiped cream from his lip and looked outside again.

"Says all the ones who come in my restaurant. You cops blab, you know."

"Well, they're Micks. They don't know him."

"You admire him, don't you?"

"Sure I do. Everyone's always down on him. Reformers, crooks, other cops. He gets it on all sides. Like me."

"At least you got good ink in *The Times*," she said, smiling. "I saw your name and kept a copy. Is that where you've been?"

"What do you care? You haven't come to see me once. You must have other 'appointments' to keep you busy?"

She crossed her arms. "Is that what you think of me?"

"No…" Petrosino noticed a row of blue bottles on a shelf behind her, and it made him think of his mother.

"Joe, what's the matter?"

"When my mother had consumption, she used to spit in blue bottles of carbolic acid, so she wouldn't spread her germs to me."

Adelina looked over at the bottles, then reached across and held his hand. "I'm sorry."

"No, it's all right. After she passed, I never realized how lonely I was. Until I met you."

Adelina smiled and kissed his hand.

He sighed and looked out the window again. The rain still fell, but the older man was gone. "How come you don't tell me much? Like what happened to your husband? And you sneak over in the middle of the night, and you don't even stay till morning. What, is it because I'm a cop?"

"I should go," she said, reaching for her umbrella. "I have a lot of cooking to do."

He said nothing, worried he'd make it worse. He just held the umbrella for her as they left the fountain and walked through the rain back to Saulino's. She squeezed his hand once and looked as if she were searching for words. The languid rain tumbled down thick as mercury, seeping through his hat, but he felt warm and content being with her.

"I was wrong to ask," he whispered.

"Joe, I don't wear this dress for my husband." She stopped on the sidewalk to look him in the eye. "It's for my daughter."

Petrosino heaved a sigh. "I'm sorry."

A hand shot out from the side and grabbed Petrosino's shoulder. He turned to see the smiling face of the handsome man from the soda fountain.

"Giuseppe Petrosino?" the man said, opening his arms for an embrace.

Petrosino stepped in front of Adelina. He squinted through the rain at the man and looked around for the other one. "Who are you?"

"It *is* you, my dear cousin! It's me Paolo from Padula. Or we say 'Paul' in America, yes? You no remember me?"

"I don't know you."

"Your mamá's uncle was married to a Vermiglio. My *nona* was a Pizzati, and she was second cousin for your mamá's uncle. You see? So this make us *cugini!*"

Petrosino motioned for Adelina to duck under the awning of a *latteria*. He turned back to Paul. "I think you've mistaken me for someone else."

Paul nodded toward Adelina. "She is angel from heaven, cousin. Your wife? Or maybe sister? Is better for me, ah?"

"Look, what do you want? If we're cousins, I never heard of you. So spill it."

Paul's voice dropped lower. "I want help you. You are in danger, *cugino.*" His smile became a leaden stare. "About the poor man they find in the barrel. You know this man's name, no? Tell to me, I help you. They want to put you out of the way…"

Petrosino opened his coat and showed his holster. "Scram, shitbird."

"Okay, *pezzonovante*. Bigshot." Paul chuckled. "But if you look so much, then maybe you find something not so good, and then you make trouble for you. And for *her.*"

Petrosino followed Paul's eyes and saw the older hounddog man chatting politely with Adelina, holding her umbrella for her. Petrosino shouted, "Get away from her!"

"That's Peter," Paul said. "He's just my *zio*. Don't worry, he's a so gentle, cousin."

"'Peter' and 'Paul,' huh?" Petrosino felt the rain dripping off his own nose, steaming in his eyes. "If I see your face again, *cousin*, I'll squash your fucking head like a turnip."

"You are *so* brave. We go now, because you make us so much afraid."

Paul retreated backward.

Petrosino stepped onto the sidewalk toward Peter, who was wiping a speck of cream from Adelina's nose. Peter licked the cream on his finger and smiled. Petrosino reached for his holster, but the two men tipped their hats at Adelina and quickly slinked away.

Piccola Italia a/k/a Little Italy

Chapter 19

"I don't know how," Schmittberger whispered across the dinner table, "but some of them had permits from 1901 to carry weapons in city limits."

"What the devil?" Deputy Commissioner Duff Piper said, stroking his thick red beard. He spooned four mounds of sugar into his coffee, took a sip, shook his head, and added another spoonful. "Who signed permits for those goddamn gangsters to carry guns?"

"Our former Chief Devery."

"Why, that Tammany son of a jackal. At least he's gone, good riddance. See, lads, that's why we have to turn out the rest of them."

Petrosino nodded from his chair to the Deputy's right, thinking of the two thugs who threatened him at the soda fountain. He didn't know why, but he hadn't told anyone about it yet, not even Max. He snapped out of his thoughts and studied Piper in the candlelight of the Lafayette Hotel restaurant. Piper lived in the Lafayette during the week, and the staff treated him like a king. The waiters even knew not to take Piper's dusty top hat. Piper kept it on his lap and constantly looked into it, making facial expressions or tossing his hair this way and that. Petrosino leaned over subtly now, trying to see what was inside the hat.

"What else did they have on them?" Piper said. "Any counterfeit notes or bad coin on the prisoners? Or the victim?"

"None that I saw," Schmittberger said. "Mind you, I haven't slept in two days, but I went through the gang's traps. Saw the usual things you might expect to find on a man, but no contraband or anything of evidence value."

"That's it?" Piper looked crestfallen. The waiter came with a tray and set down plates of thick steaks with mashed potatoes, bloody gravy, and steaming rolls. "Thank you."

"Well, I did find some droll stuff." Schmittberger picked up his steak knife. "But I didn't think you'd be interested in that."

"Oh, I am, Max. Sometimes you find the best clues in the queerest places." Piper doused his plate with salt and pepper and pocketed the silver shakers. Petrosino and Schmittberger smiled curiously at the act, and Piper spoke through a mouthful of ribeye, "Old habits of the poor. I bring them home to the wife. She collects them. Go on, Max. The droll stuff…"

"Right. So Petto had a love note to a girl, pinned inside his jacket. Inzerillo kept a small glass eye, about the size of a snake's, in his shoe. Joe says it's to ward off Italian curses. And Pecoraro had a vial of laudanum he claimed was for piles and lumbago."

"I wish the police surgeon would prescribe me some opium tinctures," Petrosino said jokingly. "My ribs feel like a bag of gravel thanks to that Ox bastard."

"What about jewelry?" Piper asked, gazing into his hat again. He sucked at his teeth and picked a piece of gristle from his gums.

"Some stickpins and a few cheap trinkets. Lobaido had an engraved watch with his initials and garnets. Morello had a similar one with an engraved M. Neither matched the old silver watch chain that was on the barrel victim."

Petrosino chewed on his steak and listened to the rhythmic tapping of rainwater on the hotel windows. "Time mocks us," Petrosino said. "Every minute that goes by, our chances go down. Clues wash away in the rain and witnesses disappear out of town or into the ground."

"Aye. " Piper ate a spoonful of potatoes. "So, Joe, what are you doing?"

"Max told you about those Sicilian union circulars from the Palermo Society. I'm working that and other angles." He nodded at Max. They'd decided not to tell anyone else about the puzzling note until they knew what it said. "The victim's gloves had the trade name 'Laird,' which is from Buffalo. So the barrel victim could be from upstate."

Piper sighed, obviously disappointed. "Well, lads, I may have done you more harm than good. I know the early hours of a case are ripe, and I'm sorry about the Primrose angle."

"That's not on your doorstep, boss," Schmittberger said, "It's not the first time a loon has confessed to something he didn't do. It had to be run down, we just got unlucky."

"I just can't stand to see Chesty McClusky and his evil Green Machine take over the Central Bureau. I'd like nothing more than to see him fail and you two solve this puzzle."

"Don't count us out yet," Petrosino said. "As soon as we leave here, we've got a meeting with one of the Morello gang. Of course, he doesn't know it yet."

"You do?" Piper's eyes flickered with anger. "That blackguard McClusky holds back when he briefs me. What's doing?"

"We turned loose the youngest gangster, Vito Lobaido. He's likely to reach The Break."

"It was Joe's idea to set him loose with a tail," Schmittberger said. "Lobaido should be in his flat by now with Jimmy McCafferty watching him. We think the only reason he didn't break already was because he was locked up with all his fellow gangsters."

The twinkle came back into Piper's eyes, and his teeth shone like ivory as he said, "And now that he's all alone, you can go thump something out of him."

"That's right."

"Well, what are you waiting for? I'd invite you to stay for brandy and cigars, but I'd rather have you squash that hoodlum! Hie thee, lads!"

Petrosino and Schmittberger wiped their mouths with their napkins and stood up to shake hands with Piper. When Petrosino stood over the Deputy, he got a clear look at the top hat and what was sewn inside of it: a small mirror. He laughed to himself.

❧

Detective "Handsome" Jimmy McCafferty was chomping Chiclets and talking to a prostitute when Petrosino and Schmittberger walked up. It was dark out, but they could see the silver coins glitter in McCafferty's hand as he leaned against a lamppost across from Vito Lobaido's rickety clapboard tenement on Stanton Street. A clock on the post read ten o'clock.

"What the hell are you doing, Jimmy?" Schmittberger said, startling McCafferty and making him spin from the lamppost.

"Just doing my job, Inspector. Why?"

The prostitute had already disappeared into a disorderly house by the time Petrosino and Schmittberger huddled under the street light with McCafferty.

"Doesn't look like it." Schmittberger thumbed at the noise from the disorderly house.

"It ain't what you think. That was just my change, that's all."

"What? You mean you've been…" Petrosino made a fist-pumping gesture.

"You fucking dolt," Schmittberger said. "And how do you know Lobaido didn't slip out while you were humping some two-bit whore?"

"Don't fret, I tailed him good. I got him up in the morning and put him to bed at night." McCafferty flashed a charming grin. "And I had a roundsman take my post when I was on her… my break."

"Aw for the love… you couldn't keep your inchworm in your trousers?" Schmittberger shook his head. "I'll have your ass in a sling if Lobaido's flown the coop."

"He's there, I said." McCafferty hiked up his trousers and put his hands on his hips. "I've been awake eighteen hours in the rain, watching the bum, and that perfume was calling to me. And you should've seen the tits on-"

"Shut your trap," Schmittberger said. "Eighteen hours? I've been awake *two days*. We're going inside. Make sure no one comes out. And, Jimmy, try not to play with your cock?"

McCafferty spat out his gum on the sidewalk.

Petrosino smirked as he and Schmittberger walked across the street and pushed in the front door of the four-story tenement. It was the kind of place that was built in a month to take advantage of the immigrant wave. Probably some wealthy politician or church owned the pile of kindling, Petrosino thought, as they creaked up the wooden steps to the second floor, the light fading in and out from a loose wire. Three layers of paint hung in peels off the wall, and the whole place smelled of yeast from the rain. They stopped in front of 2B.

"2-B," Schmittberger said, "or not 2B?"

Petrosino shook his head. Schmittberger drew out his billy club, and Petrosino held his .38 against his thigh. Schmittberger tapped the door with the billy. No answer. Schmittberger hit it harder this time, and another door down the hall opened and an angry man peeked out. When he saw it was the cops, he disappeared.

"Should we break it in?" Schmittberger whispered.

Petrosino shook his head and tried the knob. It turned. He looked at Schmittberger, who nodded, and they opened the door and barreled into the room. Two lamps were on, showing a surprisingly large place with two rooms. A kitchen in front, then a bigger room with three cots and a single window with a blanket nailed over it. They kicked at wine bottles, dirty plates, newspapers, and piles of rags on the floor.

"Probably had six or seven of 'em sleeping here."

"He's gone," Petrosino said, and just as the words came out of his mouth, he kicked a pile of blankets and realized a person was under them. Petrosino saw a tuft of the kid's brown hair and waved at Schmittberger, who came over and poked the blankets with his billy.

"Wake up, Vito!" Petrosino shouted in Italian. The floorboards groaned.

Schmittberger yanked the blankets off. Vito Lobaido was fully-dressed, shirtcollar, suit, even shoes. He was in the fetal position, hiding his head under his arms, curled up and pretending to be asleep. "Rise and shine, faker!"

Petrosino knelt down and shook the kid. "Curse the fishes."

"What's the matter, Joe? Does he need a doctor?"

"He don't need a doctor. He wants an undertaker."

Schmittberger knelt next to Petrosino. He touched Lobaido's hand. "For shit's sake. He's as cold as a cucumber."

Petrosino pulled the kid's hands away from the face and felt the neck. It was already rigid. He sniffed Lobaido's mouth and nostrils. Then he pulled the blankets aside and got down on his hands and knees, searching around the floor.

"What is it, Joe?"

"He smells like bitter almonds. Maybe you oughtta read *Tanner's* instead of *Romeo and Juliet* sometime?"

Schmittberger groped around on the floor. "What the hell are we looking for, Joe?"

"Powder. That smell is cyanide of mercury, maybe mixed with bromo."

"Damn it all, you think he was poisoned?"

"Either that or he killed himself. But he wasn't the type to take his own life. He was more afraid of Purgatory than even the mafia." Petrosino lay on the floor and saw a glass that had rolled under a cot. "There it is." He picked it up and pointed at the stains and dribbles of red wine. "There's some grains left in the wine, and see the film on the side?"

Schmittberger ripped the blanket off the wall and threw open the window. He shouted down at McCafferty in the street, "Call a wagon, you stupid ass! He's dead!"

Chapter 20

Petrosino and Schmittberger passed a flask back and forth in Petrosino's office. After they had found Vito Lobaido dead, McCafferty reported back to Chief Inspector McClusky, and the Irish dicks danced a wicked jig on the Morello gang's heads into the night. They even took Morello to the Morgue and shoved him against the barrel victim's naked corpse. But neither he nor any of the other gangsters broke. In a way, Petrosino admired them for it. It was morning now, and he and Schmittberger had just been summoned to the Chief's Oriental carpet.

They took another swig before they went upstairs and straight into his shuttered office.

"Well, if it isn't Alphonse and Gaston." McClusky wagged his leathery yellow finger at them. "It was your fine idea to turn Lobaido loose!"

"Sir, he didn't die on my watch," Petrosino said, wanting to blame McCafferty.

"No one breathes a word about Lobaido croaking." McClusky glowered at them. "I control the news from the PD, and I'll keep his untimely suicide from the press. *Me.*"

"Suicide? Chief, I think he was poisoned-"

"He poisoned himself. That's what I'll tell the newshounds, and I'll tell you two bums the same thing. Nobody prints the stuff my dicks get, not a single goddamn word from friends or enemies of the police, without correction from me first." McClusky banged his desk. "Every single thing you two have touched in this case has turned to shit. I don't know what the opposite is of the Midas touch, but you shitbirds have it. Now shut up and get out!"

They retreated back to Petrosino's office, and Petrosino tilted the flask and sipped until his throat screamed. Schmittberger took it and finished the rest.

"Max, you ever consider hopping on the water wagon, the way you drink?"

"Hell no. Water has killed more folks than liquor ever did."

"You're raving. How do you figure that?"

"Well, Joe, to begin with, there was the Flood."

They laughed. "McClusky's got it in for us now," Schmittberger said. "You think he's mixed up in this somehow? Maybe that's why he put McCafferty on the tail and why he's trying to sweep Lobaido under the rug now?"

"Or he's worried about his career. He's a climber and another body doesn't look good."

"What about Flynn? And that weasel, Ritchie?"

"I don't trust the Service either," Petrosino said. "But then I don't trust anybody."

"McClusky wouldn't shit on us if we joined the Pequod Club."

"Why the hell would we want to join Tammany's police social club?"

"It's the only hope for promotion. Everyone knows that except *us chumps*." Max lit a cigarette and inhaled with one eye closed. He pointed at Roosevelt's portrait on the wall. "Face it, Joe. The real Reform days went away with T.R. to the White House."

"What we need is a break in this case, and you'll stop harping on that." Petrosino picked up his telephone and told the T/S operator to connect him to Minerva & Company.

Steffens's voice answered, "Ready on the line."

Petrosino said curtly, "Did you figure out that item yet?"

"Hello, Joe. We're working on it."

"What's it say?" Petrosino covered the receiver and nodded reassuringly at Schmittberger. "They're working on it."

"It's not any language we've seen. In fact, we're quite sure it's a cipher."

"What's it say?"

"There's the rub. We haven't cracked the code yet…"

"All right. Please ring me if you do." Petrosino hung up and shook his head.

"See," Schmittberger said, "I told you we can't catch a break."

Rain ticked like a metronome against the window, and Petrosino could feel the wind's chilly breath on his neck. The foundation of the Palace had settled over the years, and none of the windows shut all the way. The wind and the whiskey beckoned him to sleep it off.

Schmittberger glanced at *The World* on the desk. "And to top it all off, I lost five bucks on the Giants and Trolley Dodgers game at the Polo Grounds. For shit's sake."

There was a knock at the door, and Petrosino put the flask away. "Come in."

The old doorman, Strauss, came in, crumpling his nose and holding a parcel and a letter far away from his bluecoat. "Sir, this box has been sitting by the desk sergeant all night. Stinks like the devil's breath. A letter came separate."

Petrosino took the parcel and letter, and Strauss wafted his way out of the office. The parcel was about the size of a cigar box. Petrosino shook it, and something weighing a couple of pounds slid back and forth inside. He tore open the wrapping and removed the box's lid. A dead rat lay inside, its bird-like claws extended upward. Petrosino lifted it by the smooth pink tail, and Schmittberger shrieked like a soprano.

Petrosino chuckled. "What's the matter, a big man like you? Never seen a rat?"

"I've seen plenty, and I still haven't met one I liked."

Petrosino looked at the carcass again. The rat had no eyes.

"Why the hell would someone send you that rotten thing in a bundle??" Schmittberger said in a nasal tone, pinching his nose. "What's that?"

There was a note written inside the box: *Preparati per la tua morto.*

Petrosino tossed the rat back in the box. "It's a *fatura*, an Italian bewitchment. Someone paid an old hag to put a curse on me so I'd stop doing my job." He paused and thought of the two thugs at the soda fountain. "I wonder if this has something to do with the two bastards who threatened me at the soda shop."

"Who?" Schmittberger took his hand away from his nose.

"Never seen 'em before. They were clever about it. One of them pretended to be my cousin from the Old Country. Said I should quit sticking my nose in the barrel murder."

"Why the hell didn't you tell me about it? We oughtta beat the shit out of 'em!"

"I wanted to, but Adelina was with me, and we were in the middle of the street."

"You mean Saulino's daughter? You and... I'll be damned." Schmittberger put his hands on his hips and shook his head in amusement. "How many secrets you keeping from me?"

"Less than you're keeping from me. Look, I could've pinched them, but I didn't have the goods on them. I promise you this though: if I see them again, they'll be gumming their cakes."

"You think they sent this to scare you off the case?" Schmittberger asked.

"It could be anybody. See, you and the Irish dicks don't get these nice little gifts because you're not Italian. I get hexes all the time. They usually come with a note saying, 'I cast on you the *malocchio*.' The evil eye. This one just tells me to prepare to die. Not so bad."

Schmittberger grinned. "You believe in that evil eye stuff, that Dago witchcraft?"

"Hell no. Here, hold this. I forgot to open the other thing." Petrosino tried to hand the parcel to Schmittberger, but the giant retreated with his hand up in protest. Petrosino opened the letter and found a visiting card in embossed gold lettering: *Israel Baline, Salesman Extraordinaire, Greater New York*. He flipped over the card and read a neatly written note: *I'll wait for you at my uncle's*. Petrosino grinned.

"We just might've caught a break, Max. But this stoolie likes to meet alone."

"I don't care, go. Just take that foul box with you."

Petrosino slung on his overcoat and derby hat and flew out of Police Headquarters with the parcel and visiting card in hand. Half a block down Mulberry, he tossed the dead rat into an ash barrel and pointed his index and little fingers at it. He spat out, "Phfft, phfft, phfft," sending the *malocchio* back to the *strega* from where it came, and hurried on to meet Baline.

やう

He squeezed the visiting card in his hand, worried that Israel Baline would grow skittish at any moment and disappear. At the intersection of Mulberry and Spring Streets, he scuttled faster through the wagons, hagglers, and peddlers' carts and felt his breathing shorten from the pain in his ribs. From behind a pushcart of herbs, a peddler announced in Sicilian, "Parsley is here! I have the best fresh parsley right here!" The Sicilian word for "parsley" was "*pitrusinu*," and so Petrosino eyed the peddler, unsure whether the announcement was a witty greeting or a public warning to the thieves on the street that Petrosino was among them and sniffing around.

Petrosino said to the peddler in Sicilian, "Say it again and I'll shoot you in the leg."

The peddler blinked nervously and apologized.

Petrosino walked down the Bowery beneath the rumbling thunder and floating ash of the elevated rails. He passed banks advertising postal and telegraph services, letter writing for the illiterate, currency exchange, notary public, and steamship tickets, then a row of pizzerias. At Grand he turned east, and the smells from a thousand fishmongers' carts on Hester Street carried north and swam in the air. The smells usually made him hungry, but he had only one purpose in mind. To squeeze every atom of information out of Israel Baline's greedy brain.

Bells jingled on the entrance door as Petrosino stepped inside Verdi's *Libreria* at 99 Eldridge Street, smack in the middle of a

mixed quarter of Italians and Eastern European Jews. Tonino
Verdi was hunched over a glass display case, looking at a flimsy
yellow book promising lurid stories of romance. The *Libreria* was a
shotgun style room about eight feet wide, bursting with books, sheet
music, piano rolls, and chapbooks. It was empty except for a *nonna*
looking at sheet music with her granddaughter. A small upright
piano stood against the wall opposite the display case so patrons
could play a new song from the sheet music and decide if they
liked it enough to buy. The piano rolls were stored in long boxes on
shelves, and librettos and cartoon and magic trick chapbooks were
displayed in the case beneath Verdi's frayed shirtsleeves. Petrosino
always lingered in the shop, browsing lyrics on the flip-side of new
sheet music, wishing he had a Pianola player-piano so he could
listen to live music at home.

"What is it this time?" Verdi's wild eyebrows met in a knotted
clump. "Last Saturday, he goes to Coney Island, comes back with
sixty dollars. Nobody knows how. But I know. I told my sister
to kick him in the ass a long time ago. That's what she gets for
marrying a Jew."

"What happened to your Pianola?" Petrosino moved down the
counter and squeezed between the piano and the display case to
square up to Verdi.

"Sold it to a bigshot merchant."

"Too bad. Where is he? I mean business."

"Why don't you lock him up for a few days, give him a scare?
Crooked wood is straightened with fire! Or lock up the bums he
hangs around for perverting his morals?"

"He's got no morals to pervert."

"True enough." Verdi hung his head in agreement. He glanced
at the old *nonna* in the corner of the shop, then whispered, "Stable
next door. Kick him in the ass."

Petrosino nodded, walked out. The stable next door was a pile
of rotting boards and whitewash paint held together by pasteboard
ads of Beech-Nut Sliced Bacon, White Label Guinness Stout, and
Murad's Turkish cigarettes. The splintered barn doors were cracked

open enough for a dog to slip through. Petrosino peeked into the dusky space. It took a second for his eyes to adjust, but he saw that there were no horses in the two stalls. Verdi must have hired them out. He threw one of the barn doors open to let in some light. Manure smells invaded his mouth as he crunched over straw, moving to the rear stall where sunlight splayed through loose planks. He looked over the stall's low gate and saw the sweet, dark-haired boy slumped in the corner against a water trough. He wore a brown hounds-tooth suit with a yellow shirt, brand new shoes with horseshit on the soles, and twelve hairs posing as a moustache beneath a long Russian Jewish nose. An empty beer bottle and a leather suitcase lay at those reedy and agile hands. Petrosino had never seen them lying still. He could see the magic in them now. With the boy's innocent face and sweet voice, no one would suspect that those perfect hands belonged to the fastest and most rapacious pickpocket in the East Side. Maybe in all of Greater New York.

"Izzy," Petrosino said. "Izzy, get up!"

"Who goes there?" Izzy hopped to his feet, eyes twitching alert. He squinted at Petrosino. "Shh. I don't want no one to see me talking to youse, Joe. Come in."

Petrosino looked for the clean spots and carefully stepped inside the stall, closing the gate behind. He swatted at buzzing sounds circling in the shadows and frowned. "Look at you. New duds, suitcase... agile as an accountant of a get-rich-quick concern. Your poor mama must be tearing her hair out. You oughtta be ashamed, you little leather-snatcher."

"Aw, save it for the Salvation Army." Izzy's mouth contorted as if he'd swallowed a castor bean, talking like a Bowery tough instead of the son of a music teacher and cantor. "I got more coin than my ma and pop'll ever clink. I can take in forty bucks a day, sixty on a Saturday night at Coney."

"Taking out your anger on the billfolds in the City?" Petrosino kicked Izzy's suitcase. The foot of a fine silk stocking was caught in the closure. "What's that? You a fence now, too?"

"I ain't no fence. I'm a salesman, and those are my wares. I take the money I make during the day and buy goods at a discount and resell for a profit. It's a *bona fide* trade."

"Nuts." Petrosino reached for the suitcase.

Izzy tried to shoved him away, saying, "That ain't why I wanted to talk to you, Joe!"

"Then why'd you bring me down here in all this horseshit?"

Izzy was squirming and pushing until Petrosino stepped back from the suitcase. "Because I saw in the papers that youse working that barrel murder and I mighta heard something. About the victim, see. And I might tell youse for the right price. But I ain't no stoolie. I don't want no one to think that I'm a lowdown stoolie. I gotta maintain a repute-"

Petrosino took the kid by the throat. "Listen, punk. There's a dead man on the Morgue slab right now, his throat's slashed to bits and his cock and balls chopped clean off. Now I aim to find the bastard who did it. So I'll put the idea right in front of your little nose, and I'll even put handles on it so you can get a good grasp: If you don't sing, I'll put the word out on the street that you're a first-class stool pigeon that don't know when to shut up. *Capisce?*"

Izzy got a wise look on his face and started crooning, "My sweet Marie from sunny Italy. Oh how I do love you. Say that you'll love me, love me, too-"

"Not that kind of singing, you rube." Petrosino hesistated, thinking that the kid sang pretty good. "You ain't half bad, kid. Where'd you get that tune?"

"Made it up from scratch. Now lemme go, you shit-"

Petrosino choked him again.

"Okay, wait," Izzy choked out, eyes gleaming wet. "The dead bastard's kin to an Italian by the name of . . . Giuseppe De Priemo. He's up the river now."

Petrosino loosened his stranglehold when he recognized the name. "What's the barrel *victim's* name? Is it De Priemo, too?"

"I don't know."

"What do you mean? How did you hear about this inmate from Sing Sing? How's he related to the victim? Don't make me squash it out of you, Izzy."

"I betcha'd like to mash my brains in. What's it to youse anyhow, the way I heard?"

"What's it to *me*? I'm the guy who's trailing it all the way to the killers. Whoever told you heard it from someone else, who maybe heard it from the ones who did it. So spill."

"Last night," Izzy spat out bitterly, "I heard the man in the barrel 'got his' because of De Priemo. But I was drinking whiskey at Nigger Mike's all night, and I don't remember nothing about who said which or how. Just the name and thought it was worth something to youse. I won't crack wise again, Joe, just lemme go."

"They let a kid your age drink at that Russian Jew's place?" Petrosino cocked his head and held the kid's face. "And that's all you know?"

"I swear, Joe. I told youse everything I remember. Now, youse gonna treat me on the square or gimme more of the Third Degree? Ain't that how youse cops get your confessions? Thump, thump, thump on the noggin? Bet youse beat your own kids, huh?"

"Izzy, if I had a son like you, he'd be a bass drum." Petrosino let him go and walked out of the stall, fanning away bottle green horse flies. He couldn't wait to go to Sing Sing.

"Say," Izzy called after him, "youse didn't give me nothing for my trouble!"

Petrosino felt inside his coat pocket, thumbed his wallet. "Sure I did. If you'd dipped my billfold too, then I would've broken your fingers."

Izzy smiled and flashed the dollar. "You're right, Joe, this is all I took."

Chapter 21

He rode the first car of the Hudson River Railroad to Ossining, gazing at the silver ribbon of the river. He sat as calmly as he could, knowing that a potential murder witness was waiting in a pitch black three-by-seven cell, thirty miles north. Giuseppe Di Priemo. A few months ago, he'd helped Flynn and the Secret Service put Di Priemo away for counterfeiting in Yonkers.

The one baggage car and five passenger cars emerged from the city's tunnel and roared along the tracks at twenty-five miles an hour. The train passed into the rough terrain of the northern suburbs toward Yonkers, the steel wheels beating out a monotonous rhythm. Petrosino pulled his derby low and leaned back in the oily weave of canvas upholstery, snug in his overcoat. He watched the passing landscape through the window. The train seemed to glide just above the Hudson River, its limestone currents jagged and cold. Scrub clung to the rocky edge like straggling children, and the treeline on the other side of the river was in the midst of transforming from russet to green. Some of the trees hadn't survived the winter, and their coal black skeletons were bent over in the harsh sunlight and shriveled like old men given up.

He saw his glum reflection in the glass and tried not to think of the barrel victim's face or the men who had threatened him at the soda fountain. He closed his eyes and later woke to the sound of brakes screeching and the engineer's voice, passing through the car, yelling at the flagman: "Hurry up your cakes! We got another train twelve minutes behind us."

Passengers filed off, and Petrosino straightened his derby and descended to the platform. Spring crackled through the trees like the sound of newspapers rustling. He took in the smell of chickory and turned south toward the prison. The massive stone fortress with its basin docks sat on the low ground near the Hudson. The Big House was six tiers of cells, about forty feet wide, five hundred feet long, and shaped like a barn. A man in a prison keeper uniform came up the train platform, hunched over and craggy: Keeper Shoemaker.

"Detective Bet-ye-see-no, sir, ain't seen you in a while." Shoemaker shook hands. "Let me conduct ye down to the Big House. Sorry if I'm late, just took head count."

Shoemaker led him to a sparkly motorcar that looked like a marriage between an ornate leather sofa and a small open carriage. There were two oil-burning lanterns on the glossy black frame, and shiny rubber tires that put the Police Scorcher Squad's bicycles to shame. Petrosino hopped up the step plates and into the wide seat. Shoemaker turned the start crank and jumped in. He steered the tiller and gunned forward.

"This here's the Warden's new curved dash Olds runabout," Shoemaker said proudly as they sputtered south down a makeshift road called Durston. "Got more power than a team of horses and pneumatic tires that can't be punctured no way, no how."

They hit a rock the size of a watermelon, and both were thrown a foot off their seats.

"Try to get us there alive, Shoe."

Shoemaker grinned. They traveled past the freight depot, the prison cemetery, and the twenty-foot wall and cell house. Shoemaker parked the motorcar at the end of the road in the prison barn. The familiar smells drowned Petrosino's senses. The stone walls were two feet thick, keeping everything inside festering without air and light, and the inmates' "night buckets" had recently been dumped in an open channel carved into the walkways.

Shoemaker led him to the front steps and neatly groomed lawn, inside the gate, and into the foyer. The gate slammed shut and locked behind them. A pair of guards loitered laconically on either side. Shoemaker politely asked if Petrosino would hand over his service revolver for storage in the prison magazine. Shoemaker then gave him a cup of coffee and led him to a beautifully carved cherry table in the visiting room. The table had ornate flowers and exotic birds that must have taken one of the inmates weeks to chisel in the prison workshop.

"I'll get him for ye," Shoemaker said, "he's awaitin' in the key house."

Petrosino never got over how eerie the silence was with twelve hundred inmates there. The walls were sweating green mold. It felt like a mausoleum, he thought, as De Priemo ambled in handcuffed and shackled with Shoemaker prodding him.

⁊

Giuseppe De Priemo's face looked like a parched white road that had cracked and hardened under a merciless wind. A film coated his grey expressionless eyes, and his mouth was as tight and shriveled as a raisin. The prison's barber school kept his hair cropped and his face clean-shaven. Still, he looked two decades older than his twenty-eight years. His hobnailed boots clacked across the floor, and when he sat down, a smell filled the room like a dank sack of onions and cheese. His cap and uniform hung loosely and should have been white, but they were the hue of a dingy pigeon. The uniform was decorated with just one set of black stripes. First offenders wore single stripes, two-time offenders had double, and the persistent felons had triple. Quadruple stripes were the mark of an incorrigible prisoner they called a "zebra" in Sing Sing.

De Priemo was chained to a chair beneath a string of electric fixtures that all pointed down on his head. If he were frightened or nervous, his face didn't show it. There was apathy in him and little else. Petrosino looked down at the man's Sing Sing criminal record. De Priemo's previous occupation was listed as "gardener," which Petrosino thought could be true if it meant cultivating "greenbacks." De Priemo was single, could not read or write, and he was listed as five feet five and a half inches tall and one hundred eighty-two pounds. It looked as though he had already lost twenty-five pounds in Sing Sing.

"Take off your cap, Number 5-4-0-8-8," Shoemaker said from the light's edge.

De Priemo reached his hand up, but the chains stopped his arm short.

Shoemaker knocked the cap onto the table.

"That's enough, Shoe," Petrosino said. "Let him be." Petrosino looked at De Priemo who still hadn't met his eyes. "My name is Petrosino. I'm a detective from the city, and I want to ask you some questions. I need to identify a man, and I think you might be able to help."

De Priemo said nothing.

"Maybe, there'll be something in it for you."

A sneer crossed De Priemo's pruned mouth.

"Yer welcome to throttle him a little," Shoemaker said, "if ye like."

Petrosino looked up at Shoemaker. "Let us alone for a few minutes?"

Shoemaker patted a fist against an open palm, winked. He went out and shut the door.

"You have four years on this sentence. With 'good time,' the best you could do is April 14, 1906. I can get you time outside. More than just a march to the workshops. Looks like you could use the fresh air." Petrosino took the envelope out of his coat pocket and removed the first photograph. It was the best the Coroner's photographer could do with the barrel victim's face, which looked waxen and thin but not quite dead. And nothing like the ghoul in Petrosino's nightmares. The linen collar and tie had been dressed up beneath the chin. The picture was a profile view, taken close enough to disguise the fact that the head was propped up on the Coroner's table at the Morgue. The victim's eyelids were half open. Petrosino slid the picture across the table, and De Priemo leaned forward as best he could in the restraining chair.

"You look familiar," De Priemo said and looked down to focus on the photograph.

"Do you know the man in the picture?"

Flecks of aquamarine sparkled in the grey void of De Priemos' eyes. "Is he sick?"

"Do you know him?"

"Looks like Nitto. My sister's husband in Buffalo."

Buffalo! Petrosino wanted to shout. That's where the victim's gloves were from. He felt his pulse beating in his fingertips as he held onto a second photograph. "What's his full name? And does he still have kin in Buffalo, your sister maybe?"

"Benedetto Madonnia. My sister's there."

"Is her family name the same?"

"She's a Madonnnia, but the eldest boy is Sagliabeni. Salvatore Sagliabeni. They both live at 47 Trenton Avenue. Tell me, what's the matter with my brother-in-law?"

"Take a good look." Petrosino felt the air deflating from his chest. He felt guilty because he had played a part in painting De Priemo as a squealer. And now De Priemo's brother-in-law had paid the ultimate price. "Are you sure it's him?"

De Priemo pointed with his chin at the photograph. "See that scar, the one on his cheek. Nitto got that from a fall in a quarry. Nitto's a stonemason, but he's been troubled with rheumatism and hasn't worked in months. Is he sick?"

"He's dead." Petrosino handed over the second photograph. It showed the head and torso of Benedetto Madonnia, the gaping wounds to the throat vividly centered in the frame.

De Priemo looked down again, and sweat beaded up shiny on his forehead. "They massacred him!" his voice roared like a storm tearing down a pigeon coop. The color in his face ran out, and he looked as if he'd faint. Petrosino reached across and slapped him, and De Priemo sat up and muttered, "Those sons of bitches. I should have never-" De Priemo silenced himself, saliva frothing on his lips, the wheels of his mind turning. "I don't want to see any more."

"They put him in a barrel, Guiseppe, with his balls in his mouth. In the middle of the street for everyone to see. And you know who *they* are, don't you?" Petrosino said in Sicilian, "*Cu avi dinari e amicizia teni 'nculu la giustiza*. He who has money and friends holds justice in contempt. I don't think you have either one anymore, Giuseppe. I'd wager Crocevera doesn't even look at you in here, does he? Except to give you the evil eye?"

"I told Nitto to come here."

"Where? Benedetto visited you here in prison?"

De Priemo nodded as tears traveled down the grooves of his weathered cheekbone.

Petrosino took out Madonnia's necklace and crucifix. "Are these his?"

"Yes. So this is what I get for my share? They said they would get me a lawyer."

"Who?" Petrosino held up the watch chain. "At least tell me what his watch looked like."

De Priemo quickly wiped his cheek against the shoulder of his uniform. And when his head lifted up again, the grey film had returned to blanket his eyes.

"Will you sign a statement saying that the man in the photograph is your brother-in-law?"

"I'm done talking."

"The D.A. will call you as a witness. We have Morello and Inzerillo and the others, all of them in a jail in New York as we speak. They thought you snitched to the Secret Service, and they handed you a rotten deal. It was when you were arrested on New Year's."

De Priemo clamped his chin to his chest, holding his lower lip between his teeth, mute.

"Did they go after your brother, because they couldn't get to you?" Petrosino leaned in, whispering, "They deserve justice, Giuseppe. Let me deliver it for you."

"You got it all wrong. This is *my* business now. I'll make my own justice."

"If you help me, I'll give you a square deal in return. Maybe transfer you closer to Bufffalo and your sister? Ask around about me. I never break my word."

De Priemo nodded pensively. "Let me think on it."

Chapter 22

"Chief, we got a positive ID," Petrosino said. "The victim's name is Benedetto Madonnia, an Italian from Buffalo."

Schmittberger added, "I guess we got the Midas touch after all, huh?"

"Sit down," McClusky said, brooding behind a barricade of objects on his desk. A brass lamp, an Upright telephone, a glossy humidor, and a tray of soda bottles. In the leather lounger to McClusky's left sat William J. Flynn, thumbs hooked into his vest, appearing thoroughly blasé or drunk or both. A fog of smoke clung to the yellow walls, and the room needed a window thrown open. Petrosino and Schmittberger sat.

"I've been talking to Agent Flynn here, before you two came in," McClusky said, "and it's opened my eyes to a great many things. The Secret Service is delegating full responsibility to me from now on." McClusky cut two Puerto Rican cigars, offering a fat one to Flynn. Flynn took it, and McClusky struck a match on his desk and leaned over to light Flynn's butt. Through the ribbons of sulphur, McClusky looked moodily at Petrosino, his face the color of a lizard's belly in the lamp's glow. "So how'd you catch this break?"

"An informant gave me the name of a prisoner in Sing Sing," Petrosino said. "Giuseppe De Priemo. He's a counterfeiter I ran across with Agent Flynn a few months ago."

"Sing Sing?" McClusky's jowls quivered like chicken fat. "What the hell's that got to do with this murder?"

"De Priemo?" Flynn sat up, unhooked his thumb from his vest, and snicked ashes into a water glass. "Was it that case from Yonkers?"

"What case is that?" McClusky said.

"In late December of last year, we caught three men in Yonkers with counterfeit five-dollar bills from the National Iron Bank. They were in Morello's gang, and we believed the paper they used for the bills was imported from Italy by Morello himself."

"De Priemo was one of the three you pinched?"

"That's right." Flynn puffed his cigar. "When we brought them in for questioning, I asked Joseph to pose as a suspect and listen in on De Priemo, Isadoro Crocevera, and Salvatore Romano. Joseph was disguised in handcuffs and sat down in the waiting area next to them, to see if they talked amongst themselves. I got Crocevera in my office first and spent about ten minutes with him. Not a word rolled off his tongue. Then I had Joseph come in my office to see how the others were reacting, and he had a brilliant idea. Tell him, Joseph."

"When I went into Flynn's office," Petrosino said, "I thought the first interrogation was too quick and that the other suspects knew Crocevera hadn't squealed. So I thought Bill should bring in the next one and let him stew in the chair for a couple of hours, even if he was mute as a monk. To let the others *think* he was squealing. The next one in was De Priemo."

"I gave De Priemo tea and cookies," Flynn said, "and I read the paper for two hours while he sat there like the King of Italy. Then I led him out to the hall in plain view of the other Italians. I patted him on the back and thanked him like he'd just given me a promotion."

Petrosino said, "The other two must've thought De Priemo squealed, because they started muttering under their breaths and giving each other dirty looks."

Flynn snickered. "By the time Romano came into my office, he was white as a sheet. He spilled the whole milk bottle to get his charges dismissed. He was the real rat, not De Priemo."

"I still don't follow how De Priemo fits into the barrel murder," McClusky said.

"Sir, the Morello gang follows the laws of vendetta," Petrosino said. "If they thought a gang member squealed, they would've put him in a wooden kimono. The problem with De Priemo was that he was already behind two feet of stone and watchtower rifles at Sing Sing. Since they couldn't get to him, maybe they took revenge on his nearest male kin: Benedetto Madonnia is De Priemo's brother-in-law."

"You're sure this Madonnia is our barrel victim?"

"De Priemo positively identified his Morgue picture at Sing Sing. The one thing that doesn't fit though, is why they would put Madonnia on display like that in a barrel?"

"I don't want another Primrose." McClusky tossed his cigar into the cuspidor and drew a comb out of his desk. He stood to look at his reflection in the windowpane and raked the comb across his hair. "You got any other confirmation on the ID, Sergeant? Next of kin?"

"I wired the Buffalo police to track down Madonnia's wife. She's De Priemo's sister. If she gives a positive ID from the photos, we'll bring her here for a viewing at the Morgue."

"What about a signed statement from De Priemo?"

"He was jittery. I think we ought to bring him in and have Mr. Jerome question him."

"Joe caught a hell of a break, Chief," Schmittberger said. "We thought you'd be pleased."

"Can't you see me dancing?" McClusky stopped combing his hair and turned around. He pointed the comb at Flynn. "Bill, I can handle it from here. Thanks for your help."

"Remember, George, we are fighting not against people but against demons within people. Keep faith in Jesus." Flynn shook hands with McClusky. He donned his straw boater and tipped it at Petrosino on his way out.

"Shut that goddamn door," McClusky hissed. He stared at Schmittberger as he picked up his telephone and asked to be connected to the District Attorney's office. "Mr. Jerome, it's George McClusky. How are you, sir?" McClusky's voice was cheerful. "Fine, fine. Listen, you've been asking when we're going to break the barrel murder. Well, I've hooked a big one. ...Yes, sir, I've identified the victim. ...From an Italian up the river name of Giuseppe De Priemo. I think we should bring him in so you can question him." McClusky squeezed the receiver tightly and smiled fakely. "All right, I'll make arrangements."

McClusky hung up the receiver. "I'm bringing in that Sing Sing Dago tomorrow morning so Jerome can question him. I expect you to be there, Petrosino."

"I ought to be there, too," Schmittberger said.

McClusky kicked his polished shoes on his desk, laced his fingers behind his head, and smiled at Schmittberger. "You ever have a dog, Broom?"

"Sure I have."

"You like 'em."

"Just fine."

"I love dogs," McClusky said. "When I was a boy, I had the best two hunting dogs you've ever seen. Red Setters. The runt was dumb as hell, but loyal and always came to heel when I called. The other one was big and smart and chased fox like a champ. But he never listened. He'd always run off on his own, chew shit to bits, sometimes even mess in his own house. You know what I did with the big one, Broom?"

"I don't know, Chief..." Schmittberger glanced over at Petrosino, unsure where this was going. "Did you give it away to the SPCA?"

"I put it on a wagon, and I drove out as far as I could in the middle of some woods where I knew there was all kinds of wild animals. Then I tied it to a tree with ten foot of rope. You should've heard it yelping when I drove off. I swear to this day it sounded like a child."

Petrosino felt sick to his stomach, imagining the poor dog starving to death. He looked into McClusky's hollow eyes and that's when Petrosino was sure that the Chief had some skin in the game. Something the son of a bitch was hiding in the barrel murder.

Even Schmittberger was disturbed by the story and McClusky's icy stare. It took him a moment to fire off a quip, "I take it this story doesn't end with the pup finding his way home?"

McClusky shook his head. "I luncheoned with Flynn today. Of course, I'm on the water wagon and don't drink, but Flynn had a few chianti toddies. He let it slip that it wasn't Agent Ritchie. No, it was *you* who figured out that Primrose couldn't have done the killing."

Petrosino didn't look, but he could hear Schmittberger swallow hard.

"I guess you went to that sanitarium," McClusky said, "checked the records yourself, and then fed it to the Secret Service? Course, you did all that without telling me *one fucking word*." Schmittberger stood, holding out his hands to explain. McClusky shouted, "Shut your trap! Three days' suspension for insubordination, and you're off the barrel case when you come back."

"You can't do that." Schmittberger leaned over the desk. "Deputy Commissioner Piper is the judge for police misconduct trials, and I'm entitled to a hearing."

Petrosino slowly stood. "Chief, we need Max-"

"Stay out of this, Petrosino. Go take the rest of the day off, unless you want the boot, too." McClusky turned back to Schmittberger and held out his hand.

"I've got plenty other guns," Schmittberger said and slid his service revolver across the desk. "Besides, I never needed one to pinch a crook. But you'll not get my badge. Not for three days, not for three seconds. You want it, you come try and take it from me... Chief."

"Three days penance is easy, you Jew squealer," McClusky said. "Now you can go to your temple and do whatever you heathens do."

Chapter 23

"Can you believe that fucking Irish peacock?" Schmittberger said. "We I.D. the victim, crack the case open, and what does he do? Suspends me!"

"He's crooked as a ram's horn," Petrosino said.

"Of course he is. He's a Tammany man, ain't he?"

"On this case in particular. First, he wanted it to go away when we pinned it on Primrose. Then he didn't bat an eyelash when Primrose croaked. He was almost relieved-"

"Let's do this over a drink, Joe. I need one. Or five." Schmittberger paced between an armchair and the brown velvet parlor suite in Petrosino's sitting room. He stopped and looked through a bookcase and laughed. "*Phelps on Wounds, Brundage on Toxicology, Tanner's Memorandum of Poisons*, firearms manuals, and a dictionary. Jesus, don't you ever read for pleasure? I thought you'd at least have Sherlock Holmes with all the fibs you tell?"

"Me? You're the master of tall tales. I've got Twain's *Double Barreled Detective Story* there, but it wasn't very good. Cool your heels."

Petrosino went to his kitchen and opened a beer. He split it between two coffee cups and brought it out with a loaf of black bread, a white onion, a jar of green olives, some old salami, and a hunk of fresh cheese from the best *latteria* in Little Italy.

Schmittberger was sitting in the armchair, and Petrosino settled into a rocker.

"After Primrose kicks the bucket," Petrosino said, "Lobaido just so happens to follow. And whose watch was that on?"

"His favorite. Handsome Jimmy, another potato-eater."

"Right. And now he's made some deal with Flynn so he's got full control of the investigation. Then he takes you off the case. Max, what if *he's* behind these killings?"

"Or *suicides*, you mean? Either way that Mick is trying to take this from me." Max tapped the gold Inspector's shield in his vest. "But I'm going to protect it with all I got."

"Listen, he said you're off the barrel case, but that doesn't mean you can't detail other men to work on it, right? Hell, he wouldn't even know if you were still on the job. He doesn't step foot outside the Marble Palace except to eat dinner at Delmonico's."

Schmittberger finished his beer and started in on the food. He took a bite of cheese and smiled. "You're right, Joe. I guess that means I can keep feeding you these notes?"

"*Notes*? You found another one?"

"I was going to tell the bastard, but fuck him now." Schmittberger took out a notepad and flipped it open. "Another one appeared behind that loose brick at the Star of Italy. I've had my man Stransky watching. We left it there, but I copied it down."

Petrosino took out his butcher's book and wrote down the code:

FRJOLDPR O'HUED SHU OD YROSH.

"I still can't make heads or tails of it, Max. We need to give this to Steffens-"

"I already tried his office. They're out for the day. Besides, it's after six now."

"You know where his office is?" Petrosino said.

"I followed you there once. It gets my goat that no one trusts me, you especially. That's always been your Achille's heel. You get so steamed up on a case, you let yourself get tailed."

Petrosino shook his head. He didn't know which was worse. The fact that Schmittberger had tailed him or that he hadn't known he was being tailed. "Son of a . . ."

"Aw, don't be sore, Joe. There's nothing to do until the next of kin identify Madonnia and Jerome questions De Priemo."

Schmittberger ate a handful of olives, pits and all. He smiled. "I'm on suspension so we might as well keep drinking, right? Where's the good stuff?"

"Don't follow me again." Petrosino went into the kitchen and looked in the back of a cupboard. He brought a dusty bottle into the sitting room. "You gave me this for helping you on that kidnapping, remember? I've been saving it for a special occasion, but I never have one."

"Don't be so glum. Let me see that treasure." Schmittberger read the label, "*PEARL WEDDING RYE bears the indorsement of some of our most famous physicians, because of its medicinal qualities. It is an almost infallible cure for gout and rheumatism, and used as a preventative will invariably ward off attacks of colds and la grippe!*"

Petrosino said, "I do feel a soreness in my ribs."

"Sounds like you need this medicine to me." Schmittberger's tongue raked over his lips as he opened the bottle. He poured the golden nectar halfway up two coffee cups and they toasted to the lighted apartments and the misty halo of stars shining outside the windows. Petrosino moved his rocking chair next to the Edison phonograph on the bureau, setting the cup of whiskey on a footstool. Everything within arms-length. They lit cigars and balanced them on the lip of an empty olive jar, then they took a long sip of rye and puffed on the cigars.

The smoky flavor soothed Petrosino's throat.

"That'll save many a doctor's bill," Max said. "How about some music, maestro?"

The phonograph was Petrosino's most expensive treasure, and the black canisters of wax cylinders gleamed on the bureau, all identical, so he had no way of knowing which song was which. He took another sip of rye and played the first two-minute recording.

The announcer's voice crackled through the phonograph's black and brass horn, "Selection from *Rigoletto*, played by the Edison Concert Band!" And the music tumbled out and filled the sitting room while their fingers began tapping, Petrosino's along the arm of the rocking chair and Schmittberger's on the armchair. Petrosino sang to the instrumental accompaniment, *"La donna è mobile, qual piuma al vento, muta d'accento, e di pensiero.* Ba, ba, ba, da da-da!"

Then another gold moulded cylinder. "Whistling solo, anvil chorus from *Il Trovatore* by Joe Belmont, Edison Records!" The music came out fast and frolicking.

Schmittberger tried to whistle along and almost lost his cigar. Petrosino's foot tapped to the beat. More sips of whiskey and the next cylinder. "I never trouble trouble until trouble troubles me, sung by Collins and Natus, Edison Records!"

"That's your tune, Max." The vocals and the tinkling sounds of piano started Petrosino's head bobbing and kept his foot tapping.

Max dropped two bits into the knob of the coin-slot gas meter to keep the light on, and they went through a dozen more cylinders like that: a toast of rye, a puff of tobacco, and their chairs moving farther away from the phonograph as they contorted and sang along with the baritone solo in "El Toreador" from *Carmen* and the Edison Male Quartet's rendition of "Keep on a-shing silv'ry moon" and the French tenor Bartel singing from *Aida*.

When the Intermezzo from *Cavalleria Rusticana* began playing, Petrosino rushed into his bedroom to dig out his violin case. He rosined his bow, and they listened to another dozen songs while Petrosino drew the bow softly across the violin's strings. By his seventh cup of whiskey and second visit to the water closet, his hand was pulling the bow wildly back and forth, his feet stamping as if they were putting out a fire, and his left shoulder was numb as an icebox.

Schmittberger was laughing wildly and dancing with a broom.

It made Petrosino think of dancing partners. He noticed that the lighted squares were blinking out across the street, and the stars were becoming slow comets.

The recorded voice announced the next song from the brass horn, "Adelina, the Yale boola girl, by the Edison Quartet!" Petrosino's chest swelled up, and he said, "For my dear Adelina. You're the only reason I bought this rotten record." He sung along with the cheerleading chants and music, and when the song ended, he looked out the window. She would be going upstairs soon to brush her hair and get ready for sleep. Only half a block away.

"How'd you meet Saulino's girl?" Schmittberger said, reading his mind.

"At a Saturday evening dance for the Italian Benevolent Association."

"That's a gas! You dance?"

"I did that night. She had a violet ribbon in her hair, big sad eyes, and big feet. No one asked her to dance because she wore a widow's dress. Men kept passing over her, asking other girls to dance, but she never got upset. Even danced once with her pop. So at the end of the night, I got up my courage and asked for a dance. She trampled all over my toes and, by the end of the song, we couldn't stop laughing."

"Why don't you go see her?"

"Who?"

"*Who*? Joe, you're like a brother to me, but you're a schmuck." Schmittberger put his arm around him. "I've got Sarah and the kids, and, at the end of the day, that's all that counts. So if you want that girl, go get her damn it... or I will!"

They laughed, and Petrosino said, "One more," fumbling for another cylinder.

"Stars and Stripes Forever, march, played by the Edison Military Band!"

"Dear old John Philip Sousa!" Petrosino waved his violin bow like a bandleader's baton, and they both marched in tune with the triumphant horns and the crashing cymbals, out the door and into the stairwell. Petrosino nearly slipped down the stairs, but Max caught him by the collar. They high-stepped outside as if they were in full parade march to Saulino's restaurant.

"Go on home, I can do this by myself," Petrosino whispered.

"Godspeed, Romeo." Schmittberger saluted and slipped away.

Petrosino stood beneath Adelina's window and began playing his violin, making music like a male lark. Her face appeared behind a pot of basil on the sill, hiding, but Petrosino thought he could see her eyes, big and purple as sloe berries, watching him. Smiling. His violin strings yowled over cackling from the street and a man shouting, "That sounds like a cat in heat!" Another said, "Maybe he's got a Jew's harp stuck up his *culo*!" Laughter echoed. For some reason he wasn't embarrassed. He felt alive as he strummed the bow and plucked strings and finally opened his eyes to see Vincenzo Saulino's baffled frown.

The bow screeched over the strings, and the music halted.

"My God, you've had a snootful, huh?" Vincenzo said.

Petrosino nodded silently, watching a comet spinning silver pinwheels in the night. All the Saints had turned against him.

Vincenzo Saulino looked out on life like a resentful crab peering out of its shell a few moments at a time. He put his arm around Petrosino and walked him back to his flat. "I like you, Joe, you're a good man. But she's already lost one husband. With your line of work, I couldn't bear to see her hurt like that again. Now please, don't embarrass us."

"*Signore*, with all due respect," Petrosino said as Vincenzo walked him upstairs and into his flat, "I'm going to see her whether you like it or not."

"Papa, go back home," Adelina's voice said. Petrosino was in bed now. He could hear them argue in whispers. At the end, he made out her voice saying, "Don't tell me what to do."

"Fine, look what happened the last time you went against me." The door slammed.

"You've done it now," Adelina said, staring down at him. "You and your crazy violin."

Petrosino looked up at her face and the kaleidoscope of shadows and colors and dreams on the ceiling above her, and he said, "Pearl Wedding Rye is an infallible cure for gout."

☙

He woke up dying for a glass of water, and there she was next to him. She opened her eyes, and they touched each other's faces.

She rolled her back to him, and he put his arms around her and held tight, afraid he was dreaming and that he'd hear a rooster or a wagon in a minute, and she'd vanish. But she was real. She whispered, "You stubborn bastard."

He couldn't remember every detail, but he knew he'd embarrassed himself. He kissed the back of her neck. "Are you cross with me?"

"Yes. But you were too funny for me to stay angry. Why did you get so soused?"

"Max got in hot water at work. Is your father upset?"

"It doesn't matter." She turned over and stared into his eyes. "I've been meaning to tell you something. I tried the other day at the soda fountain, but I didn't finish what I was saying."

"I remember. You said your mourning dress was for your daughter."

"That's not the only reason. I wear it so we can save face, too. My father told everyone my husband died in a mining accident." She paused and didn't say anything for a minute. "The bastard's not dead, Joe. He ran out on me."

"You don't have to tell me. It doesn't matter."

"No, I have to tell you. It will make me feel better." She sighed. "We couldn't find him when I went into labor. I was alone with the midwife for two days. I'd been so happy, dreaming of how life would be, and, when it finally happened, there was a little less of me. That happiness was born in the baby. But she had the cord around her neck." Adelina wept, and he pressed his forehead against hers. "Some of me disappeared that day, and I'll never have it back…"

He hugged her, and she whispered, "*He* came home two days later and got in bed like nothing. He'd taken the money for the midwife and went to an opium den. I got up and told him, 'If you lay your head on that pillow, I promise you'll wake up with your throat slit.'"

"Where is he?" Petrosino caressed her neck, feeling closer but also terrified that she was opening up. He'd never known how heavy her burdens were, and they were suddenly his, too.

"He went back to Italy. I heard he has a wife there, too." She set her jaw, composing herself, and her voice steadied. "So now you know my secret. You're the only one I've told."

"Adelina…" His heart broke for her, and he thought of revenge. "What's his name?"

"Edward Vinti. But I want you to promise not to do anything. I never want to see or hear of him again. I won't have another man treat me like that. Do you understand me now?"

He held her face and whispered, "Always."

BARREL MURDER UNSOLVED

Body of the Victim Has Not Been Identified.

McClusky Fears Some of the Suspects May Have to be Let Go—Secret Service Men Step in to Make Arrests.

The body of the victim of the barrel murder still lay unidentified on its slab in the Morgue last night. At least fifty persons, according to the detectives, had viewed the remains there during the day. but none had been able to make a positive identification.

While Inspector McClusky does not doubt that the murderer or murderers are among the men he has in his custody, he confesses that the failure to identify the body has sadly hampered him in his work, and that as a result he might be forced to let most of the thirteen men go when they are arraigned to-day before Magistrate Barlow, in the Jefferson Market Court, for lack of evidence. The hope of getting any of the prisoners to confess he has abandoned.

"The only trouble," said the Inspector yesterday, "is that we are a little ahead of events. We have the men who we thought killed the man before the body has been identified. If we knew the identity of the man, we could go ahead and work on a motive for the crime, and thus obtain some tangible evidence."

The Inspector will insist that Morello, who is said to be chief of the Palermo Society of the Mafia in this city, and Pietro Inzarillo, who kept the restaurant at 226 Elizabeth Street, where was found a barrel an exact counterpart of that in which the body was packed, be held. It is probable that some of the men will be rearrested by the Secret Service Agents. All of them will be kept under surveillance, as Inspector McClusky expects that by watching their movements he may be able to unravel some new clue to the mystery.

NEW YORK TIMES

Chapter 24

In the dream, Petrosino was roaming the East Side, chasing a faceless man with a gun. The man stopped at a brownstone and pointed the gun at Adelina who sat on a stoop. The nightmare transformed into Petrosino holding a set of keys and smashing them against the man's mouth until he was nothing but toothless, bloody gums. The bloodied face twisted into a smile and choked out, "I'll see you in hell, Petrosino." Then the eyelids drooped, and the face morphed into the barrel victim's death mask.

Benedetto Madonnia's eyes opened wide and his decapitated head gurgled, "Save me."

Petrosino bolted upright in bed, drenched in darkness and sweat. He sat up, shaking his head and swallowing a Beacham's digestion pill and a pitcher of water. He wobbled into the kitchen and flinched when he saw Adelina sitting on a stool. She was in her black dress and already had water on for tea and a *frittata* of egg, onion, and cheese on the stove. The dream had taken away his appetite, but he didn't tell her.

"What are you doing here?" He stood in his underclothes, dumbfounded. "Your pop?"

"He knows, Joe. He tucked you in bed for God's sake." She got up from the stool and patted his cheek. "The whole neighborhood knows after your little *concerto* last night."

He snatched her by the waist and kissed her.

"Joe, stop." She grinned. "I have my reputation to consider."

"I'm glad I ruined it."

She kissed his cheek and straightened her dress, turning for the door. She stopped and looked back at him. "Are you learning violin because Sherlock Holmes plays?"

"That's nonsense."

"I knew it." She stuck out her tongue and left.

He went to the window and watched her cross the street and slip inside Saulino's. He was content that she'd told him everything. He wanted more than anything to have children now for both their sakes. But there was one promise he'd break, if he found Edward Vinti. He sighed and filled his bathtub, thinking about the murder again. He kept seeing Madonnia's face in the picture of his father on the wall and the reflections in his bath water. He dressed slowly, putting on a fresh shirt collar and a brown suit for Mr. Jerome. Too early to leave, he thought, sitting in the front room armchair, staring at the wall clock. The clock's hands seemed to stand still. He had a feeling that De Priemo was going to sing and could hardly wait.

He cleaned and loaded his .38 Smith & Wesson, humming *Rigoletto* from the recording the night before. When daylight rambled through the windows of his sparse rooms, the morning ice truck rattled outside and the ice man sent a chip up the dumbwaiter. Petrosino was loading his icebox when a knock came at the door.

"You forgot to bill me again?" Petrosino said.

"A message for you," a voice said from the stairwell.

"I can barely hear you." Petrosino opened his door. In the dim stairwell, he saw the top of a greasy, curly head. "Who's that?"

The head bobbed away, down the steps, shouting, "A message from-" And that was when the first explosion filled his ears.

Petrosino slammed the door shut and dove to the floor. A rapid series of gunshots followed. Tinny, small caliber echoes. He pulled his pistol and scrambled to the side of the door, waiting, counting a dozen pops in perfectly timed succession. And he knew that it wasn't a gun. He ran to the front window and saw the curly head disappearing into the crowded street below, joining another man in a black suit. He couldn't make out their faces.

He pushed open the door with his gun and smelled gunpowder. Twelve spent Chinese firecrackers on the floor, and bits of paper floating in the air. His ears were still ringing as he raced downstairs. He thought the man had said, "A message from... *Il Volpe*." The Fox.

He hustled down the street, seeing only the men's backs a block ahead. He shoved through the crowds, gaining ground quickly, following them all the way to the Bowery, where they slipped into a red light club. Petrosino was desperate to see their faces. He knocked over pushcart peddlers and ignored shrieks on the sidewalks as he flew past. Outside the red light club, a stout watchman was sitting on a crate, half-asleep. The watchman's eyes nearly fell out of his head when he saw Petrosino bounding up the steps. The watchman fumbled for a silent button. A buzzer warning of a police raid.

Petrosino knocked him off the crate and barreled into the club. He found the remnants of an orgy. The air smelled of rosewood and sex, and bodies slept in various positions on lush fur rugs and flowery silk sofas. A man and two naked women drunkenly played leapfrog, oblivious to his intrusion. Another girl was splayed on the floor, singing, "*The Bowery, The Bowery. They say such things and they do strange things on the Bowery. The Bowery! I'll never go there anymore!*" A buzzer over a gilded bar counter signaled an alarm that no one heeded.

He dashed to a grand staircase in the back, nearly running over a Negro chambermaid.

"Two men," he said, "which way?"

She nervously pointed up the staircase. He gripped his gun tightly, sprinting up the carpeted stairs. A long corridor led to a sign over a red door: EXIT- SUICIDE HALL. He picked up speed, ran up, and kicked the door open. He nearly fell through and had to grab onto the splintered jamb. The door was open to the outside, no balcony, only a twenty-foot drop straight down to a grotesque pile of garbage below. Petrosino saw the two men escaping down an alley. The curly-haired one looked back. It was his "cousin" from the Old Country: Paul.

"Curse the fishes," Petrosino said.

శా

Petrosino had worked up an angry sweat chasing Peter and
Paul. He changed into a fresh suit and called into Headquarters to
check wires, which made him late. On the way to Centre Street, he
bought a copy of *The World* and skimmed an article titled, *Barrel
Murder Unsolved*. There was no mention of the victim's identity,
but there were foolish quotes from McClusky that the PD would
tail any gang member freed on bail. Nothing like letting a crook
know he was being shadowed, Petrosino thought. He hustled up
the steps of the Criminal Courts Building, nodded past the police
guard, and headed upstairs. It never crossed his mind that he
should tell anyone about Peter and Paul. He imagined what they
would say: *Firecrackers? What's next, Sergeant? Want we should make
out a report of a dog bite?* He was furious with himself for not being
more careful. What if those had been real gunshots? Was he careless
because he was with her?

Jerome's secretary waved him through the waiting room, and he
went through another door into a lingering trail of tobacco smoke.
He turned down a corridor of rooms for the assistant attorneys,
clerks, process servers, and office boys. The last office door was
blank, no stenciled letters on the smoky glass. He went in and was
surprised to see District Attorney William Travers Jerome's desk
empty except for an engraved gold nameplate and three favorite
reference books: the Bible, Bartlett's Familiar Quotations, and a
volume of celebrated speeches. In the far corner of the expansive
room, four men sat at an octagonal table with a tray of bottles
and glasses. Blue smoke and chatter curled around them and a
chandelier over their table.

A cigar in Chief Inspector McClusky's jowls stopped mid-flap,
and he nodded at Petrosino, who saluted. Deputy Commissioner
Duff Piper was in his old plum suit, sitting across from the Chief,
scratching his red beard. Garvan, the assistant district attorney,
waved a pipe. District Attorney Jerome was shuffling cards. His
light brown hair was pasted down and parted, turning white over

his ears. A pince-nez clung to the bridge of his nose, and a small moustache covered his lip. He was neatly dressed in a slate grey suit, vest, and burgundy bowtie. A man of great dash who looked like he could fight the Devil with fire, Petrosino thought. He'd never met a man as sharp as Jerome, and he was secretly intimidated by him.

Jerome stopped shuffling cards and motioned Petrosino in. There was an anthill of copper on the table, which Petrosino thought odd because Jerome had famously won his office by leading raids on gambling houses with a pistol in one hand and a hatchet in the other.

"Don't look so surprised, Joe, it's just penny ante." Jerome puffed a cigarette. "I may be a Reformer, but I like to gamble a bit myself. A man can get all the gambling he needs in a social game with friends instead of disorderly houses. Isn't that right, Deputy?"

"I suppose so," Piper said, "if he's winning. Why's the little Dago here? Did an organ grinder lose his monkey?" He and McClusky laughed heartily.

Piper's playing the game, Petrosino thought. Good.

"Have a seat, Detective." Jerome dealt out a hand.

Petrosino sat between Jerome and McClusky.

"My father and Uncle Leonard taught me the game," Jerome said. "But my mother was a very pious woman, and she said to me one day, 'A great deal of time is wasted, dear, is there not, in playing cards?' I said, 'Yes, mother, there certainly is. In the shuffling and dealing.'"

The men coughed out laughs in the smoke.

"So, Deputy, we're still in the dark about the victim's identity," Jerome said, smiling at Piper like President Roosevelt would. "Let's hope Petrosino's lead is good."

"I wouldn't be a wee bit surprised if it's another Dago," Piper said. "They're the niggers of Europe, what with all their fornicating and fighting."

Petrosino stood, pretending to sulk over Piper' insult. He put his derby back on and pointed to the door. "Should I come back another time?"

"Sit down, Detective," Jerome said. "You're not like the ones Duff's talking about."

"Thick skin, lad, you're a fine Dago." Piper smiled through the red fur of his beard. He raised the pot and flipped over three cards, all hearts. "Who'd like to see the rest of my flush?"

"Where's the prisoner?" Petrosino asked.

"We'll bring him in after this hand," Jerome said. "See if he's credible."

"Speaking of credible," Piper said. "Have I told you the story of the Dago applying for work at a dry goods house? His appearance wasn't prepossessing, and references were demanded. After some hesitation, he gave the name of a driver in his prior boss's employ to vouch for him. The driver was asked if the applicant was honest. 'Honest?' the driver says. 'Why, his honesty's been proved time and again. To my certain knowledge, he's been arrested at least nine times for stealing and every time he was acquitted!'"

They laughed and made bets. Jerome and Garvan folded. Piper bet all his copper, and McClusky called, flipping over three kings. Piper turned over four of his cards, all hearts. Then he lingered over the last card. He flipped over a red deuce and smiled dejectedly.

"Two of diamonds! You four-flusher!" McClusky scooped up the pennies.

"Time for me to go," Piper said. "You've bankrupted me, George McClusky. I'd say you were a cheat, but that's a given since you're a Democrat."

McClusky didn't like that comment and his brow sunk. Jerome chuckled and waved his hand in the air. "Come now, gentlemen. We're a bipartisan poker board here. Yes?"

"Sure, sure." Piper tapped out burnt pipe tobacco into his drinking glass. "All those pennies lost, I'll have to sell my little home, probably be living in a flophouse next week. You won't have me to kick around anymore, *Gentleman* George."

Piper picked up his top hat and looked into it as he dusted ash from his beard.

"Duff," Jerome said, "my driver can take you back to the Palace."

"I don't like to ride. I'm for walking on my two nice big police feet. But it's the fashion in my set these days to show it off when you're rich and powerful, ain't that right, George? Not to hide your light under no bushels?" Piper shook everyone's hand except Petrosino's. "Don't play cards with the Italian here, unless you want a knife in your back." And he left.

"Pay him no mind, Joe," Jerome said. "The Deputy is a Republican and a bad bluffer. So have you got the goods on this barrel murder or not?"

"I think so, sir," Petrosino said.

"Is it a copper riveted, air tight, lead pipe cinch?"

"It better be," McClusky interrupted. His breath smelled like sour milk, making Petrosino's whiskey-scorched stomach gurgle. McClusky shot his hands out from the starched cuffs of his "dude" suit and straightened himself resentfully. "Petrosino and the Jew wasted our time on a wild goosehunt to start and now that corpse is rotting away at the Morgue."

Jerome exhaled a smoke ring. "Detective, what say the Buffalo police?"

"I checked the wires," Petrosino said. "The Buffalo dicks showed Madonnia's wife a newspaper picture of the victim. She said it looked like her husband, but she won't accept that he's dead. She's bed-sick with rheumatic fever, so they're sending the eldest son. When his train gets in from Buffalo, I'll take him to view the body."

"Let's see if your witness is on the square first. Clear the cards off the table, and let's bring him in. He said he's ready to make some sort of deal."

Chapter 25

Two guards brought Giuseppe De Priemo into Jerome's office. He looked less beaten down, Petrosino thought. The fresh air and train ride had done him some good, and Warden Johnson must have seen to it that he arrived presentable. His zebra-stripe uniform was new and smelled of soap and sunshine. But his shriveled raisin of a mouth was chewing away at itself.

"Mr. De Priemo, you look harmless enough," Jerome said, leaning back, raking over the part in his hair. "Come now, have a seat. We haven't got all day. I have tea appointments with some other criminals this afternoon. They're all Tammany men." McClusky growled an objection. "Only a jest, George."

De Priemo took short choppy steps as if he were still wearing leg irons. Jerome pointed to the chair directly across from him, and De Priemo glanced sideways at Petrosino and McClusky before he sat and ran his hands along the glossy leather padding on the armrests.

"You know why you're here, Mr. De Priemo?"

De Priemo nodded, leery. "Yes, sir, but before I spill my guts. . ." He pointed at Petrosino with his chin. "This cop said I can bargain for anything I like if I talk."

McClusky snarled. "*Anything* you like? The hell you say."

"I don't like Sing Sing. I want to be in Erie County Prison close to my sister and my family. And I want more time in the yard-"

With a diplomat's smile, Jerome held up his palm, cigarette wedged halfway through it. "You're a prudent man, De Priemo. A bargain depends on you. Are you prepared to tell us everything you know about the barrel victim? To tell us the whole truth? To swear an oath in court against your friends in a first degree murder case?"

"Yes, sir, I am."

Jerome slapped the table and grinned. He called for a stenographer and lit another cigarette, smoldering away while the stenographer made ready and read the oath. Petrosino took out his butcher's book to jot down anything useful.

"Mr. De Priemo," Jerome began, "do you know the man who was found in a barrel on East Eleventh Street and Avenue D in this city on April 14, 1903?"

"I know him. He's my brother-in-law, Benedetto Madonnia, from Buffalo. He came to Sing Sing to see me Saturday last. Said he would start back to Buffalo the next day."

"What route was he taking back?"

"Said he was stopping in Wilkes-Barre, Pittsburgh, and maybe Chicago before Buffalo."

"I see. Hmm. And how do you know the victim is your brother-in-law?"

"I saw his picture in the paper, and, well..." De Priemo put his index finger on his own cheekbone. "He has a scar on his face right here."

McClusky leaned forward in his chair, fists taut. Petrosino would've expected him to react differently on hearing a positive I.D. of the victim.

"How did Madonnia know to come see you in Sing Sing?"

"I sent for him because my friends cheated me. There should've been a divvy before I was sent up the river, but it was put off. They made up a reason. Before I left for Sing Sing, I turned over a good deal of money and things to my friends and told them to keep my share for my family. They were to look after me in prison, but they rooked me, I guess."

"Let's step back. Why are you in prison? On what charge?"

"Passing counterfeit, sir."

"Was your crime committed as part of a gang you were in?"

"Yes, sir. My friends and me. Giuseppe Morello, Inzerillo, the Lobaido brothers, and some others. The ones you have in jail mixed up in this case."

"When your brother-in-law came to visit you in Sing Sing, what was he wearing?"

"Oh, Nitto fancies clothes like I fancy jewelry. I like Diamond Jim Brady. Let's see, Nitto had a nice black suit, black and white stripe pants, and. . . a green tie, I think. Checkered."

Jerome cast his eyes at Petrosino, silently asking if the clothes were the same as the barrel victim's, and Petrosino dipped his chin, yes. "All right," Jerome said, "did your brother-in-law carry any jewelry, anything valuable on him?"

"Just a crucifix. He was looking for a new watch. Can't remember nothing else, sorry."

"What did you and Benedetto discuss when he visited you at Sing Sing?"

"I told him there was much coming to me from the tricks I turned before I was caught, maybe five thousand dollars, and that the fellows ought to divvy. So I instructed Nitto to go see them and get my share of the loot-"

"Wait a minute. Did you tell 'Nitto' or Benedetto to threaten them with exposing this mafia society if they didn't pay your share of the loot?"

When De Priemo heard the word "mafia," his eyelids dropped like window shades. He slowly forced them open and pondered the question. McClusky impatiently thudded his glass on the table, and Petrosino saw the glint in De Priemo's eyes dampen with each thud.

"Spit it out," Jerome said. "Did you discuss threatening to expose the mafia society?"

"You keep saying that word. I tell you, there's no *mafia* in this thing, none at all. Not that I know of anyhow." De Priemo looked around the room like a reproved schoolboy. "I swear, it must've been a plain squabble over money, that's why they killed poor Nitto."

"Is that right?" Jerome crossed his legs, adjusting his pince-nez. He stared intently at De Priemo who chewed his bottom lip again. "So you sent your brother-in-law to New York to dun a gang of bloodthirsty Sicilians for your share of counterfeiting spoils? And he was innocent as the day he was born, eh? Did he know that The Clutch Hand was the mafia chieftain?"

"I'm sure… what I mean is, there was no mafia in this. Truly, sir."

"Was your brother-in-law a member of the society?"

"He was a stonemason, I tell you. That's how he got that scar on his face."

Jerome's eyes turned vicious. "That scar on your brother-in-law's face is twenty years old, and he probably hasn't touched a stone since then, except to skip one across Lake Erie." Jerome circled behind De Priemo. "A stonemason doesn't have fancy clothes and soft baby hands, unless… unless he made his living buying counterfeit himself and shoving it off for the gang? You don't get callouses from handling counterfeit, do you, Mr. De Priemo?"

"I'll be damned," McClusky mumbled. "The victim's a crook himself?"

Jerome said to De Priemo, "And Nitto's route home is a typical one for counterfeiters and 'shovers of the queer.' They pass off bad coin and notes as they go, don't they, Mr. De Priemo?"

De Priemo held his lip between his teeth.

"The Secret Service gave me a letter they found in Morello's rooms," Jerome said. "A few months back, some of the gang got arrested in Wilkes-Barre, and Morello asked Benedetto to look after them. Benedetto complained that the pinched gang members were left to rot because Morello didn't send enough money. So Benedetto threw the whole job over and went back to Buffalo. There was bad blood between him and Morello, wasn't there?"

Petrosino felt a cancerous rage spreading in him. Why hadn't they shared this with him?

De Priemo mumbled, "Maybe."

"I won't speak ill of the dead anymore, Mr. De Priemo. I'm going to assume you're protecting your brother-in-law's good name so as not to despoil his memory." Jerome went back to his chair and flicked ashes. He took a puff, making De Priemo squirm in the long silence. "Did Madonnia speak to Morello or the gang before he visited you at Sing Sing?"

"Nitto asked my friends for their help, but they said they didn't know anything about my money. They made jokes about me instead. Nitto said it was like Wilkes-Barre all over again, and he was sore at them."

"Who's *they* exactly?" Jerome grew impatient as De Priemo hesitated. "You're weakening. Remember, a transfer to Erie County Prison is on the horizon."

De Priemo's face blanched as he said, "Morello laughed at me. I think he's the one who double-crossed me."

"Do you think he killed your brother-in-law over this money squabble?"

The moment of truth. Petrosino watched the fear growing in De Priemo's eyes. De Priemo stuttered, "N-N-Nitto is… he *was* as stubborn as a mule. He said he'd show them. He'd make them shell out my share. He said the Sicilians here are as bad as they are back in Sicily-"

Jerome suddenly pounded his fist on the table, and De Priemo cringed. "Answer the question! Did Morello have Benedetto Madonnia killed?"

"Yes! It must have been!"

"How do you know Morello had Benedetto killed? Did he talk about it?"

"I just know. Please, sir, stop hounding me-"

"How? What evidence do you have?"

"I just know," De Priemo huffed like a frustrated child. "Everybody knows he's the bigshot. He's the *capo*. If he wants someone snuffed, they get dead."

Jerome pointed his cigarette at De Priemo and was nearly shouting, "So you don't know for sure. You don't have any proof at all except your measly gut instinct?"

De Priemo shrugged, his lips swollen from being chewed.

"Well, Mr. De Priemo, if this killing had been ordered by Morello, would he have done it himself? Would he have struck the blows that nearly decapitated your brother-in-law?"

"No." De Priemo teared up. "The Clutch Hand never dirties his own fingers. He would've had The Ox do it. That one likes to make people suffer. He's wild, I tell you."

"Now you're using monikers. By The Ox, you mean Tomasso Petto?"

"Yes, sir, I guess, but not... yes."

Petrosino sensed something in De Priemo's hesitation. He waved a finger, and Jerome nodded at him to speak. Petrosino asked, "Do these men have other names from the Old Country?"

"I know The Ox by a different name. He was always Luciano to me. Luciano Petto from Wilkes-Barre. See, we used to work together in the mines."

Petrosino scribbled down notes. "And what about the other men in the gang, do they have different names, too? Have you ever heard of Giuseppe Terranova?"

De Priemo's eyes twitched. "Not that I know of, sir."

"If you're lying to us, you'll rot in Sing Sing, you hear?" Petrosino leaned over the table and held De Priemo's gaze. "How does the gang pass counterfeit?"

"Sometimes we sell it to rich people, sometimes in bundles to church men."

"Church men?" McClusky's face contorted. "That's a bold-faced lie."

"It's true, sir. They come from far off, buy a batch, and pass it off on their flock."

"That may be," Petrosino said, "but that's peanuts. How does the gang make its money in this City? The *real* money? How do they unload all the fake bills?"

"Just like I said." De Priemo started eating his lower lip again, and it cracked and began to bleeed. "I swear on my brother's soul."

Jerome stubbed out his cigarette and said, "Are you sure Benedetto didn't threaten to go to the police? To expose the gang's counterfeiting operations? Where they made the money, the names of the shovers, where the paper and printing presses came from and the like? Come now, why else would they display him in public like that?"

"Giuseppe," Petrosino said, "that was a Sicilian gesture, wasn't it? The gang was warning everyone to keep their mouths shut or else, right?"

"I don't know, sir. Like I said, The Ox is the blackest devil I ever knew. Can we please stop now? I'm so tired, and I just want to go back to my cell. Please, sir."

Jerome looked over at McClusky and Petrosino. "Anything else?"

"One more," Petrosino said, thinking of the notes hidden in the wall at the Star of Italy. "How does the gang communicate with each other?"

"In Italian, mostly." De Priemo wiped his mouth and noticed blood on his sleeve.

"Do they pass notes, and can they do it from prison?"

De Priemo glanced at McClusky, and his head shook. "You said 'notes.' I know of political 'bills' written for the Palermo Society. But I can't read so…"

"These 'bills' you know of. Who writes and sends them out and who receives them?"

"The Clutch Hand can write the best. He's shrewd, that one."

"Does the gang ever write in code? Is there a secret way of talking?"

"Like I told you, I can't read. So how would I know, sir?"

McClusky laughed at that one, and De Priemo flashed a bit of confidence in a smile.

Petrosino tried a hunch, the name he'd overheard in jail. "What about *Il Volpe*? The Fox?" Petrosino stared at De Priemo, who suddenly fidgeted like an opium fiend itching for a fix. "You didn't think I knew about *him*, did you, Giuseppe?"

McClusky gave Petrosino an irritated look, as if to ask, *Who's that*?

"It's their boss," Petrosino said.

"The Fox?" De Priemo said, hesitating for a moment, hands together under his chin like a doomed supplicant. "I only heard of him. I don't know much, sir."

"He's not in the gang? The Fox is an outsider?"

"I know nothing about him," De Priemo said, "except that he exists and talks to the Clutch Hand about making bad coin. That's all I know. I swear, sir."

"Did the gang ever grease any rotten cops?"

McClusky jerked up in his chair and pointed at the stenographer. "Stop typing or I'll smash your machine." He grabbed Petrosino's sleeve. "Just what the hell do you think you're doing? This ain't Lexow, Sergeant. The target is this gang, goddamn it."

"Chief, what if these men have some kind of contact inside? Morello's been arrested before, but he keeps getting off scot-free, so-"

"We didn't pay off cops, sir," De Priemo interrupted. "Not that I know of. We only worked with Sicilians. Maybe a few Neapolitans and a Calabrian once…"

"Move on then," McClusky said, staring viciously at Petrosino.

"The Chief Inspector's right," Jerome said, "let's keep our inquiry focused. We've gotten positive identity of the victim, motive, two suspects, and an alias for The Ox." Jerome turned to De Priemo. "Everything you've told us, you'll say at the Inquest?"

De Priemo nodded.

"Good, now sign your statement, Mr. De Priemo."

De Priemo wiped sweat from his face and scratched an X on the transcript. Then he held his hands out instinctively, waiting to be cuffed. After the guards shackled him, he turned to Petrosino and mustered up what little energy he had left.

De Priemo spoke in Italian, "This is difficult for me, sir. To resort to the law is infamy for a Sicilian. I've always regarded it as a good thing to let alone because I'd rather see the killer set free so I can get justice personally. But I'm in prison now and no help to my poor sister who's lost a husband. And once they find out I squealed, I'll be dead."

"I won't let that happen."

"It doesn't matter if I die, because I put my trust in you now. Give them justice for me."

"I give you my word," Petrosino said.

The guards took De Priemo away, and the stenographer followed them out.

"What'd he just say, Sergeant?" McClusky's eyebrow slanted on his mottled forehead.

"He said he's going to trust us to do justice for him."

McClusky grunted. "Sounded like he said a lot more than that. You damn well better watch yourself, because I am."

"As am I," Jerome said. "Despite what this De Priemo *suspects*, we still don't know whose hand drew the knife across Madonnia's throat, nor do we know which men held him down when he was being disposed of so effactually as to keep their mafia secrets intact. And we still don't have solid evidence." Jerome smacked the deck of cards on the table. "Last year, the City had only 419 convictions out of 768 jury trials. That's got to improve under my watch. I won't take another dog to trial. You've got two days before the Coroner's Inquest or this case is in the shit-can."

"Yes, sir," Petrosino said.

"And keep your Jewish chum at arm's length," Jerome said. "The fact that he was granted immunity didn't undo the wrong he's done. Once a cheat, always a cheat, I say." Jerome went back to shuffling cards. "Good day, Detective."

EVENING EDITION **World.** NIGHT EDITION

"Circulation Books Open to All."

NEW YORK. MONDAY, APRIL 20, 1903. PRICE ONE CENT.

ER MERTES, WHO
HIS ANKLE AND CAN'T PLAY.

NEW YORKS TAKE LEAD IN THIRD.

"Mute" Taylor Is Put in the Box by Giants' Manager, and a Small Army of Other "Mutes" Cheer the Twirler with Fingers

THIELMAN SENDS THEM OVER FOR BROOKLYN.

Another Big Crowd Assembles at the Polo Grounds to See Third, Game Between New Yorkers and Trolley Dodgers

The Batting Order,

New York. Brooklyn.

POLO GROUNDS, NEW YORK, April 20.—Hoping to see the Giants again trounce Ned Hanlon's pets, another great crowd thronged to the Polo Grounds this afternoon. With a record

SUSPECTS KNEW BENDETTO, THE BARREL VICTIM.

It Came Out in Court This Afternoon that the Man Who Was Found Murdered in East Eleventh Street Had Been Associated with Some of the Prisoners Accused of Killing Him.

FIRST CLUE TO IDENTITY LED THE DETECTIVES TO SING SING.

There Was Found Joseph de Prima, Who When Shown The Evening World's Photograph of the Dead Man Promptly Exclaimed, "That's Bendetto!"—The Secret Service Men Confirm Identification.

Madonnia Bendetto, the Buffalo Italian, who has been identified positively as the victim in the great barrel murder mystery, was definitely traced to-day to association with some of the men under arrest as suspects

Chapter 26

Petrosino had a few hours to pass until Salvatore Sagliabeni's train would arrive from Buffalo. He dreaded the thought of taking a son to see what may be his father's body at the Morgue. It was the worst part of the job. He'd been sneaking a few sips of whiskey at his desk, thinking about who The Fox could be when Steffens called. The excitement in Steffens' voice made Petrosino throw on his coat and derby to meet him.

A mantle of indigo light fell on Washington Square Park as dusk filled the cracks in the city. Petrosino walked past shadows strolling through the park's glowing lamplights, thinking about the encrypted note. Although Steffens had been carefully vague on the telephone, Petrosino knew that they had discovered something about the note. What did it say, he wondered, and how had they tumbled it out?

When he entered Steffens' office, he noticed McAlpin was gone. Steffens and Tarbell were sitting in their desk chairs, laughing and drinking triumphantly.

"Good to see you, Joe, sit." Steffens patted an empty chair.

Tarbell held out her hand, and Petrosino took it and pecked her knuckles.

"Don't make me blush, Detective. The sherry's already gone to my head." She pointed at a bottle on her desk, whispering, "Amontillado Sherry."

"We were about to order Chinese boxes of chop suey," Steffens said.

"Can't stay for supper, but I could use the moisture on the side." Petrosino sat down between the two of them.

"We saw in the afternoon papers that the barrel victim is an Italian named Benedetto Madonnia. Was he in cahoots with the Morello gang like they're saying?"

"Betweeen us," Petrosino said, "I've no doubt that this Madonnia was in the counterfeit game. My witness from Sing Sing, De Priemo, is Madonnia's brother-in-law. From how scared he was, this is bigger than a money squabble. Remember I said I'd heard about a man known as 'The Fox' and maybe he's the rotten cop in your Syndicate? Well, when we interrogated De Priemo, he said The Fox was in the bad coin business with Morello and that The Fox was an outsider. I tried to ask whether the gang ever greased any cops, but Chief Inspector McClusky cut me off at the knees, and Jerome clammed it up, too."

Steffens' eyes bulged behind his spectacles. "By Jove, so you think it's McClusky?"

Petrosino shrugged. "I don't know yet, Steffens. But it scares me."

"Well, don't be too frightened," Tarbell said with a bubbly tone and poured Petrosino a glass of sherry. "The good news is I solved your puzzle. Thus, the sherry we opened."

"That's not true," Steffens said, "I solved it, too. In fact, after I spoke to Schmittberger, I conceived the acorn of the idea that sprouted into the oak of discovery."

Petrosino was drinking sherry and almost choked. "Hang on. You spoke to Max? I thought you didn't want him included in your investigation of the Syndicate?"

"It wasn't my doing. He showed up at *McClure's* and caught me after an editorial board meeting. Our wives are friends, after all. I couldn't just ignore him, could I?"

Petrosino drank more sherry and tried to digest why Max had visited Steffens. "So what did Max say to you?"

"He said the two of you were working on the barrel murder and he asked what I knew about the *mafia* society. He's the one who got me thinking about the note. I'd been reading the awful news about the pogroms in Russia, and since Max is a Jew-"

"Steffens, just tell me. I can't bear a yarn right now."

"All right, you know how we have a mezuzah on our door? Well, I have one at *McClure's*, too, and Max was looking at it. He says to me, 'This another one of your phony displays of culture, Steff?' And I said, 'No, I actually feel close to the Jew folk.' So Max asks if I even know what's written on the scroll inside the mezuzah. Of course, I never asked, so that got me thinking."

"Actually," Tarbell said, "*I* was the one who wondered if the note could be some ancient language like Hebrew. We delved into it and eventually found out that the mezuzah is written in code. There's a one letter shift of the third, fourth, and fifth words of a Hebrew prayer called the Shema. The words are '*Adonai, Eloheinu, Adonai.*' The Lord, our God, the Lord."

"See, Joe," Steffens said, "I'm a man of science, and I knew I was on the right theoretical track. The Jews wrote in code to hide the name of their God from the polytheistic Romans."

"And that's when the moment of eureka hit me," Tarbell said and sipped her sherry with a smile. "The *mafia* society fancies itself like the Roman Empire, yes? So what if they used the code that Julius Caesar used to communicate with his generals? That's what the mezuzah uses. But a one-letter shift didn't work for our note, so I thought of the triumvirate."

"You mean *we*," Steffens said. "We think three men control the Syndicate, like the ancient triumvirate of Rome. And, sure enough, shifting the alphabet by *three* did it!"

Petrosino finished his sherry and tried to wrap his mind around the idea. "Can you puzzlers show me how it was solved?"

"Cryptographers," Tarbell said. "Here let me show you our codex for the three-letter Caesar Cipher." She reached into a satchel next to her and spread out a sheet of paper that had a box chart filled with letters:

A	B	C	D	E	F	G	H	I	J	K	L	M
D	E	F	G	H	I	J	K	L	M	N	O	P

N	O	P	Q	R	S	T	U	V	W	X	Y	Z
Q	R	S	T	U	V	W	X	Y	Z	A	B	C

Petrosino said, "So the person writing a word with an 'A' would use a 'D' and so on?"

"That's right. Here's the note you gave us. I knew we were onto something when I deciphered the first word. I thought it was English at first, but you'll see." She took out another page with each of the three sentences solved:

F	R	Q	V	H	U	Y	D	C	L	R	Q	H
C	O	N	S	E	R	V	A	Z	I	O	N	E

D	O		O	D	Y	R	U	R.
A	L		L	A	V	O	R	O.

P	D		F	R	P	X	Q	L	F	D	U	H
M	A		C	O	M	U	N	I	C	A	R	E

H		G	L	I	H	W	W	R	V	D
E		D	I	F	E	T	T	O	S	A

S	H	U		O	D	Y	R	U	R
P	E	R		L	A	V	O	R	O.

L	O		E	X	H		G	H	Y	H
I	L		B	U	E		D	E	V	E

I	D	U	H		X	Q
F	A	R	E		U	N

H	V	H	P	S	L	R		G	H	O
E	S	E	M	P	I	O		D	E	L

E	X	I	D	O	R
B	U	F	A	L	O.

"It's Italian." Petrosino mumbled the message, "*Conservazione al lavoro. Ma comunicare è difettosa per lavoro. Il bue deve fare un esempio del bufalo.*"

"Well, what in the name of the Sphinx does it say, Joe? We waited for you."

"Something like, *Keep at the job. But talking is bad for work. The ox must make an example of buffalo.*" Petrosino shook his head, thinking it over. "The structure is odd, the way someone who's not Italian might word it."

"Sounds like a message for a cattle farmer," Steffens quipped.

"No," Petrosino said. "*The ox must make an example of buffalo.* That's the order to kill. The gang calls Petto 'The Ox.' And the barrel victim is from Buffalo. The Ox made an example of the man from Buffalo." A chill knifed through Petrosino.

"My Lord." Tarbell held her hand over her mouth. "Then this is a fine clue."

"Maybe. They made it hard to prove. Look how many layers of secrecy they used. Someone writes the note in Italian, in block print so we can't use a handwriting expert. Then they use your Caesar Cipher to encrypt it, and they pass it anonymously, and on top of it, they're using generalities and nicknames in the message itself."

"You're right," Steffens said. "The cipher is simple, but the method is devious. And I bet they never thought a cop would understand it either. How many speak Italian?"

"In the whole city? Maybe a dozen cops."

Petrosino took out his butcher book and flipped to the page where he had copied down the second note that Schmittberger found.

Petrosino said, "This is a another one we found."

Steffens and Tarbell leaned in, watching as he consulted the codex and wrote down each letter. He groaned when he was done and pushed the translation on the table in front of them:

FRJOLDPR O'HUED SHU OD YROSH.

COGLIAMO L'ERBA PER LA VOLPE.

Petrosino smiled as he thought of the two men who had been harassing him. "It says, *Cogliamo l'erba per la volpe.* 'We pluck the herb for the fox.'"

"That's more of a riddle than the last one," Steffens said.

"No, it isn't," Petrosino mumbled. "The gang's nickname for me is *Pitrusinu.* That's Sicilian for 'parsley.'"

Tarbell nudged Steffens. "Parsley is an *herb.*"

"And they intend to 'pluck' me, whatever that means. Maybe they don't like how close I'm getting." Petrosino poured himself a full glass of sherry and took it down.

"I'm sure you'll be fine."

Petrosino brooded and took yet another shot of sherry. The note and the sweetness in his mouth irritated him. "It's easy for you," he said. "This barrel murder is a story, and the Syndicate is a theory of corruption. After you publish your work in a magazine, you'll be done with it. But now I have to deal with looking over my shoulder."

"Are we in danger?" Steffens asked.

"Nope. They won't come after you. All the same, I should get on with my work." Petrosino checked his pocket watch, slowed by the drinking, but focused on the next task. Salvatore Sagliabeni and the Morgue. He looked at Steffens and Tarbell. A somber veil darkened their faces. "If either of you are leaving, I'll walk you to a carriage."

They walked downstairs into Washington Square and said their good-byes in the street.

"I can walk you, Minerva," Steffens said.

"I think I'd be safer with Detective Petrosino."

"Suit yourself, I'm a little scared myself, truth be told," Steffens said. "Joe, ring me tomorrow and tell me what happened with the victim's son, would you? We should stay close now that the fires of evil are stoked."

Petrosino nodded, and Steffens waved good-bye.

Tarbell took Petrosino's elbow and tried not to falter as she walked, leaning against him. He tried not to look at the tall stalk of a woman on his arm. She had seemed content in her cups, but now an air of worry and loneliness followed her. Maybe that was what drew him to her. That was what drew him to the few people he liked. The loneliness they shared. He and Max were alone in the PD, an outcast and a squealer. Adelina was a young childless "widow" in a Ghetto where women were as prolific as barn cats. And here was this modern woman on his arm who had given up old notions of companionship for achievement. Tarbell was maybe the most tragic of them all because she'd chosen her path.

"Every night as a child, I prayed to God to spare me from marriage and send me to college instead. Maybe I'm not suited for it. What do you think?"

Petrosino looked at her and smiled without a word.

"I don't know why I said that." Tarbell sighed as they walked toward a hansom cab on Sixth Avenue. "You remind me of a friend in college. There was a certain way he'd look at people. It would make you wonder what he was thinking, and then you'd just start talking to break the silence. You'd say things you'd never say to family or friends."

"I don't mean to make you uncomfortable." He opened the cab door and politely shook her hand. "Thank you for deciphering that note and for the sherry."

She was so close he could see the ridges of her lips. She held his shoulders, closed her eyes, and kissed him. He watched her, and she eventually opened her eyes slowly. Then her hands pulled away from his shoulders. The cab driver's horse pawed at the ground in the silence. He kissed her again and felt sad for her.

"You must have a gal already," Tarbell whispered. "Please be careful with those threats."

She stepped into the cab, and he closed the door as she groaned from inside. In a city of so many, they shared the loneliness of ghosts, he thought. Maybe that was what this murder was about for him, too. The poor man died alone without ever saying good-bye to his wife and boy. Left by himself in the street to bleed to death in a barrel.

"I'll fix them, Benedetto," Petrosino mumbled as he walked to Headquarters.

Chapter 27

He found Salvatore Sagliabeni asleep on the soft side of a plank in a police lodging room. The eighteen year old had just gotten in from a long train ride, and his dark boyish face jiggled as he snored. His shriveled mouth resembled that of his uncle, Giuseppe De Priemo. The rest of him wasn't so boyish. He smelled of coal and had a wiry frame and the large knotty hands of a manual laborer.

As soon as Petrosino entered the room, the boy's snoring halted, and his eyes opened.

Salvatore quickly sat up on his haunches and rubbed cheerless eyes at Petrosino.

"I'm sorry about all this," Petrosino said in Italian. "I'm Detective Sergeant Petrosino. It's a little late to go to the Morgue. We can put you up in a hotel and go at first light?"

Salvatore planted his feet on the floor, yawning and shaking his head. "No, I'm ready now, sir. The police told my mother, but she doesn't want to believe it's him."

"As you wish, Salvatore." Petrosino sighed. He'd seen this futile hope a thousand times before. "We'll take a carriage. Put your coat on, it's cold."

Outside, the horses were snorting steam into the cool stillness of the streets. Petrosino and Salvatore got inside the carriage, and Petrosino lifted the hatch to tell the police driver they were going to the Morgue. He studied the boy in the shadows as a gauze of clouds dimmed the moonlight and crows cawed from trees.

"When was the last time you saw your stepfather?" Petrosino lit a cigar to warm up. The stupor from the sherry dwindled like coals of a dying fire, and the veins in his head thrummed.

"Before he went to New York to help my uncle in Sing Sing. My stepfather wanted to see if he could be transferred to another prison closer to us in Buffalo."

"When did he leave for New York?"

"In early April. He wrote my mother on April 13, saying he was coming home, but we never heard from him again." Salvatore's eyes glistened in the carriage's grey light. "Do you think it's him?"

"You'll have to tell me, kid. Did your mother ever write back to him in New York?"

"She wrote him a note to come home quickly."

Petrosino nodded gravely. "We found a note like that on the victim. I'm sorry."

Salvatore turned to the window, looking out the carriage in silence the rest of the way.

When they entered the Morgue, Petrosino led Salvatore up to a haggard attendant at a desk and flashed his badge. The attendant wrote down their names and Petrosino's badge number 285 in an entry book. They quickly moved through dark corridors, not a soul in sight. Petrosino shoved open the door to the freezing mortuary chamber, and the poisonous air of the charnel house made them both gag. They could see their breath, and the hair on Petrosino's wrists unfurled in the cold air. Salvatore was trembling and staring at the body.

One electric globe shone down on the rotting and mangled body. The corpse had turned ghastly shades of green and violet, the face shrunken like melted wax, and the hole in the pubic mound grotesquely alien. Petrosino cursed under his breath and pulled a sheet across the body, so only the head could be seen. When the sheet settled on the body, putrid smells wafted up.

Salvatore took three short steps toward the slab and let out a gasp, "Papa." The boy crouched over Madonnia and kissed the forehead where the skin was the color of a robin's egg. His voice wailed like a funeral dirge, "I loved him very much."

Petrosino felt like crying himself. He tried to console the boy and, after a few minutes, he pulled Salvatore into the hallway. The kid stood shakily, exhausted from weeping.

"Stop crying," Petrosino whispered. "Listen, you're the man in the family now. You want justice now, don't you?"

Salvatore wiped his cheeks against his jumper. "Yes."

"You'll stay at Bettini's Hotel tonight. I want you to get some rest, because the District Attorney will want to talk to you, okay? We need you for the Inquest."

Salvatore took a deep breath and nodded. "Can I have my watch back?"

"What watch?"

"He borrowed mine because his was broken. He gave it to me for Christmas."

"You're sure he had it with him?"

"I'm sure. He looked at the watch at the Lehigh Valley depot before he came to New York. You must've found it with him? Please, it's all I have to remember him."

Petrosino hugged the boy and patted his back. He thought of the evidence bins. It must've been deep into the night by now, but he wasn't going to catch a single wink.

e/o

Petrosino got Schmittberger out of bed at the officers' quarters in Eldridge Street Station and told him about the pocket watch. They walked back to the Marble Palace and sneaked inside while the desk sergeant was nodding off. They were hoping to find Salvatore Sagliabeni's pocket watch before McClusky or any of his Irish dicks would be awake.

"The kid said it was a gold filled, hunting case watch," Petrosino said. "There's a locomotive engraved on the case, and scratches on the neck where he used his thumbnail to tighten a loose screw."

"Okay." Schmittberger yawned.

Petrosino unlocked what they needed from the evidence locker, and they went in search of a quiet room where they could dig through the evidence, somewhere other than the general assembly room for detectives. In the basement, there was a storage room that Petrosino thought would do just fine. They opened the door and heard the stilted breathing and snores of heavy slumber. Schmittberger turned on the lights, and two patrolmen blindly flailed their arms in the sudden brightness. Each was splayed across a table in his undershirt and uniform pants with brogans on the floor. It was a "cooping" nest known to every cop except the brass.

One of the patrolmen sat up and muttered with a German accent, "Dis is our coop. Find somevhere else."

Schmittberger threw a bluecoat at the stout patrolman. "Rise and shine, girls!" Then he said in German, "*Stehen sie, sie schweine auf.*"

The two patrolmen hurriedly dressed, whispering at each other, and tore out with cursory salutes against their crooked helmets. Schmittberger sat down at one table with his Baker's Breakfast Cocoa, and Petrosino sat down at the other with a steaming cup of black coffee. Schmittberger had the evidence bags from the mafia gang, and Petrosino had a box of letters collected from Morello's apartments. Petrosino wanted to read them himself to see if they connected The Clutch Hand to Madonnia and the murder. One of the naked bulbs overhead began buzzing and fading in and out as they began working.

"I hope that's not a message from above," Schmittberger said. "I oughtta throttle you, by the way. When you poked me up, I was dreaming of the Fischbein twins. They were wearing red garters and brassieres and nothing else, and they kept saying they were Little Red Riding Hood, and I was the Big Bad Wolf come to eat them. Whispering the most vile dirty talk, too, like experts. I had an erection the size of an iceberg, and you had to go and ruin it for me."

"You need to go back to that sanitarium in Queens."

Petrosino scanned through the letters and glanced up from time to time to see Schmittberger pulling out jewelry and trinkets and pocket watches. Each sack had a tag scrawled with the name of the suspect's belongings. Schmittberger stopped and looked perplexed, his face grey and heavy with lines from lack of sleep.

"What's wrong?" Petrosino asked.

"We don't have Lobaido's belongings anymore. They took his traps when he killed himself."

"Well, you told Piper that he had a fancy watch with his initials and garnet stones, remember? That's not the watch we're looking for."

Schmittberger heaved a sigh. "I knew that. Just a little test." He took out a pocket watch from Domenico Pecoraro's bin and held it up. "What about this one? It's gold. Look."

Petrosino walked over to the other table and studied the timepiece. It was a hunter's case, in gold, but there was no locomotive engraved on it. Instead a fancy 'P' with seraphs and swirls adorned the cover. He looked closely at the pin to be certain. "Different watch," Petrosino concluded. "We can ask Salvatore later to be sure, but there's no locomotive engraving, and see there on the neck where that screw is. Not a scratch on it."

Schmittberger nodded dourly, and Petrosino sat back down to the letters. Several were from Allegheny, Pennsylvania, and kept referring to 'making pastries.' Petrosino wondered if it were a term for printing counterfeit money. It didn't make much difference to him, because he was after murder clues. After two hours, he found nothing in the letters and grew frustrated while dawn broke with the sounds of roosters and dogs and wagons rattling outside. He kept tasting the grit in his empty coffee cup, thinking about sleeping for a few hours.

Schmittberger grew giddy from exhaustion and pulled out some of the useless papers found on the gang. He was trying to read in Italian, fumbling over the words, making Petrosino smile. "Say, Joe, this is a love note from Petto The Ox. What's it say? Read it."

"How do you know it's a love note if it's in Italian?"

"Well, someone drew hearts on it and a cupid's bow, and it's addressed to a 'Cara Federica.' I'm guessing that ain't his dear old mudder."

Petrosino looked at the note. "It says, 'Dear Federica, oh how I've missed your sweet kiss. Your belly is like bread dough and your hair smells like beer. I would like to get drunk in it Saturday.' What a poet. 'If you'll be my gal, I'll go to an artist on Division Street to have your initials tattooed on my arm. But he said he can't do anything to remove your sister Marie's initials. I'm sorry, do you forgive me? Kisses and embraces, The Ox.'"

"Boy, that Petto's a regular Mark Twain in love." They burst out laughing. "Let's find another one."

"Wait a minute, isn't that the names of the two gals we questioned next door to the Star of Italy? Federica and Marie?"

"That would make sense. Morello's humping one, and Petto the other."

"We oughtta pay them another visit."

Petrosino hovered over Schmittberger's shoulder as he thumbed through the documents in the bins. They went through all the suspects, finding licenses to carry concealed weapons, train schedules, Sicilian Union circulars, meal tickets, a flyer to attend barber college, a theatre program and ticket stub, advertisements for massage parlors and cheap men's suits, newspaper pictures of chorus girls and motorcars, a government form to obtain a pushcart permit, and then something caught Petrosino's eye in Petto's belongings.

"Wait! What's that? Take that one out."

Schmittberger pulled out a wrinkled ticket and squinted at it.

Petrosino leaned closer over his shoulder. "What's it say?"

"Hold the reins, Joe, let me see."

The ticket had a number at the top, *27696*. Beneath that was a weakly printed name in cursive letters: *B. Frye*. The address beneath that was completely faded except for the words, *Bowery* and *New York*.

"What's the fine print say in the middle?"

"It says, '*Contract for pledging goods for one year or less, 1903-*"

"That's a pawn ticket!" Petrosino snatched the ticket. "It's rubberstamped April 14, 1903, the same day the barrel was found. Max, I thought you already went through these things before? Why didn't you spot this?"

"Hey, don't forget your place again, Joe. What do you think, that I've been hiding it from you? I would've tossed it if that was the case, you stupid Dago."

"I didn't think that." Petrosino heard the doubt in his voice and began to wonder again.

"Wipe that look off your face. I'm tired of it. I've had plenty other leads to run down before they got cold, and I haven't gotten two nights' sleep in a week. Besides, you can't read that chicken scratch there either. It could be a ticket for anything."

Petrosino held the ticket up to the buzzing light. "I can read it, all right. It says, '*HC Watch, 1.00.*' Hunting case watch, one dollar. And it's made out to, what is that name? '*Johni.*' No last name." Petrosino held the ticket in front of Max's handsome moustache. "See it now, boss? It's not as plain as the Hebrew nose on your face, but you can decipher it. If the Chief and the DA knew about this, your head would be falling into a basket."

Schmittberger stared at him. "I oughtta lick you, you wiseacre."

"Not today you can't. You're still on suspension, remember, Inspector? If my ass ends up in a sling, I'd have to fill out a report. Wouldn't I, *sir?*"

Schmittberger smiled. "You've got cast iron balls, you sly little mutt. Of course I missed it the first time 'cause I don't think like a greasy Italian thief. What's the other side say?"

Petrosino flipped the pawn ticket over and skimmed the contract terms. "Says if the ticket's returned within one year from the pledge date, the goods can be redeemed on payment of the pawn plus twenty-five percent interest. Except, of course, the broker's not responsible for fires or burglary."

"With our luck on this case, there'll be a fire *and* a burglary before we get there." Schmittberger pocketed the pawn ticket. "Get your derby. We're off to the Bowery."

Chapter 28

A statuette of San Nicola of Bari sat in the barred window surrounded by pistols, jewelry boxes, silver hair combs, engagement rings, pearl-handled looking glasses, a shiny violin, driving goggles, and an Oriental bust of ersatz jade. The bearded San Nicola was painted dark as a Moor, and he wore a bishop's mitre and a red and gold mantle. In his left hand was a scepter and in his right were three gold spheres, the familiar symbol for a pawn shop. But the stencil on the glass had a dressed-up title: *Frye's Collateral Loan Office, 276-278 Bowery.*

Outside the entrance, Schmittberger pointed. "Lookie there, Joe, St. Nicholas is waving us inside to hock all we got. Patron saint of New York."

"And pawnshops . . . and thieves."

"That's our dear old city."

A bell on the door jingled. They walked into the dusty collection of glass display cases holding every imaginable cast-off that a desperate person could sell for a few miserable pieces of silver. The place smelled of sweat and shame. Petrosino glanced around the room full of souvenirs and noticed a well-dressed man looking at a jeweled broach the size of an egg in his hands. He looked as if he were agonizing over something, mumbling to himself. Petrosino walked up to the main counter where another man who looked like the proprietor stood. His fat moon face fell in folds over his collar. He pretended not to see Petrosino and Schmittberger and locked his cash drawer while dumbly scratching at dandruff in his hair. A few dozen wall clocks and cuckoos ticked frantically away on the wall behind him.

"You Frye?" Petrosino asked.

"In the flesh. Who'd like to know?"

"I'm Detective Petrosino and that's my boss." Petrosino thumbed toward Schmittberger who was bending over a case stocked full of pocket watches. "We're investigating a murder."

"Morning to ya." Frye leaned on elbows fat as baked hams, yawned. "Say, ain't it a little early in the year fer a *donation*? To yer fine benevolent society, The Pequod Club?"

The wealthy gentleman tripped over himself and out the jingling door.

Frye watched the gentleman exit with disgust. "That fish ain't never hocked nuttin' before. Would've given him five bucks for his mudder's brooch, too."

"I bet you would've given him five bucks for his 'mudder,' too," Schmittberger said from his crouch, wiping dust from a glass case and squinting at watches.

Petrosino said to Frye, "You're supposed to keep a broker's book with the name and address of your customers. Get it out."

Frye's eyes shifted in their fat slits. He stepped over to the drawers and leaned down, pulling out a large book. "Got a transaction in mind, Your Honor, or should I just pluck one outta me bum?"

"Crack wise again and you'll be gumming your cakes, pork chop. Look up April 14, ticket number 2-7-6-9-6."

Frye licked his sausage fingers, flipped through his book. "Here 'tis. That ticket was issued to 'Johni' on April 14 for receipt of a gold filled watch. Gave a buck for it."

"Swell. What's the fellow's full name and address?"

"All I have here is 'Johni' from Elizabeth Street."

"You didn't ask for a last name or a street number, you lousy fucking fence?"

"No, officer. Must've slipped me mind."

"Open the drawers there, let me see them." Petrosino watched Frye's hands shake as he opened all the drawers. The one that had been locked was full of money. "Why don't you keep a package of photographs in a drawer so you can see whether a customer is a known thief from the Rogues Gallery? Don't you know you're supposed to do that, unless you're a fence?"

Frye shrugged. "I ain't in the question-askin' business. If I was to do yer job for ye, then I oughtta get a salary from the Police Department. Which I ain't got yet."

Petrosino smacked Frye's face hard. "I warned you once, wise ass. What did this 'Johni' look like? Was he a big man? And what time of day did he come in?"

"Take it easy now. Me mind's all foggy." Frye turned back to the wall of clocks, hemming to himself. "He came around four o'clock, I recall. That's when I wind the clocks."

"It's that one!" Schmittberger shouted. "That's our watch, Joe."

Petrosino was champing at the bit, but he said coolly to Frye, "Take that watch out of the case for us. Quick."

Frye waddled over to the case where Schmittberger was pointing. Frye brought out the watch and laid it on a frayed velvet cloth. There it was, a gold filled hunting case pocket watch with a locomotive engraving. Petrosino picked it up and examined the surface to be sure. Curved scratches, like those from a fingernail, were all over the neck and next to a screw of the stem winding arrangement. This was Benedetto Madonnia's watch. Petrosino heard all of the wall clocks ticking and tocking, and his heart felt as if it were beating just as fast.

He wrapped the watch in the cloth and pocketed it. "We got 'em, Max."

"An Ox in the electric chair, that'll be a first." Schmittberger grinned and shook hands with Petrosino. "Good work, Joe."

Petrosino said to Frye, "Lock up shop or find someone else to run it."

"What the devil fer?"

"You'll see. You're coming with us."

As they dragged Frye out, a plump female version of Frye wobbled in, shrieking, "The pawn's one dollar and twenty-five cent! That's still our watch. Ye rooked us, ye dirty thieves!"

"We have to keep it as evidence," Petrosino said, "but we'll gladly return your husband."

☙

Schmittberger stayed behind. He was still on suspension and wanted to avoid being seen at The Tombs. Petrosino walked the pawnbroker alone into the detention center and across the Bridge of Sighs as prison keepers unlocked gates. The light faded with each step, and Frye's face was as pale and lonely as a single light bulb in a mineshaft. Petrosino told him not to speak. Shadows of silent men were crammed in the cells, their eyes glowing like tin coins behind the bars. Turnkeys escorted them around the last corner where they saw Sandy Piper, The Whale himself. When The Whale came down the corridor, the iron gates on the prison cells rattled in his enormous wake.

"Boy oh boy, it's himself, the Detective. How are ya, sir?" The Whale had a mouthful of peanuts, and empty shells clung to his uniform. He shook Petrosino's hand.

Petrosino said, "I need this man to view The Ox."

"Oh, I've been keeping an eye on him for you. On all them thieves, like you-know-who said. They're nay going nowhere's with me on the job, Detective, sir."

Petrosino nodded, anxious to get on with it. They moved into another corridor and stopped in front of a dark communal cell. Petrosino grabbed Frye's shoulders, pointing him in The Ox's direction. The pawnbroker's eyes grew big and white as egg shells, staring at the sweaty mass of Tomasso "The Ox" Petto, who was doing push-ups on the filthy floor.

"Did you get a good look?"

Frye nodded his three chins and pulled away from Petrosino like an intractable dray horse. They went into a suffocatingly small interrogation room, and Petrosino shut the door behind them.

"Well, was that him who pawned the watch?"

The pawnbroker wheezed from the excitement and walking. "I tell ye truly, I don't remember what the feller looked like." He wiped trails of sweat from his ballooning cheeks and huffed in desperation, "I swear on me mudder's grave. It's no use keepin' me here."

Petrosino thought that the pawnbroker was telling the truth and asked The Whale to escort Frye out and bring The Ox into the interrogation room.

"I've got brass knuckles if you want 'em," The Whale said.

"No need," Petrosino said, "I've got the goods on him now."

"Aye." The Whale nodded like an obedient child. "Shame we can't work him over."

The Whale went out and returned with two guards pulling Tomasso Petto at the end of his chains. Petto loped over to a bench, looking sideways at the guards and Petrosino, keeping his rubbery lips clenched. He looked as massive as ever, and his head wounds we're healing. But there was a veil of rage over his eyes. Threads snaked out of the edges of his wrinkled tan suit and blood crusted brown on his shirt collar.

Petrosino said in Italian, "That witness saw you, Petto. Wanna know where?"

Petto's eyes moved between Petrosino and The Whale. Petto's bulky shoulders shrugged.

"That was your pawnbroker," Petrosino said. "He saw you on April 14th, the day Benedetto was found in the barrel. Said you pawned a gold watch for a buck."

"He's a lying piece of shit."

Petrosino pulled his chair up to Petto's bench and sat face-to-face with The Ox. He could feel the guards and The Whale draw into a tight circle around them. Petto's eyes were as cold as the "hawk" wind off the Hudson River, and Petrosino peered into them. "I know more than you think, Petto. I know you were told to make *an example* of Benedetto."

Petto licked his lips in silence.

"They said to keep at the job and shut his mouth. *The Fox* gave the order."

"I don't know what you're talking about."

"And now we have the pawn ticket from Frye's. You pawned a dead man's watch the same day he was killed. The day *you* made an example of him. You're done for."

"I never pawned any watch."

"Then how do you explain the pawn ticket we found on you?"

Petto's eyes blinked, and his chains rattled as he squirmed on the bench. "Oh that thing? Yeah, I had a pawn ticket. A friend gave it to me for safekeeping."

"Yeah? What's his name?"

"Johni."

"How long have you known this Johni?"

"Three years. He's a countryman of mine, a friend from Corleone."

Petrosino could see the wheels turning in Petto's eyes. "Go on. And how did you come to get this Johni's pawn ticket?"

"He gave it to me for safekeeping. We stayed together on April 13th. He slept in my room with me in Williamsburg. We had breakfast in the morning, then he gave me the ticket."

"What's Johni's last name?"

Petto searched for an answer. "Don't know."

"You say you've known Johni for years, you stayed in the same rooms, but you don't know his last name? You're a bad liar even for an ugly ape."

"Don't call me that. I don't like that."

"Where's Johni live?"

"I saw the watch on Johni four months ago," Petto said. "He must've pawned it himself."

Petrosino yanked Petto's moustache. "Stop buying time. What's Johni's address?"

"Don't know."

"What's the address in Williamsburg where you stayed with him?"

"My room? That's 324-326 South Street."

"That's the address you gave when you were booked. We ran it down, and it's a vacant lot. Tell me another lie."

"No, what did I say 324? I mean 2-3-4."

"We've got a witness, the pawn ticket, and the watch from the man you killed. There's only one thing you can do to save yourself. Tell me who gave the order and why. Tell me the truth. Was a cop involved? The Fox?"

Petto's chains rustled on the bench, and he looked past Petrosino and around the circle of faces above the both of them. He stared at The Whale and frowned. "I told you the truth, Parsley. Johni gave me the ticket. To keep for him. I've never seen that pawnbroker or that dead bastard Madonnia in my whole life."

"I don't believe you, you hairy cunt-faced ape."

"Fuck you."

"Does The Clutch Hand know you were fucking his girl, Marie, before you moved on to her sister, Federica?" Petrosino watched Petto flush red. "You know, Petto, I think maybe Federica knows about you and this killing. How would you like it if I gave her a nice fuck for you? How does she like it? Let me guess: in the *culo*?"

"A Sicilian would never threaten a man's woman. And you wouldn't talk to me like that if I wasn't in chains, Parsley." Petto's stare made Petrosino feel as if cold fingers gripped his heart. "How are your ribs? I felt them snap like twigs. When I get out, I'll finish the job."

"Tough guy." Petrosino drew out Madonnia's necklace and dangled the crucifix in front of Petto. "You took Benedetto's watch after you killed him. Why didn't you take this, too? It was on the throat you slashed. You left it behind because you're afraid of Hell, aren't you?"

"Fuck you, Parsley." Petto spat in Petrosino's face.

Petrosino wiped the spit from his nose and punched Petto in the mouth. Two of Petto's teeth speared through his lip, and blood leaked down his chin. Petto laughed and licked his red lips. Petrosino's knuckles stung, but he ignored the pain.

"When they strap you in Old Sparky," Petrosino whispered, "you don't die right away. The smell is the worst part. You can smell your own hair burning. Just like you're in Hell."

"FUCK OFF!" Petto jumped from the bench, tearing at his chains. The Whale and the two guards jabbed Petto with clubs and muscled him to the door as he screamed, "I'll have a witness who'll testify to an alibi for me! You'll see, Parsley! I'll be back on the street, and you'll be the one who gets fucked in the ass!"

III

THE SYNDICATE BOSS

Petrosino (left) escorting Tomasso "The Ox" Petto (second from left) to the Tombs with two other detectives

Chapter 29

Petrosino set the pawn ticket and Madonnia's gold pocket watch on Chief Inspector McClusky's desk. McClusky looked at the items as if they were junk from an ash barrel.

"That pawn ticket was on Petto when we pinched him, Chief," Petrosino explained.

"So?"

"So we've got him dead to rights. The ticket was given for that watch. He sold it on the Bowery. Madonnia's son identified that watch. Madonnia had it when he came to New York."

"So Petto had the victim's watch." McClusky grunted. "You find anything else?"

"I'd like to talk to Petto's gal. Her name's Federica. Petto got hinky when I threatened to squeeze her. That's the only loose end." Petrosino held back on the ciphers. He and Schmittberger had discussed it again after the trip to the Tombs, and they didn't want anyone else to know about the notes until they tumbled out who "The Fox" was. And Petrosino suspected McClusky even as the Chief smirked at him now.

"I wouldn't worry too much about chasing one of these gangster's whores. This evidence will do." McClusky looked down at his polished fingernails, still smiling but in a way that unnerved Petrosino. "Did you find this pawn ticket and watch on your own?"

"The ticket was locked up in Evidence. I took it to the pawnbroker, but he couldn't identify Petto." Petrosino touched the gold pocket watch, trying to get the Chief to hold it. "Madonnia's boy said the watch had a locomotive on it. See there?"

"You didn't answer me. The Inquest is tomorrow, and Jerome needs this evidence. Hell, he's been hounding me, and now I've got something to give him. So I'll let you slide." McClusky pulled his legs off his desk and leaned forward in his chair, chin hanging just above his blotter and the pawn ticket and watch. "But don't think I don't know what goes on in my Bureau. I am God Almighty here, and I see fuck all from the rats in the basement to the Watch Commander on graveyard. . . to the dick who spied a tall Jew with you."

"Sir, I don't want trouble. All I want is to solve this case."

"Good, because I chatted with the PD lawyers. The shysters advised me that everyone gets notice and an opportunity to be heard. Due process, they call it. See, the brass has been troubled by insubordination and intemperance on the job, but I'm a fair man, and I want to go about fixing it the right way."

"Intemperance? Chief, every cop I know drinks."

"I don't, goddamn it. And besides that, I had a citizen in my office complaining about a raid on a saloon last month. Seems this good honest citizen just happened to be in the establishment by accident when one of my Inspectors tossed him through a plate glass window."

Petrosino knew where this was going. They were trying to railroad Max. "Chief, all he knows is the job. He can't do anything else but–"

"He turned Judas on his brothers. If he loses the badge and ends up a bootblack nigger shining shoes, then good riddance. I'm giving you fair warning. Keep fraternizing with a rat Jew and you're liable to get covered in rat shit."

The sound of Petrosino's grinding teeth screeched in his head. He stared at the Chief and entertained the thought of slugging him. Instead, he nodded and stood to leave.

"I haven't dismissed you yet. Is there anything else you've got on this barrel murder, anything you haven't told me?"

Petrosino turned around. "No, sir. Just some red herrings."

McClusky reached into his vest pocket and took out a scrap of paper. He unfolded it and placed it on the desk for Petrosino to see. "Handsome Jimmy found this on one of the Dagos when he was giving them the Third Degree. We think one of their whores smuggled it inside her baby's diaper. That's why the paper's a little yellow. What do you make of it?"

Petrosino looked at the familiar cipher and tried to quickly decode it in his head:

**PDQGD OD SXWWDQD D FDVD SULPD
FKH DEEDL.**

He made out only the first three words, *Manda la puttana* … *Send the bitch*, before McClusky took the note back.

"You're looking at that paper like you're studying for the Captain's exam. You understand what it means or not?"

"No, sir. Just trying to tumble it out." Petrosino reached into his jacket for his butcher's book, anxious to copy down the code. "It's not Italian. If I could study it-"

"So you can't make heads or tails of it either then?"

"No, sir."

"Uh-huh." McClusky studied him. "Take that pawn ticket and watch down to Evidence and lock 'em back up. I want to see a report on it, too, with a statement from Madonnia's son. Wouldn't want anything to go missing when Mr. Jerome calls witnesses tomorrow, would we?"

"No, sir." Petrosino placed the items in a paper sack and saluted. He gestured toward the note, but McClusky tucked it in his vest pocket and pointed at the door.

∽

Petrosino couldn't stop thinking about the note and its meaning. *Send the bitch.* Send her where and who was she? He tried to wrap his head around it, but he'd already forgotten the rest of the cipher. And why was McClusky keeping it to himself? Was he trying to solve the puzzle himself or was he trying to flush Petrosino out? What if McClusky were the conduit?

Petrosino went across the street to a public telephone booth and rang Tonino Verdi. He asked him to send his nephew, Izzy Baline, as soon as possible. There would be money in it for Izzy, but the pay-off would decrease every minute Petrosino had to wait. He loitered for a half hour at a bootblack's stand near Mulberry and Houston until Izzy came up, wearing a blue-and-white striped seersucker suit and a new grey top hat. The suit was two sizes too big for him, and he looked like an eel squirming in a picnic tablecloth as he strutted toward Petrosino. Izzy pretended not to recognize him and ducked into the entrance of a brownstone next door. Petrosino waited a second and followed the kid into the cramped foyer.

"Snappy duds, kid. Maybe they'll be back in style when they fit you in ten years."

"Up yers, Joe." A freshly-rolled cigarette stuck to Izzy's pursed lips, unlit. "So what's the rumpus? I saw there's gonna be an Inquest for that mafia gang youse pinched, huh?"

"I got a job for you, kid. But it requires delicacy."

"Swell, I used to work at a Kosher delicatessen. What's doin'?"

"The Chief gets a shine next door at 11 o'clock every day. He'll be there in about ten minutes, and he's got a scrap of paper in his suit jacket, vest pocket below his heart. It'll be a cakewalk for a maestro like you."

Izzy squawked with laughter and slowly realized Petrosino was serious. "Youse want me to dip the Chief Inspector of the Central Bureau right across from Headquarters? Why, that's loony as a wooden duck! Not a fuckin' chance in Hades, Joe. Nope."

"Remember that silk ladies' hosiery you had last time? I know the merchant you borrowed it from. Even if it wasn't you, he's a mean bastard, and I'm sure he'd swear an affidavit against you out of spite. You know what they'd do to a squealer like you at the boys' reformatory in Elmira? Awful things, Izzy."

"Oh yeah? Your pal The Broom's the biggest squealer of 'em all."

"Watch your mouth." Petrosino shoved Izzy against the wall and squeezed his face hard.

Izzy squirmed and said, "I'm sorry, Joe, wait … I heard somethin' else."

"Spill."

"That cop they call Handsome Jimmy, I heard he was there with that lady who found the barrel… that's all's I heard, I swear."

"What the devil," Petrosino muttered. Why was McCafferty at the murder scene? Petrosino let go of Izzy and said, "Get that note or else."

"Lousy copper." Izzy spat out his cigarette in protest. Petrosino watched the kid walk back out to the street in front of the shoeshine stand. Izzy started busking, his voice undulating through the street, and his feet pattering an impromptu jig. After several minutes, McClusky appeared on the front steps of the Marble Palace, and a bull kept watch as McClusky crossed the street and plunked down on the shoeshine's chair. The bootblack folded up the Chief's pant legs and carefully set the Chief's brand new shoes on the brass stirrups.

Izzy moved in front of McClusky and sang:

> *"My sweet Marie from sunny Italy,*
> *Oh how I do love you*
> *Say that you'll love me, love me, too*
> *Forever more I will be true*
> *Just say the word and I'll marry you*
> *And then you'll surely be*
> *My sweet Marie from sunny Italy!"*

The shoeshine boy was buffing the leather in tune with Izzy's voice, and McClusky's scowl softened as he listened. Izzy repeated the stanza, finished with a flourish on the last note, and took a bow. That kid can sing, Petrosino thought.

"I don't go in much for I-talian music," McClusky said, "but that was good, boy. You know any Irish tunes?"

Izzy patted McClusky's shoulder and winked. "Why, sure I do, boss. Me mudder was born in County Cork…" Izzy cleared his throat loudly, closed his eyes, and crooned:

"O, father dear I often hear you speak of Erin's Isle,
Her lofty scenes, her valleys green, her mountains rude and wild,
They say it is a lovely land wherein a prince might dwell,
So why did you abandon it, the reason to me tell."

The song's two minutes passed in what seemed like seconds. Izzy
lingered over the last few words, outstretched his arms theatrically,
and embraced McClusky: *"And loud and high we'll raise the cry,
'Revenge for Skibbereen.'"*

"Dear Old Skibbereen," McClusky mumbled with tears in his
eyes. He tousled Izzy's hair and reached for his billfold, but Izzy
pulled back and shook his head tersely.

"No, boss. I'd sooner die than take a penny from a fellow
Irishman for dat ballad."

McClusky nodded and tipped the bootblack heavy. He started
back to the Marble Palace, but stopped to let a carriage pass and
turned back. "Say, boy, you ought to be in a music hall. What's
your name?"

Izzy held his top hat against his chest. "Irving, sir! Irving…
Berlin at your service."

"I'll remember you. You'll go far."

"*Erin Go Bragh!*" Izzy waved good-bye and waited until
McClusky and his bull disappeared inside Headquarters. Then Izzy
darted back into the foyer of the brownstone where Petrosino was
waiting with a big grin.

"Irving Berlin? Where the hell did that come from?"

"Stage name, ya dope. Someday I'll be a singin' waiter in
saloons. Songs just pop into my noodle like magic." Izzy took
a scrap of paper from inside his hat and handed it to Petrosino.
"Here's the note. What a turnip the Chief is, thought I was a Mick.
My Russian Jew ass."

"You were good, kid. Maybe you'll make it out of the Ghetto
yet." Petrosino unfolded the note and translated it in his butcher
book while Izzy happily chirped another song and waited for his

tip. Petrosino mumbled the decoded message, "*Manda la puttana a casa prima che abbai.*" *Send the bitch home before she barks.* Petrosino looked up. "Federica."

"What?"

"Nothing, kid. Here's your dough." Petrosino absently shoved silver in Izzy's hand and walked straight to the Star of Italy.

Chapter 30

The patrolman that Max had detailed outside the Star of Italy had been pulled off, and now no one was watching the comings and goings of the saloon or the tenement next door where the sisters lived: Marie the pretty cross-eyed one and Federica the brute. Petrosino thought of his taunts to Petto, that he'd pay Federica a visit, that maybe she knew something about the barrel murder. What if she were the "bitch" who needed to be sent home before she "barked"?

He was leaning against a lamppost across the street from the tenement, eating a cigar more than smoking it, hoping he was wrong. He didn't like the idea of going in alone, but he didn't have a choice. He flicked the cigar into a barrel and started toward the building when he saw Bimbo Martino whistling his way down the block. The big greenhorn was in plainclothes and PD walking brogans.

"Bimbo." Petrosino waved him over. Bimbo's face brightened, and he rushed over, about to salute. Petrosino grabbed his hand, shook it.

"Detective, sir." Bimbo stood at attention.

"Knock it off, kid. How come you're not in uniform?"

"I got an hour leave from reserve to pick up fresh underclothes. We're on duty for another two weeks before our day off. I've had stick training, marching, all that stuff."

"They take you greenhorns to the basement of the Eighth Regiment Armory?"

"Did they? You know they hang pig carcasses on hooks for us to shoot at?"

"That's the closest thing to a man's body. How'd you do?"

Bimbo looked down. "Not so good with a gun, but they said I'm a champ with the billy."

"I should give you lessons. Make a real police out of you. You never know when, kid, but some day you'll be in a shoot-out. Don't play Buffalo Bill and shoot for a hand. Aim for the chest and squeeze the trigger gently, don't pull hard. If only I could teach a whole squad of Italian bulls like you." Petrosino patted Bimbo's broad shoulders and got an idea. "Say, I bet the girls go wild for you. Wanna work a murder case?"

"Would I!"

Petrosino motioned with his chin, and they crossed the street to the tenement next to the Star of Italy, and its front door sign forbidding *Hebrews, consumptives, and dogs.* A pair of toddlers sat on the ground in front, tossing fistfuls of dirt into the air. A drunk slattern hung out a second-story window, watching the children with a toothless smile. They walked up the front steps, and Petrosino pulled Bimbo into the darkened hallway where light and air vanished like condemned souls.

"A tough walnut's gonna answer the door," Petrosino whispered. "We don't have time for a warrant. So you're gonna charm her. Speak Sicilian and ask for her sister, a girl named Federica. Tell her you have a note for Federica, and only you can give it to her."

"Like a love note. What if Federica's there?"

"Then we'll pinch her."

Petrosino motioned with his hand, and they climbed three flights of stairs, passing a discarded diaper, two arrogant rats, and the sound of sewing machines whirring behind doors. On the third floor, Petrosino pointed at the first door to the left, then noticed an open door at the other end of the hall. A rectangle of copper light gleamed in the opening. Petrosino slipped down the hall and nudged the crooked door open to see a steep staircase to the roof where another door was propped open with a brick. He nodded at Bimbo and hid in the staircase.

Bimbo knocked on Marie's door.

"Who is it?" Marie's voice said.

"It's a friend of Federica's," Bimbo said in Sicilian.

"She's not here."

"I have a note for her."

Locks clicked and opened, and Marie poked her head over a chain and into the hall. "My God, what are you supposed to be, a piano mover?"

"No, just a friend of Federica's. Is she here?"

Marie's eyes scanned the hallway. "Give me the note."

"I have to give it to her myself."

"Suit yourself." Marie pulled her head back inside and slammed the door.

Petrosino motioned Bimbo over, and they both crept up the steep staircase, holding onto the walls for fear of falling backward, until they emerged on the roof. The sun reflected off the rooftops in shimmering patches of copper. Petrosino studied the scene, taking in the clotheslines and wash bins as he crossed to the short brick wall separating the tenement and the neighboring saloon. His curiosity was piqued.

"She wouldn't budge," Bimbo said.

"Shh. Follow me."

They threw their legs over the dividing wall and walked over to the neighboring roof door. Another brick sat wedged in the jamb, keeping the door ajar. They opened the door and descended into the darkness of creaky steps. Three flights down, silently, they came upon a door covered with graffiti and warnings carved with penknives. The largest scrawl read, *Beware The Black Hand Of The Mafia*, flanked by a crude carving of a skull and dagger. Petrosino thought that this dreary hole would be an easy place to stab a man, and a chill crawled up his spine like an insect. He shuddered and tried the knob. Locked. He took out a set of nippers and jimmied the keyhole. He glanced at Bimbo, put his finger over his mouth, and turned the knob. The door moved three inches before it thudded against something heavy. A short bookcase. Beyond that was the windowless back room of the Star of Italy, a makeshift office that he'd seen before when he and Max visited the place. The door was the size of a panel that matched identical panels on the wall. No handle. A secret panel concealed by the bookcase and wallpaper.

"Those women are couriers," Petrosino said. "To pass communications. They could've even used this passage to hide the gang and sneak them out in a jiffy."

"What should we do?"

"Go back up and tell that woman that you're in love with Federica, but you're afraid of her man, The Ox. You have to know where she is or you'll die. Look weepy."

Bimbo scrunched up his chin, pretending to cry.

"Not like you're gonna shit. Like you're sad." Petrosino shut the back door to the Star of Italy, locked it, and led them back across the rooftop and to the hallway of the girls' apartment.

Petrosino waited in the landing on the second floor below, listening as Bimbo knocked again. The door groaned open.

Marie snorted at him. "She's not here. Don't be pathetic."

"Please, I'm afraid of her man. But I need to see her. I'm over the moon for her."

"She likes them big, I'll give her that. You'd better take care with her man though. He's crazy like a fox. How come she never told me about you?"

"She was afraid of what *he* might do if he found out."

"Don't worry, he's in jail now. The lawyer hasn't gotten bail. So what does my sister got that I don't got? Aren't I prettier?"

"Where's Federica? Did I do something to upset her?"

Petrosino crouched in the lower landing, grinning at the kid's act. It wasn't half-bad.

"My God, you've got some fever over her," Marie said. "It's too bad, because I'm not telling you where she's staying. The only company she needs is Our Virgin Mary."

"Please, I beg you."

Marie's sigh carried down to the stairwell. She invited Bimbo inside and shut the door.

After two minutes passed, Petrosino crept downstairs and waited across the street. Bimbo came out five minutes later, tucking his shirttail in his trousers and wiping a layer of sweat from his flushed cheeks. They walked down the street until they were a block away.

Bimbo turned to him. "This is the best job in the world, Joe."

"What did she say?"

"She said Federica went to work at a silk flower factory in Paterson, New Jersey. Wouldn't say which one."

"Curse the fishes. Federica must know something. That's why they sent her to Jersey. These *mafiosi* are sharper than I thought."

"Why don't we just go pinch her?"

"Can't, she's outside our bailiwick. Doesn't matter. I've got the goods on Petto with the pawn ticket. Go home, kid, you did swell."

"See you tomorrow morning at the Inquest?"

"How's that?"

"Inspector Schmittberger detailed me to the Coroner's Court since I speak Italian. To watch the crowd."

"Bully for you, son."

Bimbo saluted.

"Plainclothes men don't salute. Now scram."

Bimbo left, and Petrosino suddenly felt sick because he was certain now who The Fox was. Izzy's tip-off about McCafferty and Federica's disappearance sealed it. He headed for Eldridge Street Station to find Schmittberger.

Chapter 31

Petrosino and Schmittberger were sitting in Minerva & Company's office overlooking Washington Square Park. The sun had set just below the tree line, and the leaves in the park had a red tint. Even the Washington Arch looked pink as Petrosino stared out the window in the awkward silence. No one had said much when Petrosino brought Schmittberger to the office. Steffens and McAlpin had been reading the afternoon papers, still warm to the touch and wet with fresh ink. But their eyes flicked above the pages and looked warily at Schmittberger.

"The Mayor's speaking at the opening of the new Stock Exchange on Wall Street." Steffens shook out folds in his newspaper. "And the Negroes joined the Italians in their subway strike. I'd like to see labor unite. All they want is a buck fifty and an eight-hour day."

"Scratch a socialist," Tarbell said, "and you'll find an anarchist underneath."

"No ma'am, anarchy is a vacuum. Socialism is a brotherhood." Steffens picked up a copy of *The World*. "Say, they've got a picture of The Ox on the front page! Ill-favored look to him. Is he as strong as they say, Joe?"

"Yup." Petrosino stared at the headline: *Mafia Murder Gang Are All In Police Net*.

"Says Coroner Scholer is having a hard time finding jurors for the Inquest tomorrow," Steffens said, reading. "He thinks men are afraid of the mafia and that, if they find cause to send the case to the Grand Jury, they might sustain some injury from the Morello gang."

"What'll he do if he can't get twelve talesmen?" Schmittberger asked.

"Scholer said he'll handpick some men from a club he belongs to. The Arion Society. Why, those men will be well-suited for the Inquest with their Teutonic reticence. If anyone's not afraid of an Italian, it's a German."

"He's right," Schmittberger said to Petrosino. "Us icy Dutchmen ain't a-skeered of you sneaky I-talians."

Petrosino chuckled, but the other three sat mute.

McAlpin finally rustled his paper. "Our new American league team is playing the Washington Senators tomorrow. I'd like to wager a few bits on them."

Schmittberger nodded at McAlpin. "So would I. They're starting that spitballer Happy Jack Chesbro. Could you put me down for a fiver on the Highlanders, too?"

Steffens sighed his disapproval loudly and shook his head at McAlpin and Tarbell.

"All right, cut the vaudeville show," Schmittberger said. "If you muckrakers are against me being here, say so. I already know about your angle on city corruption and some gambling Syndicate, so what do you think of that?" Schmittberger turned to face Steffens. "Go on, Steff. You think I'm still a grafter on my old Steamboat Squad? That was in 1894, damn it, and I was given full immunity! Is it because I wanna bet on a baseball game? Don't be yellow, say it."

"The less people who know what we're doing, the better," Steffens said. "This is the kind of story that could bring many powerful men down. But if they get us first, then it would surely bring us and our magazine down."

"And why can't I help you? At least Joe and I get our hands dirty. We risk our necks to get crooks off the street. What do *you* do with your gold specs and your little pencil?"

"I came to New York with only a hundred bucks and my father's order to make it or starve. I've made my own way, and my writing does as much good as any flatfoot cop!"

"You're nothing but a wormy muckrake."

Steffens popped up from his chair and shook his fist. "The journalist is a true servant of democracy. The best journalist is like a prophet of old: he cries out the truth!"

"Nuts! You're on the make for success, ignorant of your inadequacies, and only interested in your destination. Like Lexow. I still owe you a licking for what you did to me-"

"You did that to yourself," Steffens said. "You chose the crooked path-"

"Humbug, gentlemen!" Tarbell rose from her chair and hushed them all like a daunting schoolmarm. "Let's not behave like children. I'll speak plainly, if you don't mind, Inspector."

"It's about time for plain speaking, ma'am," Schmittberger said.

"Good." Tarbell sat back down calmly, adjusting her dress and holding her knees. "The reasons we were reluctant to include you are threefold. First, you were a grafter in the past, and sometimes there's a risk of backsliding. Not that you're on the take, but it was a risk. Second, we can't have any leaks. Although you're reformed, you could've been tempted to tip off colleagues still in the game. And last, it was *my* idea to keep you at arm's length because of the strain between you and Steff, which was evidenced so clearly just now. If we can't get along with our allies, we can't slay the dragons, can we?"

Schmittberger crossed his arms and squinted at Tarbell. He said loudly, "I like you, Miss Tarbell. If it's any consolation, I've heard from reliable sources, including Joe here, that the PD brass and Tammany villains are coming after my badge. They want me off the job because I've been pushing for the truth behind this murder. Of course, I have two of the most ruthless Hasidic lawyers to defend me if need be, and they make vultures look like peace doves. So I mean to fight for my job tooth and claw, because I'm no crook. I swear on my seven kids' hearts."

"I believe you." Tarbell raised an eyebrow at Steffens. "Now, can everyone else bury the hatchet with a handshake?"

Steffens stood up with an apologetic smile and walked over to Schmittberger with his hand outstretched. Schmittberger took Steffens hand and squeezed until Steffens whimpered.

"Easy, Max." Petrosino pulled Schmittberger's hand away.

They all sat down again. McAlpin threw open a window, and the smell of leaves and spring swept through and lifted their spirits.

"I'll go first then," Petrosino said, "and I'll be blunt. There's something fishy in the Bureau. McClusky has every clue we found, except Max and I held back the notes in Caesar code. At least I thought we did. McClusky got hold of a third note."

"What?" Steffens inched forward on his chair.

"He asked if I could translate it, but I played dumb. I tried to decipher it in my head, but he was quick to take it back from me and wouldn't let me copy it down either."

"How'd he come across the note?"

"He said McCafferty found it on one of the gang. But that can't be. The only way the Chief could've gotten that note was if he was the conduit. Then a stoolie told me that McCafferty was at the murder scene when that woman found the barrel. He doesn't so much as sneeze without the Chief's okay. So..." Petrosino swallowed hard. "I think McClusky is The Fox."

Tarbell whispered, "The Chief of the Central Bureau is in league with a mafia gang?"

"And he's probably the third member of your Syndicate."

"How so?"

"McClusky had the third note because he's either writing them or helping pass them. I got my hands on the note, and it was a message to 'send the female dog home before she barks.' I'd just interrogated Petto and told him I'd pay a visit to his gal, Federica, to see if she'd squeal. Next thing I know, McClusky has this note, and he's testing me to see if I can decipher it. Then I go to Federica's rooms on Elizabeth Street, and she's flown the coop."

"I knew it was that lace curtain Irish peacock," Schmittberger said. "McClusky made sure his bootlicker, McCafferty, was there to cover it up. That's his do-it man. It all fits now. McCafferty carted

Primrose off to the Tombs, and what happened to the lunatic doctor? *Suicide.* And Jimmy was the one tailing Vito Lobaido, too. Lobaido ended up drinking poison. Another *suicide,* so they say. It's easier for the PD to have one less murder case, especially a witness who might squeal about a link to an organized crime racket. So the Chief spins it like Lobaido killed himself out of guilt over some part in the barrel murder. It's perfect."

"The Chief also pulled Max's man off the Star of Italy," Petrosino said, "and McCafferty ratted out Max when we were going through the gang's traps. See, Max is on suspension…"

"By Jove, this is astounding." Steffens licked his pencil, taking notes. "I always wondered if Primrose was a red herring."

"What we're talking about is just that: *talk,*" Schmittberger said. "We don't have any solid evidence that McClusky is mixed up in the Morello gang."

Petrosino nodded. "I aim to connect him up as The Fox."

"How?" Tarbell asked.

"I don't know yet. But we've said the Syndicate would want the Chief Inspector because he could quash almost any investigation in the City. And if he couldn't stop it, he could tip off raids and arrests." A thought jolted Petrosino. He snapped his fingers. "Max, remember how he tells stories about his dogs and *fox* hunting? See… *The Fox.*"

"That's right."

"I'm not convinced," Steffens said. "I haven't heard that McClusky has any real pull in Tammany. If anyone, it might be George McClellan, Jr., who's got the Green Machine financing his Mayoral campaign this year. Tammany hopes McClellan won't enforce the Raines laws restricting gambling and liquor, which is good for the Syndicate. And I still don't understand how the mafia gang fits? The loyal Irish thugs have been Tammany's muscle for decades."

"I'm working on that," Petrosino said, thinking about the gang's expertise. "You know who knows something? Petto's gal. That's why they shipped her to Jersey."

"If we're right," Schmittberger said, "and the gang's already muzzled up Madonnia, Primrose, and Lobaido, why wouldn't they have snuffed this Federica gal, too? Morello killed a woman in Sicily after all."

"But Federica is Petto's gal and the sister of Morello's woman. Sicilians don't have many scruples, but one thing they don't do is knock off their own women."

"Joe, we won't be able to do much digging before the Inquest tomorrow."

"I'd like to hunt down Federica," Petrosino said, "but I'm on crowd detail at the Inquest in the morning. That's only a few hours from now."

"I'll find her," Schmittberger said.

"Max, you oughtta lie low. You're on suspension-"

"Not in Jersey, I'm not. Look, they're coming after me anyhow, right?" Schmittberger took out his hip flask and toasted with a grin. "*Oh what a tangled web we weave…*"

"*When first we practice to deceive,*" Tarbell replied. "Are you a scholar of the classics?"

"Just because I'm a flatfoot doesn't mean I don't read The Bard."

Tarbell smirked. "That's not Shakespeare. That's the Scottish poet, Sir Walter Scott."

Petrosino and Steffens laughed.

"Touché, Miss Tarbell." Schmittberger sipped whiskey and rose with pinkened cheeks. "Let me ask you something though, Steff. If we find the dirt on rotten cops and politickers in your gambling Syndicate, what do you intend to do with it?"

"Expose them in our magazine, of course. They'll be shamed off the job and put on trial."

"Just like me. Almost. Good, I guess." Max turned for the door, stopped, and called to the back of the room. "Hey McAlpin, don't forget to put five on the Highlanders for me."

"Sure thing."

Petrosino had another idea and said, "McAlpin, where do you place your bets?"

"A club a couple blocks east of here. Next to Snigglefritz's Saloon."

"I know that place. Alderman Murphy owns that whole building. Put five down for me, too. The other way though, on the Senators. We'll see which one of us wins."

Steffens cocked his head. "Why are all of you contributing to this Syndicate's coffers?! Is everyone going bad as sour milk, or am I missing something?"

"You're missing something," Petrosino said. "It's a theory I'm playing on the Morello gang's part in this."

PETTO, "THE OX," THE WATCH WORN BY MADONIA, AND THE PAWN-TICKET FOUND ON HIM WHEN HE WAS PLACED UNDER ARREST.

THE WORLD

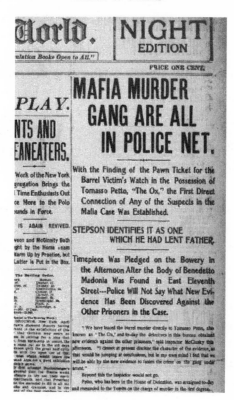

MAFIA MURDER GANG ARE ALL IN POLICE NET.

With the Finding of the Pawn Ticket for the Barrel Victim's Watch in the Possession of Tomasso Petto, "The Ox," the First Direct Connection of Any of the Suspects in the Mafia Case Was Established.

STEPSON IDENTIFIES IT AS ONE WHICH HE HAD LENT FATHER.

Timepiece Was Pledged on the Bowery in the Afternoon After the Body of Benedetto Madonia Was Found in East Eleventh Street---Police Will Not Say What New Evidence Has Been Discovered Against the Other Prisoners in the Case.

Chapter 32

The Inquest was a great flypaper to the East Siders, Petrosino thought, watching them swarm the courthouse as the morning sun reddened their faces. He'd gotten little sleep the night before, staring at the ceiling of his office with each minute blurring into the next until he dozed off for an hour and dreamt of Benedetto Madonnia's decaying face again. He woke up shivering and put on his merchant's disguise, a worn olive suit, bow tie, and cap. He walked to the Criminal Courts Building where Centre Street was overrun with East Siders and police reserves.

At the courthouse entrance, Bimbo Martino towered like a blue colossus in his tall helmet and PD overcoat. The lines of gold embroidery on his sleeves and the silver badge on his chest shimmered like Christmas ornaments. He was shouting in Italian and English, directing the crowd, tipping his helmet at women, and waving his billy at men.

"Move along!"

Petrosino watched silently and admired the cop young enough to be his son.

At nine o'clock sharp, a caravan of chatter snapped him out of his trance. Chief Inspector McClusky and his lackeys, McCafferty and O'Farrell and two guards, climbed the courthouse steps en masse followed by a pack of reporters. The Chief was barking at the newsmen with the *de rigeur* assurance of a political incumbent, "It's bosh to say that anyone can get a confession. There's not one instance in criminal history of a confession being obtained from an Italian without the application of torture." Some of the reporters laughed. "And these crooks are *Sicilians*, that's like an Italian with rabies. They'd just as soon die in the electric chair as by their vendetta. But we don't need a confession, what with the pawn ticket, the watch, and Sagliabeni. Now, if you don't mind, I'd like to go see Mr. Jerome crucify these Dagos."

Petrosino pulled his cap low and slipped inside the courtroom ahead of McClusky, who swaggered with his entourage into a PD box next to the press. Petrosino elbowed his way near the jury box of a dozen fair-haired German men. Dented copper cuspidors on the floor were already brimming with spit and tobacco beneath a large sign: *All rise when the Coroner enters and leaves. Bondsmen are requested to sign all deeds to property. No spitting at prisoners.* The common folk crammed together on long benches, watching with the reverent anticipation of a Catholic congregation. On the podium above, clerks scurried like drones around the honey colored wood and its ornate hive of paper stacks and desk lamps.

District Attorney Jerome sat at one table parallel to a longer table of defense attorneys led by Chas Le Barbier, Jerome's former clerk. The sight of Le Barbier worried Petrosino. He was just as sharp as Jerome, but unrestrained by the burden of scruples.

A bailiff appeared on the podium and called out, "Case number 4-2-8-4-1. All rise for the Honorable Coroner Gustave Scholer!"

Everyone rose and leaned sideways for a peek as Scholer hobbled in with glasses and a white moustache that matched a white fedora tilted up on his forehead. Scholer absentmindedly clutched his hat and handed it to a clerk before he sat between a pair of flagpoles festooned with Old Glory and ivory eagleheads. He waved everyone to be seated, and the benches screeched and groaned with the shifting weight.

As a score of police guards led the eight prisoners in, a woman gasped. With their bruised faces, the Morello gang looked more like Bellevue patients than a dangerous band of killers. Except for Tomasso "The Ox" Petto. He carried himself like an executioner instead of a victim, as if he could mete out death with one blow. Petrosino watched him intently as the other gangsters filed in behind him, dwarfed by comparison. Police guards sat them down at the defense table and hovered behind them while the crowd chattered at the sight.

Coroner Scholer rapped his gavel on the bench and said with a thick guttural accent, "The District Attorney may call witnesses."

"Your Honor," Jerome said, rising, "the People call Salvatore Sagliabeni."

As Salvatore came into the courtroom, Petto bolted from his chair, chains and all, and violently upended the defense table. In the cloud of papers and cigars flying in the air, he lunged after the boy, and the courtroom echoed with screams of panic.

Petrosino started for the podium, but then held back. He was there in plainclothes to spy on the crowd. He edged closer to the gate as women shrieked, and men stood on the benches to get a better look. Even in shackles, The Ox threw guards off of him as if they were children. Petrosino reached in his suit jacket for a sap when Bimbo Martino dashed into the courtroom.

Bimbo sprinted down the aisle, bowling men over, and leapt over the gate. He grabbed Petto by his hairy neck and threw all of his weight against Petto's body. They tumbled in a heap over a table, somersaulting to the floor. Petto grabbed Bimbo's hands and tried to free himself, but Bimbo dragged The Ox backward. The Chief signaled from his box in press row, and Handsome Jimmy McCafferty jumped into the fray, shoving The Ox back to his chair while Bimbo pulled on the chains.

"I'll fix you," Petto growled at Bimbo, "when I get out, you're a dead man." Petto shouted to the crowd in Italian, "IT TAKES TWO OF THEM TO HOLD ME!"

"And one to do this," Bimbo said, punching Petto's kidney.

Petto laughed as they forced him into his chair and guards bound him with more irons. By the time they were finished, Petto grunted with amusement and sunk low, docile as a milking cow. The crowd chirped at Bimbo like fans at a prizefight, and the thrill warmed Petrosino's veins like hot whiskey. He wished Max had been there to see the kid tangle with The Ox.

Coroner Scholer sat up from the bench like a squirrel testing the environs, and his gavel brought the room to order. An eerie hush followed as Salvatore Sagliabeni was ushered back into the courtroom between two guards and a gale of menacing looks from the Morello gang.

Salvatore stumbled into the witness box. His large knotty hands clutched at the wood railing, and his eyes were full of dread. He looked lost, like a forlorn ghost to Petrosino, but there was nothing he could do to help him. This was the moment of truth.

Jerome started with simple questions, trying to calm Salvatore. He asked how he came to America and how he was related to Benedetto Madonnia, and he gave the interpreter and Salvatore plenty of time to answer. Throughout the room, a murmur began as those in the back passed on the testimony to dozens in the hallways and then hundreds on the street outside.

"I know this is difficult, Mr. Sagliabeni, and I apologize." Jerome approached the witness stand and held up a morgue photograph of Madonnia. "But is this your stepfather, Benedetto Madonnia?"

"Yes, that's him." Salvatore's eyes watered.

"Thank you." Jerome gave him a few seconds to compose himself, then held up a gold hunting case pocket watch for the jury to see. "Is this your stepfather's watch?"

Petrosino saw Morello lean over defense counsel's table. His deformed hand had been hidden inside a loose sleeve, but now it slinked out and rapped loudly against the table to get the boy's attention.

Salvatore fixated on Morello's claw and stammered.

Jerome followed Salvatore's gaze and stared angrily at Morello. "Mr. Morello, if you make any gestures to this witness, I'll seek contempt against you."

Le Barbier popped up in his double-breasted frock. "Objection, Your Honor! Mr. Jerome is threatening my client. This is an outrage."

"Pipe down, Chas," Jerome said. "Your client is the one who's trying to intimidate my witness. Maybe you should counsel him on obstruction of justice. You're an expert at it."

"Look who's squawking, Jerome. You've got more tricks than Saks has suits."

The crowd chuckled.

"Everyone sit down," Scholer said. "Mr. Morello, if you do that again, you'll be blindfolded and gagged. Go on, Mr. Jerome."

Jerome smiled at Le Barbier, adjusted his pince nez, and said, "Mr. Sagliabeni, I want to remind you that you have nothing to fear. You're under the protection of this Court and the Central Bureau detectives. Now, once again, is this the watch you loaned your stepfather?"

"Well . . . it looks *just like* mine. My father's watch was out of order and he carried mine from Buffalo on his trip to New York."

"What do you mean 'just like' yours? It's *yours*, is it not?"

"It l-l-looks like my watch, but . . . there may be many others like it in the world." A tear started down the fuzzy curve of Salvatore's cheek. "I can't say it's mine for certain."

The Ox snorted from beneath his chains, and Petrosino felt as if the whole courtroom were turned upside down and all the blood gravitated to his head. He bit his lip and fought the urge to go over and shake some sense into Salvatore.

"Wait a moment," Jerome said. "When you saw this watch in the hands of the police, when you met with Detective Petrosino, didn't you tell him, 'That's papa's watch'?"

"I may have. I'm just not sure now." Salvatore glanced at the Morello gang.

"Come now, didn't you say that this was your watch, that you scratched the neck with your thumbnail because of a loose screw? Mr. Sagliabeni, you're weakening, sir."

Salvatore seemed on the verge of a convulsion and couldn't speak. Petrosino groaned, watching helplessly as the boy unraveled on the stand.

Jerome smiled uncomfortably at Coroner Scholer. "Your Honor, Mr. Sagliabeni's prior affidavit positively identifies this watch as his stepfather's. Given this mafia gang's transparent efforts to intimidate the witness, the People move to publish said affidavit to the jury."

"Granted," Coroner Scholer said. "The jury should conclude that Mr. Sagliabeni positively identified the watch found by the police as the watch loaned to his stepfazzer. It was described by the witness as a gold hunting case pocket watch engraved with a locomotive."

"Thank you, Your Honor," Jerome said. "Now, Mr. Sagliabeni, I know this is difficult for you, but I must ask: when did you last see your stepfather alive?"

"At the Lehigh Valley train depot." Salvatore paused. "I'll never see him again, will I?"

"Thanks to these mafia hoodlums here, I'm afraid not, son."

"Objection!" Le Barbier said. "He can't say that, Your Honor!"

"No further questions," Jerome said.

A bailiff helped Salvatore off the witness stand, and the gang's unblinking eyes stabbed at the boy as he left the courtroom.

Jerome stood before the jury box and lifted up his finger in silence, drawing everyone's attention before he announced: "We call Giuseppe De Priemo as our next witness."

Petrosino watched The Ox shift tensely in his chair, and Bimbo put his hands on the gangster's enormous shoulders, bracing for another outburst.

∾

Petrosino squeezed the leather sap in his pocket and prayed that Giuseppe De Priemo would fare better than Salvatore. If there were saints in heaven, he thought, they should help De Priemo. He took out a handkerchief to wipe his brow. The room had become stifling with De Priemo's entrance. The bailiffs threw open windows, but the stagnant air was infected with malevolence. Babies cried out in frustration, and police guards grew irritated and stood closer to the sweating gangsters.

De Priemo was the only person shivering in the room. His prison stripes quivered as he stared down at his own lap.

"How, if at all," Jerome said, "do you know the suspects in this case, Mr. De Priemo?"

"We made plenty of bad coin together, printed false notes. Things like that."

A hissing sound like an angry teakettle came from the back of the room. Petrosino turned, but couldn't see who was making the noise.

"Who was in this band?"

"The men you have in chains there." De Priemo pointed without looking.

"And you reside in Sing Sing now for passing counterfeit?"

"Yes, sir." De Priemo glanced at the gang. "They let me go up the river and never gave me my share of the spoils. Before my trial, they said they'd get me a lawyer. But I guess they double-crossed me. They were happy to let me rot in Sing Sing."

"I see." Jerome nodded with satisfaction, then held up a large photograph for the jurors.

Petrosino could see that it was one of the more grotesque Morgue pictures of Madonnia. His head was lopsided in the photograph, and tendons fell out of his neck like red strands of pasta. For the first time, the laconic German jurors made noise. They mumbled and groaned at the picture, and the crowd whispered at the reaction.

"Please take a look at this photograph." Jerome handed the photo to De Priemo. "Do you know the poor dead soul in this picture?"

"My God, yes, I know him." De Priemo's whole body cringed. "It's my brother-in-law, Benedetto Madonnia."

"Did Benedetto know the other men in the gang, this counterfeiting gang here?"

"Yes."

"And how did he know them? Strike that. Do you know if he ever spoke to them on your behalf? About getting your share of the counterfeiting loot and getting you a lawyer?"

"Yes, he did. He went to that man there, Giuseppe Morello, and asked for my share of the loot. And they all laughed at him."

"Did your brother-in-law threaten to expose the gang if they didn't pay you what you were owed? Did he threaten to squeal?"

"I . . . I don't know about that?"

"Come now, sir, didn't you tell me that before? Didn't Benedetto say that they'd pay one way or another or he'd expose them?"

"I don't know. I don't remember."

"Well, why do you think your brother-in-law ended up this way?" Jerome took the photograph and held it up again, this time for the audience. The crowd gasped in disgust. "Why do you think they stabbed him to death, cut his throat, and shoved his manhood in his mouth?"

"Objection, Your Honor!" Le Barbier boomed. "This is vaudeville at best. And Mr. De Priemo's opinion as a layman is utterly irrelevant! There's no foundation, he's no expert-"

"Overruled," Scholer said. "The witness will answer."

De Priemo paused before directing his words at Petto, "I think Benedetto was killed to shut him up and keep him from going to the police."

Petrosino nodded and thought, *Keep going, De Priemo, don't crack.*

"The man you're looking at right now," Jerome said, "do you know this Tomasso Petto?"

"I knew him once." De Priemo's cloudy eyes strained at Petto. "But not by that name."

"You know Tomasso Petto by a different name?"

Chair legs screeched on the floor as some of the Morello gang moved in their seats, but the police guards held the suspects still.

"Mr. De Priemo, answer the question. You knew him by another name? What was it?"

De Priemo's shriveled lips mumbled, "I knew him as 'Luciano' . . . Luciano Petto from Wilkes-Barre, Pennsylvania."

Jerome nodded and leaned on an elbow against the jury box railing. "Did you know that Luciano Petto stabbed a miner in Scranton?"

"Objection, hearsay, Your Honor. It's irrelevant and prejudicial-"

"Overruled. You may answer."

"Yes," De Priemo said, "I heard that he stabbed a man in Scranton."

"Did you also hear that the police found a pawn ticket for Benedetto's watch on Petto when he was arrested, after Benedetto was also found stabbed? Like the fellow in Scranton?"

"Yes, sir."

"Do you have any reason to believe that your brother-in-law would have voluntarily given that watch to the likes of this Petto?"

"No, sir, he wouldn't have done that. Never."

"So then, do you believe Petto murdered your brother-in-law in cold blood, stabbing him with a knife as he'd done before and then stealing the watch from his still-warm body?"

"Objection! This is ridiculous, he's leading his own witness-"

"Overruled," Scholer said. "Answer the question."

De Priemo looked away from Petto's black stare. "Petto was a friend of mine once, and I didn't want to believe he killed my brother-in-law. But now I think... yes, I think he did it."

Petrosino exhaled his anxiety and mopped a handkerchief across his face.

"Does Giuseppe 'The Clutch Hand' Morello tell Petto what to do?" Jerome asked. "Is he the 'head' or *capo* of this gang? Is he the one who ordered Petto to kill?"

The Clutch Hand shifted in his chair, and De Priemo looked over at his former *capo*. Morello eyed De Priemo, lifted his deformed hand to his own lips, and mouthed the word, *Shhh.*

A man in the crowd shouted in Sicilian, "Say good-bye to your family, De Priemo!"

De Priemo's eyelids draped shut, and he collapsed into a heap of jelly.

The bailiffs tried to gather him up, saying to Coroner Scholer, "He's out cold, sir!"

Another voice in the crowd yelled, "They gave him the death sign!"

Coroner Scholer banged his gavel and shouted, "CLEAR THE COURTROOM!"

The guards clubbed the Morello gang's heads, shoving them out the prisoners' entrance, and spectators scrambled for the courtroom door. Petrosino jostled through bodies, looking for the culprits and muttering, "When I find out who's behind this, there won't be ambulances enough for you." Then he saw them. One had dark curly-hair, handsome but in a menacing way. The other looked like an unshaven drunk. Paul and Peter from the soda fountain.

The two men looked back at him tensely, then shoved their way outside. Petrosino caught Bimbo's arm at the courthouse entrance, pointed, and shouted, "STOP THOSE MEN!" But the crowd moved like an irresistible tide, pouring onto White Street, then spreading north where Walker Street converged with Canal. By the time it thinned out, Petrosino and Bimbo were in Harry Howard Square still in sight of Paul and Peter. They dodged two carriages and a trolley car and kept running, the air burning Petrosino's lungs like a cheap cigar.

When the sidewalk cleared out and they had a bead on the two crooks, Bimbo pulled a baseball out of his bluecoat and held it up as if to ask Petrosino's permission. Petrosino shouted, "Do it!" Bimbo twisted into his wind-up and whipped his arm forward with all his strength. The brown leather sphere whistled through the street like it was on a clothesline and cracked the back of Paul's head, sending him tumbling forward into a pile of straw and manure.

Petrosino and Bimbo caught up just as Peter managed to hoist Paul back to his feet.

"If it isn't the soda jerks," Petrosino said over his cocked .38. "I told you if I ever saw your faces again, I'd squash you like turnips. Guess what? It's squashing time, boys."

Chapter 33

"I'm gonna teach you what a 'sweatbox' is, boys," Petrosino said in Italian. "Show you the true Third Degree." He shoveled more coal into the old-fashioned stove in the cell at Eldridge Street Precinct. The black iron stove rattled like an elevated train as the flame grew in its belly. "You won't catch a cold that's for sure. Maybe a fever, but not a cold."

Peter and Paul sat in the brick cell, chained to the plank bench against the back wall. Sneering. The room was the smallest of any precinct, less than six feet high, maybe a few feet bigger than a Sing Sing coffin cell. A bulb the size of a lemon flickered in the ceiling and bluish-orange light bubbled from the coal's embers. Smoke spiraled through the cracks in the stovepipe and climbed the air like a black serpent. Peter and Paul's expressions didn't change. They sat in their wool suits and iron bracelets, stoic as wooden Indians in a pipe shop.

"Joe, is this on the square?" Bimbo asked. His broad silhouette was only ten feet down the basement corridor. "They said in training we can't do sweat boxes or shower baths anymore, because shysters are making a stink about the Third Degree and the Constitution."

"You're right, kid. But the law isn't black and white. It's full of grey areas." Then Petrosino spoke loudly to the two prisoners. "Lots of holes in the law. Isn't that right, Peter and Paul? Nobody's used this sweat box in a while, at least since that one prisoner died. He was a tough bastard, skin thicker than a rhino's hide. I wasn't surprised when they couldn't get a word out of him. They said when the ambulance took him away, he weighed thirty pounds less than when they first pinched him. It was all the water he lost."

Bimbo's face twitched, and he looked back at the stair door at the end of the corridor.

"Don't worry, kid. These men are rougher than that fellow. Aren't you, Peter and Paul?" Petrosino lifted the rusted shovel from the bin and added more coal to the stove. He stoked it until the flames were white hot. Then he took off his cap, his suit jacket, his tie, and unfastened the top three buttons of his shirt. "I'm not so tough myself. I'm gonna wait out here."

Petrosino went into the corridor, closed the cell door and and sat on a stool. He kept the coals burning and watched through the iron bars of the door as Peter and Paul went through the stages. First, they laughed at him until their faces turned shiny and wet like bronze. As the minutes passed, their cheeks ballooned, and their bodies pulled at their chains. They cursed at him, trying to wriggle out of their suits. Their hands had only so much slack in the chains, so barely a button was loosened. They used their mouths to try to undress, teeth gnawing at the fabric, but their bodies began to slump lethargically. Sweat fell from their noses as they bickered, trying to move the plank bench away from the stove, scuttling to the corner of the cell.

Petrosino said, "What are your real names?"

They shook sweat from their eyelids and glared at him, saying nothing but curses.

Petrosino reached between the door's iron bars and shoveled more coal in the stove until it felt like the inside of a baker's oven. He flapped his suit jacket at the acrid black smoke, forcing it to envelop the two thugs.

"Who are you? Mafia? Is that why you were threatening witnesses at the Inquest?"

They ducked their heads between their knees, coughing for air. Paul choked out, "Fuck you, Parsley. Give us a lawyer."

Bimbo shuffled closer and stared at the two men melting away in the brick cell. He whispered timidly, "Joe, please, this ain't good. We're supposed to give them-"

"These men have been threatening me, kid, and I think the witnesses at the Inquest, too. They're mixed up with the Morello gang. So to hell with them." Petrosino stared at them. "The fellow that died in here, it wasn't all sweat. It was vomit and piss, too. Even the snot in his nose and the water in his eyes. I guess at some point, he lost his mind. The doc said his brain got cooked like a hardboiled egg. So he lost control of all his functions."

Peter looked up, his hounddog eyes crossed with dizziness. "No more... stop."

"Tell me who you are, and I'll shut the stove off. And I'll pour this on you, too." Petrosino reached for a bucket behind him and showed them the water. He cupped his hand and took a slurp of it, exaggerating the taste, smacking his lips. "Nice and cold." He flicked cold drops at them. "Who are you? Is your boss The Fox?"

The door at the end of the corridor swung open, and one of Schmittberger's best plainclothes men, Moses Weiss, catapulted down the corridor. The young Jewish sleuth grabbed Bimbo by the shoulder and hissed, "We got company!"

Petrosino quickly opened the cell door and closed the stove. "Stall 'em."

Weiss disappeared back through the corridor door, and Bimbo looked back at Petrosino with a pleading look. It was obvious he wanted to follow Weiss out.

"Get the hell out of here, kid. I'll handle it."

Bimbo left as Petrosino put his suit jacket and his tie back on. He wiped the sweat from his face with his cap and tossed it into the shadows behind him. Then he threw the bucket of water on Peter and Paul. They gasped with relief and baptized themselves in the salve of wet clothes. The ugly one even sucked moisture from his sleeve.

"Curse the fishes," Petrosino hissed at the approaching shadow in the corridor. "With all your complaining about the PD, you were the last man I expected to see."

Chapter 34

Secret Service Agent William J. Flynn sauntered down the basement corridor with a tall man behind him. Flynn had a gloomy look on his walrus face, as if he'd just gotten word of a death in the family. He had his straw boater in hand and didn't offer Petrosino a handshake as he came up to the brick cell and examined the pair of exhausted men in chains. He looked at their condition and sighed. Their will to live almost sluiced out of their boiled skin.

"Joseph, what the devil's going on here?"

"PD business. What's this got to do with you and this fellow?"

"This man is a foreign dignitary, he works for the Italian Consulate." Flynn waved his hand at the tall man. "*Don* Vito Cascio Ferro, this is Detective Sergeant Petrosino of the New York police. I'm sorry, I forgot your title, Mr. Cascio Ferro."

"I'm the aide-de-camp of *Signore* Rafaello Palizzolo, the Deputy of the City of Palermo, and I'm ambassador to the Inglese and Ferrantelli families."

"Swell, another Sicilian," Petrosino said as he studied the man.

Cascio Ferro had a regal air. He was in his forties, tall but made more elongated by his black suit, plain black tie, and white shirt. His chestnut hair, blondish beard, and curved nose made him look like an Italian Mephistopheles. His eyes absorbed the jail surroundings with a hint of sadness.

Flynn tapped Petrosino's hand. "Joseph, I need you to turn those men loose."

"What for?"

"They work for Mr. Cascio Ferro."

"So what?" Petrosino finally turned his eyes away from *Don Vito*. "How'd you know they were even here, Flynn?"

"I don't know, Joseph. Someone must've called the Consulate and they called Treasury. I was ordered to come straight away and free them. What did you pinch them for?"

"You of all people?" Petrosino shook his head with a mocking laugh. "I would've never suspected you with the likes of these men. Did your boys help the gang pass notes, too?"

"I don't know what you're talking about. I'm just doing my job. Maybe you ought to do the same. Now I've got orders to have these men walk. Shake a leg."

"Can't do that. They're arrested for obstruction and threatening witnesses."

Flynn sighed and glanced anxiously at Cascio Ferro, who seemed completely unruffled as he reached into his pocket for a pipe and chewed on the stem. "Do you have any evidence against these men, Joseph? Because I heard you don't have a thing."

"You've got quite an information source. Did your tip-off tell you these men gave the death sign to witnesses at the barrel murder Inquest?"

"Did anyone see them do that? Do you have witnesses?"

Petrosino shook his head. "I know it was them."

"Did you find weapons on them?"

"No, but I've seen them before…" Petrosino thought of the soda fountain and the firecrackers at his apartment. "I know a crook when I see one. Why'd they run, answer that?"

"Everyone runs from you, Joseph. Don Vito here is an upstanding man. He's helped get Italian observers at the polls in the immigrant wards. He's the kind of man who doles out holiday dinners and buckets of coal at Christmas time, and this is an election year, mind you."

"Nuts. If we hold them until I Marconigraph a message to Italy, I bet you a thousand dollar bill that the Italian authorities will have rap sheets longer than your arm-"

"Excuse me, Detective," Cascio Ferro interrupted, "but these gentlemen you arrested are no more crooks than I could fly over the moon."

"I wasn't talking you to, *amico*," Petrosino said.

"Joseph," Flynn said, holding his elbow, "you've got nothing on these men. It's already been cleared from Mr. Willkie at Treasury down to the Central Bureau. You're out of line. This is politics, not crime. We have to cut them loose."

Petrosino shoved Flynn aside and squared up to Cascio Ferro. "Who are you anyhow?"

"I already told you that, Detective, or maybe your English isn't so good?" Cascio Ferro repeated it in Italian.

Petrosino listened to the man's elocution. By comparison to the Morello gang who spoke and carried themselves like shepherds and bandits from the hills, Cascio Ferro could pass for bourgeois. "When did you come to this country, Vito?"

"Shame what goes on in these places." Cascio Ferro looked around, caressed the Belgian rabbit fur of an exquisite Borsalino hat in his hand. "I came here two or three years ago."

"Which port did you come through?"

"New York. A steamship from Genoa or Le Havre." Cascio Ferro's bony fingers played with the rim of his black fedora. "First class passage."

Le Havre was a well-known port for smuggling, Petrosino thought. He studied Cascio Ferro's hand and noticed a gold ring in the shape of a snake coiled around his middle finger.

"Joseph," Flynn said, "if you don't turn them loose, I'll have to proffer charges against you for interfering with a federal officer and then the brass will get wind of what you're doing here, too. Torture of all things. Now do the Christian thing and let it be."

Petrosino handed Flynn the keys to the shackles. "Here, you want to free your new chums? Go ahead, I bow to Treasury. Or Tammany. Or whoever snapped the whip at you."

Flynn snatched the keys and slipped inside the brick cell.

"What are the names of those men in there?" Petrosino asked Cascio Ferro.

"Pietro and Paolo Rizzatto."

"How do you know them?"

"I'm their *padrino*. I baptized them in our Church in Corleone."

"Sure, I bet you baptized those nice altar boys. In the ways of the dagger."

Flynn came out of the cell with Peter and Paul listlessly following. The pair of soaked prisoners stood behind Cascio Ferro, scowling painfully at Petrosino.

"Joseph, what the devil were you doing?" Flynn asked. "They look like barge rats."

Petrosino ignored Flynn and kept staring at Cascio Ferro. There was something about this man that turned his hairs endwise. "Do you know Giuseppe Morello and Luciano Petto?"

"Never heard those names before."

"What about Benedetto Madonnia?"

Cascio Ferro shook his head, pipe smoke curling out of his nostrils.

"Then why are your nephews threatening witnesses at Madonnia's murder Inquest?"

"I don't know what you're talking about. I vouch for these men. They work for me, and they've never threatened a fly on a horse's tail."

"You know nothing of the barrel murder case in this city? Someone stabbed Madonnia to death and shoved his balls in his mouth. Sounds like a crude Sicilian message, doesn't it?"

"Sicily has an unfair reputation in this country, but you wouldn't understand that."

Petrosino played a hunch. "I heard they make the best counterfeit in Sicily. It would be easy to import that business here. Smuggle what you need into New York, get the right men, start passing it off as you go. But you wouldn't know anything about that, would you, *Don* Vito, emissary of the honorable Sicilian government?"

"Blast it, Joseph," Flynn erupted, "that's enough. This man is a guest of the Consulate. Let's go, Mr. Cascio Ferro. I'm sorry about this. . . misunderstanding."

"Sometimes these things happen when a little man thinks he has big power." Cascio Ferro smiled at Petrosino and turned to leave, but Petrosino grabbed his arm.

"I never forget a crook's face, *Don* Vito. If I see you in my city again, I'll fix you up."

"Joseph, knock it off!" Flynn said.

Petrosino watched Cascio Ferro's eyes turn cold, exposing a glimpse of venom in the elegant Sicilian. He set his Borsalino fedora on his head, towering over Petrosino. His long features and silhouette gave him the air of belonging to a superior ancient race. "I'd like to see you in Sicily, Detective. I'll give you a welcome a man of your stature deserves."

"You would, would you?" Petrosino stepped forward, but Flynn stood in the way until the three Sicilians filed down the corridor and out the door.

Petrosino's stomach turned as he watched the trio walk out, scott-free.

"What the devil's the matter with you, Joseph?"

"I could ask you the same thing, Flynn, but I already know. You always complain that the PD is a 'chamber of horrors,' but now you're rolling over for these scum."

"I don't know what you're talking about. He's just an I-talian politicker with pull, and those two puppets are nobody in your murder case." Flynn turned to walk away and muttered over his shoulder, "You've cracked up, Joseph."

BASEBALL
SPORTING ⚡ RACES

" Circulation

PRICE ONE CENT.

JURORS IN TERROR OF THE VENGEANCE OF THE MAFIA.

Coroner Declares He Had Trouble to
Secure Enough of Talesmen to Act
at the Inquest Into the Death of
Benedetto Madonia, the Victim of the
Barrel Murder Mystery.

The terror of the Mafia has already laid hold of the men who are a
part of the law's machinery in the effort to fasten the murder of Benedetto Madonia, the barrel victim, on the guilty slayers.

When the inquest in the case was called by Coroner Scholer to-day
many of the men subpoenaed to serve did not respond to the calling of
their names. They had answered the subpoenas and come to the Coro-

(Continued on Second Page.)

THE WORLD

Chapter 35

The Inquest was moved from the courtroom to Coroner Scholer's chambers, where it was barred from the public. Jerome had rested his case for indictment at five o'clock in the afternoon with an array of sensational exhibits: Dr. Weston's pronouncement of murder, the pocket watch, the pawn ticket, the stilettos and knives found on the gang, the gruesome Morgue photos, and the barrel itself. Scholer sent the twelve German jurors into the deliberation room and told them not to come out until they had reached a decision. It had been two hours since, and Petrosino had grown anxious waiting at the Criminal Courts Building. Schmittberger found him at the back entrance, and they shared a few slugs from Schmittberger's hip flask.

"As of five o'clock," Schmittberger said, "I'm officially off suspension and on the job."

"How'd Jersey go?"

Max winked. "Did the ole train trick."

"You pinched Federica? In New York?"

"Damn right. Tracked her down waiting for a train in Jersey. I put on a conductor's cap and pointed at the northbound train and yelled, 'Next stop PATERSON! All aboard!' She and a few other folks looked confused, but they got on. Of course, the next stop was Suffern. So as soon as the train crosses into New York, I put the bracelets on her and she starts squawking."

"Did she talk?"

"Nope. She's a tougher walnut than her man Petto. But I got her on ice. How'd our witnesses do?"

"Almost fell apart like the Dewey Arch. Let's not loiter here waiting for the jury. I'll get dyspepsia. I want to collect my winnings anyhow. Remember?" Petrosino took out his betting stub. "The Senators licked our Highlanders 7 to 2."

"I saw. The sports pages are calling the Highlanders a bunch of damn Yankees. Hell, that Bimbo could pitch better than Chesbro. Why'd we bet both ways on that game?"

"You'll see."

On the way to the gambling parlor next to Snigglefritz's Saloon, Petrosino explained what had happened at the Inquest and in the sweat box with the Rizzato brothers and *Don* Vito Cascio Ferro, and how Flynn must be a grafter for springing them from the Eldridge Precinct jail.

"I knew Flynn when he was on the Police Board," Schmittberger said, "and he never struck me as a Tammany man. Remember that house burglar stoolie I had in Satan's Circus? Boob Sidensheiner?"

"I liked Boob. Wasn't he a dwarf?"

"He crossed Flynn's path once. A rich family left their home in Gramercy for the summer, and Boob and his pal drove up a stevedore wagon and pretended they were movers. They picked the lock and started unloading the family's furniture. They had trouble with a big armoire, and Boob saw Flynn and a couple strawboaters coming along. He knew they were the law and was leery at first because he said Flynn looked as hard as the eye of a Customs House officer. But instead of acting shifty, Boob said, 'Could you lend a hand to a fellow Christian?' Flynn smiled, said something about Jesus, and directed his Secret Service men to help load the armoire. Boob said he made off with a fortune and had Jesus and The Law to thank for it..."

Petrosino laughed. "I wouldn't have pegged Flynn as a grafter either. But he must be."

When they made it to Mercer Street, they saw a dead horse on the side of the road beneath a lamppost. Its mottled grey legs were sprawled across crooked cobblestones, and its shoes were falling off in the gutter. Six little boys sat on the curb, dangling their feet in the brown puddled water, poking sticks at the carcass. One of the boys was leaning next to the horse's toothy head and comparing a marble to its opaque lifeless eyeball. A swarm of flies and mangy dogs gathered for their turn at the flesh. The sight put Petrosino in an even fouler mood.

"Look at them making a playground of that carcass. Already numb to death. Get away from that horse! Skedaddle!" Petrosino grabbed the slowest straggler by the collar. "Not you. You take this stub into that parlor there and bring me back the dough." Petrosino handed him the stub. "I'll give you a tip. Go on now."

The little boy's blackened hands snatched the stub, and he darted into the gambling parlor. He came back with a five-dollar certificate and four silver dollars. One buck had gone to the house for its rake. Petrosino bit each coin and flipped one to the boy who grinned and ran off. Petrosino moved under the lamppost and held the certificate up to the fuzzy globe.

"So?" Schmittberger said.

"This batch is top-notch, Max. It would fool most folks. And look, it's the National Iron Bank of Morristown."

"Same bank as before? The Morello gang's handiwork?"

Petrosino nodded. "Let's go see if Steffens is in his office. He'll want to hear this."

☙

Steffens paced in front of the tryptich of windows overlooking Washington Square Park as the moon glimmered. Tarbell and McAlpin watched intently as he recited a few lines from what must've been a draft article: "Tammany is bad government; not inefficient, but dishonest; not a party, not a delusion and a snare, hardly known by its party name – Democracy; having little standing in the national councils of the party and caring little for influence outside the City. Tammany is Tammany, the embodiment of corruption."

"You might want to say something like, *Hypocrisy is not a Tammany virtue*," Tarbell said, " *but rather Tammany proclaims its genuine intentions: Tammany is honestly dishonest.*'"

"*Honestly dishonest.*" Steffens paused to jot it down. "I like that one, Minerva."

Petrosino and Schmittberger stood in the entrance and began clapping. The other three started from their chairs, then grinned, beckoning them inside.

"Come in." Steffens adjusted his spectacles. "I was just working on my article, *New York: Good Government In Danger*. I thought you two would be in Court."

"No patience for waiting," Petrosino said. "But we found some things of great interest."

"Do tell, Detective?" Tarbell rose up and offered her hand, and Petrosino took it and handed her the five from the gambling parlor.

She looked at the bill. "This is bigger than my last book advance."

Petrosino smiled and said, "That's the money I won betting on a baseball game. It was paid off at one of Alderman Murphy's dives."

"I see. So, Mr. Schmittberger, you lost your money on those damn awful Yankees?"

"Why, Miss Tarbell, my ears are red from such salted language."

Steffens got up and looked at the bill. "What of it?"

"The five is counterfeit. My original bet though was with good money."

"You mean the gambling houses are printing this stuff?"

"No, Steff. You remember you couldn't figure out why the Syndicate would use an Italian gang. Now we know. The Sicilians are experts at manufacturing counterfeit. They never had two coins to scratch together in the Old Country either, so it was a cinch for them to import it here. In fact, that's some of the best work I've ever seen."

"I see." Steffens took the note and sat down in his chair, examining it under the green shade of his desk lamp. "Remarkable.

You know, I haven't told you this, but we have records from government hearings where Alderman Murphy, Big Tim Sullivan, and the Liquor Dealers Association met with the city council about the Excise Laws. See, Murphy's getting protection at his establishments to not only sell liquor but also games of chance."

"And with the Sicilian gang, his Syndciate wins all the way around," Petrosino said. "First, they fix the odds in their favor. If you lose, they collect good money. If you win despite the house edge, they pay your original bet in good money and your winnings in bunco notes. And what gambler is gonna complain if they ever found out? That's what the Sicilian enforcers are for. It's a two-way profit scheme and a brilliant way to circulate the phony money."

"Then the gambling racket must be even more than the six millions I estimated before."

"Joe and I call it 'money laundry,'" Schmittberger said. "Washing out the bad with the good coming in. And we think they use the Italian gangs for a lot more than counterfeit. Like extorting protection money, collecting bad debts, and pushing a button on rivals to make 'em disappear. After all, who's better with a knife than an Italian? We even think they're using the Morello gang to get out the Italian vote. Tell 'em, Joe."

"Flynn came to the Eldridge Station with a bigshot Sicilian named *Don* Vito Cascio Ferro, and made me release two Sicilians who threatened me and a witness at the Inquest. I think the Secret Service could be getting a share of the spoils while they look the other way. Flynn said something about Italian poll watchers, and we all know there must be three hundred thousand Italians here from the Old Country. That's a lot of votes…"

"Well, I'll be Darwin's monkey!" Steffens shook his head. "So it was a federal law man then? That strait-laced, goo-goo Flynn is mixed up in this Syndicate?"

"He denied it of course," Petrosino said, "but it would explain how Morello's always gotten off scott-free from the federals. And remember the notes in Caesar Code? The Secret Service said the gang believed they were born leaders, *like Caesars*."

"So you think Flynn wrote them?"

"Or maybe he helped pass the info. And I think Cascio Ferro is an advisor to the gang, calls himself their Catholic 'godfather.' He looks like he could pull the strings of these ruffians."

"But do you have proof?" Tarbell asked. "If we were selling gossip for *The World*, we'd quote you anonymously. But *McClure's* is a serious magazine. Where's the evidence?"

"We've got the code and the counterfeit," Schmittberger said. "And whatever documents and government records you three have found. Hell, if we got Steff's pals in the Society for Prevention of Crime to send undercover Pinkertons into these parlors, we'd have a mountain."

The telephone rang and shook papers on Steffens' desk. "I have a man down at the Criminal Courts." Steffens lifted the earpiece to his cheek, held the candlestick stem. "Hello?"

Petrosino moved closer, but could only make out crackling on the other end.

"They're in." Steffens looked gravely around the room. He repeated what his man was saying, "Upon recommendation of the jury, the Coroner found that Benedetto Madonnia's death was done at the hands of a person or persons... *unknown* at this time."

"Curse the fishes."

"The Coroner also found that the crime of murder in the first degree was committed in violation of Section 1-8-3 of the Penal Code and that there's sufficient cause to believe the following are guilty of being accessories thereto... Tomasso alias Luciano 'The Ox' Petto, Giuseppe 'The Clutch Hand' Morello, Pietro Inzerillo proprietor of the Star of Italy café, and Vito Laduca. Defendants shall be held to await the action of the grand jury and committed to the city prison on ten thousand dollars bail each, except for Petto who shall be held without bail."

"Hot damn!" Schmittberger said, shaking Petrosino's hand.

"Hold on," Steffens whispered, then spoke into the phone. "Come again? What the devil are they going to do about it? All right, yes. Ring me if you hear more."

Steffens hung up the earpiece and sighed deeply.

"What is it? Spill it." Petrosino tugged on Steffens' sleeve.

"Some lawyer and a kid came up, like an altar boy at Communion, and gave the Coroner a cloth wrapped around an enormous wad of bills. Morello made his ten thousand dollar bail *in cash*. Scholer was set to release him, but then the Secret Service showed up with a federal warrant to take custody of Morello on counterfeiting charges."

"You think that's a ruse, Joe?" Schmittberger said.

Petrosino stared vacantly, digesting it all. "I don't know. Maybe Flynn's on the square after all. If Morello posted bail on the state charges, why would Flynn pinch him for federal ones? If Flynn were crooked, he'd just let Morello fly the coop. That's the wise play."

Steffens' telephone jangled again, and, this time, everyone froze in silence. On the third ring, Tarbell plucked up the phone and spoke calmly, "Yes, go ahead." She listened intently to the buzzing voice on the line, her eyes wide. She said nothing and hung up, turning to the men.

"Detectives, get to the Tombs fast. They say the prisoner who says he's Petto, he isn't Petto at all. Some kind of switch?"

"Son of a..." Schmittberger grabbed Petrosino's arm and pulled him to the door. "Let's go see what in the name of the Seven Sunderland Sisters happened."

❧

"Where the hell is The Whale?" Schmittberger asked a dozen Tombs keepers. "Don't play dumb or I'll lick every son of a bitch in the house. Now where's Sandy Piper?"

"He's as big as a shithouse," Petrosino said, "you couldn't miss him if you tried."

"He ain't here," one of the Tombs keepers mumbled.

"So a murderer switches out with a drunk ringer, and nobody saw a goddamn thing?"

"We don't know how it happened, Detective."

The prison keepers stood outside of a long communal cell, scratching their heads at one man snoring in the corner among twenty terrified sober prisoners. Petrosino shoved his way through and looked in at a burly drunk curled up like a newborn on the cell floor. The ringer wore Petto's clothes, using his yellow fedora as a pillow. He could pass for a brother of The Ox, but with less muscle and thinner lips compared to The Ox's rubbery, simian mouth.

"Wake up!" Petrosino shouted at the ringer. The drunk snorted and turned over, giving Petrosino his back. Petrosino turned to one of the keepers and told him to unlock the cell. He went inside, Schmittberger trailing him, and grabbed the drunk by the hair.

Petrosino said, "Who the hell are you?"

The drunk's eyes opened and trained the room foggily. He belched an intoxicating cloud of cinnamon and fermented molasses.

"I said, who are you!" Petrosino slapped his face. "Who told you to do this?"

"Howdy, Cap'n." The drunk smiled queerly and pinched Petrosino's cheek. "That was good rum, too. When can we have some more? Say, where's my dough?" The ringer's eyes rolled back and came down again. "I'm supposed to get a hundred bucks for every month I have to stay here. I been dreamin' about it."

"I'll give you something to dream about." Petrosino grabbed the man by his suspenders and slung him head first into the bars. His skull clanged against the metal, and he crumpled onto the jail floor. Petrosino toed the man aside. "What do we do, Max?"

"The *mafiosi* who bailed are scattered under the floorboards by now like roaches. We could roust the bail bondsmen at Biaggio Cassese's office, but they won't know squat. Wait." Schmittberger whispered in his ear, "*She* would know where The Ox is."

"I got an idea to make her talk, Max."

Schmittberger nodded and led them out of the Tombs as one of the keepers gave them an oily smirk. As if he knew they'd been tricked and he enjoyed it. Petrosino punched the wind out of his gut and shoved him in an ash barrel full of burnt tobacco and spittle.

"What was that for, Joe?"

"He didn't give us a proper salute."

"That gets my goat." Schmittberger donkey-kicked the barrel over on his way out.

Chapter 36

Vincenzo Saulino's back was folded over and withered like a branch burdened with the overripe fruit of his head. He muttered, "*Merda*," when he opened the door.

Petrosino said, "I need to see Adelina if you don't mind?" A lump formed in his throat. He was ashamed that he hadn't spoken to Vincenzo yet about what had happened, about his secret courtship of Adelina.

"I don't want her to see you, if *you* don't mind?" Vincenzo blocked the doorway of Saulino's Restaurant, guarding the empty tables and chairs sitting scattered and lonely between the lunch and dinner hour. Vincenzo liked to use eggplant dye to hide his six decades, but when he was angry or hot, purplish-black droplets would trickle from his scalp down his temples. He wiped them now and whispered, "Did you hear me? Go away."

"I need to see her. We have this woman at Headquarters, she's a tough walnut to crack, and I need Adelina's help." Petrosino held his hands out. "It's important-"

"You've got some balls coming here."

"I never meant any disrespect." Petrosino pushed on the door, but Vincenzo held his ground. "Can we talk about this inside?"

"You louse. Do you even know what happened? A man came looking for Adelina because of you. Now leave us alone."

"What? Who?"

"It's a good thing I keep a *lupara* under the counter." Vincenzo wiped black sweat from his brow and mimicked holding a shotgun. "And where were you? Nowhere to be found. *You* put her in danger, and now you need *her* help? To hell with your police business."

Petrosino pushed the door open harder and stepped inside the restaurant. He whispered, "Please, I didn't know. What happened?"

"Last night, when I was closing, I turn around, and there's a big man standing right here. He had a hat pulled low and a bandana over his face, and he asked after Adelina. You wanna know what he called her? 'Parsley's woman.' Where is she, he asked me. I took out my shotgun and told him to go to hell or I'd send him there myself. The scum laughed and said he'd come back. Thank the Saints he left, because I don't know if I could've shot him. I didn't tell Adelina what he said, and I'll put a hex on you if you do."

"What did he look like? Was it one of the ones mixed up with the Morello gang?"

"I don't know, but do you see why I don't want you here?" Vincenzo shook his head and sat at one of the empty tables. His chalky face suddenly looked a hundred years old, staring at his shaking hands. "You ask me what the man looked like? Not if my daughter is all right?"

Petrosino bit his own lip. "Where is she? Did something happen-"

"She's fine, no thanks to you. She went to your place last night after the man came, but you weren't there. I'm asking you as her father, leave my child be. Please."

"Damn it, Vincenzo, why didn't you tell me? Why didn't anyone call for the police?"

"Sure, we'll whistle for the cops. Because I need them like I need the plague. What's the matter with you, Joe? You been a cop so long you forgot how things work in the Ghetto?" Vincenzo stopped looking at his hands and stared up at Petrosino. "This man, he was like death himself. His eyes had no soul. And you think he's afraid of the police? He's not even afraid of you, goddamn it. Just leave us be."

Petrosino put his hand on a chair to steady himself. He wondered if it were Petto. Footsteps clipped quickly and angrily down a stairwell in the back. Adelina appeared with a hesitant smile that seemed to fade the closer she got.

"Are you all right," Petrosino asked, holding out his arms to her. He wanted to embrace her, but Vincenzo's trembling hands reached out for Adelina. She hugged her father.

"I'm fine, Joe. It was nothing. Probably someone looking for the cash box at the end of the night. Papa, what did you tell him?"

"The truth. Just like a cop, he's never around when you need them."

Adelina turned to Petrosino. "It's nothing, I'm sure. Did you come to see me?"

"Yes," Petrosino said. "I was going to ask you to help me. It's about this gang, maybe it has something to do with the man who came here last night. I don't know." Petrosino paused, wondering if he should just let her be. He'd caused enough grief as it was, but still he couldn't help wanting to find Petto even more now. The thought of a gangster stalking Adelina made him sick with rage. "Petto escaped from jail. It could've been him."

"He came for *me*?" Adelina asked. "Because of *us*?"

"*Porco Dio*!" Vincenzo stood up and squeezed her hand. "I don't want you mixed up in this mafia business, Adelina. No good will come of it. You listen to me, I'm your father."

"Papa, I'm not a child. I want to hear him out. What do you want me to do, Joe?"

Petrosino looked at the black beads of hair dye clinging like a rosary on Vincenzo's forehead. "Your father's right. This was a mistake-"

"Joe, I'll help you." She let go of her father and grasped Petrosino's hand tightly. "I don't want those bastards coming back here either."

Petrosino nodded and glanced at Vincenzo. "I promise I won't let anything happen to her. I'll do right by you."

"Save your promises, they mean nothing to me. You two do whatever you please. Get yourselves killed." Vincenzo pulled up his trousers and made his way to the stairs.

"I love you," Petrosino whispered to Adelina. "You'll have to change clothes."

☙

Adelina wore her best Sunday dress, a huge hat festooned in silk flowers, and a lace parasol. In the interrogation room in the Eldridge Street Station, she sat on one side of a long table, legs crossed in her fine yellow dress, doting on two boys who played with a new spinning top on the floor. For a dime each, Schmittberger had recruited the boys from the ugliest newsies he could find. One was seven, and the other was only five but had a stocky build. Both were keeping their mouths shut and playing along, just as they'd been coached. A pitcher of lemonade, caramel candies, and cookies sat on trays on the table. The boys had already torn through half the sweets, and wrappers and crumbs littered the room.

An empty chair waited at the other end of the table.

Petrosino poked his head in the room and nodded at Adelina. She nodded back at him.

Petrosino led Federica into the room as the boys kept chasing the spinning top. Adelina made a stern face when she saw Federica, who looked back at Petrosino with a confused frown. Petrosino sat Federica down in the empty chair. She looked ragged, weary from all the questions, but she kept a stony façade. She watched the boys, and her frown dwindled. She clapped at the boys and smiled at them, but they ignored her.

"You don't know who they are, do you?" Petrosino said, putting his hands on his hips, shaking his head sympathetically. "That bastard…"

"What do you mean?" Federica asked, eyeing Adelina now, examining her fancy dress and her parasol. "Who are they?"

"You probably made the silk flowers on her hat," Petrosino said to Federica. "Are you gonna tell me where he is? Because I don't think he loves you like he said, my dear. He's no good, I tell you. Rotten as the devil himself to do something as low as this to you."

Federica snapped her head at Petrosino, then back to Adelina and the boys on the floor.

"You told me you loved him," Petrosino said, "and that you'd die before you gave him up to a lousy copper like me. Right? Well, I'm here to tell you, my dear sweet girl, I don't think he loved you very much. No, in fact, I don't think he loved you at all."

Federica started shaking with anger. Petrosino could see the malevolent cloud of jealousy pass over her face and blacken her stare. Federica hissed, "Who's this woman?"

"I didn't want to tell you, because I see how much your heart breaks for him. He did you dirty. He lied to you."

Federica leaned over the table, clawing her hands in the wood. "Who is she?"

Petrosino waved the younger boy over and lifted him up, groaning at the weight of him. "Look at this one's face. His shoulders. My God, he's built ike a Brahma bull, Federica."

She looked at the boy, and a panicked smile quivered on her lips. Her nails gouged deeper into the table. "He does look just like him, doesn't he?"

"This is Eugenio." Petrosino put the boy back down. "He named him after Eugen Sandow, the strongman. And the older one, well that's Junior. *Luciano*, Jr."

"Luciano?" Federica whispered.

Petrosino nodded at Adelina for her cue. She looked down her nose at Federica, brushing a crumb of cake from her dress, and asked in a haughty voice, "Detective Petrosino, who is this dreadful troll of a girl?"

Petrosino could feel the table vibrating now as Federica quaked. He said to Adelina, "Why, *Signora* Petto, this girl claims to know your *husband-*"

"YOU BITCH!" Federica shrieked as she leapt across the table. But Petrosino had her by the hair, and Adelina threw a quick slap, fattening Federica's lip.

"Mrs. Petto," Max said, appearing in the room. "Come outside, I'm sorry about this." He held his long arm out, guiding Adelina and the two newsies out of the room. The smaller boy swiped cookies off the table and stuffed them in his pockets, disappearing in a trail of sugar.

The door slammed and locked from the other side. Petrosino could see Schmittberger's face pressed in the viewhole. Petrosino and Federica stood alone in shock. Hers real. She mumbled, "They looked just like my dear Ox. Big and handsome." Then she quivered like jelly, weeping in Petrosino's arms, muttering, "That bastard, how could he?"

Petrosino patted her back, making cooing noises until the waterworks dried up, and she firmly pulled away from him.

"All right then," she said, snarling with a vicious gleam in her eye, "I'll tell you everything I know about that two-timing blackhearted bastard."

Chapter 37

"He's what they call a slugger, a button man," Federica said, sitting at the interrogation table across from Petrosino and Schmittberger.

"Your English is just swell now that the jig is up, huh?" Schmittberger said.

"Yeah." The color had drained from her round face, and her cheeks sunk with heartbreak and exhaustion. "They say he's the best in New York. Everyone's afraid of him, even across to Chicago and down New Orleans. If the boss wants someone put out of the way, he pushes the 'button,' and my Ox takes care of it."

"Takes care of it?" Petrosino said. "You mean *kills*."

"Depends. Sometimes, I suppose. I'm sure whoever got it, had it coming." She wiped a tear from her red eyes. Still defending her man, Petrosino thought. "It's not like my sweet Ox is a bloodthirsty man. He's just bigger and stronger than everyone else, you see? So it came natural that he could do that line of work."

"Did you think Benedetto Madonnia had it coming?"

"I don't really know about that business. Maybe he did."

"Did your sweet Ox kill Madonnia?"

"I don't know. They wouldn't tell a woman such a thing."

"Sure, because your sensibilities are so dainty, huh? Did you hear about a money squabble in the gang? That Madonnia was the brother-in-law of another *mafioso* in Sing Sing named De Priemo, and Madonnia wanted his brother's share of some loot?"

"That must've been why." She nodded vigorously, too vigorously for Petrosino's taste.

Petrosino asked, "Who's the *boss* that would push the 'button' on a man?"

"Little Finger." Federica made a gesture with her hand. A claw.

"The Clutch Hand? Morello?"

She shrugged. "I only know him as Little Finger. He scares the hell out of me."

Petrosino slammed his fist on the table. "Don't feed us chickenshit! We know your sister was running with him. That bastard baby she's got is probably his spawn. So don't go halfway. You go all the way with us or you get mashed like everyone else."

"You'd hit a lady, too, wouldn't you, you bastard?"

"Not without taking my brass knuckles off first!"

"Okay, don't yell. Everyone knows he's the *capo*. It's the *Morello* gang, ain't it?"

"Yeah, it is. But I wanna hear you say it. So how did you meet Petto?"

"Through my sister, Marie. She goes with Little Finger, like you said, and my Ox is Little Finger's bodyguard. We ran into each other all the time, and he said how much he liked my hair. He would say it all the time. I like to wear a lot of silver combs." She preened the sloping bird's nest on her head. "It looks awful now, but I have pretty hair. I do."

"What's his real name? It' not *Tomasso*, is it?"

"I don't know what's real anymore. He told me he didn't have a wife and kids, that he only wanted me. So how do I know what's *real*? All of you men are pigs. That's real."

"Yes, we are, from the snout to the tenderloins," Schmittberger said, "but what did he tell you his name was?"

Petrosino tried not to smile. Federica was drowning in a lovesick puddle, after all.

"He said his name was Luciano Petto. I knew he was from Corleone. They all are. He said when he made enough coin working for them he'd take me away. We'd run off and get married, and he'd do his own carnival shows."

"Where would he go if he was on the lam?" Schmittberger asked.

Her eyebrows arched up, and a hopeful smile curled her lips. "He got away then?"

Schmittberger glanced over at Petrosino and sighed. "Yes, my dear. But I should tell you that he sent a coded message to his wife that he'd be coming for her and the boys soon."

"With steamship tickets back to the Old Country," Petrosino added with a nudge.

"And he didn't mention you once."

"That bastard, he's going to take that witch instead of me?" Her eyebrows sunk, and her smile grew teeth. "Sure I know where he'd go hide. He always said that, at the first sign of trouble, he'd go to Pittston. He used to work in the mines there in Pennsylvania. He said he's got a place in the woods where no one could ever find him. Or dare try. He told me one time, after he said how much he loved me. Pfft! He said, if I needed him, to write to the Pittston Post Office, special delivery to Luca Perrino. And my message would find him."

Petrosino and Schmittberger gave each other poker glances, not wanting to give away their glee over the flush hand she just dealt them. Petrosino wrote down the alias, Luca Perrino, and the details of Petto's hideout in his butcher's book.

Schmittberger said, "Is there any other place he might go? Besides the mines?"

"I don't think so. You go to Pittston and see for yourself. I bet you all the tea in China the two-timing bastard's there!"

"Did you visit him at the Tombs after he was arrested?"

She nodded, growing angrier. "The things I did for him, too! Do you know how a woman has to smuggle things inside a jail? It's no stroll in Central Park."

"The course of true love never runs smooth, does it, sister?" Schmittberger said, nudging Petrosino. "*Midsummer Night's Dream.*"

"What did you say?" Federica crossed her meaty arms.

"Nevermind that," Petrosino said. He imagined Federica making trips across the Bridge of Sighs, visiting Petto in the Tombs, and proclaiming her undying love while he passed her notes to have witnesses poisoned. Notes she likely hid in her crotch. "You said you hid things for him. When you visited the Tombs, did you help them pass information to the outside?"

"Am I going to be in trouble for this? I can't go to jail. I'll die in there."

"You'll go up the river for a long time. Unless you tell us everything. If you talk, the Inspector could fix it so they turn you loose. So spill. The gang passed notes, didn't they?"

She nodded, her fattened lip giving her a permanent pout.

"So you can read the code they use then?"

"No. My sister told me what was going on. There was a guard at the Tombs who knew the gang. From before. I don't know how."

"What's his name?"

"I don't know, I never met him. You think they'd tell me? Besides, they pay off turnkeys all the time. Cops, too." She smirked at Schmittberger. "Or didn't you know that?"

"Watch yourself, butterbean," Schmittberger said, his eyes boring through her.

"The Fox is one of those cops you're talking about," Petrosino said, "isn't he?"

Her eyes froze, glued between her eyelids. "Who?"

"The Fox. He's a cop, isn't he? Someone with police pull, mixed up with the gang?"

Schmittberger grabbed her hand before she answered. "Don't you lie, butterbean. I can see the wheels of deception spinning in your eyes. Not one damn lie or you'll be doing hard labor till your nice pretty hair is old and grey and falling out of your little head."

She nervously tucked a skein of hair behind her ear. "He used to work at a Turkish bath."

"Who? The Fox?"

"No. My man. Luciano. When he came to New York, he wasn't making any coin at first. He did physical culture shows at Coney Island, but they were only once or twice a month. So he made extra money as a rubber."

Petrosino and Schmittberger looked at each other. "Where? Which bathhouse?"

"Different ones on the East Side. I don't know." Her head shrunk back into her body. She looked down at her lap, trembling. "I can't say it. You'll say it's horrible."

"What do you mean? Which bathhouse was it?"

"I don't know! It doesn't matter." She put her head in her hands, pulling at her hair.

"Listen, woman," Petrosino said, thinking of ways to harness her anger, "you've got more trouble coming and it's not just from us and the law."

She peeked up from her lap. "How do you mean?"

"His wife wants to prefer charges against you. Oh, don't look so surprised. She's a decent woman. You know what she called you? 'A bilge-sucking whore that makes Scotch Ann look like the Virgin Mother.'"

"What! She thinks she's better than me, does she, with her fancy clothes? I didn't do anything to that evil bitch! What's she got against me? What charges?"

"Alienation of affection and adultery. She said she's gonna fix it so that you never see him again. She said you ought to be burned at the stake like the *strega* you are."

"Let her try it!" Federica hammered her fist down on the table. A tuft of her own hair was in her fist, ripped from her scalp. "Then I'll tell everyone that her husband likes men, too!"

Petrosino stared straight ahead at her, not wanting to turn and see the look on Max's face.

A teakettle whistle escaped Schmittberger's mouth.

"So your great big man, The Almighty Ox, is a boylover?" Schmittberger said.

"Go to hell. It wasn't like that. You don't know a thing about him. He's a good sweet-"

"Shut up and listen," Petrosino said. "It doesn't matter if he was raping chickens. I asked you who The Fox was, and you're going on and on about a bathhouse and your man's cocksucking ways. Your man met The Fox in a bathhouse, didn't he? He was his rubber. SAY IT GODDAMN IT!"

"YES!" she hissed, clawing at her head again.

"Why was The Fox mixed up in the gang? And what's his real name?"

"I don't know. I never knew."

"What did he look like?"

"He said it was a man with a beard the color of a fox. That's why he called him *Barbarossa*, too. No one else called him that. He said he was crafty like a fox, too." She tore at her head again, wildly tossing black shafts of hair on the table. "Look what you made me do now. They're gonna kill me, you bastards!"

Petrosino dashed around the table and snatched her flailing arms, clamping her wrists back to her shoulders. "He was behind the the barrel murder, wasn't he? This cop? That's why Benedetto Madonnia was killed! It was more than a squabble over gang money, wasn't it?"

"ANSWER HIM!" Schmittberger roared.

"I don't know!" Federica screeched.

Petrosino slapped her face back and forth, as hard as he could. Her fat lips were bleeding, and she laughed insanely. "He liked it rough, too!"

"Answer me, woman! Why did they put Madonnia in the barrel?"

"You want to fuck me, don't you? Here!" She kept cackling and tried to pull up her petticoats. "I'll fuck you both, right here on the table. Do it, you limp-dick bastards!"

Petrosino held her wrists behind her back, holding her down, and shouted in her face, "WHY DID MADONNIA DIE?"

"BECAUSE HE WAS GONNA SQUEAL TO THE POLICE ABOUT THE FOX!"

Chapter 38

Black tumbleweed clouds rolled across the horizon. Petrosino and Schmittberger could see their breath as they strode to the Deputy's lair at the Lafayette Hotel. Petrosino felt like he might vomit. He and Schmittberger didn't want to believe it, but they knew that Federica had told the truth.

Sandy "The Whale" Piper was outside the Hotel, tilted against a lamppost, gobbling vivid green jelly candy from a brown bag. Almost as if he were waiting for them, knowing they were coming. His pudgy face had lost its dim smile, replaced by a hardened smirk in the pink taffy of his skin. Two men were standing behind him, grey marionettes in overcoats. They looked like washed-up Pinkertons. Before Petrosino said a word, The Whale winked a pink eyelid and motioned him inside the Hotel. Petrosino and Schmittberger glanced at the overcoats and then each other.

"Shouldn't you be at the Tombs playing with keys?" Petrosino said to The Whale.

"My day's ended."

"Who are these turnips with the pretty coats?"

"Private guards for my uncle. Isn't he a public figure, the Deputy Commissioner, and shouldn't he have them like everyone else? Only the City's too tight to pay, shame on them."

"They can wait outside."

"No, it's all right, Joe. The bigger the audience, the better." Schmittberger waved at a hulking shadow crossing the street toward them.

Bimbo Martino in his bluecoat, waving his billy as a greeting.

"Inspector, sir," Bimbo said, out of breath. "I came as fast as I could-"

Schmittberger said, "Nevermind the apology. Come join the party."

The Whale looked Bimbo up and down, and Petrosino could see that he was sizing him up. The Whale looked a little irritated.

"What's the matter, chubby?" Schmittberger said. "There's three of us, and three of you. We can play cards after. Joe likes a Dago game called *scopa*, but I'm a poker man myself, play a little *skat*, too. Now why don't we scat inside and see your uncle?"

The six of them went inside the hotel, eyes constantly watching each other, passing a bellboy, and into a private parlor in the restaurant. Deputy Commissioner Duff Piper was sitting alone at a table, feeding tablescraps to a black Scottish terrier. He looked up at them and beamed through his tawny beard and shabby old suit.

"Good to see you, lads! Come have a seat." The codger cleaned his hands on his napkin and looked down into the tiny mirror in his top hat, wiping his mouth. "Well, what are you waiting for, lads? Sit. *Begorra*, look at the size of the greenhorn with you, too!" Piper eyed Bimbo and tapped a new walking stick against the side of the table. Petrosino noticed that it had an ivory figurehead on the cap, could have been a dog or a jackal. Or a fox.

Piper said, "You've both got faces longer than a cat's tail. What's the matter?"

"We did a little digging," Schmittberger said, "and found out that you and Dr. Dold from River Crest Sanitarium are both members of the The St. Andrew's Society. *Et tu, Brute?*"

"Me and about a thousand other Scots in the city. What of it?"

"You sold us a false bill. You used that lunatic to cover it up." Schmittberger crossed his arms and stood towering over Piper's table. "And one of my men said you've been running me down behind my back. You said, 'The Broom is a big dolt.' That I was being used like a stick, not to sweep up crooks, but to enforce the law against backsliders in your little Syndicate."

"Sit down." Piper smiled like a grandfather listening to a child's tale. He patted the chair next to him, but neither Schmittberger nor Petrosino moved. "I didn't say that, Max, not exactly. What I said was that you were a big dolt, but that I admired you. And that your Sergeant here is a little dolt whom I love, too. And I also said that I could beat the both of you at any game, crooked or straight, any time I pleased. That's what I said."

"You're a Republican, Duff. How could you throw your lot in with Tammany?" Max leaned forward, putting his palms on the dining table. The two overcoats hovered close by. "How could you goldbrick *me* like that? You introduced me to Sarah for shit's sake."

Petrosino held Schmittberger's shoulder and spoke up, "That rancid tub of lard you call a nephew over there, he was the one who put Primrose out of the way. It all tallies. He's the Deputy Keeper at the Tombs, he can pass notes in and out, and he can even have a man strangled and make it look like suicide. I bet if I get a handwriting expert like Bill Kinsley to look at Primrose's suicide note and the gang's Caesar Code, he'd say it was Sandy's penmanship here."

"Caesar which? You sound touched in the head. You've been reading your name in the papers too much, Joe, and now you think you're Sherlock Holmes." Piper put his terrier on his lap, stroked the dog gently, and looked up with wide enchanted eyes. "Keep going, lad. I love a good fable. Let me know when I'm supposed to be frightened, and I'll cover my eyes."

"You're The Fox," Petrosino said with a finger point. "I haven't figured out how you got to Vito Lobaido and poisoned him, but I know you're the third boss in the Syndicate. Benedetto Madonnia knew about you, and he was going to rat you out along with the Morello gang to the police. The *real* police. It would've destroyed you. So you made an example of him. You let the whole City know that only you could do the destroying, not the other way around. You put his manhood in his mouth to silence anyone else who might rat. It was a Sicilian message."

Piper smiled. "*Real* police. I'm as real as the sun, lads, I assure you. But I'll never get catched because if you get too close, you're liable to burn. And there's the difference betwixt-"

"We know your nephew turned Petto loose." Schmittberger thumbed at The Whale. "It couldn't be anyone else. We heard one of the bondsmen came in with a big stack of bills folded up in a hanky. So what in the name of the Seven Sutherland Sisters happened? Did Petto climb down their hair? Or did the gang give you and this fat pig extra 'sugar'?"

"Well, lad," Piper said, "you're the confessed grafter. Not I. And Petrosino's Italian. Maybe he knows how that Ox got out of The Tombs? They're all thick as thieves, Dagos."

"You met Petto in a Turkish bath," Petrosino said, "and that's how you recruited the gang for the Syndicate. You got your Whale here to switch Petto out of jail with a ringer, just when he got indicted for the barrel murder. Because you were *sweet* on him, weren't you?"

Petrosino watched Piper's eyes flicker. He'd struck his weak spot. No one else knew that Piper was a boylover, Petrosino thought. Why would they?

"Lads," Piper said, grinning and waving his walking stick at The Whale and the two guards, "would you step outside? Leave the Inspector and the Sergeant with me. It's all right."

"Uncle, I'm nay goin' nowhere. That Jew *clype* just called me a grafter." The Whale loosened the buttons on his tight-fitting uniform and rolled up his sleeves. He pointed at Petrosino and Schmittberger. "T'aint no filthy money here, boys. Why, we take it down to Chineetown and have it laundered after we get it. Ain't that right, Uncle?"

"No," Petrosino said, "that's why you threw your lot in with the Morello gang. It all tallies. For years, they've have been making counterfeit for Sicilian aristocrats who pass it off on peasants. They're the best at the job, so why not have them do it here? Your Syndicate takes in clean money from gambling houses and saloons, then you pay out with the Morello gang's counterfeit. That's how you do your *laundry*."

"Jings, that's a fine thing!" The Whale said. "Ye of all people calling *us* 'grafters'! Your Jew boss here was a bag man for Clubber

Williams in the Tenderloin, and we all know that yer a dirty little Dago yourself, ain't ye? A low-down, motherless, *clarty* lot of bog scum-"

Out of the corner of his eye, Petrosino saw a colossal fist slam into the billowing white cheek of The Whale. There was a cracking sound like a horsewhip in everyone's ears, and The Whale's face contorted with a rush of air escaping from his mouth. He toppled and rolled to the floor, his arm extended up to the ceiling, frozen in unconsciousness.

Bimbo stood, fist still clenched, hectoring over The Whale.

The puppets in overcoats reached for pistols, but Schmittberger already had his army issue Colt .45 pointed at them. Big as a fire poker. Petrosino slid sideways, hand on his .38.

Piper started laughing, and everyone slowly looked over at him. An old chuckling Santa Claus with a silvery red beard, shaking his head, giggling. "You're behaving like wee toddlers. Put the guns down, lads!" Piper clacked his walking stick on the floorboard, and his guards showed their hands and helped The Whale back to his unsteady feet.

Schmittberger put his .45 away.

"That was a helluva a right, lad," Piper said to Bimbo. "You could've licked John L. Sullivan with that one, I'll say." They all stared at each other for a moment and snickered at the truth of it. "It was the insult about *motherless* that got you, wasn't it? Did you lose your mum?"

Bimbo nodded. "Yes, sir. Scarlet fever."

"I'm sorry about that, lad. You Italians are all mama's boys, eh? It's quaint. Tell me, are you gonna knock out every man who calls you a Dago?"

"You're damn right I am. Sir."

"Well, you're gonna need a new set of hands every week then, and you're gonna have the shortest career in PD history if you don't wise up. This is an Irish world we live in. Even the Inspector and the Detective will vouch for that. You better learn to love potatoes, lad, and fast."

"Maybe," Petrosino said, "but you forget that America was discovered by an Italian."

"The fun's over, lads," Piper said. "You children go outside and let us adults have a word. Me and the Inspector and Detective Sergeant. Go on now."

Piper's guards each hefted an arm and helped The Whale out. Bimbo followed them.

❧

"Do you believe in God?" Piper asked.

Schmittberger and Petrosino hesitantly nodded.

"Well, see, that's where you've gone astray as policemen, lads. This isn't about right and wrong. It's a game, and the sooner you realize that, the sooner you might win."

"Duff," Schmittberger said, "you had a man butchered because of a crime racket. They cut off his cock and put it his mouth! And now you're in with Big Tim Sullivan to boot!"

"I've been in this game a long time, lads. Only on the losing end, and I've seen honest men with nothing to show for it. The rich fight over the fattest pieces of meat while the poor never even get a sniff of the bones. Does that seem fair to you?"

"Listen to yourself. Talking just like a goddamn Tammany man now."

"I certainly am not. I'm Republican to the end. But thanks to men like you, Reformers and Fusion Goo-Goos, we've all changed our ways. We're a bipartisan board now, and we all play along. Now we have the shrewdest Tammany *and* Republican men aboard, and Italians are 'getting out the vote' for *our* politickers. You must render unto Caesar what is Caesar's, lads."

"I loved you like my own uncle, Duff, I always did," Schmittberger said, sagging into a chair at the dinner table. "But if I can prove this, I'll put you down myself and throw dirt on your coffin. I'll even swallow my pride and go to McClusky if I have to."

"Chief Inspector McClusky despises you both now," Piper said. "I made sure of it. I couldn't lose either way with that gambit.

Either no one would notice, and Primrose would catch the charge, or you'd make a pig's ear of it, which you did by being 'honest,' and McClusky got egg on his face. No, lad, McClusky likes you very little and trusts you even less. The amusing thing about it is that he was trying his best to solve that murder, to build his stature as the Chief. And you crossed him from the start." Piper reached inside his jacket and took out a rolled-up document bound at the top. He pushed it on the table to Schmittberger. "Consider that service on you personally, Max. It's a Police Court complaint, something about insubordination, assaulting a citizen, intemperance, and other sundry derelictions of PD duty. It's got statements from the Chief and from a Detective Sergeant McCafferty against you. I held onto it because, as Deputy Commish, I'll be the judge at the misconduct hearing, and I want to give you a chance to redeem. But I think we're past that path in the rose garden, aren't we?"

"I knew this was coming, Duff. You'll have to do better than this. I won't chuck up the sponge easy. I've got lawyers that circle vultures to death, so you and McClusky can go to hell."

"And we've got the goods on you, Duff," Petrosino said, pounding his fist on the table.

Piper's terrier bolted from Piper's lap and disappeared.

"Do you? I've done nothing. What have you really got, lads? Think it through. You two are going to make a report against the Deputy Commissioner of the PD? For what? You'll say I'm some kingpin named 'The Fox'? And you'll make up some nonsense about Caesar Code and Italian counterfeiters and grafting from a crime ring? What kind of weight would your word have against me, a decorated veteran of the Union Army and PD, wounded in the line of duty? A *real* American. This city was made for me and *my* kind. You Jews and Italians are grist that comes through our mill. Lads, I like you both, but you'd ruin yourselves."

"But what we're saying is true, and you *know* it."

"No, I don't, Inspector. I'm the Deputy and I swore an oath to do my job." Piper looked into his hat on the table, admiring himself in the mirror. "This is the truth I see, the way I figure the barrel murder case. You, Max, went back to your old grafting ways. You took Big Bill Devery's place in this so-called Syndicate. I'll have proof of it, too. Down the line, someone will find a stack of dirty money, maybe in your desk at Eldridge Street or in your wife's coal bin or even Max Jr.'s toy chest. It won't matter. Once a rotten cop, always a rotten cop. The good folks of this city know you from Lexow as the squealing crooked cop, and they'll have your head on a pike this time. T.R.'s gone, and not even Lincoln Steffens will save you."

Petrosino turned and looked at Schmittberger. Max's bristly moustache sagged into a despairing frown, and wrinkles gouged his forehead, making him look ancient.

Piper continued, "But this time, Max, you brought in your chum, Petrosino. He's I-talian, and, of course, like all I-talians, he has an evil, lying bloodthirsty streak in him. He can't help himself, nay, it's Eugenics. So he's the one who got mixed up with the Morello gang, he's the one that wrote notes in code or Italian or whatever gibberish it was, and he's the reason Petto's escaped and poor Madonnia's dead. See, Madonnia was going to expose the two of you."

Petrosino's veins boiled as he poked Piper in the chest. "You're worse than the goddamn devil himself. You're no cop. You don't even deserve to wear a White Wing's uniform-"

"There's that Italian temper again. This isn't personal, Joe. It's a game."

"It got personal when they threatened me and my woman. That Vito Cascio Ferro and his thugs. Is he your *godfather*, too? Is that how you got the Secret Service to turn a blind eye?"

"High stakes, lad, high stakes. Maybe he's the fox among us hens? Imagine if the *mafia* had a charismatic leader and if he 'unionized' the crooks in the lingo of the socialist labor movement. That would create a gang of Italians that could hush up any man in a minute. What did I tell you before? That I could beat you at any game, straight or crooked, underground, overhead, or on the level. Which I could and did. Get me? I said back of your back and I'll repeat it in front of your face – you two ain't going nowhere unless you bend to what we want."

"The hell you say." Schmittberger stood up, wringing his fedora in his hands. "We'll go to the Mayor if we have to, Duff."

"The elections are nigh upon us, and Mayor Seth Low will be gone soon. We've handpicked our candidate. General McClellan's son, George Jr., is running as a 10-9 favorite over Low. You'll like Georgie Jr., he's a Princeton man, speaks I-talian. Doesn't know a damn thing about *the game* though, which is why we like him. And Junior's already told the press that, if he's elected, he won't continue General Greene as Commissioner. Hell, he may not keep anyone in office: commissioners, captains, or even a certain *Inspector* and *Detective Sergeant* of the Central Bureau. We'll tell him who to keep and who to send to the sticks."

"You're a real cocksucker, Duff. I mean that sincerely."

"That's the spirit, Max. That's putting ginger and Tabasco in you!"

"You're gonna lose this fight, I promise you that."

"No, we'll win, and it will be a credit to the Reformers. You taught us that the last system didn't work. All the matter with police business was that it was mismanaged, too democratic, every cop in on it somehow. We fixed it, concentrated it so only a few are in charge now. The system's cinched up so squealers like you, Max, won't even know there's anything to squeal at."

Petrosino studied Piper in the candlelight. If the old codger had a conscience, it had given up the ghost a long time ago. There was nothing but a smile beneath his red beard, light and airy, as if he were laughing at saloon jokes.

"So what's it gonna be, lads? Bend like limber trees until the storm passes. That's all we ask of you. It's the smart play."

Schmittberger heaved an enormous sigh, nearly blowing out the candle on Piper's flickering dinner table. Petrosino looked at his friend, and they mulled it over with their eyes. Petrosino could feel the rage churning inside of him, and he recognized it in Max, too.

Piper laid a cigar on an ivory ashtray, the smoke dancing in his smiling eyes, waiting.

"Well," Petrosino said, "I guess we'll go after every crook in the game, one by one."

"You will, will you? You're a chessmaster then? Start with the pawns first?"

"No, we'll start with your *queen*. We'll find your precious Ox and bring back his head."

"We'll get you, Duff," Schmittberger said.

"Not till I've got you first, lads."

Chapter 39

"He's right, you know," Schmittberger whispered into the chill of night as they walked north on the Bowery. "They'll massacre us if we go against him with what little evidence we got. He's dangerous, Joe, and cagey. 'The Fox' was the right name for that fucking turncoat."

"And you were right about Tammany coming back on us," Petrosino said. "You'll never let me hear the end of it now, will you?"

"Nope. Hell is empty, and the devils are here."

"Let's even the score. What if I went to the mines in Pittston?"

"Like when you went to Jersey before the Pan-American Expo?"

Petrosino nodded, thinking of the weeks he had spent undercover in immigrant mining camps in 1901, breaking his back over a pick and shovel, spying on suspected anarchists. He'd told T.R., who was Vice President then, that he'd heard of an assassination plot against President McKinley. But McKinley brushed it off, saying that the anarchists were gunning for monarchs, not men elected in a free democracy. One month later, Leon Czolgosz walked up to McKinley at the Pan-Am Expo in Buffalo, pistol hidden under a handkerchief, and shot McKinley twice.

"No one listened to us then either," Petrosino said.

Schmittberger shook his head. "Pennsylvania is outside our bailiwick."

"We'll play the anarchist angle. They're worse now than they were then. There's Italian terrorists talking about setting off bombs on New York ships."

"I know you think you've got a roving commission, Joe, but you can't just set off without orders. Someone's gotta fend off McClusky."

"Max, if I get Petto, then we get two birds with one stone. He's the killing hand of the Morello gang and he's Piper's... I don't know what you call it... his paramour. We strike at the heart of the gang and the Deputy at the same time."

Schmittberger sighed, squeezing the Police Court complaint in his hand. "What the hell. I might as well detail you myself since I'm getting the boot. But I don't see how you can roam that far. The last time you were working with Federals."

"Now that everyone's treating the barrel murder as a lost cause, we have other cases, right? I'll send you my report that informants say Italian anarchists are plotting to bomb ships at port here, which is true. I know of talk that the steamship *Umbria* is a target. The word is that the anarchists are operating in the mines on the border of New York and Pennsylvania. So it only makes sense that you handpick me and Bimbo for the job."

"You want to go to Pittson with that rookie?" Schmittberger mulled it over. "I suppose a six-foot-five Jew would stick out in the mines like a naked gal with tits the size of honeydews?"

"I'll say. The kid's Italian, speaks the language, and I need the extra muscle. Remember the last time we pinched The Ox? If we find him, we'll say we pinched him in New York."

"You'll fib that you nabbed him in New York? You'll sign that affidavit?"

"I'm not signing it. That's what rookies are for."

"Once you cross those lines, Joe, they fade away. It's easier to cross 'em next time. Trust me, I know. And if we start a war with Piper and these Sicilians, it may never end."

"This isn't just about the barrel murder anymore. Sure, I want Petto to roast for it, but they came after me. And Adelina, too. One of them showed at Saulino's in a mask. I think Petto. Who knows what might've happened if her father didn't scare him off with a shotgun?"

"You didn't tell me about that. Maybe you're not thinking straight here."

"I want that bastard. You'd feel the same way if they threatened Sarah and the kids."

Schmittberger looked at a trio of Ghetto urchins sleeping on a stoop under flaps of burlap. He nodded. "You're right, I would feel the same way. This may be the last thing I do as a cop before Tammany gets me, so it might as well be for a lost cause. I'm in."

"You're real police, Max. And a true friend."

"Don't get blubbery, you little Dago. They haven't chucked us in the East River yet. Some have greatness thrust upon them, Joe. If that 'some' ain't me, it better be you."

Petrosino looked up at Max's blue eyes, wet from the chill in the air maybe, and he wondered if the Green Machine would push them both out of the PD. "What will you do?"

"Spend a lot of coin on shysters and fight to the end. We probably won't see much of each other, Joe, till the courts decide my fate." Max stopped outside a loud saloon and put his arm around him. "Just remember: '*Revenge should have no bounds.*' That's Hamlet."

༄

Two days later, Petrosino addressed a red envelope to Luca Perrino care of the Post Office in Pittston, Pennsylvania. Inside was the message he had written in Caesar Code:

WXWWR H VLFXUR. ULPDQHWH OD SHU RUD.

TUTTO È SICURO. RIMANETE LÀ PER ORA.

"*Everything is safe,*" Petrosino whispered to himself. "*Stay there for now.*"

Daylight was coming, but he hadn't been able to sleep all night. He played another Edison record, the "Overture to William Tell," while he packed mining gear in a rucksack with his .38 service revolver, a .22 Derringer, a .32 Colt he'd taken off a horse thief, two pairs of handcuffs, a leather sap, a knife, a canteen, beef jerky, and extra clothes. It had been two days since he'd seen soap, and his skin had begun to itch all over, but he couldn't bathe. He sat on his bed with a bottle of wine now that everything was in place. The dusky room grew brighter as he drank and stared out his window at the stars softening in the dense blue horizon. Footsteps began slithering on the walks and wagons purled over cobblestones and the clock chimed.

He put on coveralls, a flannel jacket, a slouch cap, a bandana, and the rucksack on his back. He nervously rubbed granules of stubble on his face as he checked the window and the stairwell before he made his way out. He slipped out the back door of his building and into the foot traffic. Bimbo was waiting for him on Spring Street, dressed as a pick-and-shovel man. A large carpetbag dangled from the kid's hand.

"What did you shave for?" Petrosino said.

"I forgot. Don't worry, Joe, the way my hair grows I'll have a beard by supper."

"I told you not to shave or bathe, damn it. You'll get yourself killed if you don't fit in." Petrosino frowned, feeling his chest tighten. "Here, keep this inside your jacket."

Petrosino slipped him the .32 pistol. Bimbo took it carefully into a pocket.

"You know the plan. Are you ready, kid? You're doing a man's job now."

Bimbo nodded, and Petrosino motioned for them to walk. He thought he'd be picturing how he was going to catch Petto, but Adelina was the only thing in his head. He circled around the block and stopped outside Saulino's. She was dumping trash into an ash barrel when he whistled her over. She squinted at first, then suddenly recognized him and smiled at his disguise.

She came closer, and the smile disappeared from her face. "Where are you going?"

Petrosino whispered to Bimbo, "Give us a minute. Go stick your hands in an ash can and rub soot on your face."

Bimbo nodded and walked away, glancing back at them.

She said, "You're going after him, aren't you? And you're using that boy to help you?"

He wanted to tell her that they had boys as young as six years old working in the mines, but that wasn't her point. He reached for her hand. "I'll be back in a day or two."

"Will you? Is this how it's going to be if we're together? I haven't seen you in days, and now you come to say good-bye with a face for a funeral."

Petrosino looked over her shoulder and saw Vincenzo's bent shadow in the front window. "That sounds like your pop talking. You know who I am. You know I have to do this."

"Why? What are you trying to prove?"

"They'll try to hurt you, Adelina. They won't stop."

"I don't want you to go. Do you want to be just like them with their vendettas?"

"No." Without thinking, Petrosino squeezed her hand too hard until she whimpered.

She pulled her hand loose. "Don't go."

"I have to. I'm afraid. Of Petto and the rest of them, too. I'm afraid they'll take you away and then I'll have nothing."

"After everything I told you… I told you I didn't want you to leave me, and now look what you're doing."

Petrosino caught Vincenzo's scowl in the window. "Damn him… Adelina, I'm not leaving you, you know that. This is just who I am."

"Whatever demons you have, get rid of them now. For me." She put her hand on his cheek. "I love you, Joe."

The first time she'd said it. He kissed her hand and let go of it.

"When I come back," he said, "I'll speak to your father."

છ

They took an omnibus to Grand Central Depot without saying a word, Petrosino trying not to think of her. The further away from the East Side they got, the more his head cleared. He and Bimbo had already confirmed the pick-up times for the mail and scouted which sub-station to use. Trains were whistling and churning, and people were scurrying on the platform in the cool morning air. He ambled up to the postal sub-station and handed the clerk the red envelope and some silver. "Registered mail, please," Petrosino said.

The clerk looked at the letter, handed it back. "You want a return address on it, case it comes back, Diego?"

Petrosino nodded, wrote down *226 Elizabeth Street, New York. The Star of Italy.*

"Why, you can write English. Bully for you." The clerk smirked, tossing the envelope in a mailbag marked 'PITTSTON.'

Petrosino lingered for a moment, dreaming of knocking the clerk's teeth out. He and Bimbo moved to the platform, next to the tracks. He heaved a great sigh while Bimbo paced nervously behind him like a hunting dog. Petrosino watched the kid's shadow and brooded over what Adelina had said. One thing struck a chord as soon as she'd said it. He *was* using the kid. Their train approached on the arc of metal. It took three minutes before it finally screeched to a stop in front of them, and men unloaded and loaded baggage and parcels.

"Ain't this the one to Pittston?" Bimbo asked.

"I don't think so. Next one." Petrosino pointed to a man holding a long stick stacked with bagels at the end of the platform. "Get some bagels to fill our stomachs on the train."

Bimbo looked confused, like a child struggling over a puzzle, but he walked reluctantly toward the pushcart. Petrosino feigned indifference and looked at the ornate bustle of a beautiful woman passing by. Then he quickly looked back to see Bimbo moving far enough away. Petrosino stood at the steps of one car, watching as the mailbags from the postal sub-station were loaded on board, one-by-one. The conductor made the last call, "ALL ABOARD!" A whistle sounded, a couple ran past him onto the train, and Petrosino took a deep breath and slipped on behind them. He looked out the window, trying to find Bimbo's face, whispering to himself, "It's for your own good, kid."

A shadow lurched in front of him, hanging from a leather strap, smelling of sweat and enthusiasm. Bimbo smiled and gave him a bagel. "I saw you get on. This was our train, wasn't it? Good thing I'm fast, huh, boss? Like circling the bases at the Polo Grounds."

"Yeah, kid, good thing." Petrosino shook his head, tearing his warm bagel in half.

They rode on the train carrying the mailbag with the red envelope on its way to The Ox.

Chapter 40

The Laurel Line Depot sat on a hill overlooking a billboard for Franco-American Soups and Grape Nuts and an array of rooftops that eventually gave way to the Susquehanna's grey snake of water. The mailbag was dumped on the station platform, and Petrosino stood by it, taking a deep breath of the sulphur wafting from the coal collieries. He surveyed chimneys and church spires below, the nearly empty dirt streets, the slow trolley cars, a swath of mills closer to the river, and the undulating shadows of the Poconos. It was colder than New York, and there were few people in town except what miners called "tenderfoots."

He and Bimbo paced near the mailbag, pretending to be lost, anxiously checking a clock above the ticket office. A mail wagon clattered up next to the platform, and an adolescent kid set down his horsewhip and hopped off. As the kid chucked the mailbag into the wagon, Petrosino summoned up the thick Italian accent he once had as a child and asked for a ride into town. He flashed a piece of silver, and the kid grinned and told him and Bimbo to hop in, next to the mailbag and loose parcels.

As the wagon rumbled downhill through town, Petrosino took in Pittston with one hand on the mailbag. They rolled by telegraph poles, school buildings, a stone watchtower, and a handful of elegant Victorian homes that must have belonged to coal bosses. There were small shops and businesses and the Flatiron Building on Main Street, which was even more narrow than the Fuller Building in Manhattan, but not as tall.

When the wagon stopped outside the small Post Office, Petrosino crawled out with his rucksack, and Bimbo carried the mailbag for the boy. They passed a drunk on the steps, asking for a loan to sharpen his mining tools. Inside, the boy took custody of the mailbag with an officious wave of his hand, lugging it to a thin postal clerk behind the counter. The clerk leveled his banker's visor and sorted speedily through the letters, slotting them in different cubbyholes. He raised an eyebrow at the red envelope, then tucked it into a cubby designated, *Registered*. Petrosino and Bimbo sat on the waiting bench, and the clerk asked if they needed help. Petrosino said a few words in broken English about a steamship from Italy and waiting for a cousin. With a blasé nod, the clerk disregarded them.

This was always the tedious part of a shadow job. The waiting. Petrosino watched as Bimbo took out a new brown leather baseball with black stitches. He was practicing different grips. Though the kid had square features and a thick shadow of facial hair, he stilled looked green. It was in the eyes. They weren't clouded with age and defeat yet. Crystal clear and twinkling.

"You nervous?" Petrosino said in Italian. Bimbo shook his head, trying to master a three-finger grip on the ball. "You sure you don't wanna play for the Trolleydodgers instead?"

"Nope. But I wonder if the boys play though? Do *we* have a team?"

"No, but we have a marching band. Perfect for a young virgin rookie like you."

Bimbo stopped gripping the baseball and held it in front of his heart like a tit. He grinned. "You kidding? I grew up in the Ghetto, remember?"

"When was the first time you had cunny?"

"When I was twelve. On the rooftop where my mom used to work."

"Jesus, twelve? You're joking. No, you're not." Petrosino hunched over the bench with a newfound respect for the kid. It reminded him of how he discovered the great mysteries of sex. In dark stairwells and rooftops at night. The rites of passage on the East Side. "When I was twelve, I couldn't even talk to a girl without blushing. I was so shy, when I turned sixteen, my pop took me to a swank bordello. He must've saved up for it, now that I think about it."

Bimbo looked at Petrosino. "What was it like having an old man?"

Petrosino patted the boy's knee. "It was good when I was younger. The older you get, the more bitter things taste. But I'll never forget the time he took me to the Tenderloin. I had read about a red-haired damsel in a book, and I kept insisting on it, even though my father said red hair was bad luck. *Malpello.* But he gave in and took me to the place, and there was this big woman with pretty red hair and soft skin and breasts the size of cannons.

"But the thing I remember most was this suave fellow in a White Wing suit, deciding which girl to pick, making them all giggle. I wanted to be like him. I mean, I also remember when I was alone with the redhead and having a hard time finding, you know, where to stick it. Afterwards, my father patted me on the back and asked how I liked it, and I told him I wanted to be a White Wing. He laughed his head off about that."

"Your papa sounds like a good man."

"He was," Petrosino said. Bimbo looked down at the floor, his expression lost in some memory he didn't share. "I should take you to a bordello sometime, get your little worm wet, kid. What do you say?"

Bimbo's face tilted up, grinning. "Sure, that'd be swell. But won't we get in hot water?"

"No, it'll be an undercover job. So to speak." They laughed.

"What's it like being the first Italian dick in the Bureau?"

"Watch what you're saying. We're in public." Petrosino looked around the Post Office. "I wasn't the first. I can think of at least two Italians before Roosevelt appointed me in 1895. Ben Tessaro and Antonio Perazzo. Perazzo died with his 'boots on,' which means while he was on the job. Both were murder men."

Bimbo whispered, "How do you investigate a murder? Is it easy to learn?"

"Sure, it's only two parts. First, establish a killing's been done, then hunt the killer."

Bimbo smiled. "You're teasing the greenhorn."

"The first step in solving a murder is the picture of the scene. You remember every clue and keep it in your noodle. Usually that's the best start a dick's got."

"You think I could be a murder man?"

"Stick with me, kid. I'll bring you up right. Now back to business."

Petrosino rested on his rucksack and quietly eyed the red envelope in the cubbyhole behind the postal clerk's counter. Petrosino pulled the slouch hat low over his forehead, just enough to shroud his vigil over the envelope, while Bimbo ate jerky and sipped from his canteen.

Townsfolk and miners came in and out all day, doing their business without so much as a blink at them. The benefit of looking like lost unkempt immigrants, Petrosino thought. He leaned back further on the bench and watched everyone. But no one claimed the red envelope. He began to wonder if his hunches were wrong, if the clues he had pieced together were for a different puzzle. Maybe Petto was nowhere near Pittston. Maybe Federica had made up the whole story about The Ox hiding out as "Luca Perrino" to throw them off the scent. The doubts gnawed at him as each hour passed, and his guilt over bringing Bimbo made it worse.

Near the end of the day, he began feeling his chin bobbing up and down, dancing with a tempting slumber. He gnawed on jerky and took small sips from Bimbo's canteen to revive himself, convinced that he was wasting his time.

Then a boy walked in and cracked something wise to the clerk. The clerk turned and drew out the red envelope from its cubbyhole.

 భ

The boy was no more than ten, but his face held the world-weariness of a sage. His nose and mouth were blackened from breathing coal dust, and he wore a sullied pair of denim overalls, thick work gloves in his back pocket, and a cap with an unlit gas torch on the bill. He bit off a wad of tobacco, stuffed it in his shirt pocket, and snapped two fingers at the postal clerk.

The clerk said, "Got any papers to identify you, young master?"

The boy snorted contemptuously, pulled out a crumpled piece of paper, and slapped it on the counter. The clerk looked at it and held open a book. The boy momentarily looked like a real child when his tongue lingered in the corner of his mouth as he signed. The clerk handed the red envelope to the boy, who shoved it inside his overalls with a cluster of other envelopes and papers. Petrosino conjured up the image of The Ox playing marbles with boys outside of Morello's tenement. The boy probably even wrote and decoded for him. It made sense.

Petrosino whispered in Italian to Bimbo, "This is it. You stay here."

"Why?" Bimbo sat up on the bench.

"You're not ready, kid. Besides, I need you to stay here to help me if and when we need to put him on the train. Don't argue."

Petrosino turned from Bimbo's pout and focused only on the soot-faced boy as his little legs scissored out the door. Petrosino followed him onto a trolley car, scanning the faces on board as the car lurched off. The boy sat by himself, staring out with a detached look. Petrosino sat nearby and paid little attention to anything else for a while. The trolley rolled further along the Susquehanna and away from town, and the landscape grew barren. There were fewer buildings, and those few turned into shanties and stores that were little more than rotting piles of lumber. After a long while, the only men left on the car, laborers young and old, hopped off the trolley. Petrosino followed them.

The air was thick with smoke, and the sulphur so strong that it seemed like a fire was burning everywhere. Ash floated in the sky, and the ground under Petrosino's feet was brown and rocky. Along the railroad tracks, the boy avoided puddles of silt and walked past a weatherbeaten building with the sign, *Stonehill Iron and Coal Company*. It advertised itself as a dry goods store, tool rental, sharpening shop, and bank rolled into one, but it looked deserted except for two chestnuts tied to the porch rails. Further on was a makeshift hospital and a rocky lane marked *Church Street*, where a whitewashed Roman Catholic church stood.

Then a sea of small shanties where the miners' families lived amid a strong smell of shit. The boy kept walking, past a haggard man at a stable beating a bony mule with a sprag. Petrosino didn't turn his head, eyes fixed on the boy's jean coveralls ahead. The sickening sounds of the mule's braying faded as they went around a bend and down into a valley streaked with large veins of coal.

There were deep holes cut into the valley with heavy wooden beams and splashes of paint denoting mine numbers and wagons pulled by goats on rail tracks. They passed several tunnels where soulless husks of men shambled about the Stygian desolation. All with the same dead eyes and black-sooted faces from scraping rock out of the earth's womb.

None paid the boy or Petrosino any attention.

More miners emerged from the tunnels, turning over their empty canteens, and shouting, "No water!" They joined a pilgrimage heading toward a massive breaker building carved into the side of a hill. Petrosino stayed close to the boy, mixing in unnoticed. A long line of men spilled out of the building onto the railroad tracks, where their women and children waited in their "best" clothes. Pay day, Petrosino thought.

He kept following the boy's scissoring legs, wondering where he was going with the red envelope as the sun descended in the ashen twilight. Out of the corner of his eye, Petrosino saw a trio of "coal and iron cops" on horseback. They weren't real policemen, only ruffians hired by the coal bosses to keep order when the drinking began. They would be no help to him.

Petrosino surveyed the enormous line from the paymaster's office on the front porch to the railroad tracks while the boy made his way to the front. As each paid miner came out of the office, he bitterly gave some coins to the boy. When nearly all the men had been paid and the singing and drinking began, the boy separated from the miners and ambled across the black dustbowl to a stand of woods a quarter mile away. Petrosino waited a few seconds and watched intently to mark the exact spot where the boy entered the woods. Then he made for the spot.

When Petrosino entered the woods, he looked back to see if anyone followed him, feeling as if he heard noises. The sun was almost gone as he weaved through the tree trunks and bramble, looking for any sign of the boy. He found a small pair of fresh tracks and pursued them. For nearly half an hour, he slipped deeper into the woods and the coming night until suddenly the tracks were gone.

He said a silent prayer to St. Anthony. Then he dropped his rucksack and spun in a circle until he noticed a patch of fallen branches. He kicked them aside and found an opening to a narrow footpath. The boy's tracks were turned over on themselves to rearrange the camouflage of branches. Petrosino crossed himself and followed the wending tracks again as crickets chirped in his ears. There was little sun left, and he realized that he had no torchlight. He plodded feverishly through the thickening bramble, sickened by the thought of losing the boy. And the red envelope. Where could he have gone? There was nothing out in these woods. The tree trunks slowly shrunk in size and number until he stood at the edge of a clearing.

A rustling in the woods, and Petrosino froze, digging in his rucksack for his .38 pistol. A rabbit darted past. He let out a relieved sigh and smelled fresh firewood burning. He quickly got off the footpath and crawled into the brush to conceal himself. The smoke came from a roof stovepipe on a small windowless cabin, like a trapper's lodge, tucked against a knoll.

He watched the cabin door for what seemed like an eternity, feeling the ground cooling beneath his belly. The door finally opened, and the little boy appeared. A thick arm tousled the boy's hair, then disappeared inside the cabin. The boy was counting coins as he entered the woods again. Tree branches shuffled ten yards from Petrosino. Then a short bowlegged man came out of the cabin and took a different path into the woods toward the mines.

Petrosino didn't move, listening to the growing calls of animals and insects. He imagined Petto was inside that cabin, opening up the red envelope and decoding the message:

EVERYTHING IS SAFE. STAY THERE FOR NOW.

If Petto bought it, Petrosino thought, he'd be off guard.

Smoke funneled from the stovepipe into the night, and light flickered above the cabin door where it hung unevenly in the frame. When the light went out, Petrosino waited another hour. Then he looked up at the moon hanging in the sky like a yellow skull and said a prayer before he rose up, clenching the gun.

Chapter 41

His mouth was dry as he approached the cabin. It was small, maybe twenty feet square with no windows. But now that he was closer, he saw a slit next to the door. Just wide enough to point a gun out and take a shot. He crouched low and circled the cabin. The front door was the only entry, and each wall had a gun slit. Petrosino crawled on his hands and knees to the rear of the cabin, pressed his ear against the knotted logs, but heard nothing.

He crawled through dirt and fireflies to the front and reached the crooked door. There was a keyhole, but he could only see splotches of shadow and light from what must have been the stove's fire. He put his ear against the iron keyhole and thought he heard deep breathing and a fire crackling. Curse the fishes, he said to himself. If only he had his nippers, he could pick the lock. But what if jiggling the lock woke the man inside? Or what if the occupant were a paranoid gangster and had jury-rigged a trap at the door? A hair-trigger shotgun could have been waiting on the other side.

Petrosino shook his head and crawled twenty yards away from the cabin. He considered crashing through the door with his gun drawn, but that could have gotten someone killed, including him. And there was a good chance that, if someone were inside, he might not be Petto at all. Petrosino turned toward the sound of a coyote's howl in the distance and noticed the smoke still coiling thickly from the stovepipe into the slate sky. He moved low to the ground, back to his rucksack in the woods. He put his pistol in a pocket, then dug through the sack, finding fresh undermuslin. He stuffed the clothing into the front of his coveralls and carefully went back to the side of the cabin closest to the stovepipe.

He crossed himself, then found his first toehold in the wall of logs. He grabbed with both hands and clambered from one log to the next until his torso was above the roof. He reached for the stovepipe, but his arm wasn't long enough. He carefully threw one leg over and crawled on his belly to the stovepipe. The smoke twisted right above us head. He took the extra clothes out from his overalls and shoved them deep into the pipe, packing them quickly and tightly. Then he dangled his legs over the roof's edge and slid quietly down to the ground.

He quickly circled to the front door and drew out the heavy lead sap. Smoke corkscrewed out of the keyhole. Coughing came from within the cabin, then choking sounds, and a man's voice cursing. Heavy footsteps, metal clanging like pots falling from a stove, then a crash of iron and a hissing sound, like water snuffing a fire. The cabin door burst open with a cloud of smoke, and a hulking man in a bearskin coat came stumbling out. His bearded face was concealed by hands rubbing at his eyes and by fits of coughing. A grey funnel of smoke sucked out of the cabin and past the man into the darkness.

Petrosino saw the man's great size, but hesitated as the man bent over, gagging and spitting on the ground. When Petrosino clearly saw him, Petrosino raised the sap. Petto's face was just looking up when Petrosino brought the sap down on his scalp. The blow disoriented Petto, and he staggered back with his hands up in self-defense, bleary eyes still blinking through tears. He coughed out a curse and threw wild punches in the air. Petrosino swung the sap at his crotch, and Petto doubled over, clutching his groin and wheezing desperately. Petrosino smashed him again on the head, then pushed him back inside the cabin's haze. The room was only visible in patches as he struck Petto across the mouth and shoved him onto a bed. Petto tried to sit up, holding up his arms as a shield, gasping to speak.

Petrosino took out his .38 pistol and lit a small lamp while Petto tried to get his breath. On a side table were coins, lists of miners' names, a loaded silver pistol, and the opened red envelope. In the weak light and dying embers from the woodstove, Petto's bloodshot eyes thinned at Petrosino, and his grotesquely bearded face contorted violently.

Petto sputtered out, "I'll. . . kill . . . you."

"I got a .38 full of lead. What do you bid?" Petrosino took out the handcuffs, tossed them at Petto's crotch. The air was still murky, but he saw clearly enough. "Put those on."

"Fuck you, Parsley." Blood trickled from Petto's chipped teeth into the bristles of his beard. He rested on his elbows, and his right arm went under a pillow.

Petrosino whispered, "You think you can threaten me and my family and get away with it? You and your *husband* from the bathhouse? I know all about the Deputy, and I got news for you: you're both fucked now. You're gonna fry in the Chair."

Petto's face became a wolfish grin. "You have no right here. We're in Pennsylvania."

"That's true. And you're Luca Perrino here. But, when we get off the train in New York, you'll be Petto 'The Ox' again, and I'll say I found you hiding in the City. You have to pay for what you did to Madonnia." Petrosino sat on an overturned washtub, resting his gunhand on his knee, still aimed at Petto's head. "Now put those handcuffs on."

"You're alone, aren't you?" Petto shook his head in disbelief. "Big balls."

"I have men waiting for me in town."

"You're lying. How do you think you're gonna make me go anywhere?"

Petrosino saw Petto's eyes searching for the silver pistol on the table, and he knew there was no bringing this man in. Maybe he'd known it all along, and that's why Adelina didn't want him to go. She could read him better than anyone. He blinked her out of his mind and could see beads of sweat stippling Petto's nose, could hear their shallow breathing, could smell the burnt air. His senses were sharpened. It felt as though he were on the edge of a cliff staring down into Petto's cruel smile. Petrosino cocked the hammer on his .38 Smith & Wesson. "Be a man for once in your life, you gutless coward, and put the cuffs on. You'll never make it to that gun, Petto."

Petrosino felt as if someone were watching him, and his stomach gurgled when Petto suddenly grinned.

"I think I'll stay right here, Parsley," Petto said.

A floorboard creaked from behind, and Petrosino turned his head to see the bowlegged man from the woods, pointing a gun at his back.

Petrosino slowly raised his hands up, still holding the .38, but pointed at the ceiling.

"Now we'll try the cuffs on you, Parsley, and have some fun," Petto said. "You know why you have such a hard cock for us Sicilians, Parsley? Because you're not good enough to be one of us. Take his fucking gun."

The bowlegged man said, "Who the hell is this bastard?"

Bimbo's voice said, "That's Petrosino." And a gunshot rang out. The bowlegged man clutched his shoulder, reeling forward and firing his gun into the floor. Petrosino spun from the washtub and fired his .38 once into the bowlegged man's head, and the man collapsed.

Another gunshot thundered from the bed, and Bimbo looked down at a hole in his shirt, saw the blood come, and fell backward. Petrosino dodged sideways as he and Petto exchanged fire. Thunder seemed to shake the cabin, pillows exploded into feathers, and tunnels of air whizzed through the room and splintered the wood. Then a calm.

Petrosino squinted through the floating feathers and the fog of gunpowder. Petto was sprawled out on the bed, motionless. His right hand was blown clean off, bits of flesh and bone caking the wall and the silver pistol on the floor. There were two holes in his massive chest, and blood and air gushed out of the wounds with a chilling hiss. Petto's lips and eyes were the only things moving. The lips mouthed silent words, and the eyes rolled frantically in his skull.

Petrosino lowered his gun and moved closer to the bed.

Petto looked up at him and said, "*Nell'inferno.*" *In hell.* Blood gargled and choked into the sound of the death rattle.

Petrosino rushed over to Bimbo's body in the doorway. The baseball had fallen out of the kid's pocket and sat in a thickening red puddle. He lifted Bimbo's head up. Bimbo's eyes blinked open and twinkled for a moment. "I told you I could do it, Joe," he mumbled. "I even shadowed *you*. How's that for detective work?"

"You stupid kid." Petrosino hugged him tightly. "Stay with me, son."

"Are we still going to a bordello…"

Petrosino felt Bimbo's last breath in his ear and said a prayer for his soul.

Chapter 42

Petrosino sat in his cubbyhole office at Headquarters, tearing through newspaper after newspaper, cutting out the articles that mentioned The Ox's death and hoping to find Bimbo's name. If he couldn't find his name in print, he felt like the boy's memory might slip away. He collected all the newspaper articles and locked them in his desk with Bimbo's St. Anthony medal and the new baseball the kid had bought with his first pay. Then he took out a lock of hair he'd cut from Petto's head and put it in an envelope addressed to the Lafayette Hotel with a note for Piper: *This is what's left of The Ox. I thought you'd like to have it.* He hoped it would sting the bastard's heart. Piper would've called the gift "Italian vendetta," but it made Petrosino feel better for a short time. And when the feeling ebbed, Petrosino made for the nearest saloon and drank for two days straight.

The first night, he paid an extra ten cents to sleep at the saloon's table. And, when he woke in the morning, he went through the same routine. By the third day, he hated himself and went out into the East Side in a stupor. He saw kids playing stickball and young bulls in uniform, and he couldn't bear to watch. He could only imagine what it must've felt for Adelina to lose a child, and now he realized how much he wanted a son of his own. He had no one to turn to. Max was in hiding, preparing for trial with his lawyers, so he wouldn't see him for months, if at all. He walked and walked until he ended up in Central Park in a downpour, watching a shepherd move the meadow sheep into their Sheepfold house. And when no one could tell, he buried his hands in his face and wept. After he was drained of all his guilt and sadness, he walked home, picking up *The Times* and *McClure's* magazine along the way.

He cleaned himself up and read Lincoln Steffens' article, *New York: Good Government In Danger*, and then an article in *The Times*: *Head of Morello Gang Released From Federal Custody on Bail*. He knew he was sober and in his right mind again, because he was enraged. He put on his derby, took the copy of *McClure's*, and walked to Washington Square Park. He found both Steffens and Tarbell in their office drinking tea and frowning over splays of newsprint on their desks. Before they could even say hello, he laid into them.

"Not a single goddamn word about the barrel murder! You didn't even mention Alderman Murphy, Big Tim Sullivan, or Piper. No one would even know that Madonnia was butchered because he threatened to expose their gambling Syndicate and the Morello gang's counterfeiting game! Damn it to hell, Steffens!"

"Joe, calm down."

"The hell I will. You rehashed the evils from the 1890s that Lexow already uncovered. So what? This isn't a prosecution of Tammany's new crooks! Why, it's just a toothless prayer for reelecting the Reform ticket!"

"Joe, why are you all in a lather?" Tarbell stood up and held Petrosino's hand. "What ever is the matter? This isn't about Steff's article."

"I lost someone dear to me. And it was my fault." Petrosino slumped into a desk chair. "Then I read that Morello's on the street again. The two of you sold me a false bill of goods. You said that if I helped you tumble out who was in the Syndicate you'd go after them. You said, 'The pen is mightier than the sword.' And I was damned fool enough to believe you."

"Now hold on a minute, Joe." Steffens stood with his palms up. "We wrote that article the way we said. Mr. McClure vetoed it and made us change it all."

"What?"

"That's right. We put in the details about the Syndicate and the Deputy Commissioner, but he said we didn't stand a chance agains the libel laws. He said it would ruin *McClure's* and every one of us for good. I never would've-"

"I don't care what that yellow bum says. You still owe me. Both of you. Put your coats on and let's go. We'll try it my way now and see if the pistol is mightier than the dagger."

"What the devil are you talking about?"

"Where are we going?" Tarbell stood, unconsciously reaching for her overcoat.

"The two of you and all your friends, the Reverend Parkhursts and the Goo-Goos and all the Park Avenue folks in the City Club. You've got a lot of pull with Seth Low. See, I don't want to answer to Tammany men in the PD anymore. I want to answer *only* to him."

"Mayor Low?" Steffens adjusted his specs.

"That's right. The Clutch Hand's back on the street. His whole gang is back, except for The Ox. I'm outnumbered, Steffens. Don't you remember when you said that if I had ten men, real *men*, then I'd whip the whole crooked lot of them? You remember that?"

"Of course."

"Well, the three of us are going straight to City Hall. You're good at *shame*, Steffens. You're gonna tell Mayor Low that he'll be judged by the cops he appoints and that the reporters know that Tammany's been putting a list of crooks over on him. You're gonna shame Low into giving me an honest squad of ten Italian cops or else you'll start writing articles about how his ass will be booted out next election. Isn't that so, Miss Tarbell, pardon my language?"

"Damn right, Detective." Tarbell put on her coat and pulled Petrosino's hand, leading him to the door. "Let's go raise hell."

"Say, that could be a story," Steffens said. "You could call it *The Italian Squad.*"

Max Schmittberger

Joe Petrosino

Special thanks to Detective Mark Warren and the NYPD Commissioner's Office, Leonora Gidlund and the Municipal Archives of the City of New York, Correction Officer Arthur Wolpinski of Sing Sing Correctional Facility, the New York City Police Museum, the New York Public Library, the New York Transit Museum, the Lower East Side Tenement Museum, the New York Historical Society, the Ossining Historical Society Museum, the NYPD Columbia Association, the Joe Petrosino Museum in Padula, Italy, the U.C. Santa Barbara Davidson Library, Kevin Smith, Penn Whaling, the Ann Rittenberg Literary Agency, and my family in the United States and Sicily.

72269435R00201

Made in the USA
Middletown, DE
04 May 2018